BOOK 4

An
Ivy Malone
Mystery

Stranded

Lorena McCourtney

Revell

Grand Rapids, Michigan

© 2006 by Lorena McCourtney

Published by Fleming H. Revell
a division of Baker Publishing Group
P.O. Box 6287, Grand Rapids, MI 49516-6287

Printed in the United States of America

Library of Congress Cataloging-in-Publication Data
McCourtney, Lorena.
    Stranded / Lorena McCourtney.
        p.   cm. — (An Ivy Malone mystery)
    ISBN 10: 0-8007-3138-7 (pbk.)
    ISBN 978-0-8007-3138-0 (pbk.)
    1. Malone, Ivy (Fictitious character)—Fiction. 2. Women detectives—Fiction. 3. Older women—Fiction. I. Title. II. Series: McCourtney, Lorena. Ivy Malone mysteries ; bk. 4.
PS3563.C3449S77 2006
813′.54—dc22   2006017014

1

Squawk. Scr-e-e-e-ch.

Not good.

Thud. Thump. Thunk.

Worse.

Clankety, clunkety, clank-clank-CLANK!

The clanks vibrated right up through the driver's seat of the motor home, jarring my teeth and rattling my bones. Only one sound is worse, and it came next, right after a dying wheeze of engine.

Silence.

I'd automatically braked at the screech, but it was an unnecessary gesture. The motor home was dead on the highway. Motionless as a dinosaur fossil. Lifeless as roadkill.

Abilene woke and jolted upright in the passenger's seat. She'd been traveling with me since Oklahoma. "What happened? What's wrong? Where are we?"

She shook her head and blinked, looking disoriented and bewildered as she peered out at the heavily forested mountains rising into a whiteout of falling snow on either side of the road. Where were we? We'd been in a Wal-Mart parking lot when she'd fallen asleep, after being awake most of the night with a toothache. Now we were smack in the middle of a narrow, winding highway somewhere in the mountains of Colorado on a winter afternoon. With falling snow rapidly obliterating the yellow dividing line ahead.

"When did it start snowing?"

"About half an hour ago. The engine just quit—"

I broke off as lights shot out of the veil of falling snow behind us and blazed in the rearview mirror. Panic froze my hands on the steering wheel. The car barreled straight at us.

With no more than inches to spare, the driver squealed his brakes, screeched around our stalled vehicle, skidded across the highway, and careened back into the right lane. The angry blast of a horn trailed the red taillights as they disappeared into the falling snow.

"Thank you, Lord," I whispered gratefully. I used the fingers of one hand to pry the cramped fingers of the other off the steering wheel. My possum-gray hair felt as if it were standing on end.

Abilene's knuckles gleamed white as she clutched the armrest beside her seat. "We've got to get out of the middle of the road before someone hits us!"

Right. This had all the makings of a demolition derby. I tried the starter. Maybe those weren't fatal clunks. Maybe they were just warning twinges or a temporary glitch.

Wishful thinking. The engine momentarily made a sound like a garbage disposal trying to chew up a stray spoon, and I quickly turned the key off again.

But we did have lights, at least until the battery gave out, and I turned on everything from turn signals to warning blinkers so other vehicles could see us.

Abilene unbuckled her seat belt. Koop jumped from her

lap to the ledge below the windshield, lone eye alert, orange stub of tail twitching.

"Maybe we can roll backward to a turnout and at least get off the road," she said. "I'll run back and see what's there."

She grabbed a jacket, and an icy flurry of snowflakes swirled inside when she opened the door. Another car came up behind us but spotted our carnival of lights in time to pull around. I offered another thanks that traffic was not heavy on this mountain highway, and that it was only midday. But where was a patrol car when you needed one? One had showed up quickly enough to give us a warning ticket when a taillight had gone out a few days ago.

I slid out of the driver's seat and went back to turn on lights within the motor home in hopes they'd help make us more visible.

When I returned to the seat I spotted something I'd been too shaken to notice before. A red light on the instrument panel, a red light where no light should be. A red eye glowing like some evil messenger of doom.

Abilene returned a minute later. "Nothing back there. The shoulder is barely wide enough to stand on."

"Look." I pointed to the red light. She leaned over, and we studied it together.

"It's the oil pressure," she said.

"Right. There isn't any."

"We'd better call for help on the cell phone."

Yes, the cell phone! We'd bought it only a couple of weeks ago, one of those prepaid kind where you purchase so many minutes and use them as you need them. This was exactly the kind of emergency for which we'd bought the phone. I congratulated myself on our foresight.

Abilene grabbed the phone from the drawer and handed it to me. I yanked up the little antenna and hit the "on" button. After a series of blips, the two words I got on the tiny screen were both chilling and final: no signal.

The reason was fairly obvious. We'd been on a downhill stretch, but the road rose steeply ahead of us. We were deep in a valley here, surrounded by high mountains, modern cell phone technology zapped by geography. At this point the cell phone was no more useful than a battery-powered salami. Foresight, shmoresight.

"Now what?" Abilene asked. She peered ahead. "Maybe I should start walking. How far since we went through a town?"

"I'm not sure. Twenty miles anyway."

"How far to the next town?"

"I'll have to look at the map." I was stalling, of course. The idea of Abilene hiking even a mile or two along the narrow shoulder of this mountain road in the swirling snow gave me cold shudders.

She grabbed a map out of the pocket behind the driver's seat, and we studied it together.

"At least ten or fifteen miles," I said. The map showed the next town as a minuscule dot with the unlikely name of Hello.

Abilene peered out the windshield, but she didn't rush off to start walking. I was relieved she could see that even with her youthful strength and energy, hiking off into the snow was not a wise course of action.

"I take it this is one of those times we're supposed to pray and depend on the Lord?" she suggested finally, her tone on the disgruntled side.

Since Abilene has joined me in my travels, with a reason as good as my own for keeping on the move, we've had several discussions on Christian matters. Sometimes she seems to be heading toward the Lord, but the path is definitely circuitous and potholed.

"I think that's a good plan." The Lord has seen me through a good many problems and trials over the years. His promise never to leave or forsake us was surely good here on this snowy mountain road. I offered the prayer.

We sat there. Abilene impatiently rubbed a forearm across a steamed-up window. A few more cars detoured around us, some quietly, some blasting complaints. The motor home was already beginning to feel chilly. Abilene turned up the thermostat, and the propane heater kicked on. The fan would run down the battery fairly quickly. I clicked the switch that turned on the generator to provide electricity and keep the battery charged.

"The Lord seems to be taking his own sweet time," Abilene muttered.

True, I had to admit. How long had we been stuck here? Logic said a few minutes, nerves screamed hours. But God, I reminded myself, isn't tied to time the way we in this realm are.

Several more hour-long minutes passed. The motor home warmed comfortably. The propane tanks had been filled only yesterday. We had food in the refrigerator and gasoline for the generator. In the wilderness, disconnected from modern services, we could probably survive for a considerable length of time.

How long we could survive stranded in the middle of a mountain road with cars and trucks coming at us from both directions was another matter.

2

More minutes trickled by. Koop prowled restlessly from one end of the motor home to the other, occasionally jumping up on something to peer outside. Abilene tapped a toe on the carpet and fingers on the dinette. She looked at the battery-operated clock over the door. Another car screeched around us, and I wondered apprehensively if we'd be safer standing out there in the snow under the trees.

"Does depending on the Lord mean sitting around twiddling your thumbs until he does something?" Abilene demanded suddenly.

"Sometimes it does mean waiting. Sometimes it means listening for his guidance about what he wants us to do—"

Abilene jumped up. "Good. Because what I hear is that I should get out there and flag someone down. We need *help*."

"That could be dangerous!"

"This isn't?" she retorted when a truck roared by us close enough to vibrate the motor home into an oversized version of shake, rattle, and roll. Before I could say more she ran to a closet, grabbed something, and slammed out the door.

The rate of snow falling had let up, I realized thankfully as I peered out a window. *Lord, keep her safe out there!* Visibility was up to maybe a hundred feet now.

And Abilene was definitely visible. What she'd grabbed was a bright red towel, and she jumped up and down and flapped it as if practicing for matador tryouts. In spite of Abilene's energetic waves, the first three vehicles ignored her, but finally a motor home slid to a stop behind us.

Abilene dashed around to their door. Several minutes of conversation ensued. Then the motor home, one of those big, expensive diesel pushers, went on, and Abilene returned.

"Their cell phone wouldn't work either," she reported. "But they'll send help back from the next town."

"Good."

She leaned over to shake the snow out of her short blond hair. "I suppose we owe God thanks for making them stop."

I was surprised and gratified by this comment, even though it did sound a bit grudging. Though I suspected she might be thinking, *Why didn't God just send a tow truck instead of going the long way around?* I waited a moment, hoping she'd offer the thanks herself, but when she remained silent I did it. One step at a time.

"Now," she added in a grimmer tone when I was done, "all we have to do is survive traffic until help arrives."

I made coffee. I can't say I was serenely unworried about being squashed by a truck or rear-ended by an SUV before rescue arrived, but I was out of panic mode. And a couple of minutes later two guys in a beat-up green pickup stopped. Unasked, they set out warning flares in front and back of the motor home and then stood out in the snow directing traffic around us. I was amazed. No more ear-shattering screeches or bone-rattling near misses. Abilene took them coffee and cookies.

The two guys stayed until the tow truck arrived, although I never did get to thank them myself. One minute they were there, the next they were gone.

Can angels come disguised as two scruffy guys in beat-up boots and baseball caps turned backward, both scarfing down peanut butter cookies as if they were new and improved manna? Could be.

The tow truck driver was fiftyish, uncommunicative and unsmiling but efficient. He did not ask what our problem was, but he did peer underneath the motor home. A grunt apparently meant the motor home was at least in towable condition. Within minutes he had the motor home's front end hoisted in the air, like a big, dead fish dangling on a hook. We rode in the cab of the truck with him, me in the middle, Koop in the kitty carrier on Abilene's lap.

I made a couple of attempts at conversation. Printing on the side of the tow truck said "Hello Trucking, Luke Martin, Owner," so I said, "You're Luke?"

"Nope."

"Then you are . . . ?"

"Paul Newman."

"Like the movie star? The one married to Joanne Woodward?"

"I've heard of that guy," he said darkly. "Don't seem fair, these movie people grabbin' real folks' names to use."

So far as I knew, movie star Paul Newman's name was his own, but this did not seem like an overly productive line of conversation, so I switched subjects. "Have you lived in the area long, Mr. Newman?"

"Yep."

"Where are you taking us?"

"Nick's Garage."

"In Hello?"

"Yep."

Apparently his own name was the only subject on which Paul Newman got beyond one- or two-word answers. I'd run into taciturn types before. They always made me want to say something such as, "Have you stopped making moonshine in your backyard?" Try a yep or nope on that one. Instead I shushed myself and asked politely, "Is Nick a good mechanic?"

"Yep."

With that glowing recommendation, how could we go wrong?

We passed through a couple of heavy snow flurries, but the storm clouds had lifted to expose snow-clad mountaintops and a few splotches of blue sky by the time we dipped into the narrow valley where the town lay. Nick's Garage was on the north side of town, so we didn't get to see the main part of Hello before Paul Newman dragged the motor home into a big yard enclosed by a solid wooden fence. Doors yawned open on a metal shop building, doors I was relieved to see were large enough to accommodate the motor home.

The place wasn't spotless, but it looked as good as most such establishments. Junk engines and other dismembered vehicle parts lay off to one side of the shop, near them a red pickup with the silvery figure of a bucking Brahma bull mounted on the hood. Oil and grease spots decorated the puddled ground between patches of snow. A newer Dodge Durango was up on a hoist inside the shop. A couple of guys were working under it.

No one came out to meet us. Apparently Nick was accustomed to nonworking lumps of machinery being dumped in his yard. Paul Newman unfastened the motor home, accepted my money, and departed.

Abilene, Koop in his cat carrier, and I went in through an

13

office door. Inside was a cluttered counter and cash register, a row of red vinyl chairs, a coffee maker, and shelves of car parts and supplies. An older man with bifocals, thinning gray hair, and a plaid shirt crisscrossed by green suspenders stood at the window, regarding our motor home with interest. A vintage *Newsweek* magazine lay open on a chair.

"Looks like you got troubles."

"I'm afraid so. But the tow truck driver told us Nick was a fine mechanic. Are you Nick?"

"No, Nick's out there working on my Durango. Been having brake troubles, but it should still be under warranty. Unless they squeak out from under some way. You know how those big car outfits are. Get your money, and then it's bye-bye, sucker. You folks from . . ." He leaned closer to the window and adjusted his bifocals to peer at our license plate. "Arkansas?"

I sometimes wished we could have a license plate that read "None of your business where we're from." Since that wasn't possible, and I did use a mail-forwarding address in Arkansas, I said, "More or less."

He turned to study us instead of the motor home. "Just the two of you traveling alone?"

"Us and Koop here." I motioned to the cat carrier Abilene had set on a chair. Koop's one good eye peered out suspiciously.

"Snowbirds headed south for the winter?"

"We don't seem to be going anywhere at the moment." As usual, I didn't want to leave a trail of information about where we were headed just in case anyone came inquiring. In the interest of avoiding further questions I added the same question I'd asked the tow truck driver. "Have you lived around here long?"

"Oh, yeah. I was the police chief in Hello for over twenty-five years." His voice held pride. "Name's Ben Simpson. Retired now." He stuck out a hand, and Abilene and I both shook it. He gave me a questioning look, obviously expecting our names in return. He didn't seem to take offense when I didn't oblige, however, and continued cheerfully. "I've got some friends who spend winters at an RV park down at Apache Junction, out near the Superstition Mountains in Arizona. You ever been there? I can get you the name of the place if you'd like. Good rates and a nice pool, they say."

"We haven't been to Arizona before, but we've heard about a place called Snowbird's Retreat down near Tucson—"

I broke off as I realized what I'd just done. Told him where we were headed. He'd probably been a very good police chief, I decided grumpily. With that garrulous, disarming manner he'd likely had the crooks spilling their secrets before they realized what they were doing. And he was probably more shrewd than his somewhat hayseedy surface appearance suggested.

Nick himself came in through the shop door, a young, tall and skinny, red-haired guy in grease-stained coveralls with his name embroidered in red on a pocket. I explained what I could about our breakdown noises and the oil light. "We're hoping you can take a look at it before too long . . . ?"

The retired police chief gave a generous wave. "Go ahead and have a look at their rig. I'm in no rush on those brakes. Help these good folks get on their way to Arizona before they get snowed in here."

"Thank you." I felt guilty about my unkind attitude toward Ben Simpson's curiosity, though I didn't appreciate his spreading the word that we were headed to Arizona. I grudgingly offered a smidgen of further information. "We're hoping to make it as far as Gallup today." And desert warmth and sunshine by tomorrow.

All Nick said was, "We'll get right on it, then," but something about his reserved tone made me suspect Gallup was not on our itinerary for today. Those noises I'd described had told him something.

Okay, a day or two's delay here in the snow wouldn't hurt us. Desert sunshine would still be there when we arrived.

The three of us stood at the window and watched while a younger, dark-haired guy got behind the wheel of the motor home to steer it while Nick used the red truck with its over-sized bumper to push it into the shop.

I decided to forestall more personal questions from Ben while we waited by asking my own. "So, tell us about Hello. For one thing, how did it get its name?"

"Good question." He looked pleased that I'd asked. "No one really knows. That's why there's this contest every summer. It's called 'Why Hello?' and everyone submits these stories, three hundred words or less, about how the town maybe got its name. I won one year," he added modestly. "Got an oil change here at Nick's and a fancy dinner at the Café Russo, and a free carpet cleaning. Really tickled Edna." He missed a beat in his garrulous chatter. "But she's up there in High Cemetery now."

Abilene had been prowling the small room restlessly, and now she touched my arm lightly. "Do you think we have time for me to walk around and take a look at the town?"

I was afraid she might have time to do a census count on Hello, but all I said was, "Sure. If you see a grocery store, get some plastic wrap, would you? We're almost out. How's your tooth?"

Her tongue probed a molar on the right side. "Not bad."

Ben Simpson peered at Abilene's jaw with interest. A man who was never bored, I guessed, and a little nosy about everything. I shouldn't be critical of his curiosity, however, I reminded myself. My own "mutant curiosity gene," as a friend once called it, was always primed for action.

"We got a great dentist here in Hello," Ben said. "Dr. Li. But his place is too far to walk. He's out on the other side of town, out there in the Safeway shopping center."

Abilene zipped up her jacket and headed out the door. My

next question to Ben wasn't just to keep him from asking questions. I was really curious.

"High Cemetery, that's its name?"

"No. It's all the Hello City Cemetery, but, as you can see"— he waved toward town—"we're kind of jammed in a narrow valley here. So when the cemetery started getting full, they started another section up higher on the hillside. So now we have Low Cemetery and High Cemetery."

"Nothing to do with, ummm, social status then?"

"Well, most people would rather be buried in High Cemetery, all right. Low Cemetery has a lot of old miners and crooks who shot or stabbed each other back when this was a booming mining town. Some ladies of the night too. Though everyone knows some of the early-on respectable wives started out as ladies of the night."

I picked out one bit of information from that oversupply. "Hello isn't a booming mining town now?"

"There's still a little mining going on, but it's mostly gold panners workin' the creeks in the summer. Everyone thought something big was going to happen out at the Lucky Queen. Would of been a real shot in the arm for Hello. But it's probably not going to happen now, with ol' Hiram dead. Tourists and antique shops and bed and breakfasts are about all that keep Hello going now. We don't even have any big ski area right close by to bring people in."

"Any RV parks?"

"Two over on the south side. But only one's open this time of year. Lots busier in the summer here. You oughta come back then. Or if you want to stay for a while now you could see the Roaring '20s Revue. The Ladies Historical Society puts it on every winter, and it's pretty lively. I played the police chief in a skit last year. That guy who towed you in, Paul Newman, is usually the master of ceremonies."

With uncommunicative Paul as master of ceremonies, the

Revue sounded about as lively as a sales pitch for funeral insurance.

Ben Simpson looked me over with a critical eye. "Paul's wife is in the chorus line. You might make it into the chorus line too if you hang around."

I was startled. Me, in a chorus line? "Aren't the chorus-line ladies somewhat . . . ummm . . . younger?" To say nothing of taller and more shapely.

"Some are even older." He tilted his head as he inspected me further. "You're kinda short, but they might put you on the end."

"It sounds like a lovely little town." I felt rather bowled over by all the information, especially this assessment of my qualifications for chorus-line membership. It was, at the moment, more than enough to fill even my usually bottomless abyss of curiosity. And even more especially since what I really wanted to know about was the status of the motor home.

"Yes, it is. A lovely little town." A meaningful pause and a sideways glance. "Mostly."

Mostly. I could see that he was deliberately dangling that tantalizing tidbit, and my curiosity couldn't let it go, of course. I bit and repeated the word. "Mostly?"

"I wouldn't exactly call murder 'lovely.'"

"There was a murder here in Hello?"

"And an ugly one it was too."

"When was this?"

"Oh, 'bout a month or so ago."

I thought he was going to say more, but just then a vehicle turned through the gate and pulled up in front of Nick's Garage. Ben Simpson's eyebrows shot up.

"Well, well, isn't this a coincidence? We're talkin' murder, and here comes the prime suspect now."

18

3

The blue and white Ford Bronco had a dent in the hood, a crack across the passenger's side of the windshield, and enough mud splatters to qualify as some avant-garde work of art. I expected a tough miner or cowboy type to emerge, but the person who stepped out was petite, blond, and female.

"She's a murder suspect?" I asked doubtfully. Although I knew I shouldn't be doubtful on the basis of looks. Past experience has taught me that appearance has nothing to do with a capacity for murder.

Ben nodded. "Right up there at the top of the list."

"For murdering whom?"

"Her uncle, old Hiram McLeod himself. Hiram's father and grandfather made a fortune with the Lucky Queen back in the early years. Smart about investing the money too, so even though the mine shut down years ago, Hiram was always one of the richest people in Hello. Though he was generous to a fault, you know? And all those wives must have been expensive."

I had a vision of generous old Hiram tossing hundred-dollar bills to strangers, with wives standing around like potted plants. Ben might be talkative, but he knew how to give just enough information to suck you in. No way I could not ask, "All those wives? As in polygamy?"

"Oh no, marriages and divorces, just a lot of 'em. One wife died, I think. Anyway, there were eight of 'em altogether. Although there could have been more we never knew about, since Hiram spent some time away from Hello in his younger years." Ben nodded as if he considered this a shrewd observation.

"Maybe one of them murdered him," I suggested.

"Could be, I suppose." A vague gesture of Ben's hand dismissed ex-wives as suspects, however.

"Was he married at the time of his death?"

"No, but his fiancée is all broken up over it."

"Fiancée? He was planning to marry again?"

"Some men don't like being alone. Me, I don't mind. I'd never find another Edna." He peered in the cat carrier. Koop hissed at him. He frowned. "Edna never cared for cats."

I didn't mention it, but I knew right then that Ben was a smoker. Koop has this hissing-snarling-clawing phobia about smokers.

"So no one thinks an ex-wife could have murdered him?"

"It's the niece who hit the jackpot with his death. Everyone knows she did it."

The young woman bypassed the office and headed for one of the big shop doors. She was wearing tight, light-blue jeans, heavy laced boots, a bulky blue jacket, and sunglasses. A purple knit stocking cap with a fuzzy knob on top covered part of her long blond hair.

"Grandniece, actually," Ben went on without any prompting from me. "Her grandma and ol' Hiram were brother and

20

sister. Well, half-brother and sister, technically. Hiram's father never quite got the hang of being a one-woman man either. Hiram and the half-sister, Gypsy, fought like a couple of hungry bluejays, from what I've heard."

A grandma named Gypsy. Ancestors with too many wives. Murder. Not your run-of-the-mill niece.

"And this woman's name is . . . ?"

"Kelli Keifer. She's a lawyer."

A lawyer? I was surprised. Ski bunny would have been my guess. Then I reprimanded myself for jumping to conclusions based on appearance. "And she supposedly murdered her uncle because . . . ?"

"To acquire his assets, of course."

"But if old Hiram and Kelli's grandmother never got along, why would he leave his assets to Kelli?"

"Mostly because he didn't have anyone else to leave them to, I suppose. Though I guess he and Kelli got along okay." The admission sounded reluctant. "But it was more a business than personal relationship. She was taking care of his legal and business affairs when it happened." Ben nodded sagely, as if this were a significant point in Hiram's death that canceled out the fact that the young woman and her uncle hadn't exchanged gunshots at sunrise on Hello's main drag.

"Does this suspicion of her affect her local career as a lawyer?"

"Would you want to entrust your legal affairs to a murderer? Although she wasn't exactly Miss Popularity even before the murder." Another sage nod.

Kelli Keifer was beginning to sound like the underdog in all this, a lone woman with a whole town against her, apparently without proof, and I felt myself leaning toward her side. "Old Hiram didn't have children of his own?"

"Not unless one no one knows about suddenly turns up."

Ben Simpson was a good-hearted man, I was almost certain of that. He'd loved his Edna, and he'd willingly let me go ahead of him here at Nick's. But I could also hear glee in his voice, as if he'd be delighted if some heretofore unknown heir suddenly appeared to set off fireworks.

"Do you, like everyone else, think she did it?" I asked.

The blunt question seemed to catch him off guard. He straightened his back and assumed a Retired Police Chief attitude. "Well, nobody knows for sure, of course. Innocent until proven guilty. I guess it isn't a cut-and-dried case, because Kelli's never actually been arrested. But everyone knows she did it," he repeated with a dogged stubbornness that contradicted the "innocent until proven guilty" statement.

Not me, I thought with my own stubbornness. I didn't know Kelli Keifer had done it. "No one else had a motive?"

"Like I said, ol' Hiram was generous to a fault. Everyone appreciated that. He donated the land for High Cemetery, and for the town square downtown too. And personally paid for the statue in it and the street lighting around it. And last year he not only gave his entire library to the Ladies Historical Society, he donated enough money to add a wing to their building to put the books in."

"That's very impressive," I said, although I also thought it dodged the issue of other people with motives.

"But there were people who didn't appreciate all he did, I suppose," Ben went on reluctantly. "Hiram was a shrewd businessman, and probably stepped on a few toes along the way. But in all these years, no one ever killed him. He was alive and kicking till Kelli came to town."

"You mean one day she arrived, and bingo! The next day he's dead?"

Ben frowned at what he apparently considered a flippant attitude on my part. "No, not that fast. She's been here, oh, six months or so now."

"So maybe someone else used her presence to try to make it look as if she did it."

Ben gave me a cool stare. "You some kind of private eye or something?" he scoffed.

Well, no. My only claim to detective knowledge is that I read a lot of mysteries. Plus the fact that my busy mutant curiosity gene has involved me in the solving of a few murders.

Now I ignored Ben's question and said, "Maybe she has a good alibi."

The door from the shop opened just in time for the young woman to hear my last word. It didn't take diagrams for her to figure out what the topic of discussion was. *Alibi* isn't a word that fits into most ordinary conversations.

"Talking about me?" she inquired pleasantly. Though the pleasant tone was definitely laced with acid. She yanked off the sunglasses as if prepared to stare us down.

The cold had pinked her cheeks, but I thought her eyes were probably that spectacular shade of blue no matter what the weather or temperature.

Ben's weathered face reddened with embarrassment and guilt. He plunked into a chair and suddenly became very busy looking for a page in the old *Newsweek*.

I faced my guilt head-on. "We were gossiping," I admitted to Kelli Keifer. "I'm sorry. Gossiping isn't directly named as a no-no in the Ten Commandments, but I'm pretty sure it's included as a footnote somewhere."

"That's okay." Her dismissive wave looked a little weary, but she smiled. "Everyone gossips. At least you're honest about it. Gossip about me is currently the main pastime in Hello, but no one has ever actually admitted it before." She gave Ben a baleful glance, then looked me up and down. "But I don't think I know you."

23

"We're just passing through. That's my motor home out there in the shop. Are you having vehicle troubles too?"

"I think something's messed up with the carburetor on the Bronco, though it hasn't actually conked out yet. But Nick doesn't have time to look at it today. He's coming in to check his appointment book for tomorrow."

She spotted Koop in the carrier and knelt down beside him. She touched the wire mesh, and he purred and rubbed the side of his big orange head against her fingertips. "Friendliest reception I've had in weeks," she muttered as she stood up.

Nick came in and pulled a spiral notebook out of a drawer. It looked as if it was written in grease by someone wearing mittens, but I was surprised he had an appointment book at all. He planted a finger on a space empty except for an oil spot. "Two o'clock tomorrow?"

I couldn't tell from his tone if he shared Ben Simpson's opinion that Kelli Keifer was a murderer, but he didn't sound what I'd consider small-town friendly.

"I'll be here. Thanks. Nice meeting you," she added to me as she turned toward the door. She ignored Ben Simpson. "I hope there's nothing too seriously wrong with your motor home."

"I don't know." I looked at Nick. "Is there?"

Nick launched into an explanation about oil leaking out of the pan, which meant there was no oil in the system to lubricate the rods and cylinders and crankshaft. "So everything just seized up—"

"Seized?" I repeated blankly.

I guess he could see that my knowledge of engines rivals my understanding of the national debt. He started over. "Froze up, you might say. Though it has nothing to do with cold. It's just that nothing in an engine can keep moving without oil to lubricate it. Everything just grinds to a stop."

Grinds. Yes, that was how the engine had sounded. "But where did the oil go? I had both the oil and filter changed a few days ago. I'm sure they put in something like five quarts of it."

"The oil plug is missing. Could be whoever changed the oil didn't get the plug screwed on tight after draining the old oil, and road vibration worked it loose after a while. When it fell out, oil would of drained out like pulling the plug on a bathtub. Must of left a big streak on the road back there somewhere. And it would've happened fast. The red light wouldn't have been on more than a few minutes before everything froze up."

"So you can put more oil in, and then it will be okay?" I asked hopefully.

Nick gave me a pitying look. "No, ma'am. I'm afraid not."

I jumped to the bottom line. Or maybe *plummeted* would be a better word. "So how long is this going to take to fix, and how much is it going to cost?"

My bluntness got an equally blunt reply. "At least a week, maybe two. At least $3,500, maybe $4,000."

I gaped at him.

"The engine is blown," he said. "Shot. Kaput. Unrepairable. Those thunks and clunks you heard were the rods tearing up the cylinders because no oil was getting to them. You need a new engine."

"A new engine?" I repeated faintly.

"I'll have to order one, and I don't know for sure how long it will take to get here. Or the exact cost."

There was something else Nick didn't know. I did not have $4,000 jingling in my checking account. Not even $3,500.

"Couldn't you maybe get a used one . . . or something?"

"Possible. But that means contacting wrecking yards everywhere from Denver to Albuquerque and Phoenix. Finding a good used one may take longer than ordering a new one. And you don't really know what you're getting."

25

"I see."

"I'm sorry. If I could repair this one, I would. But . . ." He lifted one shoulder regretfully. "I take Visa and MasterCard. Discover too, if that's any help."

"I don't use credit cards." I'd heard too much about how traceable they were, and traceable was not what either Abilene or I could afford to be.

Suddenly another chilling thought occurred to me. "Could someone have deliberately loosened the plug?"

Nick looked surprised. "Well, yeah, I suppose. But why would someone do that? Anyone who knows enough to do it would also know it could ruin the engine."

"Malicious vandalism." Ben Simpson nodded wisely. "You never know what some people will do these days."

"That's right." Kelli's tone suggested personal experience.

I looked around. I wasn't surprised that nosy Ben Simpson was still there and listening with interest, but I was surprised that Kelli Keifer had paused with her hand on the doorknob to listen to the details of our disaster. Even more surprised that a little frown between those blue eyes suggested concern about our predicament.

"So, you want me to start tearing out the engine right away, or . . . ?" Nick left the question open ended.

"Not just yet. I'll have to . . . see what I can do."

"We'll just pull the motor home out of the shop for now, then."

I nodded. The money numbers swung in my head like a hangman's noose. Warm desert sunshine was now a mirage shimmering on the far side of an uncrossable wilderness spiked with dollar signs.

Because, as far as I could see, the here-and-now fact was that we were stranded in Hello until I found $4,000 I'd tucked away and forgotten in my billfold, or a new motor home engine dropped out of the sky. Whichever came first.

4

"After Nick gets through with the Durango, I can give you a lift to a motel or one of the bed and breakfasts," Ben offered. "There's a couple of 'em stay open during the winter."

I hesitated. More expenses. I probably shouldn't have told Abilene to buy that plastic wrap.

I looked back at Nick. "Perhaps we could stay in the motor home right here until we figure out what to do?"

Nick shook his head regretfully. "City passed an ordinance a while back. No occupied RVs except in RV parks within the city limits." He hesitated. "I could probably get by letting you stay in it here for one night. But no longer."

"Thank you. We appreciate that." I turned to Ben. "I think we will stay here for tonight, then. But thank you for the offer to take us somewhere. That's very nice of you."

For the moment I blocked out worries about what we'd do after tonight. Kelli Keifer, apparently deciding we were taken care of, opened the door and went on out to her Bronco. I stood at the window and watched Nick and his helper use the truck to pull the motor home out of the shop and drag it over to a space by the fence. Motor homes are unknowing, unfeeling lumps of metal, of course, but ours certainly had a dejected look at the moment.

"Tough break," Ben said.

"God probably has something in mind."

Ben nodded. "That's kind of what Edna used to say when things went wrong."

I picked up Koop's carrier and sloshed across the puddled yard to the motor home. By now I was beginning to worry about Abilene. She'd been gone a long time. Inside the motor home, I let Koop loose, turned on both the furnace and generator, put water on to heat for tea, and sat down to consider our predicament.

The big question, next to "What are we going to do now?" was whether someone had deliberately loosened that oil plug. Because there were two definite "someone" possibilities. The Braxton clan was out to get me. I'd been the star witness in sending one of their own to prison for murder. They'd already retaliated by trying to burn my house, with me in it, back in Missouri. They'd located me in Arkansas and booby-trapped my old Thunderbird with dynamite. They'd chased me across a couple of states and almost caught up with me again in Oklahoma. They were vindictive, murderous, and determined.

Then there was Boone Morrison, Abilene's abusive husband. She'd incurred his wrath when she accidentally wrecked his treasured Porsche while trying to escape from him before he escalated the abuse, which included a broken arm and threats of murder, to actual homicide. He, with the help of a sheriff cohort, had tracked her to Oklahoma, where we'd barely managed to elude him before he had a chance to carry out his threats.

I didn't doubt that both our menacing shadows were still

28

on our trail, persistent as prison-break bloodhounds. They were why we'd kept on the move ever since leaving Oklahoma, and why we tried to leave no clue where we were headed next.

But there was one reason to think neither the Braxtons nor Boone Morrison had caused our present predicament. Just pulling a vital plug on the engine wasn't malicious enough.

The Braxtons had vowed to make roadkill out of me. Boone Morrison had sworn to make mincemeat out of Abilene. The wording of their threats got low points for originality, but the threats themselves were all too real.

Sabotaging the engine on the motor home would mean a big inconvenience as well as a financial disaster for us, true. But it wasn't likely to have fatal consequences, and neither the Braxtons nor Boone Morrison would settle for merely inconveniencing us. They were out for blood. Our blood.

So, I decided with a certain relief, I could safely rule out Braxton or Boone involvement in our present predicament. We were here because of carelessness on the part of the guy who had last changed the oil, or perhaps even because of a simple mechanical malfunction. These things happen.

Which didn't mean the Braxtons or Boone Morrison wouldn't take advantage of our sitting-duck situation if they caught up with us here in Hello . . .

But what to do? I didn't want to get Nick into trouble for illicitly harboring two women and a cat on his property, but where could we go? And where, I wondered again, was Abilene? It'd be dark before long.

I poured a cup of tea, dumped some liver-flavored crunchies in a bowl for Koop, and sat down to think again.

I had a little money in a CD, but I needed the small amount of interest income it supplied to supplement my Social Security. There'd also be a painful penalty to pay if I took anything out of the CD. And there was always the possibility of some even more drastic emergency than this one for which I'd need the money. It might be *me* going thumpety-thump-clank-clank-clunk next time, and there was a big gap between Medicare coverage and total medical costs. But what other solution was there?

Sitting on a street corner with a sign reading "Will work for motor home engine" did not strike me as a likely solution. Nor, in spite of Ben Simpson's generous assessment, did I think I had a big future as a chorus-line dancer.

So, some mundane job in Hello until we saved up enough to pay for an engine transplant? I'd had a couple of housekeeping/caretaking type jobs recently, and I had been a librarian back in Missouri for some thirty years. I'm industrious, dependable, and curious. Also a reasonably quick learner.

Character traits which, I suspect, could also describe anything from a con artist selling snake oil to a bag lady going through dumpsters, and I don't see many job openings for either.

I'm also rather over-the-hill in the eyes of most employers.

Feel free to jump in here anytime, Lord. Got any ideas?

And where is Abilene? She should have been back by now.

A vehicle pulled up outside, and I peered out the window. I was surprised to see Kelli Keifer's muddy Bronco, even more surprised when she headed for the motor home door rather than Nick's shop. I opened it before she knocked. The sun had dropped over the mountains now, turning them to cold blue silhouettes. Kelli wasn't wearing the sunglasses now. An icy breeze tousled her long blond hair.

"Hi," she said. She didn't strike me as an uncertain sort of person, but there was something tentative about the greeting. Perhaps as if, given her status as Hello's designated murderess, she wasn't certain of her welcome?

"Hi." I tried to sound friendly.

Then words came out all in a rush. "Maybe it's none of my business, but I got to thinking after I left . . . You're going to need someplace to stay after tonight, right? Apparently you're stuck here for a while, and I got the impression your finances might be—" She broke off as if not wanting to sound nosy or insulting.

"Shaky?" I suggested. "Tight?"

"Whatever."

"I'm afraid so. Definitely tight and shaky finances."

"Anyway, I have a house. It's empty, and I wouldn't charge anything if you'd like to stay in it for a while."

"A free place to live?" I asked, astonished. "Just like that, you'd let us stay in your house? You don't even know us."

"I know you were honest enough to tell me you and Ben were gossiping about me. And nice enough to apologize. No one else has done that. You and your cat don't look like you'd throw big, drunken parties and wreck the place. Not that wrecking it would probably be much of a loss, under the circumstances."

"The circumstances being this was the house in which your uncle was murdered?" I guessed. "And everyone is acting as if it's tainted?"

She smiled. "I should have known you'd spot the worm in my apple."

"I've lived in a house where someone was murdered." Two someones, actually.

"You have?" Her head jerked back as if she were startled, and I wondered if she was reassessing her generous offer. Probably most inconspicuous little old ladies don't come with murder in their resume.

"Not anyone I murdered," I assured her.

"I wasn't thinking that," she protested. She smiled and made a gesture of putting forefinger and thumb together with a narrow space between them. "Well, maybe just one teensy little thought. I saw a rerun of *Arsenic and Old Lace* not long ago."

"Although I don't have any references to offer," I had to admit.

"I didn't kill anyone either," she said suddenly, her voice unexpectedly fierce. "No matter what Ben or the townspeople think. I didn't do it."

I didn't know Kelli well enough to jump in with a resounding echo of belief in her innocence, but I was certainly leaning in that direction. Does a murderer offer down-and-outers a free place to stay?

"Do you have any idea who did?" I asked.

"Unfortunately, no one who makes as good a suspect as I do."

"Maybe we can talk more about this sometime," I said.

She regarded me thoughtfully. "Maybe we can."

I briskly returned to the matter of the house. "It's not just Koop and me who need a place to stay. A younger woman, my friend Abilene, is traveling with us. Though I don't know where she is at the moment."

"The more the merrier. Uncle Hiram isn't going to mind. And I think the house would be better off occupied than sitting there empty. You know how old houses get when they're empty. They start smelling strange. And they get broken into."

"Has this house been broken into?"

Reluctantly, as if she were afraid it would scare me off, she said, "Somebody shoved in the back door and went through things, though I don't think anything was taken. But I'm sure that wouldn't happen if the house was occupied. There isn't much crime in Hello."

"Do you have time to come in and wait until Abilene gets back? I just made tea."

She instantly pulled off the stocking cap. "That'd be nice."

Kelli was sitting on the sofa, under inspection by Koop, and I was pouring tea for her when the door burst open. Abilene's cheeks were pink with exertion, and excitement lit up her eyes.

"Ivy, you won't believe what happened—" She broke off when she realized I wasn't alone in the motor home.

"Kelli Keifer . . . Abilene Tyler," I introduced. Abilene had stopped using Boone Morrison's last name. "And I guess I haven't introduced myself yet, either. I'm Ivy Malone." To Abilene I added, "Kelli has offered us a place to live."

"We're staying here?" Abilene said, and I remembered she hadn't yet heard the bad news about the kaput engine.

I briefly explained our problems and the probable cost of a new engine. She dropped into a seat at the tiny dinette, obviously as shocked by the figure as I was. Yet at the same time, she didn't look as disappointed or panicky about this change of plans as I was afraid she'd be, which surprised me. So far, she'd been as eager as I to keep on the move.

We all contemplated that $4,000 figure for a moment, until Kelli said, "You've been out for a run?" Abilene wasn't really breathing hard—she's in too good physical shape for that—but her breathing was still fast enough to suggest exertion.

"No. Well, I did run back here. I'd been gone so long that I figured Ivy'd be getting worried."

"I was." Abilene is kind of the granddaughter I never had, and I do worry about her. I took her under my wing back in Oklahoma. Although I have to admit that sometimes she's the wing, and I'm the one under it. "Where have you been all this time?" I added, trying not to sound as if I were scolding.

"I walked downtown, past all these little antique-y places and a city square with a statue of a miner with a gold pan, and then I looked down a side street and saw a palomino horse rearing up on its hind legs."

"A horse? In town?"

"I was surprised too. I thought it must have gotten loose from somewhere."

Kelli laughed delightedly. "Dr. Sugarman's horse." She spoke the name with unexpected warmth, considering her chilly attitude toward the other residents of Hello. "And the horse does look real, doesn't it? But it's made out of fiberglass."

If there's an animal of any species within jogging distance, Abilene will find it or it will find her. Maybe that includes fiberglass varieties.

"So I walked over there to look, and by the time I got there I saw what it was. It's in front of a veterinarian's office. And there was a sign in the window saying 'Assistant Wanted.' I wondered what kind of experience or training a veterinarian's assistant would need, and I decided I'd just go in and ask."

"What did you find out?"

"Nothing right then. The door was locked, and there was one of those clock-face signs in the window, with the hands showing the vet would be back at four o'clock."

"Dr. Sugarman does mostly small animals," Kelli explained, "but in an emergency he'll go out to a ranch for a sick horse or cow. Or over to Stella Sinclair's, if she gets in a tizzy about her potbellied pig eating too many Godiva chocolates." Kelli rolled her eyes, apparently not overly sympathetic to the plight of a pig on a chocolate high.

"Anyway, I didn't have a watch to know what time it was," Abilene went on, "so I was just standing there trying to decide whether to wait for a while, when an SUV screeched up. A little girl jumped out with a cat wrapped in a blanket, and her mother jumped out right behind her. And both of them

34

were frantic when they found the vet wasn't there, because the cat was unconscious."

"Oh no—"

"They'd had some old Christmas lights out and were testing them. The cat chewed on the electrical cord and got shocked."

"And it was still alive?" Kelli said. "That's a wonder."

"I didn't think it was alive. It was *limp*. Then I remembered seeing on TV about how this fireman gave CPR to an unconscious cat he'd pulled out of a burning building."

"You gave CPR to a cat?" Kelli asked.

"I wasn't sure exactly how to do it, but I figured I couldn't hurt the poor thing. It wasn't breathing at all. So I tried to remember what I'd seen on TV, and I closed the cat's mouth and put my mouth over its face and breathed into its nose. It's different than how you do CPR on a person," she added.

"A whole lot different," Kelli said, which I had to echo. Then Kelli added thoughtfully, "But I guess I could do it if I had to. If it were my Sandra Day . . ."

Now it was my turn to be astonished. "You named your cat for a former Supreme Court judge?"

Kelli smiled self-consciously. "Not many people make the connection. It's kind of a lawyer thing."

I nodded toward Koop, who was busily kneading Kelli's lap. "He hates smokers. His name's Koop."

Kelli looked blank for a moment, then awareness lit up her face with another smile. "After the surgeon general who was such a fanatic against smoking!"

"Not many people make that connection either."

It's odd how bonds form between people. You wouldn't think cat names would do it. But we smiled at each other, and I felt a definite link here. It didn't prove Kelli Keifer wasn't a murderer, but it was going to take more than Ben's "everyone knows she did it" to make me think she was.

I turned back to Abilene. "So what happened with the cat?"

"After a little while it started breathing on its own."

Kelli clapped. "Hey, that's awesome!"

"I was really surprised when it worked," Abilene admitted. "And then the vet drove up, and the woman told him what I'd done. So he asked if I'd like to go inside and wash out my mouth—"

"Good idea!" Kelli said, and we all laughed. I was still trying to decide if I could do what Abilene had done.

"So I went in and washed out my mouth, and then I watched while the vet checked the cat to see if it was going to be okay. Its name is Mittens. The woman had a camera with her and took a picture of the little girl and me and Mittens all together."

"Do you know who these people were?" Kelli asked.

Abilene shook her head, and I had to smile. She knew the cat's name but not the people's. Or why the woman had a camera with her. Typical Abilene. "After they left, the veterinarian said I'd done . . . good."

Abilene is a modest person, not given to bragging. I guessed she was being modest now about what the vet had said.

"And then he offered me the job as his assistant."

"Dr. Sugarman will be a great guy to work for. I always take Sandra Day to him. This is great!"

I echoed the thought. A job involving animals would be a perfect job for Abilene.

"Everyone likes Dr. Sugarman," Kelli added. "He does everything from teach Sunday school at a church to run a 4-H club for the kids."

A Christian, an animal lover, and good with kids. I right away wanted to know if he was married, but Abilene jumped in before I could ask. "I told him I couldn't take a job because we were just passing through, but . . . ?" She looked at me questioningly.

"I don't think we're just passing through."

"Then maybe I'll go talk to him again about the job. He said he'd train me and teach me whatever I need to know."

She spoke in an offhand way, but I could see she was bubbling with eagerness. She clapped a hand to the side of her face. "Oh, but I forgot all about the plastic wrap!"

And, temporarily, the toothache too, apparently. "I think we'll survive without it," I assured her. Probably neither Abilene nor Kelli could, but I could well remember back to the days when we did without plastic wrap because there was no such thing.

I envisioned Dr. Sugarman as young and handsome, though I doubted that mattered to Abilene. The chance to work with animals was what was important to her. And there was that big barrier to a romantic relationship for Abilene anyway, a barrier in the form of brutal, vindictive Boone Morrison, who was still, unfortunately, her legal husband.

Kelli jumped up. "Okay! Good. Do you want to go over to the house now or wait until tomorrow?" She answered her own question. "Actually, tomorrow would be better. Uncle Hiram had the place modernized with a heat pump a few years ago, and I have the heat on to keep the pipes from freezing, but it's down really low. I'll go over now and turn it up, so the house will be warm tomorrow. Okay?"

"Sounds good," I said.

Kelli offered to come pick us up, but I said we could walk, so she drew a map of streets and suggested we meet at the house at ten o'clock the following day. She said it would be quite a walk, but I said we didn't mind.

"But we don't want you taking time off from work just for this. Ben Simpson mentioned you're a lawyer, and I know how busy lawyers are. We can come earlier or later."

"I'm surprised he didn't also mention that I'm not exactly overwhelmed with business." Actually Ben had pointed that out, but I didn't mention it now. "I'm still working on Uncle Hiram's estate, and I'm handling a couple of real estate things, but I let my receptionist go a few weeks ago." She gave us a little wave as she went out the door. "See you tomorrow."

Nick closed and locked the gate when he left for the night, and I felt comfortable and secure behind the wooden fence. I fixed pork chops and microwave-baked potatoes for dinner, and Abilene added a salad. Koop snuggled up at my feet when we all went to bed, me in the bed up over the driver and passenger's seats, Abilene on the sofa. I'd offered numerous times to switch with her because she's so much taller than I am, but she always insisted the sofa was fine.

I crossed my hands behind my head on the pillow and reflected on the day. It had been stressful, no doubt about it, and I knew we might be stranded here for who-knew-how-long. But the Lord, working in his usual mysterious ways, was looking after us. A dream job for Abilene. A house to live in.

Thank you, Lord.

And an intriguing, unsolved murder lurking in the wings . . .

5

Kelli's Bronco was already parked in the driveway when we arrived, me huffing from the climb, because the house was well up on a steep hillside on the east side of town. This had no doubt been a lone-wolf, power position overlooking all of Hello at one time, and the view of town below and mountains beyond was still spectacular, but homes of more recent vintage rose on the hillside above the house now.

The house looked like a late Victorian, maybe built in the 1890s or early 1900s, I guessed, although it had probably been modified since originally built. We'd seen other Victorians on our climb up here, but this one, though not as well-kept as some, showed evidence of past glory. A steep roofline topped the three stories, with odd angles and juttings here and there to accommodate dormer windows and other projections. A round tower rose from each front corner of the house, which struck me as unusual. Perhaps built that way because other houses constructed locally in that time period had only one tower, and whichever McLeod ancestor had built the house felt the need to proclaim his superiority with two?

The tower on the right was open on the third floor, making it a circular balcony with a fancy railing below a peaked roof rising to a weather vane of a trotting horse. The tower on the left had a semicircle of tall, narrow windows with arched tops and a graceful roof that matched the opposite tower. When we peered through the tall hedge surrounding the front yard, I saw that a brick walkway outlined each tower.

Subtracting from the elegance of the tower on the left was a chunk of unpainted plywood covering one of the windows. A pillared porch loaded with gingerbread trim ran across the front of the house between the towers. Most of the house was painted a dreary mold-green, but an impressive brick chimney rose beyond the right tower. An addition appeared to have been built on the back side of the house at some time, a flat-roofed oblong unfortunately tacked on with no regard for architecture or style.

I felt, as freeloading tenants, perhaps we should go around to some servants' entrance, but Kelli had been watching for us and swung the front door open.

"A rather grand old gal, isn't she?" She motioned us up the front steps. "Too bad it has this pall of doom hanging over it. Like a curse or infectious disease, and anyone who gets too close might catch it."

"People will get over whatever prejudice they have against the house because of the circumstances. It's a beautiful old place."

"It needs some work, but it is beautiful, isn't it? And if you live here and don't get murdered, maybe the death-taint will be defused."

If we didn't get murdered? Not a reassuring thought. But free is free, I philosophized. Can't be fussy about details.

Apparently realizing how what she'd just said sounded,

40

Kelli smiled ruefully. "That didn't come out quite right, did it? But I'm sure you'll be perfectly safe here."

"You didn't live here with your uncle?" I asked as Kelli shut the door behind us. The heat pump had brought the interior temperature to a comfortable warmth.

"No. I stayed here for a short time, but it wasn't working out. Now I have a little log cottage over on the other side of town."

The front door, with a heavy oval window of etched glass, opened onto a large, hardwood-floored foyer centered with a broad stairway leading upward. An archway opened to a living room, or perhaps it was called a parlor at one time, on the right. A door to the left was closed. I looked at it curiously. There's something magnetic about a closed door, at least for someone as curious as I am. I could almost feel, as my good friend Magnolia back in Missouri would say, vibes coming off the room. Was that where Hiram had been murdered?

Kelli ignored the closed door and led us into the living room, brushing aside a spider web draped catty-corner across the archway.

"Living in the same house wasn't working out because . . . ?" Okay, it was a nosy question. But little old ladies can often get away with nosiness, and I'm willing to take advantage of any perks available to LOLs.

"The rumors are rampant, of course. One is that Uncle Hiram didn't want me living in the house with him because he was afraid I'd poison him. Another is that I didn't want to live here because it would cramp my lifestyle. I'm from the Los Angeles area. Which to the local imagination could mean anything from nude dancing on tabletops to throwing cocaine parties with my friends from the Hollywood Mob. It's all so outrageous that it would be funny, except . . ." She shook her head and blinked, and I guessed the town's suspicions hurt her more than she wanted to let on.

41

"And the real reason you didn't want to live in the same house was . . . ?"

"A big reason was that Uncle Hiram didn't like cats, and I have my Sandra Day. I didn't care for his heavy smoking, and we also had some . . . philosophical differences." An intriguing comment, I thought, but she moved on without elaborating. "I also prefer something a little more cozy than this."

She waved toward the distant ceiling, the molding and elaborate crystal chandelier liberally draped with more spider webs. The enormous fireplace had been covered over at some time and was now just a blank brick wall beneath an elaborately carved mantel. The mantel would still be a nice place to hang a child's stocking at Christmas, and I felt an unexpected wave of nostalgia about a fireplace mantel hung with stockings back in my son Colin's childhood. Sometimes it's hard to believe how old Colin would be now if he hadn't disappeared in a ferry accident while on a military peacekeeping assignment in Korea so long ago.

A round tower room opened off this larger room, a charming, airy space, lace-curtained but quite devoid of furniture. Actually, both living and dining rooms were rather skimpily furnished, though a few impressive and no doubt valuable antiques remained. A lovely grand piano and a grandfather clock dominated the living room, and a heavy, claw-footed oak table and matching hutch stood in the adjoining dining room. A number of oversized portraits and photographs of various stiff-backed, bearded gentlemen hung on the walls, a couple of the men accompanied by wasp-waisted women in enormous, elegant hats.

Abilene, hands stuffed in the back pockets of her jeans, studied one of the photos. Although I suspected she was less interested in the people than the woman's hat, probably looking to see if the feathers were from some endangered species. Abilene notices things like that.

"Are any of these pictures of Hiram?" I asked.

"No. That was his father." She pointed to one elaborately framed oval photo of a wiry man with an unexpectedly rakish look in spite of an unsmiling countenance. The cane in his hand looked more like a stylish accessory than a necessity. "But I'm not certain who the others are. Various grandparents and uncles and cousins, according to Hiram. But he could be mischievous. I wouldn't put it past him to just pick up some old photo in an antique store and blithely claim it was a distinguished or rascally old McLeod."

An odd but probably harmless peculiarity of character.

Jarring next to the classic lines of the piano was a modern sofa with a purple and green pattern that looked as if it had been overrun by some virulent species of jungle fungus. Folding metal TV trays doubled as end tables, and most of the fringe on an old-fashioned floor lamp was missing. Blotchy gray paint covered the wallpaper on one wall, as if in preparation for some remodeling project that had never materialized.

In total, not the elegant rooms or furnishings you'd expect in a big old Victorian house with a wealthy owner. That thought must have zipped across to Kelli.

"There are more antiques stored upstairs, but what usually happened was that one wife would move in and change things to suit herself. Then another would come along and redo everything. Except for the first two, who he married when he was quite young, the wives were always much younger than Hiram. Maybe Ben Simpson mentioned there had been eight of them?"

I nodded.

She didn't comment on Ben Simpson's eager dispersal of gossipy information. "Apparently the wives always wanted things different than how they were, and Uncle Hiram was happy to humor them. The most recent wife threw out most of the previous wife's furniture, but she didn't last long enough to replace anything, so that's why it's so bare in here. I'm not sure where that came from," she added with a nose-wrinkle of distaste at the sofa.

There was nothing good to be said about the sofa, so I didn't say anything. "Did Hiram play the piano?"

"Oh yes, and he was quite good at it. I was always surprised when I'd come over and hear this wonderful Mozart floating out to the street. I think it relaxed him."

No doubt he needed relaxation after eight temperamental, furniture-tossing wives.

Kelli led us on through a swinging door into the large kitchen. "He did most of his living in here in his last couple of years."

This did not look like the world of a quite good, grand piano player, even a mischievous one. Actually, it looked . . . sad. And lonely. An enormous big-screen TV blocked most of one window, and a single cot covered with layers of khaki blankets stood against the opposite wall. A tiny microwave sat on the kitchen counter beside a huge combination refrigerator/freezer. A folding card table apparently served as Hiram's eating area. It was set up near an electric fireplace. A lone yellow silk rose stood in a cheap vase on the windowsill over the sink, beside it a mayonnaise jar filled with feathers.

"Uncle Hiram hated to shop, so when he did do it he bought enough to last for a while. Like the thirty-four TV dinners, all Mexican enchiladas and tamales, that I found in the freezer. Plus seventeen cans of chili in the cupboard and rotten tomatoes in the refrigerator. Because he'd bought something like twenty pounds of them, way more than he could use."

"He was a bit . . . ummm . . . eccentric?" I asked, curious but not jumping to conclusions on the basis of thirty-four TV dinners. Before living in the motor home full-time, where space is limited, I'd been known to stock up on good buys too. I've also discovered that a bit of eccentricity, like the invisibility that comes to many of us with the advance of years, can occasionally come in useful.

"Living like this, it looks that way, doesn't it? But I think it was more that he considered his present living conditions temporary and irrelevant. He really wasn't concerned about the details of everyday living." She smiled. "But maybe that's one definition of eccentricity?"

"I wonder why he didn't hire a housekeeper?"

"I wondered too. I even suggested it, but he got all huffy, as if I were implying he was getting incompetent and couldn't take care of himself. So I just dropped it. I don't think many people knew he lived like this. He always dressed very well and cut quite a distinguished figure when he went out."

"Did you know any of the wives?"

"They were all past-tense by the time I moved here. One is still around, though she's elderly now and I think would rather no one knew she was once married to Hiram. But he was planning to marry again this spring. I suppose Ben told you that too?"

I nodded. I glanced around, wondering how a new wife would react to all this. "Hiram was an optimistic sort of man, then."

Kelli surprised me by laughing with delight. "I hadn't thought of it in exactly that way, but yes, that's true. Uncle Hiram was an optimistic man. He always had big, sometimes grandiose ideas, and he never gave up on marriage. And I think he had a right to be optimistic in this case. The next wife was to be Lucinda O'Mallory. She's the widow of a man whose early family established the first bank in Hello."

"Not as young as the others?"

"She's about Uncle Hiram's age, late sixties. By far his

45

best choice in wives, I think. Actually, it's quite a romantic story."

"Oh?"

"Lucinda was his old flame way back in their high school days here in Hello. I don't know what happened, but something did, and she married the banker and Hiram married someone else. She stayed married to the banker all these years, but he died a few years ago, and she and Hiram got together again not long ago. I sometimes wonder if the reason none of Hiram's marriages worked was because, deep down . . ." Kelli smiled self-consciously as if embarrassed to be caught romanticizing about the endurance of lost love. "Maybe I should be trying to write syrupy romances instead of a legal thriller."

"You're a writer?"

"I've had a considerable amount of free time since coming to Hello. I figured I might as well try to use it constructively." Her tone was wry, but her smile unexpectedly mischievous, perhaps a trait that ran in the family. "Also a perfect opportunity to fictionally skewer a few local personalities."

Hastily she jumped back to the story of the upcoming marriage that was not to be. "Lucinda has a beautiful home on the other side of town, a Victorian like this, only much better kept up. They were planning to live there."

Wise Lucinda, I thought. "What did Hiram intend to do with this place?"

"He talked about selling it after they were married, though I'm not sure he'd ever actually have done it. He had a sentimental streak."

"You approved of the marriage?"

"Oh yes. Lucinda's a wonderful woman. Very upbeat and cheerful. Active in local charitable and civic affairs, and very health minded too. I've seen her working out at the local health club. She's in incredible shape for someone her age. She'd have taken good care of Hiram."

"Too bad, then, the way things worked out."

Kelli nodded. "I know he must have had enemies from business dealings or personal differences over the years. He was a shrewd businessman. But it's hard to believe someone could have hated him enough to kill him. He was so generous to the town. To me too. He bought my little cabin for me. And then to have people think I murdered him . . ." She swallowed hard.

"Does Lucinda think that?"

"No. She says anyone who claims I killed him should be forced to write 'Kelli Keifer is not a killer' 349 times. She's always been wonderfully kind and nice to me, both before and after Uncle Hiram's death. We worked together on his funeral arrangements." She gave an unladylike snort. "Their upcoming marriage was another reason people think I murdered him, of course. I had to kill him before he and Lucinda married, otherwise I might lose out on some or all of the inheritance."

"There's a lot to inherit?"

She hesitated slightly. "I'll be working on that for some time yet."

"Hiram was still mentally okay?"

"Oh yes. He had an excellent memory. He could tell wonderful stories from when he was a small boy and spent time with his father out at the mine. Like when his father shot an attacking bear out there. And another time when he was playing in a creek and found a gold nugget as big as his thumb."

Abilene, always quiet, hadn't said anything all this time, but I knew she was anxious to get out of here and go talk to Dr. Sugarman about the job in his vet clinic.

"So, what do you think?" I said to Abilene, thinking we'd hurry this along so she could be on her way. She still needed to see a dentist too, but I knew that for her that came second in importance to the job with Dr. Sugarman. "Look okay to you?"

Although it was an unnecessary question, of course. We didn't have a smorgasbord of free living quarters from which to choose while we were stranded here in Hello. Abilene nodded approval. I knew Koop would love the place too, with its various nooks and crannies and, undoubtedly, plentiful supply of mice.

I turned to Kelli. "The house looks wonderful, and we really appreciate your generosity, so—"

"Let me show you the bedrooms first. I don't want there to be any unpleasant surprises."

Actually I was more curious about the murder than the bedrooms. I hadn't noticed any blood stains or other signs of violence so far. How had Hiram been murdered? And where? Who'd found the body?

Yet I thought tact and sensitivity required waiting until Kelli offered the information rather than my demanding it, so I merely followed when she opened a door from the kitchen to a hallway.

"This part from here on back is an addition that was put on in the '50s, I think it was. Hiram's mother, or maybe it was his grandmother, was bedridden, and they needed rooms for more nursing and household help."

The long hallway led to a windowless back door. The first two rooms Kelli opened in the addition were empty, but the next one held an impressive array of workout equipment, a treadmill, a stepper, barbells in graduated sizes, and various weight machines.

"Hiram worked out?" I asked, surprised.

"No, some wife had all this stuff moved in. I've heard she had a trampoline out in the yard too, and she liked to work out on it in her bikini. I heard there was a big jump in the sale of binoculars locally about that time."

48

Yes, I decided, Hiram definitely needed an older woman such as Lucinda O'Mallory.

The next room looked as if it had been Hiram's discard room. Or maybe it was his save-it, I-may-need-this-some-day room. Piles of newspapers and magazines, a mountain of wadded-up plastic bags, plastic jugs, bits of old, broken furniture, cardboard boxes of all sizes, various-sized chunks of Styrofoam, sacks of old rags, even a couple of old bicycle tires.

"I've been putting it off, but one of these days I'll have to rent a truck and haul all this stuff to the dump."

"Some of it could be recycled."

"Just don't drop a match in here, or the whole town might go up in flames."

"We'll be careful."

"There are two furnished bedrooms on this floor," Kelli went on as she turned and led us in the opposite direction down the wide but dim hallway. "There are also various rooms on the second floor that I suppose were bedrooms. The second floor hasn't actually been closed off like the third floor has been for years, but I haven't had the house checked for structural reliability yet, so it would probably be best to use these."

She opened a door off the hallway and stood back to let us see inside. "This is the smaller bedroom on this floor. I've wondered if it may have been a nursery at one time. There isn't a private bath, just the bath down the hall."

The bedroom may have been a nursery at some time, but the furniture now was old and heavy, probably antique but mismatched and rather worse for wear. Two single-wide beds, a tall chest of drawers, and two nightstands. Two generic, English hunting scenes hung on walls papered with cabbage roses. The carpet, of entwined dark flowers on a blue background, had a faded elegance, and there was also an impressive armoire of more dark, carved wood, probably rather valuable.

The room was clean, but the beds looked carelessly made up. A crooked sheet hung below the bedspread on one. A book, *I Married an Alien*, with a picture on the cover of a big-eyed, hairless being, lay on the nightstand. The open door of the armoire revealed a couple of plaid shirts, one with a hole in the elbow, and a pair of scruffy, sheepskin-lined slippers. A faint scent of old smoke clung to everything.

"Did Hiram spend some of his nights here rather than in the kitchen?" I asked.

"No. Norman, the caretaker out at the mine, came to town once in a while, and Hiram always let him stay here. Hiram and he liked to smoke and drink tequila and argue about everything from politics to UFOs. It was a rather unlikely friendship, but they were good buddies."

"Was this buddy around when Hiram was murdered?"

"You're seeing Norman as a murderer?" Kelli smiled and shook her head. "No, I'm sure he wasn't, though the police did go out and question him. Not that anyone would suspect ol' Norman anyway. He's a bit odd, but harmless. He was terribly upset by the murder. He even showed up at the funeral in a blue suit. Although the tie with a palm tree on it detracted a bit from the effect."

Harmless or not, I wouldn't automatically dismiss someone who was apparently here at the house often. Could the authorities know for certain he wasn't here at the time of the murder? Sometimes even friendly arguments exploded into violence when old buddies drank together. And sometimes murderers were, too late, upset by what they'd done.

The next door opened on a much larger bedroom furnished with impressive antiques that had apparently escaped the wives' toss-'em-out energies. A huge, canopied bed draped with red velvet curtains stood in regal splendor against the wall. Scattered around the room were several wingback chairs, a graceful, old-fashioned chaise longue, a mirrored dresser, several chests of drawers, and an antique trunk. More red velvet drapes framed an airy bay window.

But all that paled in comparison to what stood in the far corner.

Carousel horses. Three of them. Necks arched, hooves prancing, eyes gleaming, nostrils flaring, tails flowing. One was white, one ebony, one golden. Their saddles were blue and scarlet and purple, bridles and reins of gold-colored leather. Each was mounted on a brass pole, and they stood on a round wooden base, as if poised for the lighthearted tinkle of calliope music to bring them to life. Harley and I had ridden a merry-go-round once, oh so long ago . . .

The carousel horses were so astonishing, so totally out of place here in this bedroom, that I didn't know what to say.

"Aren't they amazing?" Kelli said.

"They're beautiful! Are they antique? Something that's been in the family for years?"

"They're old, and they're original carousel horses that have been restored, not modern copies. Lucinda knows enough about antiques to confirm that. Real carved wood, not plastic or fiberglass. But I have no idea where they came from or anything of their history. Hiram never mentioned them, and I never saw them until after he died."

"How strange." But the carousel horses unexpectedly gave me a warmer feeling toward Hiram. I'd been put off by all those wives, but here I saw a hint of small boy deep inside the man. Maybe he'd wanted to ride a merry-go-round as a boy and never had the chance. Another thought occurred to me, a more romantic one.

"Maybe he meant them as a surprise for Lucinda. Maybe they rode a carousel together when they were young, and it held nostalgic memories."

51

"If so, I'm afraid Lucinda doesn't remember. She seemed as astonished as I was to find them here. She says they're quite valuable."

Abilene had already crossed the room to run her hand over the sculptured lines of the wooden animals. "Look! The manes and tails are real horsehair."

I went over to join her, marveling at the level of workmanship carved into the wooden animals. Then I looked down and shrieked.

6

Abilene grabbed my arm protectively. "What is it? What's the matter?"

I pointed to the carpet under my feet. Abilene isn't a shrieking person, but even she gave a small squeak. Blood stains, enough blood stains for an ax murder, were seeping out from under the base of the carousel horses. The stain hadn't been noticeable earlier, mixed with the floral pattern of the carpet, but now . . .

I clutched Abilene's hand and looked at Kelli. "This is where . . . ?"

"Oh no. I'm sorry!" She waved her hand and gave an embarrassed laugh. "I'd forgotten. I should've warned you. It isn't a blood stain. At least I don't think so."

"It isn't?" I said doubtfully.

"I thought it was blood too, when I first saw it," Kelli admitted. She walked over and peered down at the stain with us. "I even wondered if I should check back to see if one of the wives had mysteriously disappeared sometime. But then

I got to looking closer, and I think it's just a wine stain. I'm guessing one of the wives threw something like a bottle of burgundy at Uncle Hiram sometime. He tended to marry the hot-tempered kind."

I knelt and examined the irregular stain and decided Kelli was right. Part of the stain was under the base holding the carousel horses, which meant they'd been moved into the room after the bottle-throwing incident, probably fairly recently. But why? Why would old Hiram bring something as unlikely as expensive and beautiful carousel horses into his bedroom? Especially when, with a wedding coming up in only a few months, he wouldn't have been living here much longer?

"I don't know if the stain wouldn't come out, or if he decided it wasn't worth the bother," Kelli added. "In any case, it hasn't anything to do with the murder."

"And so," I asked, figuring I'd earned the right to take a flying leap over sensitivity and tact, "where did the murder occur?"

"I'll show you. What do you want to see? The beginning or the end?"

While I was wondering what that meant, she made the decision herself and motioned for us to follow. Abilene hesitated. I recognized her dilemma. Curiosity runs deep in Abilene, maybe almost as deep as it does in me. We've both read enough mystery novels to write our own *Murder for Dummies* manual, with footnotes. But now she was torn. Dr. Sugarman or murder mystery?

Dr. Sugarman won. Which told me again how much the job meant to her. She glanced down the hallway toward the front door. "Would it be okay if . . . ?" she began tentatively.

"You run along. We'll see about moving our things from the motor home over here later."

Kelli looked at her watch. "I have to take the Bronco in to

Nick's for that two o'clock appointment. We can do it right after that."

Abilene wasted no time heading for the door. I followed Kelli at a slower pace down the hallway to the foyer and stairs. I was certain we were heading for that closed door. I was even anticipating a shivery *Inner Sanctum*–type squawk when it opened.

But Kelli turned toward the stairs leading upward. She noticed my questioning look at the door. "Nothing happened in there. It's just Uncle Hiram's office and library. I've already moved his records and papers over to my office, so it's just books in there now."

So much for my vibe-recognition abilities. "I thought Hiram had donated his books to the Ladies Historical Society."

"He did, but they've never picked them up. They spent every cent he gave them on getting the new wing for the library added onto their building. When they ran out of money, he said he'd donate another bundle for maintenance and to hire someone to organize and catalog the books, but he hadn't yet gotten around to that before he was murdered." She paused, frowning slightly.

I jumped right in with a possibility. "Could there have been some connection? Someone didn't want him to make that next donation?"

She groaned but also laughed. "Don't say that. If the town hasn't already thought of it, they'll be adding that on as another black mark against me: I had to murder him before he gave more assets away. Of course the ladies of the Hysterical Society would have had enough money without another donation from him if they hadn't acted like kids turned loose in a video arcade when they built the new wing."

As a longtime librarian, I'm also a longtime book preservationist. "They had to have a good place to put the books,"

I protested. "Books deteriorate in poor conditions, and temperature is important."

"But did they need 175-dollars-a-yard carpet and imported teak shelving, and bringing in some artsy guy from New York to do a mural?" Kelli snorted in disapproval.

"May I go in and look around later?"

"Sure. Help yourself. The door isn't locked. I keep thinking there must be more records concerning investments or accounts that I haven't located yet, but I don't know where else to look."

"I'll keep an eye out for anything like that."

"Anyway, there are tons of old books about Colorado history and mining and various other subjects that interested Uncle Hiram."

The spindlework supporting the railing on either side of the stairway looked too delicate to hold up the thick, molded railing, but the rail felt solid under my hand. A green ribbon blocked access to the hallway at the second-floor landing, although it was mostly symbolic, because the ribbon wouldn't actually keep anyone out. Beyond the ribbon, a haphazard collection of junk and/or antiques lined the hallway. On the third floor landing, a bare piece of plywood lay to one side. Holes and splinters in the wood showed where it had been yanked from a nailed position across the doorway.

"Didn't you say the third floor was closed off?"

"It was, until Uncle Hiram decided to open it up for some unknown reason."

We stepped into an enormous, unfurnished space. Dusty light streamed through uncurtained windows. A maze of footprints decorated the dust on the floor, polished hardwood gleaming through them. "A ballroom?" I guessed.

"Hiram said that when he was a small boy his parents held wonderful fancy-dress balls here, but it's another part of the house that I was never in until after his death."

She led the way across the bare floor to a round tower room, the one with windows. A solid, although slightly warped, door closed off the balcony tower room, but only an archway separated this room and the ballroom. There had once been carpet in the circular room, but it had been ripped up, leaving only shreds on the floor. A smell of old wood and musty carpet hung in the stagnant air.

"That's where he went out." Kelli pointed to the raw plywood covering one long, narrow window. "He landed on the brick walkway below. I had the window boarded up temporarily until I get new glass installed."

I went to a window to the left of the plywood. The bottom sill was no more than a few inches above floor level, not all that difficult to plunge through. Kelli stayed back, as if she'd rather not look out.

Nothing showed that a body had once crashed to the bricks below. No chalk outlined where the body had landed, and the old bricks were too discolored by long exposure to the elements to reveal any blood stains now. Bare-branched trees hung over the yard like dark skeletons leering over a tragedy.

I had a sudden, dizzying awareness of how it would feel to crash through the window and plunge headlong through open space to death below. I grabbed the framework around the window to steady myself, then jerked my hand away as I realized a grayish powder clung to the woodwork.

"The police checked for fingerprints?" I asked, looking at the residue on my hand.

Kelli nodded. "Yeah. They called in people from the county sheriff's office and were quite thorough. They went through the house with the proverbial fine-toothed comb."

I dug a tissue from my pocket and wiped at the fingerprint powder, which resulted in more smearing than removal.

"What made the authorities decide he was murdered?"

I asked. "With the sill so low, couldn't he simply have tripped or stumbled and fallen through the window accidentally?"

"The police think that's how the murderer wanted it to look. But Uncle Hiram had an injury that was, as they put it, 'inconsistent' with how he landed on the bricks. If he'd landed differently, maybe they'd never even have suspected it was murder."

"What kind of injury?"

"He landed face down, but there was an injury to the back of his head. The medical examiner said he'd been hit with something, although they've never identified what. At least not publicly. The weapon has never been found." Wryly she added, "Although they got a warrant and spent enough time searching my place for it."

"And the ripped-up carpet?"

"There wasn't any visible blood on the carpet, but they took it off for laboratory testing anyway. And the tests did show specks of blood. Uncle Hiram's blood, according to the analysis."

"Which gives further weight to the conclusion that he didn't stumble and fall through the window on his own. The blood came from the blow to the head."

"Right."

"So, the theory is that when he was hit on the head, he fell forward and plunged through the window, breaking it?"

"I'm not sure if they think that's how it happened, or if they think the killer hit him and then picked him up and shoved him through the window after he was unconscious."

"That would take a fair amount of strength."

I glanced back at Kelli. She smiled without humor. She struck a bodybuilder's pose and flexed a bicep under the gray sweatshirt. "They seemed to think I could have done it easily enough. Uncle Hiram wasn't a large or heavy man."

"Was it the blow on the head or the fall that killed him?"

"The blow on the head was vicious, but it wasn't fatal, according to the autopsy. Landing on the bricks was what killed him. The only good thing—" She broke off and swallowed. "If you could call anything good in all this, it's that he was probably already unconscious from the blow and didn't know he was falling or feel the impact on the bricks."

"What were he and the killer doing up here together, if the third floor was usually closed off?" I went back to the window, noticing what I hadn't before. The view of the town from here was truly spectacular, the narrow main street lined with picturesque old brick buildings.

"Good question. The police didn't lay out details for me, but from their questioning I gathered they thought I removed the plywood blocking off the third floor, lured Uncle Hiram up here on some pretext, and whacked him with some heavy object. But, since I know it didn't happen that way, I have no idea why he was up here." Again that bitterness in her voice, along with an undercurrent of frustrated helplessness.

"Or who was with him," I murmured.

"Exactly."

"Hiram, or whoever removed the plywood, must have used some tool to do it. I wonder what happened to it?"

"There was a hammer. The police took that too, but it turned out to have only Uncle Hiram's fingerprints on it, and no trace of blood. They said it wasn't the weapon."

"So the killer didn't just grab whatever was readily available to kill Hiram. Which means the killing wasn't a spur-of-the-moment impulse. It was planned, with the killer thinking ahead to bring his own weapon."

"I guess so," Kelli said, although she sounded uncertain, as if she hadn't thought of that particular angle. "Even though I

59

know it happened, I-I still find it hard to believe that someone could deliberately kill him."

"You've never been officially charged with the murder?"

"Much to most people's annoyance and exasperation, no."

"Why not?"

"Except for the motive of grabbing Uncle Hiram's assets, they haven't any real reason to charge me. There's no solid evidence. They couldn't find any weapon at my place. My fingerprints weren't anywhere up here. Which doesn't remove me from the top of the suspect list, of course, because everyone figures I could have dumped a weapon out at the mine. There are old shafts out there you could probably shove a Volkswagen in, and it would never be found."

"Motive looks like the big thing, then. But someone else must have had a strong motive too."

"It's all speculation. Unfair speculation," Kelli added on another note of bitterness.

"Do you have an alibi?"

"I have the truth. Which is that I was working on my book manuscript, at home with Sandra Day, the evening it was probably done. Unfortunately, a cat alibi doesn't carry a lot of weight with the police." Kelli tried to speak lightly, but the words snagged on a convulsive swallow. "Sometimes I get . . . afraid. I know I'm innocent, and I-I believe in our legal system. I wouldn't be a lawyer if I didn't. But people do get convicted of crimes they didn't commit."

I reached over and squeezed her hand, her very cold hand, and tried to think of something reassuring and helpful. But she was right. Sometimes innocent people were convicted. "Do you work on a computer with your book?"

"When I'm at the office. That's where my computer is. But at home I just fill up these big, yellow, legal-size tablets. Then I transfer them to the computer, revising as I go."

60

Which shot down my idea that some expert could go into the internal workings of her computer and prove that she'd been using it at the time Hiram was killed.

"No fingerprints anywhere?"

Kelli shook her head. "Nothing up here. And too many prints of all kinds of people downstairs. I guess prints can hang around for a long time."

"Did you find the body?"

"No, it was Lucinda, his fiancée. She'd been trying to call Uncle Hiram for a couple of days. When she kept getting no answer she decided to come over and check on him." Kelli moved over to look down now, as if pulled by something stronger than the revulsion that held her back.

"She waited two days before coming over? Didn't they keep in closer touch than that?"

"They weren't like teenagers on the phone half a dozen times a day. It also wasn't unusual for him to go out of town for a day or two. He was dealing with some big mining outfit about reopening the Lucky Queen, or he may have been trying to round up some private investors. He didn't discuss any of that with me. In any case, he was too independent to think he was obliged to keep anyone informed of his whereabouts."

"Not even a fiancée?"

"Not a fiancée, and certainly not me, either."

"How long had he been dead when she found him?"

"Probably two to three days. With the body outside, and the variable weather conditions we've had, they couldn't pin it down exactly."

I studied the street in front of the house. It was not busily traveled. Only one car went by as I watched. There were no houses beyond the far side of the pavement, just a concrete curb. The narrow street followed the curve of the hillside, the ground falling off steeply beyond the curb on the far side, only roofs of houses below visible. It was a large lot, houses on either side at least a couple hundred feet away, trees between. Ideal setting for a murder.

"No one spotted the body in all that time?"

"The hedge blocks view of the yard from the street, so someone would have had to actually come into the front yard to see him lying there on the bricks, and I guess no one did. Oh, there's Chris!"

She waved wildly at a man getting out of a red Mustang, but he didn't look up to see her. "Be back in a minute," she called as she dashed for the stairs.

I didn't see any point in lingering at the window. Not because I wasn't interested, but because, since we were going to be living here, I could return for a closer perusal any time. Which I definitely intended to do.

I reached the foyer just as the guy stepped inside. He and Kelli greeted each other with a light kiss. Kelli introduced us—full name Chris Sterling. "Well, Christopher Sterling II, if you want to get technical," she said, and he grimaced lightly. She explained our motor home predicament and that Abilene and I would be living in the house for a while.

He smiled as we shook hands, but he afterward looked at his hand with a grimace of distaste. With good reason, I realized guiltily. I'd left fingerprint powder residue on his hand. He got out a clean white handkerchief and, frowning, rubbed at the smear. At the same time, when he said, "Do you really think it's a good idea having someone live here? It's such a rickety old place," I could see that he wasn't overjoyed with the news about our living in the house.

I figured I knew the reason, and it wasn't a "rickety" state of the house. He was afraid we were of questionable character and were taking advantage of Kelli's generous nature. Not an unreasonable assumption, I had to admit. Or maybe he was afraid one of us intended to fall down the stairs deliberately and sue for neck or back injury. After he stuck the handkerchief back in his pocket, he put a protective arm around her shoulders and looked at me. I tried to think of something to ease his concerns.

"Kelli and I haven't discussed it yet, but I'm thinking we can do some cleanup work in the house in exchange for living here."

He glanced at the dust-covered piano in the living room. "Well, you've got your work cut out for you. Although my own thought is that someone ought to just strike a match to the place and be done with it."

I thought Kelli might be put off by that attitude toward a house that probably had some sentimental family value for her, but she just smiled tolerantly. "Chris isn't into old. He's always saying what Hello needs is a good computer and electronics equipment store, not another antique place selling more useless old knickknacks, dreadful lamps, and ugly jewelry."

Chris was looking at me, and I had the feeling he was perhaps classifying me in there with all the other useless old antique stuff.

"Have you gotten Hiram's office cleaned out?" he asked Kelli.

"I think so. Although he sometimes squirreled things away, so I'm not sure I have everything."

"Yeah, I thought a lot of the old guy, but he was a little strange sometimes. You feeling okay now?"

"I'm fine." With a glance at me she added, "I ate something a couple nights ago at the Russo that didn't agree with me."

I wanted to know more about Chris Sterling. I could see that he was tall, blond, and well built, his angular jaw and deep-set eyes handsomely sculpted. Although, as a complete package, he was a bit too Greek-goddish for my taste. I rather like some small imperfections. My friend Mac MacPherson's knobby knees, for instance. And the blue motorcycle tattooed on Mac's forearm has an unexpected appeal. No tattoos on Christopher Sterling II, I was sure.

Chris was well dressed in a dark business suit with light blue shirt and diagonally striped blue and silver tie, a bit more urbane than I'd have expected in Hello. I could also see from the way Kelli looked at him that she was probably in love with him.

Oddly, I felt a sense of protectiveness of my own. I barely knew Kelli, but I didn't like the way the town seemed to have unfairly ganged up on her. This man seemed different, caring and concerned about her, but, with the disdainful attitude toward the house and that picky way he'd wiped his hand, did he deserve her love?

"I tried to call you at the office and home, but I couldn't reach you. So I decided I'd run over here and check before I left town."

"Is something wrong?" Kelli asked.

"No, I just wanted to let you know I can't make it to lunch today. Something came up with the Swenson case, and I'm going to have to make a quick trip up to Denver," he said, and I gave him points for thoughtfulness. "Unless you'd like to come along?"

"Thanks, but I have an appointment with Nick about the Bronco, and I want to help Ivy and Abilene get moved in."

"Mom wants us to have dinner with her tomorrow night. Okay with you?"

"Sure. I have to run out to the mine tomorrow afternoon, but I'll be back in plenty of time."

Chris's dark gold eyebrows edged together. "Kell, don't you think you're doing too much for that old guy out there? He can't expect you to be his personal errand girl. You were out there only yesterday."

64

"I know, but his pickup's broke down, and he needs some feed for the chickens and something for his stomach problems. And he was coming down with a cold too."

"For which he wants you to bring him what? A couple bottles of that tequila he and Hiram were so fond of? Or maybe some eye of newt, snake oil, or powdered lizard tongues?"

Kelli pounded her fist lightly on Chris's arm, a gesture that looked more affectionate than angry. "There you go again. Ol' Norman's not into weird stuff like that."

"They don't call him Nutty Norman for nothing. And I'm not so sure the old coot isn't dangerous. One time when I came over to talk to Hiram about something, he and Norman were yelling bloody murder at each other."

"Norman's just a little eccentric, and their arguing didn't mean anything. All he needs are cough drops and Nyquil, and some blackberry balsam for his stomach. Perfectly ordinary stuff. And he's no more dangerous than my Sandra Day."

"Your Sandra Day always looks at me as if she's thinking about clawing my eyes out. I don't want you going out there alone."

"Okay, maybe I won't go alone. Ivy, you want to come along?"

I knew nothing about Nutty Norman, or what this trip entailed, but I promptly said, "Of course. I'd love to."

Chris rolled his eyes, and I could see he figured I'd be as much help to Kelli in a dangerous situation as a month's supply of lizard tongues. He didn't argue anymore, however. Just a put-upon expression and another light kiss. "Be careful," he said and headed back to the Mustang. I looked at Kelli after he was gone.

"Someone special?"

She smiled. "Very much so. Though he worries too much.

You don't really have to go out to the mine with me tomorrow. The road's pretty rough."

And muddy, I suspected, from the condition of Kelli's Bronco. But, after two seconds' thought, I knew, if she hadn't invited me, I'd have tried to finagle a way to go along. That mutant curiosity gene in action, of course. "I'd really like to go."

7

By that evening, Abilene had the job with Dr. Sugarman, plus an appointment with the dentist, Dr. Li, for the following day. She and I had cleaned out the refrigerator and freezer in the motor home while Nick adjusted the carburetor on Kelli's newly washed Bronco. I arranged with Nick to drain the water system on the motor home so it wouldn't freeze up and break something. Kelli had then ferried everything we thought we'd need over to the house. We could always come back later for anything we'd forgotten. I'd told Nick I'd let him know as soon as we figured out how to pay for a new engine.

"No rush," he said generously. "I'll just drag the motor home around behind the shop where it'll be out of the way." After an odd little hesitation he added, "You be careful over there at the McLeod house, okay?"

"Careful of what?"

"Well, you know. Old Hiram got murdered there."

"I doubt his murderer has anything against Abilene and

me. And I certainly don't believe in spooks or ghosts or anything like that in old houses."

Nick looked uncomfortable and suddenly became busy searching a drawer for something, as if he wished he'd never brought this up. "I just know I wouldn't want to be living there," he finally muttered.

"We're looking forward to it," I said firmly.

At the house, I cautiously let Koop out of the cat carrier, making sure all the outside doors were securely closed. I didn't want him to get frightened and bolt. But I should have known Koop was too laid-back a feline gentleman for that. On a busy but calm tour, he investigated the jungle-fungus sofa and jumped to the piano, leaving delicate cat tracks in the dust. He checked out the windowsills in the tower room and prowled under the dining room table. In the kitchen, he hissed at the khaki-covered cot, which still commemorated Hiram's heavy smoking habit. He checked out the bedrooms, including a foray into the depths of the armoire, then left us to continue his tour upstairs.

Abilene chose one of the single beds in the smaller bedroom for her living quarters. I debated between the other single in the same room and the master bedroom. The master bedroom, I finally decided. It was a bit gaudy for my taste, but what other chance would I ever have to sleep in a velvet-canopied bed with three carousel horses for company?

We found a serviceable washer and dryer in a utility room beyond the kitchen and caught up on laundry, including the sheets and blankets from Abilene's room. Ol' Norman, Nutty Norman as Chris Sterling had called him, apparently scorned showers as city-folk nonsense. Both beds in that room smelled of unwashed body, old smoke, and garlic, with a scattering of gritty sand in the foot area. We turned the mattresses too.

The sheets in the master bedroom were crisp and new, delicately patterned in tiny yellow roses, almost as if prepared and waiting for someone special. Lucinda? No, because after the wedding they'd planned to live in her place, not here. Perhaps just leftovers from the last wife who had occupied the room. They didn't look as if they needed washing, but we washed them anyway.

We moved the cot from the kitchen to one of the empty rooms and dined on TV dinners from Hiram's plentiful supply. A few minutes later I answered the unexpected chime of the doorbell and was surprised to find Kelli standing there. From the front door, town lights winding through the valley below looked fragile and insignificant beneath the black silhouettes of mountains looming against the star-studded night sky.

"I just wanted to make sure everything was okay," she said brightly. She waved a sack. "I thought a housewarming party might be in order. I hope you like double-chocolate pecan crunch ice cream and Twix cookies? And I brought a copy of the *Hello Telegraph*. It's the local weekly newspaper."

Ice cream and newspaper were a sweet and thoughtful gesture, but at the same time I suspected an ulterior motive on Kelli's part. Not a *bad* ulterior motive. Just a bit of loneliness in a town that obviously hadn't taken her under its protective wing. I wondered if she intended to stay on in Hello after she got Hiram's estate settled. I wondered, too, why she'd come to Hello in the first place. Maybe I could work those subjects into the conversation on the way out to the mine.

I led her through to the kitchen, by far the most homey room in the big old house. We'd turned on the electric fireplace, and it put out both heat and flickering flames, which, though imitation, added a nice aura of coziness. A scent of perking coffee rose from the old, blue-enamel pot on the stove.

Kelli lifted her nose and sniffed appreciatively. "There's nothing like coffee from Uncle Hiram's old blue pot. He said the wives were always wanting him to switch to some fancy coffeemaker, but that was where he put his foot down. They could change the furniture all they wanted, but his coffeepot stayed." Again I heard that note of affection in her voice. If I wasn't already convinced Kelli couldn't have murdered her uncle, this settled it.

"I'll get dishes for the ice cream," Abilene said. Dishes were one thing in plentiful supply here. The cupboards were full of them, from a set of delicate old Meito china, with a platter just like the one my mother used to have, to a modern set of black, octagonal plates made of something I suspected could survive anything from temperamental wives to chemical embalming, plus a shelf of orphaned irregulars.

"We're fine, settling in nicely," I assured Kelli. I pointed to Koop, who'd already claimed as his personal domain a miniature-sized, imitation white bearskin that we'd found in the bedroom and moved out here in front of the electric fireplace for him. "Have you heard from Chris?"

"He called and said he was going to dinner with the client and would drive home in the morning. You might want to check out the photo on page 3 in the newspaper," she added.

I did. "Abilene, come look at this!" She came over, and we stared together.

The photo was of Abilene and a little girl holding a wide-eyed cat, the caption identifying Abilene as the person who had just saved the cat's life with CPR. The smiling little girl was Mindy Carchoun, daughter of a regular features writer for the newspaper, which no doubt explained why she'd had a camera handy for the occasion.

"You're a local heroine now!" Kelli said.

"I've never had my picture in a newspaper before." Abilene sounded rather overwhelmed but pleased.

Then she looked at me, and the wonderment in her eyes

changed to uneasiness, and I knew what she was thinking. This was nice, but the last thing either of us needed was publicity, not with a vindictive Boone Morrison on our trail. Yet I didn't want that worry to spoil her joy in this.

I squeezed her arm. "It'll be fine. I doubt the newspaper's circulation goes beyond the outskirts of Hello."

"I wouldn't say that," Kelli said. "It got written up in some tourist publication last year, and orders for subscriptions poured in from all over the country. I guess people like all the folksy stuff. How many newspapers report 'news' such as Maude Evans chasing a skunk through her laundry hanging on the line, getting tangled in a sheet, and calls coming in to the police about a ghost running through the neighborhood?"

"I'm sure it'll be fine," I repeated to Abilene.

Kelli gave us an odd look as if she wondered what that was all about, but I didn't enlighten her.

Abilene set dishes with big scoops of ice cream for each of us on the card table, along with a plate of Twix, and I poured coffee. The card table had numerous circular burned spots in the center. Hiram apparently didn't bother with such niceties as protective hot pads.

"Ummm, good," I said after letting a creamy spoonful melt in my mouth.

"I'm kind of a closet ice cream eater," Kelli confessed. "Chris won't eat dessert, unless it's fresh fruit, and he doesn't think I should either."

Commendable, I suppose, but somehow not a trait I found endearing. My friend Mac eagerly chows down on everything from my peach cobbler to jelly beans to anything chocolate. However, this was a nice opening. "Tell us about Chris," I suggested. "He seemed quite thoughtful and concerned about you."

"Oh, he is, a very thoughtful man. He was born and has

71

always lived right here in Hello, except for the years he went away to law school."

"He's also a lawyer?" I don't know why I should be surprised, but I was. I guess I have to admit I've always had a cold spot in my heart for lawyers, ever since a frivolous lawsuit about a pill-bottle lid was filed against Harley and his pharmacy back in Missouri.

"He and two other men are partners in the biggest law firm here in town. He handled all of Uncle Hiram's legal affairs before I came." She laughed at something in my expression. "So Chris should be furious because I stole his important client, right? He should be resentful, and we should be meeting at high noon, legal briefs drawn and subpoenas loaded, for a shoot-out on Main Street?"

"That would seem likely."

"Well, actually, it kind of started out that way. Things were pretty tense the first few days when Chris was transferring everything over to me. But after we'd spent some time together and talked and got to know each other, we both realized there was an attraction between us that was more important than rivalry."

"Is this a relationship that's going somewhere?"

"I think so." She smiled. "If it were up to Chris, we'd elope right now. He keeps suggesting it."

"Wouldn't you prefer a nice church wedding?"

"Not necessarily." She tilted her head thoughtfully. "Well, maybe. But either way, I'm inclined to take things more slowly than Chris is. I love him, but I want to be sure it's going to last a lifetime before I jump in with both feet. I don't want to wind up with a track record like Uncle Hiram's."

Good thinking. Unexpectedly, the doorbell chimed again.

"Would you like me to get it?" Kelli asked.

"It must be someone looking for you. We certainly don't know anyone here."

8

Kelli disappeared through the swinging door and returned a couple of minutes later with a trim, petite lady with curly gray hair, bright hazel eyes, raspberry colored sweats, and Nikes. She walked with a jaunty bounce, and cheerful laugh lines bracketed her mouth. Kelli made introductions and explained our presence.

"I'm so glad to meet you." Lucinda O'Mallory reached out and clasped my hand and then Abilene's in friendly handshakes. "The old house needs someone living in it. Your bad luck in being stuck here in Hello looks like Kelli's good luck."

Lucinda O'Mallory had probably never been a great beauty. Her skin was ruddy, her features ordinary, and wrinkle cream would surely find her face a challenge. But sharp intelligence and good humor gleamed in her hazel eyes, and I had the feeling Lucinda was the kind of woman you quickly forgot wasn't all that beautiful, because her energy and the charm of her personality bubbled through. She seemed to be coping well with the loss of her fiancé.

"I didn't mean to intrude. I just happened to see the lights on and thought I should investigate." To me she added, "Someone broke in once, as Kelli probably told you. But don't let that scare you! Everyone knew about all that tequila Hiram kept on hand, and we figure it was just some kids looking for it."

"Not that they had any chance of finding it." Kelli and Lucinda exchanged conspiratorial smiles.

"You removed it?" I asked.

"We . . . ah . . . disposed of it." Lucinda stuck out a hand, squinted one eye, and cocked a finger. "Pow! Pow! Pow!"

They both giggled, and I looked at them, amazed, as I realized what Lucinda was saying. These two ladies, one young, one old, had dismantled Hiram's liquor collection by using the filled bottles for target practice. I've never done any shooting, but with these two I could probably learn to enjoy it.

Kelli primly swallowed her giggle. "Lucinda's house is on the hill on the opposite side of town. It sits at an angle, so even if only the kitchen lights are on here, you can see them from her living room." To Lucinda she added, "I should have called and told you Ivy and Abilene had moved in. But you shouldn't be running over here just because you see lights," she scolded. "What if you ran into a burglary or wild teenage party in progress?"

"Then maybe I'd get to try out some of these karate moves I'm learning." Lucinda punched the air with her right fist and followed with a thigh-high kick with her left foot. The fuzzy pink balls on the end of her shoelaces snapped briskly. Somehow, in spite of the huge difference in their ages, something about Lucinda's vitality reminded me of my grandniece Sandy, who is given to exuberant backflips now and then. "I told you I'd started karate lessons at the health club, didn't

I? That's where I'm headed now. How are things going with Hiram's estate?"

"Slowly. Very slowly."

I thought I detected something in that uninformative answer, although I couldn't decide what. Kelli certainly wasn't hinting to Lucinda that Hiram's estate was none of her business, but neither was she actually telling her anything. Kelli had, I realized now, given Chris's question about Hiram's affairs a similar detour.

"Well, it's nice meeting you two," Lucinda said to Abilene and me. "I'm glad you aren't letting what happened here disturb you. It's ridiculous, the way so many people are acting as if the place has suddenly turned into a House of Horrors."

She spotted Koop on the rug and went over to kneel beside him. Koop's only reaction was a lazy opening of his one good eye. A good recommendation. She gave him the kind of petting he likes, long swoops from head to tail. A few orange hairs clung to her raspberry colored sweats when she stood up, and she didn't make some fussy attempt to brush them off. I liked that.

"Oh, hey, I know who you are!" she said suddenly, a raspberry-tipped forefinger targeting Abilene. "You're the one who saved Edie Carchoun's cat with CPR! I saw your picture in the *Telegraph*. Such a wonderful thing to do."

Abilene is so modest that she flushed at the unexpected compliment. "I'm working for Dr. Sugarman now."

"He's lucky to have you," Lucinda declared. "How many people could or would do CPR on a cat?" She pushed back her sleeve and looked at her watch. "Okay, time to get to my class. Oh, I almost forgot. Victoria said to tell you that they'll be sending a truck to pick up Hiram's books within the next day or two."

"What are they going to do, just dump them on the floor in that new room and hope the book fairy comes to straighten them out?" Kelli inquired in a tone that matched her facetious words.

"It seems there's some money in an emergency fund that most of the Society members didn't know about. Doris Hammerstone was hoarding it. Anyway, they're going to dig into that to hire someone who knows how to organize books and catalog them on the computer. Although how they're going to find anyone who knows anything and is willing to work for the pittance they want to pay beats me."

My ears perked up. "I was a librarian back in Missouri for some thirty years. I'm not an expert on the computer, but I know a little. I'm looking for a local position, and I'd be willing to work very reasonably."

"A real live book fairy!" Lucinda clapped her hands. "Could you go down to the Historical Society building and talk to Victoria Halburton tomorrow morning?"

"You're a member?" I asked.

She touched her chest, looked down at me from her superior height of an inch or so over my five-foot-one, and in an exaggerated voice of hauteur said, "My dear, everyone who is *anyone* in Hello belongs to the Historical Society."

"Which means I don't," Kelli muttered.

"They invited you when you first came."

"And then made it plain that I was uninvited after my remarks about the Lucky Queen at their big meeting."

"Um, well, yes, that's true," Lucinda agreed. "And just for your information, we do know that you call us the Ladies Hysterical Society." Her tone was severe, but her hazel eyes twinkled with good humor. Ah-ha! So I wasn't mistaken when I thought I'd heard Kelli use that term earlier.

"Oh dear." Kelli put on a mournful face. "If they know that, I'll never win the Miss Popularity contest. And I was so counting on it."

They looked at each other and grinned. Then Lucinda

turned back to me. "Yes, I'm a member, but I don't care for the CT & G sessions, which are the mainstay of the group—"

"CT & G?" I interrupted.

"Coffee, Tea, and Gossip, which is really what the Ladies Hysterical Society is all about. But I've helped get a couple of historical booklets together, and I've more or less managed the Roaring '20s Revue for years. Although this may be our last year. We've always had it on the stage in the old Hello Hotel, but the place is about to collapse. Hiram was going to buy the old place and fix it up for us, but that isn't going to happen now, of course."

"Sounds as if Hiram was indeed a generous man," I commented.

"Can you spell b-r-i-b-e?" Kelli said.

"Bribe?" I repeated with interest.

"Now, Kelli," Lucinda said, her tone reproachful. "Hiram had a strong sense of civic responsibility and was always concerned about the welfare of the town."

"Okay, okay," Kelli muttered. "The saint with a cigar."

No one seemed inclined to enlighten me, but now Lucinda looked me over appraisingly. "Would you like to be in the Revue? We have a full lineup of sixteen for the chorus line at the moment, but someone always has to drop out. We're into rehearsals now, but Sophia Ledger is already saying her arthritis is never going to last through those high kicks."

There was that chorus line again. "Thanks, but I don't think so."

"The costumes are very modest, if that concerns you."

I couldn't see myself kicking up my heels in a costume of any sort, but . . . "Maybe there's something else I could do, something behind the scenes?"

"Could be. It's always tough finding people for the behind-the-scenes work, so I'll keep you in mind. Anyway, be at the Historical Society building tomorrow morning. It opens at ten o'clock. Oh, by the way, Kelli, I took daisies to Hiram's grave this morning, and we should see about getting the hinge on that gate fixed."

"He'd appreciate the daisies. They were his favorite flower, weren't they? I'll see about the hinge."

"Is he buried in High Cemetery?" I asked.

"No, he's in Low." Lucinda looked a bit surprised that I knew about the cemetery division. "The old family plot is there, with all the old rascals tucked inside a wrought-iron fence."

Impulsively I sneaked in another question. "Was Hiram planning to move those carousel horses over to your place after you married?"

"I have no idea where those carousel horses came from, or what Hiram planned to do with them." Lucinda shook her head. "There's no place in my house where they'd fit. They're a mystery to me."

Odd.

"What do you think of Lucinda?" Kelli asked after Lucinda was gone. "Isn't she a doll? It's too bad things didn't work out for her and Hiram years ago. Both Hiram and this old house would probably be in better shape if he'd had Lucinda all that time."

A little warily, because I didn't want it to sound like criticism, and I surely didn't mean it as such, I said, "She seems to be holding up well, under the circumstances."

"You mean because she laughs, and she's out shooting up Hiram's tequila bottles instead of making some sentimental monument out of them?"

"Something like that, I guess."

"Lucinda's a survivor," Kelli said almost fiercely. "One of

the strongest people I know. She lost her husband five or six years ago, and then a couple years later, one of her two sons was killed in an avalanche on a ski slope up north. She lost a baby daughter to polio years ago, just before the vaccine became available. She managed to keep going through all those terrible times, and she's done the same after losing Hiram. She grieves him, very much so. But she isn't going to do it by taking to her bed and covering her head and crying all day."

Hearing all that, I felt an instant bond with Lucinda. I too had lost both a husband and son. I wondered if it was faith that had carried her through, as it had me.

Kelli smiled, a reminiscent look in her eyes. "You probably wouldn't know it to look at her, but Lucinda can have quite a temper. Uncle Hiram was rather casual about time, and when he was late for dinner at her place for about the umpteenth time, she went down to the tavern and rounded up a couple of ratty old guys she knew from when she interviewed old miners for a Historical Society booklet. So when Hiram finally arrived, he found these whiskered old guys eating up the last of his favorite tamale pie, and all that was left for him was a cup of cold coffee, an empty plate, and an icy stare from Lucinda. I don't believe he was ever late again." Kelli nodded with satisfaction. "She'd have kept Hiram in line."

"She isn't a smoker." Koop's reaction to her told me that, although her health-conscious exercise regime also suggested it. "What about Hiram's smoking? Was he going to give it up?"

"No, but they'd already settled that he could smoke only on the back porch at her place. Though she did say she was going to have it glassed in for him."

Kelli told me how to find the Historical Society building in the morning, and then we agreed that she'd pick me up at the house at 1:00 for the trip out to the mine. She left a few minutes later, and Abilene, eager to start work at Dr. Sugarman's in the morning, showered and was in bed by 10:00. The master bedroom had a private bath, quite an elaborate one, modernized with lots of gold fixtures and white tile veined with gold. There were too many mirrors for my taste. I'm not fond of seeing my sags and bags from all angles. But I enjoyed a leisurely bath with passionflower-scented bubbles, courtesy of my grandniece Sandy.

Sandy is always giving me little things I'd never buy for myself, things that usually startle me. She sends them first class to the mail-forwarding outfit in Arkansas, and they send them on to me when I call and give them an address. A toe ring. Fake fingernails. Skimpy Victoria's Secret nightwear. A perfume called "Catch Your Man." Sandy thinks I should catch Mac before someone else does.

I hadn't really intended to call Mac, but, thinking about Lucinda and her latest loss, I felt an unexpected surge of gratitude that Mac was alive and I could call him.

Mac MacPherson and I don't share the kind of relationship Lucinda and Hiram had; we certainly aren't into marriage plans. There's something between us, although it's about as substantial as a puff of hair spray. But it's there. The thing is, we never seem to be in the same place at the same time in our lives, and I mean that in more than physical location. Yes, our physical locations are often far apart. Mac has been traveling all over the country in his motor home doing articles about places and events for various travel magazines for several years now, and I never know where my efforts to dodge Braxtons may take me.

But the real difference in "place" has more to do with where we are in our outlook on life at any given moment. If I'm thinking commitment might be the way to go, Mac is in a don't-fence-me-in stage. If he's in a settling-down mood, I'm backing off, thinking it's too late in life for this.

And, of course, the Braxtons and Boone Morrison are a constant factor. A few months ago, Abilene and I had intended to spend some time in the town where Mac was recuperating from a yak attack (and don't you have to love a man who could get attacked by a yak?), but that was when we had to take off and run from Boone, and I haven't seen Mac since.

So our relationship is definitely indefinite. But there's enough to it that I felt a real longing to connect with him tonight. I got the cell phone out of my purse, looked up his cell phone number on the menu, and punched the call button. I was pleased that I wasn't getting the "no signal" message here in town.

But I was also getting no answer to the ring, and for the first time the dismaying thought occurred to me, What if a woman answered? He could have up and married someone, just like Sandy, and my good friend Magnolia Margollin, warned he might do.

Then his voice, muffled and grumpy. "Hello? Hello. Is someone there? I thought I'd turned this blasted thing off for the night—"

"Mac? It's Ivy. Did I wake you?" I hadn't considered that my 10:45 p.m. call might reach him well after midnight if he happened to be on the East Coast. He wasn't usually an early-to-bed person, but you could never tell where Mac might be. "Where are you?"

A brief hesitation, as if it took him a moment in his sleep-interrupted state to figure out not only where he was but who someone named Ivy was. Not too flattering.

"Alabama . . . No, that was yesterday. Today it's Florida. I'm on my way to do an article about Spongeorama."

"About *what*?"

"Spongeorama. In Tarpon Springs, where the sponge is king."

"Mac MacPherson, are you sure you're awake?"

"You woke me up, so you should know." He sounded more normal now, less as if he were talking through a pillow, though still a bit grumpy. "I tried to call you a couple times, but you never answered."

"We keep the cell phone just for emergencies and don't have it turned on most of the time."

"Is this an emergency?"

"Well, no, not really." But sort of. Isn't feeling a real need to reach out and touch a special someone an emergency?

"Where are you?" he asked.

At least he did know who I was now. But I hesitated a moment about revealing location information. Not that I want to hide from Mac, but I've always been a little concerned that the Braxtons might know about him and try to use him to get to me. Yet wanting him to know won out, and I said, "Colorado."

That made both of us pause for a moment to consider the distance between us.

"Come see me," he wheedled unexpectedly. "The skies are blue, the sand is warm, the palms are swaying. I will gift you with sponges for all occasions, and we will eat stuffed grape leaves and spanakopita and baklava."

"Why would we do that?"

"Because it's a Greek place. I guess the Greeks are great sponge catchers or diggers or chasers or however it is you capture a sponge. You'll love it."

I think, if the motor home hadn't been marooned in the yard at Nick's Garage, I might well have picked up and headed for Florida. With only a few words, even if they're about sponges, Mac can be quite persuasive.

"I'd like to, Mac, I really would. But we're kind of . . . stuck here for a while. Waiting on some repairs on the motor home." That was the truth, without getting specific. I didn't want to burden Mac with our problems. "I don't suppose you'll be coming through Colorado anytime soon?"

"It isn't in my plans." He paused as if considering the matter. "But sometimes plans change. Where in Colorado?"

"A little mining town called Hello."

"Hey, I've been in Hello! I did a magazine piece about that funky little newspaper they have there. The editor told me later that it brought in subscriptions from all over."

Kelli had said an article in a touristy magazine had brought lots of subscriptions for the newspaper. And Mac had written that article! Small world.

"I can't say for sure . . ." Mac's wary beginning didn't surprise me. I was feeling an unexpected nesting instinct coming on, weary of coping with the complications of a home on wheels, which meant Mac was undoubtedly in a cagey stage, not committing to anything. "But I might get out that way before long."

"That would be great! Family okay?" I asked.

"Everyone's fine. Grandchildren growing like tadpoles."

"Wrist and back okay?" Those were the areas the yak had injured.

"Aging like the rest of me but doing fine."

"Have you heard anything of Magnolia and Geoff?" These were longtime friends from back in Missouri. Magnolia was enamored with genealogy, but she scorned Internet research, and they spent considerable time in their motor home chasing down distant relatives. She had, in fact, introduced me to Mac, whom they'd met on the road.

"They were in Southern California the last time I talked to them, but that's been a while. Magnolia believes she's found a connection to some Middle Eastern ancestor. So don't be surprised if she's into belly dancing the next time you see her."

I laughed. Magnolia did tend to take on some aspect of

whatever ancestor she'd most recently uncovered. Magnolia's majestic shape in a belly dance would surely be a sight to see.

"Should I tell them where you are?" Mac asked.

As usual, I hesitated. I always figured the Braxtons could be quite ruthless when trying to obtain information about my whereabouts, and I didn't want Magnolia and Geoff caught in the cross fire.

"Better not," I said regretfully. "But maybe we'll see you later on, if you get out this way."

"Abilene still with you?" Mac and Abilene had met when we were all in Oklahoma.

"She's here. She starts work in a veterinarian's office tomorrow."

"Hey, great! She'll like that." Small pause, and then he said warily, "You're not involved in any more murders, are you?"

"What do you think, that just because I've encountered a murder or two in the past that they follow me around like a cloud of doom?" I said indignantly. Although to be honest, I had to add, "One happened before I got here, but I'm hardly involved."

Living in the house where the murder occurred isn't necessarily being involved, right? Although I prudently decided there was no need to inform Mac of that particular circumstance.

"Okay. I miss you, Ivy."

"I miss you too."

A wind came up in the night, and the old house creaked and groaned, and, with a little imagination, I could think the branches scratching the walls were something trying to get in. Or something inside trying to get out . . .

But I didn't let my imagination roar into overdrive. Instead I thought about Mac and had a rather lovely dream about the two of us riding carousel horses together, gently rising and falling to a lovely tinkle of calliope music.

At least it was lovely until a dead body plummeted out of the sky and landed on us. I do seem to attract them.

9

I was at the impressive double doors of the Historical Society's brick building at 10:10 the following morning. The sign carved in concrete overhead didn't specify Ladies Society, but, given the name everyone used, apparently the ladies had claimed possession at some time. The day was sunny but chilly, streets bare but yards still covered with snow, and ice clung to shadowy spots on the sidewalks that sunshine hadn't yet reached. I'd worn a denim skirt, thinking that should fit the pioneer theme of a historical society, and my heavy down jacket.

Inside the high-ceilinged room, glass cabinets held exhibits of smaller items of old mining equipment, such as gold pans and a gold scale, plus another cabinet of Indian arrowheads and beadwork. Larger exhibits of a metal ore cart, a long, wooden sluice box, and part of a stamp mill for pulverizing gold ore stood alone, surrounding photos showing how the equipment was used. In one corner, an old miner's camp was set up, complete with life-size figures of a grizzled miner and his gray donkey, with an old blue enamel coffeepot just like Hiram's on a grate over an imitation campfire. A display of books and pamphlets about local history stood on one side of the entrance, a rack of touristy brochures about local accommodations and activities on the other.

Two doors led off to the right. One was open, but from this angle I couldn't see inside.

An impressive archway opened to the left, a sign over it reading "Hiram L. McLeod Memorial Library." Beyond loomed a room of impressive size with tall, polished bookshelves and the ceiling covered with some sort of murky green mural. From this distance, the mural gave the feeling that you were underwater and looking up at the underside of trash floating on a layer of pond scum. But perhaps it looked better if you were directly under it. A faint scent of new wood and plaster and paint emanated from the room. The most notable feature of the "library," however, was the fact that the shelves were as empty as old Mother Hubbard's cupboard.

I suddenly realized I was being watched. An old oak desk stood at the rear of the main room, a couple of wooden filing cabinets behind it. Two older women were at the desk, one sitting in front of a computer, one standing. I approached them. Often, as an inconspicuous older woman, I feel quite invisible, but that was not the case now. Both women were staring at me as if I were quite fascinating, and I wondered if I'd unknowingly had a major wardrobe malfunction, and the thong panties Sandy had sent me were tangled around my ankles. More likely, I reassured myself, it was just that since I was the only visitor, I was the only one to watch. But perhaps I shouldn't have chosen today as the first day to try wearing the thong panties. They did feel quite peculiar.

I approached the desk. "Hello. I'm Ivy Malone. Lucinda

O'Mallory told me you were looking for someone to organize and catalog the books for the new library."

"Yes, we need someone to do that, if we can find someone with suitable qualifications. Lucinda called me about you, but we were thinking of"—she gave me a critical appraisal from my possum-gray hair to my short legs and sensible shoes—"someone somewhat younger. It's a challenging position."

The woman who spoke was the standing one, a tall, thin lady about my age, with a formidable beak of a nose, severely pulled-back hair dyed crow-black, large diamond earrings, and a stark black pantsuit. She'd probably been aiming for a look of elegance and sophistication, but, unfortunately, the effect was more scarecrow-in-mourning. I thought about nicely reminding her about laws concerning age discrimination, or not so nicely asking what a skinny old scarecrow like her was doing acting as if age were a blight on a person's abilities and character.

However, because I needed this job, I diplomatically said, "Did you have some particular qualifications in mind?"

"Can you revive a computer?" the one with her plump fingers on the keyboard of the older computer asked. Brick-red lipstick and fingernail polish matched her improbably brick-red hair, but the blue eyes she turned on me had an unexpected girlish friendliness. "I think I've killed this one. See?"

She angled the screen toward me. The plump fingers raced over the keyboard, hammering haphazardly at letters and numbers and control keys. The arrow on the screen ignored her spirited activity, like a child blithely ignoring a screaming mother.

"Does it do this often?" I asked.

"I don't know. Marianne usually runs the computer, but she's down in Texas visiting her daughter, and this important letter needs to go out. You want to give it a try?"

Skinny Scarecrow protested. "Stella, I don't think—"

"Oh, come on. How much damage can she do? It's already on its last legs. Or last kilobytes, or whatever it is computers have." She stood up and smiled. "By the way, I'm Stella Sinclair, and this is Victoria Halburton. You said your name was Ivy?"

"Yes. Ivy Malone."

Stella held out her plump hand, enviably unveined or age-marked, and we shook. The name Sinclair sounded vaguely familiar, and after a moment I placed it. Perhaps this was the Mrs. Sinclair Kelli had mentioned, with the Godiva-chocolate-guzzling potbellied pig. "You're new in town?" Stella asked.

"Yes." I hesitated briefly. I didn't want to jinx a job possibility, but neither did I intend to dodge my connection with the young woman who had befriended us, a woman whom I was convinced was quite innocent of the accusations against her. "Kelli Keifer is letting us stay at the McLeod house." Out of the blue, words came out of my mouth that I hadn't even thought about saying. "I've had some experience in criminal investigation, and I may be able to help in determining the identity of her Uncle Hiram's killer."

Stella's blue eyes rounded, and I felt a little guilty. I had indeed helped uncover some killers, but I was no Jessica Fletcher of *Murder, She Wrote* expertise. And Skinny Scarecrow was not impressed.

"There's little doubt about the identity of the killer," she said loftily. "It's just a matter of the authorities gathering the proper evidence, which I'm sure they'll have before long."

"In the meantime," I said, "innocent until proven guilty."

Victoria frowned, but she could hardly deny that axiom. "Of course," she agreed stiffly.

"So, let's have a look at that computer," I said as if I knew exactly what I was doing and could whip the computer into shape with a few keystrokes.

I circled the desk, removed my heavy jacket, and hung it on the back of the chair. I resisted the urge to flex my fingers, as if I were about to give a command performance at the piano, and gave the computer the standard ctrl-alt-delete key combination. No response. It was froze up solid. Grandniece Sandy had said the best thing to do in a situation such as this was turn everything off and start over. So, still pretending I knew more than I did, I briskly shut everything down, waited a few seconds, and turned it on again. The screen disapprovingly informed me that the computer hadn't been shut down properly, but after a brief scan to check its internal condition, it revved up nicely. Not only was the computer old, I realized, so was the program they were using. Windows 98. Stella hadn't saved anything before the computer froze up, but she had a hand-scribbled copy of what the letter should say. I briskly typed it out and printed two copies on a noisy old inkjet printer. It was a letter to a company complaining that the new coffeemaker had died only two days after the warranty expired, and the Society, as a worthy nonprofit organization, hoped it could be replaced. An "important" letter indeed. The Society must not be without its coffee.

Stella pressed her hands together when she read the printed letter. I'd fixed up a couple of problems with punctuation and grammar. "Oh, that's wonderful!"

Even Victoria seemed mildly impressed. "Indeed, this is very helpful."

"Perhaps I could fill out an application for the position?" I briefly ran through my qualifications.

"I say we hire her," Stella declared.

"I'm not sure we can do it without calling a membership meeting and voting on it," Skinny Scarecrow (no, no, I must think of her as Victoria) demurred.

"Oh, cabbages. That will take too long. Ivy is perfect for the job, and she might have something else by then and not be available."

Stella looked at me, and I nodded, liking her. (How not to like someone who indulges a potbellied pig in chocolate treats, substitutes cabbages for some unacceptable word, and even says you're perfect?) "Yes, that's possible," I agreed. Although privately I suspected there was about as much chance of my instantly finding another job in Hello as there was of the president tapping me for a position on the Supreme Court.

"Here comes Charlotte!" Stella exclaimed as the front door opened. "We can make a committee of three with her and do it."

A tall woman, mid-fiftyish, which put her somewhat younger than Victoria and Stella, smartly dressed in narrow taupe skirt, slim-heeled boots, and fur-collared jacket, walked briskly toward us. I doubted her long blond hair was natural, but the coloring and highlights were expertly done, and it had a bouncy swing as she walked. She set her oversized leather purse on the desk. It had a prominent metal initial on it, which I supposed meant something expensive, although I wasn't knowledgeable enough to know what.

"Stella, hon, do we have anything about the history of the old Randolph place over on Mountain Street? I've just listed it, and buyers are always fascinated by historical details."

"Really, Charlotte, we can't use the Society computer for personal projects," Victoria huffed.

"All they need to know about that old place is that if the termites stop holding hands, it'll fall down around them," Stella stated.

The woman named Charlotte drew back her head. "With a little imagination and effort, the Randolph house could be made quite charming. I think we should take pride in our old structures."

It was an admirable enough statement, but the woman came off sounding stuffy, pretentious, and holier-than-thou.

"Okay, I'll see if I can find anything." Stella waved a dismissive hand. "Right now we have something more important. We have the perfect candidate for our librarian position, and if we don't grab her right now we'll lose her."

I doubted that, but I didn't contradict her.

Stella pointed at me. "This is Ivy Malone. She was a librarian for thirty years. And she knows all about computers."

Charlotte gave a small blink, and I realized that until then she hadn't even noticed me behind the desk at the computer. So I hadn't lost my invisibility after all. Good. Sometimes it comes in handy.

"This is Charlotte Sterling," Stella added to me. "She works part-time for Cutter Realty."

Charlotte shot Stella a sour look, as if she thought her position warranted a more complimentary description than that. But what I was thinking was, *Sterling. Some relation to Kelli's boyfriend?*

I held out my hand and took a chance. "I believe I met your son yesterday." Okay, lay it on thick. I needed this job. "The prominent lawyer, Chris Sterling? Kelli Keifer introduced us."

"You're the people living in her uncle's house?" She gave me a sharper examination, and I nodded. "Chris mentioned Kelli was letting someone live there when I stopped by the office a few minutes ago."

"She's going to help investigate the murder," Stella volunteered brightly.

"Really?" Charlotte asked. "Would you have time to do that and work here for the Historical Society too?"

I was a little surprised that none of the three women seemed to question the investigative capabilities I'd so rashly claimed, and that Charlotte was more concerned about the time element, but I was happy to take a detour down this path. "Actually, we haven't discussed working hours yet. Or pay," I said with deliberate emphasis.

Stella said they opened the Historical Society Building only three days a week at this time of year, Thursday, Friday, and Saturday, with hours from ten to four, which is when I'd be expected to work. Victoria produced an hourly payment figure that was indeed at pittance level. No health insurance or other benefits, she emphasized. At that rate of pay both the motor home and I might turn to dust before I could buy a new engine.

I couldn't produce cheers of joy, but a job is a job, and I said, "That sounds satisfactory." We all looked at Charlotte Sterling as if she held the deciding vote.

"Sounds fine to me, if that's what everyone else wants." Surprising me, Charlotte turned to me and smiled with unexpected warmth. "I'm sure Ivy can handle the position most capably. Welcome to Hello." She shook my hand with continuing warmth. "I think you'll like it here."

Maybe she thought I'd be buying real estate soon.

Stella told Charlotte she'd let her know if she located anything about the Randolph house, and Charlotte, with a brisk tapping of high-heeled boots, departed. I noted now that the open door to the side of the main room revealed a well-equipped kitchen, a TV set, and a number of round tables. Perhaps this was where the important business, CT & G, of the Society took place.

Stella was now poking through desk drawers. "There are probably some forms to fill out, but I'll have to call Marianne and find out what they are. And where."

"You can tell Kelli that we'll have a truck at the house to pick up the books first thing tomorrow morning. You'll be there to let the driver in, I presume?" Victoria said.

"Yes. And I'll come down here and get started immediately afterward. Although it may be necessary to acquire a new software program for the computer to catalog the books properly."

"Well, we'll see about that," Victoria agreed, although her lack of enthusiasm for such an expense was obvious.

"See you tomorrow, then."

I walked home feeling quite buoyant and energized. I had a paying job! *Thank you, Lord.*

10

I made a tuna sandwich and ate it with leftover coffee from the old blue pot for lunch. Abilene didn't show up, so I assumed she was getting lunch elsewhere. Kelli arrived at the house at ten minutes after one. She picked up several books, including the UFO one from the bedroom, to take out to Norman. She apologized for being late, saying she'd gotten stuck on a lengthy phone call with a bank in Denver about one of Hiram's accounts. A sack of chicken feed lay behind the backseat of the Bronco, plus several sacks of groceries and a copy of the latest *Hello Telegraph*.

We drove out past Nick's Garage and turned right on a narrower but paved road, with a sign reading Lucky Queen Road. I told Kelli about getting the job.

"Congratulations! I'm glad to hear it. And I'll be glad to get all those books out of the house too. Maybe when they're gone I'll find more of Uncle Hiram's papers and records. I keep thinking there must be something more than I have." She frowned. "For a man who dealt with wealth all his life and made plenty of shrewd deals, he seemed to have gotten careless about details in his old age. Or maybe it was his eyesight, which was definitely failing."

"Abilene and I will still be doing cleanup work on the house even if we're both working." I didn't want her to think we were planning to freeload off her. "We can start there in the office/library after the books are out."

"Don't worry about it. Sometimes I think Chris has the right idea. Just put a match to the place." She suddenly sounded gloomy.

"But then people would assume you're trying to destroy evidence that would incriminate you."

Kelli glanced at me and laughed. "Well, I wasn't really serious about the match. But you're right. That's exactly what everyone would think."

"Oh, I almost forgot to tell you. I met Chris's mother while I was at the Historical Society. She was looking for information about a house she has listed. The Randolph place, she called it."

The pavement ended with an abrupt edge that clattered my teeth when we bounced over it. There had been a few houses near the highway, but here there was only scenery. Incredible scenery, if you didn't count the potholed road. Green forest, branches laden with snow that occasionally thundered to the ground, leaving the branch bouncing as if glad to be free of the load. Rushing creeks cut through the occasional snow-covered meadows, and sharp outcroppings of rock stuck out at odd angles on the hillsides, as if some giant hand had flung them just to see where they'd stick.

Sometimes I wonder if we take God's plan of creation too seriously; I think he probably had great fun at it. Cutting a Grand Canyon here, lifting a Mount Everest there, stirring a cauldron of bubbling lava in a Mount Kilauea. And right here, covering rugged mountains with blankets of green trees, decorating them with a frosting of snow, adding a pair of deer drinking at a stream. *Good work, Lord!*

"Mrs. Sterling seemed very nice," I said tentatively, basing that mostly on her surprisingly warm welcome near the end of our meeting. "Good mother-in-law material?"

"Oh yes. She told me once that if ours was a culture where parents picked a wife for a son, I'd have been right at the top of her list."

"That's good. Married life is easier if the mother-in-law likes you."

"Speaking from experience?" She gave me a sideways glance.

"Blessedly, Harley's mother and I were the best of friends."

"I guess I should feel lucky, because Chris's mother wasn't all that fond of the woman he was seeing before I came along."

This was a subject that aroused my nosy interest, but we hit a washboardy section of road that rattled my teeth, jitterbugged my feet on the floorboards, and nearly crossed my eyes.

"Charlotte is a good real estate person," Kelli continued after we were off the washboard and into rutted mud. "But I doubt she can do anything with that place before next summer when the tourists come through. I don't think anyone local will buy it."

"Not another murder!"

"Oh no. It's just that Hello is an 'economically challenged' area, as one city councilman likes to put it. Economically dead might be more accurate. In any case, it's especially bad in winter. Nothing sells. The unemployment rate goes out of sight. Most of the kids pick up and leave as soon as they get out of high school."

"A few must stay or come back. Your Chris did."

"But he had something to come back to. His father was a partner in the law firm, so Chris had a good spot waiting for him. Although I never knew his father. He'd passed away before I came."

"You came back to Hello too."

"I'd never lived here," Kelli corrected. "I came because the law firm I was with in California was big, and everyone in it cutthroat competitive. Who could win the biggest awards in court, whose office light burned latest at night, who could bill clients for the most hours. They were also willing to take on cases I thought were ridiculous. Maybe I'm narrow-minded, but I do not want to be involved in helping a crook sue when he's injured burglarizing a home."

"Couldn't you have changed law firms and stayed there?"

"I decided I wanted to be on my own. I wanted a slower pace of life and cases that were more meaningful. Hiram wanted me to come too, and I thought here I could be the kind of lawyer I wanted to be." She smiled grimly. "It looks as if I was wrong."

The road was getting ever rougher, the gravel only in scattered clumps between stretches of bare, bumpy bedrock or muddy holes. Branches had been laid across one bad spot. In another, a shallow stream of water ran right across the road. Kelli stopped and got out to put the wheels in four-wheel drive before we churned through that.

"I don't understand about Hello," I said. "In all honesty, you seem like a nice young woman, and I don't see why people have decided you murdered Hiram, instead of giving you the benefit of the doubt."

Kelli gave a wry snort. "Some of them were ready to lynch me well before the murder."

"I presume there was a reason?"

She sighed. "I'll have to tell you about the mine."

"First off, how far is it?" I was beginning to feel as if we'd left civilization far behind, maybe even stepped back a century. Out here, it felt as if at any moment we might meet a stagecoach dashing down the road, maybe with outlaws in pursuit.

"About twenty miles from town. About four miles to go yet. I'm hoping we can get all the way and not have to carry this stuff in to Norman." She dodged a mud hole that looked as if it could bury a stagecoach. "Okay, about the mine."

"The Lucky Queen."

"Right. Hiram's grandfather discovered the gold and made good money off it, but it was Hiram's father who actually developed it as a mine and got rich. A lot of gold came out of it. Norman still pans a little gold dust and sometimes even finds a nugget, but, as a producing mine, the area gave out years ago. But there's still gold there. It's just that it's microscopic in size. It can take forty tons of ore to produce an ounce of gold."

"Not practical to mine it, then."

"That was true for years. But now, there are new techniques and equipment available that make it both possible and profitable to get the gold out. And that's what Uncle Hiram wanted to do, reopen the mine. He was dealing with some big mining corporation that was interested. Although he didn't confide in me about that."

"Why not?"

"Because I was so strongly against it."

We hit a huge bump in the road, a chunk of bedrock rising through the surface like the beginning of a new mountain, and only the seat belt kept my head from colliding with the roof of the Bronco. I reached around and tightened the belt a notch.

"Why was that?"

"Because it would totally devastate the area again, even

worse than the earlier mining did. Look around. We're within a mile or so of the mine now. See how the trees look different? They're all much younger here. The area was scalped when the mine was operating. They needed trees, lots of trees, to make support timbers for the mine shafts. And out of those shafts came huge, ugly piles of bare tailings where nothing will grow. The wildlife disappeared, their habitat destroyed. Because the trees were gone and there was nothing to hold the ground together, water runoff cut huge, raw gulches. I've seen photos from back then. It looked like a bombed-out war zone, and it's taken all these years for nature to bring it even partway back to what it once was."

I could hear the passion in her voice even over the roar of the engine. The road, if it could be called that, was solid mud now, chunks and spatters flying from the churning wheels. I expected any moment that we'd flounder to a halt and instantly sink to the door handles. Kelli didn't seem to see anything unusual in the situation, however. She just shifted to a lower gear and tromped down on the gas.

"It would be different now," she went on. "Different and much worse. This time it would be an enormous open-pit-type mine rather than shafts. It would cover acres and acres of ground, like some huge meteor crater destroying everything. There'd be huge equipment to dig out and move the ore, and they'd have to build a big processing plant. From an environmental viewpoint, it would be total disaster."

"You're an environmentalist?"

"I never thought much about it before, but maybe I am now."

"And this had something to do with the town's antagonism toward you?"

"The townspeople, the Historical Society, the town council, the businessmen, practically everybody, were all in favor of Hiram's project. They were extremely unhappy that I opposed it. They were afraid I'd talk Hiram out of it and ruin all their big plans."

"I still don't understand. It would seem the Historical Society would be against this sort of thing, that they'd want to preserve everything as it was and keep development out. That's the stand historical societies usually take, isn't it?"

"I think, before I came, there were a few rumbles of dissent. But, in the long run, money rules. Uncle Hiram gave all that money to the Historical Society for the new library. And, as Lucinda said, everybody who's anybody in Hello belongs to the Society, so it has a lot of influence. Hiram made promises about fixing up the old hotel, and then said he'd give more money for the job you have. I think he promised money to individual businesses that are floundering too."

B-r-i-b-e. Now I understood what Kelli had been getting at. Under a ruse of civic generosity, Hiram had been bribing the town to go along with his huge project.

"But you can't bribe everyone," I protested. "Surely some people are immune."

"Uncle Hiram certainly tried. Although I'm not sure he had enough money to live up to all the promises he made, such as restoring the old hotel." She frowned slightly but didn't elaborate. "And he had plenty of other pie-in-the-sky promises. He convinced everyone the mine would bring economic sunshine and blessings to Hello. There would be jobs, and businesses would prosper. Everyone would benefit. He got a state senator to come and give a glowing endorsement. The good times would roll. Dale Halburton saw dollar signs on big new profits at his hardware store. The bank president saw deposits rolling in. One of the town councilmen saw Uncle Hiram backing him for a state political office. New industries would move in. Property values would soar. Practically everyone saw advantages for themselves personally."

"Would that have happened?"

101

"I think at least some of it would," Kelli agreed reluctantly. "There surely would have been jobs at the mine. And I can see that the town desperately needs an economic boost. I just didn't think that what reopening the mine might do for the town was worth the destruction it would cause."

"There are a lot more environmental laws and restrictions now that they'd have to follow."

"Money talks," she repeated grimly. "And people saw whatever damage the mine would cause as way out here, not right in town where they'd have to see and live with it."

"People knew how strongly you opposed reopening the mine?"

"Oh yeah. Shortly after I came, Uncle Hiram gave a talk at a big town council meeting to give the project another boost. He had all these statistics and wonderful reports about how the town would benefit, even hired some guy to come in with a Power Point presentation. He didn't quite promise everyone would be driving BMWs and sending their kids to Harvard, but that's what they got out of it. He had everyone all charged up. Then, during the question-and-answer period, I got up and spoke. I'm sure people at first assumed I meant to endorse everything Hiram wanted, so this big shock wave rolled through the crowd when I gave all the reasons the mine shouldn't be reopened, that an ounce or two of gold wasn't worth ripping up forty tons of ore. Forty tons multiplied many times over, of course."

"This was not what people wanted to hear."

"Not then, or at a couple of later meetings. From the reaction, you'd have thought I was opposing motherhood, apple pie, and the flag. People saw me as personally out to destroy their prosperity. People are not happy campers when they think you're snatching away prosperity that's within their reach."

"And now, with Hiram dead, the mine will not be re-opened."

"Exactly. For which everyone blames me. And they're right, of course. As long as I control the Lucky Queen, it will never be reopened. But I didn't murder Uncle Hiram to keep it from happening, which is what some people think!"

"So, knowing you would inherit the mine if Hiram were dead, and also knowing you were against its reopening—"

"Vehemently against," Kelli emphasized.

"So anyone who also objected to the reopening of the mine and wanted to stop it from happening could reasonably expect that if Hiram was dead it wouldn't happen. All this person had to do was get Hiram out of the way so you'd be in control. And if you got blamed for the death, it was a 'so what?' as far as this person was concerned."

"I suppose that's true," Kelli said. An exceptionally large chunk of mud flew up and clunked my window, and I automatically ducked. "But there weren't all that many who opposed what Hiram wanted to do. And certainly no one I'd suspect of killing him to make certain the mine didn't reopen."

"So who did oppose it?"

"I was certainly the most vocal and loudest opponent. Lucinda was against it. Norman, too, here at the mine. A few newcomers in those big, new places on the hill above Hiram's place. People who moved in with money, whose prosperity is independent of whatever happens with the town, and don't want it to change. And one of Lucinda's sons who lives out in California wrote several strong letters to the editor against it. He grew up here, but he's an outsider now, someone with California ideas, and no one paid much attention to him."

"Lucinda was opposed?" I asked, surprised.

"She never publicly came out against it, and I don't think she ever would have. But I know she and Uncle Hiram argued about it in private."

"And Norman was against it too?"

"He and Uncle Hiram butted heads about it all the time. Norman even went to a meeting once, and got up and talked. But not too much attention gets paid to the opinions of a man with spinach in his beard and pieces of tin can wrapped around his shoes to reinforce the soles."

Understandable, I suppose.

"Norman's lived out here for at least fifteen years, maybe twenty. It's not really a caretaking job, mostly just a free place to live. Though Hiram gave him a few dollars now and then. He gets a little Social Security and manages to survive. Hiram assured him that he could keep on living here as long as he wanted, but it would change Norman's entire life along with the landscape, of course, if the mine reopened. Huge equipment, people, noise, dust. His old shack might well have been swallowed up by the pit from which they'd be excavating the ore. Even if it weren't, he likes his peace and quiet, and he doesn't want to see the area devastated and the wildlife driven off any more than I do. Most people call him 'Nutty Norman' and consider him an environmental disaster of his own, but, in his own way, he really is an environmentalist."

I thought about how Norman used to stay in that bedroom at Hiram's house, how their arguments and drinking could have gotten out of control. "Maybe Norman felt even more strongly about all this than you realize," I suggested.

"Strongly enough for him to hit Hiram on the head and push him out the window? Is that what you're saying? Oh, Ivy . . ." Kelli shook her head and smiled. "Wait until you meet him. Wait until you see his cemetery. See what you think then."

Up ahead I could see Norman's shack sitting on the crest of a hill. A rusty metal roof topped walls of weathered, unpainted wood. A spiral of smoke drifted from a tall stovepipe. A wooden porch with ramshackle steps ran across the front, firewood stacked beside it. An honest-to-goodness outhouse stood off to one side, a shed that I guessed was a chicken house just beyond it. A rooster, crowing mightily, paraded on the roof of the house, and hens scratched where the ground wasn't covered with snow. Norman had shoveled pathways to road, outhouse, and chicken house.

"Does he ever get snowed in?" I asked.

"Sometimes. This winter hasn't been bad so far, but Uncle Hiram said Norman had to snowshoe to get to town some winters. When he did that, he'd sometimes stay at the house several weeks at a time. A bone of contention, I'd guess, if a wife happened to be in residence. But Hiram had his loyalties and wasn't about to budge concerning Norman."

An old pickup surrounded by snow stood a few feet from the house. The fenders were muddy brown, the hood a faded blue-green, the bumper a length of rusty metal pipe. It looked as if it had been cobbled together from stray parts of various other vehicles. A block of wood supported one wheel with no tire. A brown hen flapped her wings on the roof of the cab.

"That's Norman's Dorf," Kelli said.

"Dorf?" I repeated, not certain if she meant the vehicle or the hen.

"It started out as a Ford, the hood anyway, but Norman rearranged the metal letters to turn Ford into Dorf."

I suspected Ford would appreciate that. I doubt they'd want their name on this strange conglomeration of parts.

"I think the chicken on the pickup is Ginger, of Ginger Rogers fame. Marilyn is one of the other brown hens."

I took a wild guess. "Marilyn as in Monroe?"

"Right. She's one of Norman's favorite actresses. Unfortunately, Julia died a while back."

"Julia as in . . . ?"

105

"Julia Roberts. Norman's favorites are not limited to long-ago ladies."

I didn't think we'd make it all the way to the house, but Kelli churned right on up the last steep section and slammed to a stop within a dozen feet of the porch.

Norman opened the door and stepped onto the porch, one hand lifted in greeting, big smile on his face. He had a bushy gray beard, a skimpy ponytail, dark pants held up with red suspenders, a plaid shirt of some indeterminate color, and unexpectedly, rather expensive-looking, sheepskin-lined leather slippers. A gift from Kelli or Hiram, I suspected.

"Kelli, halooo!"

Kelli slid out of the Bronco. "Hi, Norman," she called. "I brought some feed for the chickens and some blackberry balsam for your stomach. How's it feeling today?"

"Can't complain." He rubbed his skinny midsection.

She reached back in the Bronco for a sack. "And some reading material too."

I didn't know whether to stay in the Bronco or get out. Norman didn't look like your average suburbanite, and I wouldn't be surprised if the chickens wandered into the shack on occasion, but were there even more reasons why people called him Nutty Norman, reasons of which I should be wary?

Well, you know me. Too curious to just sit there, I slid out. Directly into a muddy puddle, of course.

"Norman, I brought someone along to meet you. This is—"

Kelli didn't even have a chance to get to my name. Norman spotted me, and his eyes targeted me like a security camera in a parking garage. Paying no attention to the sloppy snow/mud mixture on the pathway, he bore down on me like a bearded freight train.

11

Norman had his own cemetery, Kelli had said. Who was in it? The last unwelcome visitor?

I caught a few more details as Norman thundered closer. A bit of egg caught in his whiskers. A few too few teeth in his yellow-stained smile. A grease stain the size of a handprint on his pants leg. Big, calloused hands.

Then I realized Norman wasn't advancing on me in hostility. Norman was looking at me as if I were the biggest gold nugget he'd ever seen, his eyes lit up like Christmas lights, smile warm enough to boil the puddle around my feet.

"Glory be," he breathed. "An angel is come among us."

Norman was apparently pleased to see me, delighted even. A generous attitude, even a bit poetic with his angel statement. But I wasn't sure but what hostility might be preferable, since I also wasn't sure what he had in mind here. A big bear hug, at the very least. I thwarted that by stepping behind the Bronco door and thrusting my hand out for a shake.

He shook it enthusiastically. "I ain't seen nothin' the likes of you 'round here in twenty years." He tilted his head, the egg in his beard undisturbed by the movement, and studied me with open admiration. "Glory be," he repeated. He also continued to shake my hand. "I'll have the Dorf runnin' in a few days. I'll drive into town, and maybe we can take us in a movie."

"They tore the movie theater down several years ago, remember, Norman?" Kelli said gently.

"Oh yeah, I keep fergettin'. Well, maybe we could get us some dinner at that fancy Café Russo. Hiram and I been there. Last time I had me some fancy I-talion thing with everything but the kitchen sink in it. Anyway, I'm a-comin' for you," Norman assured me with a solemn nod. "You can count on that."

Not a time waster, ol' Norman. When he wanted something, he zeroed in on it. Unfortunately, at the moment, that something appeared to be me.

Kelli came to the rescue. "Now, Norman," she chided, "Ivy just got into town a couple days ago, and she's not even settled in yet. She's living in Hiram's house, and she's going to be librarian for his new library at the Historical Society. She's also done some private investigative work, and is looking into the circumstances of Hiram's death, so she's very busy."

"Private investigative work" exaggerated my abilities, but I didn't bother to correct her. I was mostly thinking uneasily about Norman's obvious amorous attentions. But another glance at the pickup reassured me. The Dorf didn't look capable of an excursion into town anytime soon.

"Ivy? That's you? Ivy," Norman repeated wonderingly. He was down to my fingertips now, but he wasn't letting go. "Now ain't that the prettiest durn name ever? I planted me some ivy once, right there by the side of the house, but I think maybe the chickens ate it."

Ginger had jumped off the pickup and was now pecking

at my shoelaces. I had the uneasy feeling she might have in mind eating this Ivy too. I don't know all that much about chickens.

"Okay, let's get these groceries and this chicken feed unloaded." Kelli handed Norman and me each a sack and wrestled the bag of chicken feed to the door of the Bronco.

Norman looked at my plastic bag and said solicitously, "Now, that looks a mite heavy for a delicate little thing like you." He took my moderately sized bag as we headed for the house, ignoring Kelli struggling along behind with the fifty-pound bag of feed slung over her shoulder.

I tried to protest, but Norman was having none of it. He gave me a little elbow push toward the porch. I remembered that unwashed-body-cigarette-smoke-and-garlic odor on the sheets at Hiram's house, and here I was getting the full-strength, original version of it. The inside of the shack smelled even more strongly of garlic.

"Makin' spaghetti and meatballs," Norman said. "Raccoon meat, best they is. Maybe you two can stay fer supper?"

"I think Kelli wants to get back to town before dark." And if that wasn't Kelli's plan, and it came down to a choice between eating raccoon and striking off for town on my own, I decided I'd strike.

"That's too bad. Got some good garlic biscuits too."

Kelli had carried the feed over to the chicken house, and now she came in with the last two bags of groceries. Norman was stirring his pot of spaghetti on the old woodstove, and Kelli poked me in the ribs.

"I think you've made a conquest," she whispered. "Norman seems quite smitten."

"Glory be," I muttered.

He headed back toward us, and I instinctively ducked behind a chair. I wasn't sure but what he'd try for a bear hug yet. From this point I had a good view out a grimy window.

Across a small valley, snow had melted, revealing piles of old mine tailings sprawling down the mountainside like dirty avalanches. They were still bleak and barren, but trees had grown up around them, softening the raw ugliness. Trees and brush had filled in the eroded ravines too, and three deer were following a trail twisting along the edge of the trees. I could see why both Kelli and Norman dreaded the destruction a huge, open-pit mine would bring. Peace and serenity and beauty truly did reign here now, even though there was a certain undertone of garlic.

Then I spotted something closer. Off to one side of the chicken house a picket fence enclosed a square with pieces of board poking up through the snow. Kelli saw me looking.

"That's the cemetery," she said.

"Who's in it?"

"Rita, Marlene, Betty, and I don't know who else. Most people, when their chickens stop producing, have roast chicken or chicken stew or something. But Norman can never bring himself to do that. Of the chickens scratching around out there only a half dozen are still laying. The others are retired, and if the coyotes or something don't get them first, they'll wind up in the cemetery with their own little headstones."

A chicken cemetery. This gave me pause for consideration. Sometimes, when it seems likely I'll never be able to go back to Madison Street in Missouri, I think about settling down out West on a couple of country acres with a few chickens and space for Koop to roam. But now I saw that what to do with chickens gone elderly might be a problem. I'm fond of chicken in any form, fried, roasted, or fricasseed, but I doubted I could bring myself to chop off the heads of my little fowl friends any more than Norman could.

So, how did this affect my suspicions about the possibility of Norman's involvement in the murder? Could a softhearted old guy who couldn't even kill his chickens for food kill an old friend even in the heat of a tequila-fueled argument?

Kelli could read my thoughts; I knew by the way she was smiling at me. *See?* her knowing gaze said. *No murderer here.*

I had to admit that was surely the way it looked. But then, I reminded myself, that raccoon hadn't swan-dived into the spaghetti pot on its own. Norman had put it there, which suggested his softheartedness had its limits.

"We'd better head back right away," Kelli said. "That road isn't improving any."

"Oh, don't go yet." Norman sounded distressed. "Maybe . . ." His gaze cast around the two-room shack as if searching for something to entice us to stay. "We could play us some cards or something until the spaghetti's ready."

"We really do need to be going." I was pleased to hear the firmness in Kelli's statement.

"Okay." Norman gave a sigh of resignation. "I got some books out in the Dorf to send back with you. I'll go get 'em."

We stood on the porch to watch him. The rooster was on the hood of the Bronco now, peering through the windshield, or maybe admiring his reflection.

"The rooster is John Wayne, of course," Kelli said. "Actually, probably about John Wayne the 10th, since the roosters are always named John Wayne."

"Of course." I glanced back toward the pickup. "Norman has the books in the pickup because . . . ?"

"He just likes to sit out there and read."

Norman approached the pickup on the driver's side. But instead of opening the door, he grabbed hold of the top edge of it and with a surprisingly agile twist of body propelled himself through the window.

Kelli didn't appear to consider this unusual. "The doors haven't opened for years," she explained.

111

Norman definitely had his peculiarities. But there was also a certain practicality to elements of his lifestyle. If human friends aren't available, why not chickens? If your pickup doors don't open, why not go through a window? If raccoon is what you have available for meat, why not give it a try? Different, yes, but nothing that necessarily warrants a branding of "nutty."

He tossed the books in the Bronco. "Heard anything more from that big-shot mining guy?"

"I think I convinced him they had about as much chance of getting hold of the Lucky Queen now as I have of being voted in as mayor of Hello."

Norman grinned. "Good. I been listening to a talk show on the radio about a place down in South America where they got chemicals running outta some big mine like soda pop out of a can. Poisoning and polluting hundreds of square miles of jungle."

"That isn't going to happen here."

"Don't know why Hiram could never see what damage it could do here." I think Norman frowned, though it was hard to tell with all those egg-speckled whiskers.

"It'll probably be at least a week or more before I can get back again. Anything in particular you need?"

He opened the sack of books Kelli had brought. "No, don't think so. Hey, all right! You brought the book by that woman who married the alien. They was here again last night."

Kelli didn't say anything, but I ventured, "They?"

"Spaceship that flies over here regular." Norman nodded knowingly. "They're watchin' us, you know. Keepin' track. I send 'em welcome signals all the time." He tapped the side of his head, apparently to indicate how he was broadcasting the signals. "One of these nights I think they're gonna land and offer me a ride, maybe take me back to their planet."

Kelli still didn't say anything, and I gathered she had decided silence rather than reasoning or argument was the way to go with Norman on this subject.

Well, maybe he was just a teensy bit nutty, I had to admit. But who was to say with absolute certainty that no UFO aliens were circling the earth, maybe even getting ready to offer an invite or share a bowl of raccoon spaghetti?

"Okay, we're going now," Kelli said briskly. "You take care of yourself, okay?"

Norman followed us out to the Bronco, coming around to my side as I got in the car. "It's been a real joy meeting you, Ms. Ivy." He blinked suddenly. "It ain't *Mrs.* Ivy, is it?"

I was tempted to say it was indeed Mrs. and let him assume there was a current Mr. to avoid complications, but my tongue always freezes up on untruths, even if they'd be helpful or convenient. "No, I'm a widow."

"I'm right glad to hear that." Then, realizing that wasn't exactly the tactful thing to say, he added, "But sorry about your loss." He put a hand over his heart.

"Thank you."

"You come on out again, anytime. I'm looking forward to it. Might be a while afore I can git the Dorf runnin' and git to town," he added on a regretful note of realism concerning his transportation. He peered through the open window of the Bronco, and I think he was searching for a hand to shake again, but I was prudently sitting on both of them.

I thanked him for the invitation also. Kelli backed down the steep part of the hill. Norman, flanked by a chicken on either side, waved good-bye. Marilyn's brown feathers, I now saw, had a golden tinge, as befitted a chicken named for a blond goddess.

"Well, you have to say one thing for Norman," Kelli said as we slipped and slid down the steep hillside.

"What's that?"

She patted my leg and smiled. "He has excellent taste."

113

A truck and two men arrived at the house to pick up the books the following morning. I helped load the cardboard boxes they'd brought along, a bit dismayed at the men's cavalier attitude toward books. I've always been one to cherish books, to treat them with loving care, and these guys tossed them around as if they were indestructible widgets. I even yelled at one of the men, and I'm not generally a yelling person. "Be careful! You're tearing the pages in that book!"

These were guys, I reflected sourly, who probably figured the best use for the pages of a book was exactly what the pages of old Montgomery Ward catalogs had been used for long ago.

After two truckloads, with me accompanying the second load like just another widget, everything was scattered around the floor of the Hiram L. McLeod Memorial Library looking as if an earthquake had struck. Two different women were on duty today. One was Doris Hammerstone, a tiny, bent over, pink-scalped lady who regarded me rather grumpily, apparently blaming me for encroaching on the emergency fund she'd been guarding so zealously. The other was Myra Fighorn, who spent her time dusting industriously. I had the feeling I'd better not get in her way or I'd be dusted too.

Neither, beyond initial introductions, invaded my domain, and I spent the day getting an overview of what Hiram's library contained and doing a preliminary separation of books into major categories. The overhead mural was a bit oppressive. I was sitting directly under it, and the trash floating on the pond scum appeared to be old vegetables, eggplant prominent among them. If there was an artistic message in the mural, I was missing it. But I soon found I could ignore the overhead vegetables and went happily about my work.

I walked home at four o'clock feeling quite pleased with the situation.

Abilene was also pleased with her situation and told me about helping care for the half dozen animals Dr. Sugarman was boarding, plus the two cats he was trying to find homes for. Stella Sinclair had brought her pig in because it wasn't eating satisfactorily, in her estimation. Dr. Sugarman had spayed two cats, and someone had brought in a dog with a peculiar skin condition that both Abilene and Dr. Sugarman found most fascinating. Personally, talking about it made me feel more itchy than fascinated, but I'm not quite the animal person Abilene is.

"Oh, and Dr. Sugarman gave me this," Abilene said as we sat down to spaghetti and meatballs, made with good ol' ordinary hamburger, for supper. She set a booklet about traffic laws in Colorado, information people had to know to pass the test for a driver's license, beside her plate. "He says I need to have a driver's license, so I'm going to study this and get one. I can, you know, kind of drive already."

Back in Texas, she'd had to operate the tractor out on the farm, but Boone wouldn't let her drive a regular car, so she'd never had a license.

"Good idea. You need a license. Then you can drive the motor home too, when we're on the road again."

"Do we have to take off again?" She gave me a hopeful sideways glance. "Maybe we could, you know, just stay here for a while?"

"We might, unless the Braxtons or Boone locate us. But surely they'll all give up sooner or later," I added when she looked so crestfallen. I was certainly hopeful of that. "Can you take the test for a driver's license here in Hello?"

"Dr. Sugarman says I'll have to go down to some other town, Hayward, I think he called it. He said I can use his pickup to take the test."

115

As an unimportant aside, she also mentioned that she'd gotten that bad tooth filled today and it wasn't hurting anymore.

Abilene spent the evening with her nose buried in the booklet. I went through an old phone book looking at the choice of churches available in Hello. Tomorrow was Sunday, and I wanted to attend somewhere. Whatever was closest, I decided, since I'd have to walk. Then I had a different idea.

"Didn't Kelli say Dr. Sugarman teaches Sunday school? I wonder where he goes?"

"Mountain View Community Church," Abilene answered, surprising me with her ready knowledge. I doubted she'd asked him, so he must have volunteered the information. Good for him.

I found Mountain View Community Church in the listings in the yellow pages. It had an address on the hill on the other side of town. I changed plans about picking a church on the basis of distance. "That's the one I'm thinking about going to too. Want to come along?"

When we're on the road, and I just pick a church at random, Abilene sometimes goes with me, sometimes not. I know she occasionally reads the Bible I gave her, and sometimes she asks hard-to-answer questions. But she's never shown any sign of making a real commitment to the Lord, as I've hoped. Now she kept her finger on her place in the driver's license book and looked off into space for a moment.

"Sure," she said, and went back to the booklet.

I wasn't certain how long the hike across town would take, or how slippery the sidewalks might be, so we started out early on Sunday morning. The day was brilliantly sunny but frigid, and a light layer of new snow had fallen overnight.

No tire tracks had yet marked many of the streets. The hike was all downhill going down to the main street that wound through town, all uphill going the opposite way up to the church on the far side.

I was delighted when I saw Mountain View Community Church. It looked as if it had jumped straight off a Christmas card. I guessed it was built in the same era as the McLeod house; it was a narrow white building with an old-fashioned steeple and a crisp frosting of snow clinging to the steep roof. Even a melodious bell that rang out as we approached. The parking lot was minuscule, and cars lined the sidewalk-less street on both sides. Peering back across the narrow valley, I could see the McLeod house on the opposite hill, looking rather grim and Gothic from here.

Inside, an older couple was handing out programs at the door to the sanctuary, she in a pink polyester pantsuit, he in a slightly too tight dark suit. They weren't nosy but, in a friendly way, wanted to know all about us. Their approving nods suggested Abilene's job with Dr. Sugarman, and mine with the Historical Society, were excellent recommendations. There was one awkward moment when I said, "Kelli Keifer is letting us live in the old McLeod house."

The woman looked a bit taken aback by the announcement, but then, after exchanging a glance with her husband, she patted me on the arm and said, "It's a grand old house. Everyone misses Hiram." No comment about Kelli.

There was no choir. The music, played by a young woman on a piano and a guy on a guitar, was unexpectedly lively, music that started your foot tapping even if you were in church. Halfway through an energetic chorus, Abilene nudged me and whispered, "There's Dr. Sugarman."

I looked in the direction her head tilted. Dr. Sugarman wouldn't stand out in a crowd. He was medium height, brown-haired, comfortably plain-faced, with a hint of ruddiness to his skin. *Farm boy*, was my first thought. I think he'd started out in a suit, but he'd taken the jacket off somewhere, probably in the kids' Sunday school class he taught, and now he was in a light blue shirt, sleeves rolled up, dark blue tie slightly askew. Even more or less dressed up, he looked as if he was ready to jump in and help birth a calf or colt. As I watched, he hastily rolled the sleeves down, as if he'd just become aware of their impropriety in the service. Then he tried to smooth a lick of hair that persisted in sticking out above his ear. Without success. His voice boomed out in the chorus with more enthusiasm than musical talent.

I liked him.

The sermon was from the Sermon on the Mount, solidly Christ centered. I spotted Ben Simpson, the garrulous guy we'd met at Nick's Garage, but he didn't see us. Dr. Sugarman came over to our pew right after the closing song. Abilene introduced us.

"I'm so glad you both came." He shook my hand and said, "Call me Mike." Then he looked at Abilene. "You too."

We chatted for a minute about the old church, and then he said to Abilene, "I'm going to drive out to the Harmon ranch this afternoon. Jake and I have a Quarter horse we're planning to race this coming year, and I want to see how he's doing. How about coming along?"

Then Dr. Sugarman realized what he'd just done. "Maybe you'd like to come too?" he said to me, and he actually blushed at what he apparently perceived as his own rudeness for not including me in the invitation to begin with.

I could almost read Abilene's thoughts as she eyed Dr. Sugarman warily. Was this a date-type invitation? For all the abuse Boone had given her, plus the fact that he had made plain he was willing to escalate the abuse to homicide, Abilene was much aware that she was still legally married to him. For her this meant the dating game wasn't an option.

She swallowed. "I guess not."

"If you've studied that booklet, you can practice driving out at the ranch, off the public roads. You really need a driver's license for errands when I don't have time."

Abilene's face relaxed and brightened. A business trip concerning the driver's license, nothing personal. "I studied the booklet last night, but I do need some real driving practice."

Good. I was looking forward to an afternoon alone to prowl Hiram's now empty office/library. And take another look around up there on the third floor. I graciously declined when Dr. Sugarman repeated his invitation to me.

Nothing like a quiet Sunday afternoon for a little nosy sleuthing.

12

Mike Sugarman drove us home. I invited him to stay for the pot roast I'd put in the oven before we went to church, and he ate with farm-boy gusto after first asking if he could offer the blessing. Afterwards Abilene changed clothes, and they took off for the ranch in his pickup, Abilene clutching her driver's booklet.

I put on old gray sweats, figuring whatever I did would involve dirt and dust, and climbed the stairs to the third floor. I examined the piece of plywood that had once blocked access to the third floor. Just an ordinary piece of plywood, as far as I could see, yanked off the opening without any particular care. I scrutinized every inch of the round tower room, up on my tiptoes to inspect window frames and down on my hands and knees to study shreds of carpet. I tried to open a window, but they'd long ago been painted shut.

A few tracks showed in the dust on the ballroom floor, although it appeared the police hadn't made any extensive investigation in that area. I made a brief excursion around the perimeter of the room, finding only a pile of beat-up chairs in one corner and a bathroom and a couple of small, empty rooms at the far end. The room gave off no nostalgic vibes of turn-of-the-century dancers twirling gracefully. It was just a big, dusty, long-unused room with a creaky floor. Although I did have a brief urge to take off my shoes and whiz across the ballroom floor in my stocking feet. I quickly squelched that. This was not playtime; this was murder.

But if I thought there'd be an "ah-ha!" moment when I'd cleverly spot something the police had missed, I was wrong. My lone accomplishment was to do away with much of the fingerprint powder remaining in the tower room, which I did by transferring it to my sweats in big, dirty smudges.

I gave up on the third floor and went down to Hiram's office/library. What I really wanted to do was snoop, but as soon as I opened the door my conscience told me I should clean. Because what we had here was dust in all its elemental forms. Dust marks outlined where books had stood on the shelves. Dust bunnies dotted the floor like small, fuzzy creatures grazing on the carpet. Dust motes surfed merrily in shafts of sunlight.

I marched out to the utility room where I'd spotted a vacuum cleaner and dragged it back to this museum of dust, along with a can of Pledge and a handful of rags from the discards room.

I tackled the dust bunnies first. The big old vacuum cleaner was awkward as a battleship to maneuver, but it was also powerful enough to suck up everything in its path, including a large screw, several small chunks of rock, and a yellow something that disappeared before I could grab it.

However, I quickly realized one unexpected benefit: snooping and cleaning are a compatible combination. Vacuuming the carpet, I snooped under an old leather sofa and felt around in its nooks and crannies as well, producing a penny and a paper clip. Fallen, or perhaps tucked, in a large crack behind bookshelves I found several letters from an irate tenant about some property Hiram had owned back in 1989, and in the corner of a picture frame was a printed receipt for a mining book he'd bought in 1991. Was tucking things in odd little places part of Hiram's filing system, or simple carelessness?

I shoved an upholstered chair aside and pounced on a scrap of yellow paper with a few words written on it. Jackpot? No, just a torn scrap with an enigmatic scribbling of "gget at 3:30, Tu," the partial words and ragged edges suggesting it had been torn from some larger message. I didn't see of what value it could be, but as a longtime saver of this and that, I tucked it in a pocket.

I cleaned my way to a metal filing cabinet, empty, then to the big old rolltop desk where I conscientiously Pledged every surface. I opened all the drawers and found, not surprisingly, that they were also quite empty. The desk and filing cabinet were no doubt the first place Kelli had looked for Hiram's records and papers. I removed desk drawers so I could look under and around them and check for false bottoms. I also inspected for discrepancies in size of pigeon holes and compartments that might suggest a hidden compartment behind one of them.

I had no idea what I was searching for, of course, but what Kelli had said earlier certainly suggested she thought something was missing. But why, I now wondered, would Hiram bother to hide anything important? Who would he hide it from? He lived here alone, and as I understood it, the only people who came here in recent years were Kelli, Norman, and, rarely, Lucinda.

Yet wasn't it interesting that these were the same three people who had most opposed Hiram's big plans for the mine . . .

Ivy Malone, it's a wonder you're not suspicious of your own foot,

I chided myself grumpily. I switched the vacuum cleaner on again. No suspicions, or even coherent thoughts, were possible with that monster running.

The first-floor tower room on this side of the house opened off the library/office, but it was empty except for an oversized table and a long-dead plant in a Mexican pot. I was on my knees, vacuuming under the table and looking upward to see if anything was taped to the underside, when a touch on my foot made me jump.

I backed out and discovered Lucinda standing beside me. I shut off the vacuum cleaner.

"I knocked, but I knew you couldn't hear me with the vacuum running, so I just came on in." She peered around the room, then pushed a lace curtain aside to look outside. Here we were only a few feet from where Hiram had landed when he plunged. "Finding anything interesting?"

"Just dust and more dust."

"You need a phone."

"We have one of those buy-minutes-as-you-need-them cell phones for emergencies." While a regular phone here might be convenient, what we did not need was a phone listing that would show up for any Braxton prowling the phone listings on the Internet to see.

"Since I couldn't call, what I came over for is, there'll be a rehearsal for the Roaring '20s Revue tomorrow afternoon at the old Hello Hotel. I thought maybe you'd like to come since it isn't a day you'll be working. You might find it interesting."

"Sure. Sounds great. Would you like some coffee? I think it's time for a break." I felt my hair, and my hand came away cobwebby.

"Love some."

We went out to the kitchen. For speed, I used the electric coffeemaker we'd brought from the motor home.

"Abilene and I went to church this morning, over at Mountain Community Church. I was hoping you might be there."

"I used to go, but I haven't been in several years." Lucinda's tone dipped into a remote, I-don't-want-to-go-there zone. She crossed to the window and made a point of being engrossed in rearranging the feathers in the mayonnaise jar.

I barged ahead anyway. "I miss it when I don't go for a while. I know God is everywhere, but I start feeling disconnected from him if I'm not in church."

"I am disconnected from God. Permanently," she stated with harsh finality.

All those losses, I knew without being told. Husband, daughter, son. "I lost my only son and my husband too. God was all that got me through those bad times."

She looked briefly surprised but then shrugged, although I had the impression the indifference was more pretended than real. "God got me through the first couple of losses. But I guess I'd just . . . had it with God by the time he took my son too."

"I'm so sorry. Do you mind if I pray for you?"

"Pray away. In my experience prayer never makes any difference one way or the other. I did enough of it that never had any effect."

I cringed when I heard that, but I sent up a small prayer right then and there anyway. Because I do believe prayer makes a difference. God listens. Lucinda, however, perhaps afraid I was going to plunge right into a sermon, changed the subject abruptly.

"Have you had a chance to look around town yet?" she asked.

"No, but I went out to the mine with Kelli yesterday." The coffee was ready, and I poured a cup for each of us.

Lucinda scooted a chair up to the card table. "Ah, so you

met our local character." She smiled, and I sensed a real fondness for old Norman. "He still has his chickens?"

"Oh yes. I didn't get the names of all of them, but I met Marilyn and Ginger. Julia died." I didn't mention how Norman was, as Kelli had put it, "smitten" with me. I'd just as soon that didn't become public knowledge.

"Hiram's death hit Norman as hard as any of us, I think. People call him Nutty Norman, you know, and everyone thought he was definitely 'nutty' when he brought that jar filled with chicken feathers to the funeral and put it beside the flowers around the coffin." She nodded toward the jar on the windowsill. "But Kelli and I understood. Hiram always loved the fresh eggs Norman brought when he came to town. The two of them might eat a dozen of them for breakfast after drinking tequila half the night." Her gaze lifted again to the feathers on the windowsill, and she blinked back tears, but she also shook her head with a hint of exasperation. "Stomachs of iron, both of them. Stubborn as old mules too. And they liked salsa on those morning eggs. I sometimes thought Hiram could eat Mexican food morning, noon, and night."

"No health problems for Hiram, then?" I remembered Kelli had taken blackberry balsam out for Norman, so maybe the iron in his stomach was rusting a bit. Or maybe he wasn't getting enough salsa these days to keep it tuned up.

"His eyesight was slipping a little, and he was getting more forgetful and putting on a little weight. But basically, no, he wasn't having any health problems."

Would forgetfulness on Hiram's part result in a misplacement of papers and explain why Kelli hadn't found everything she thought should be there?

I leaned forward at the table. "Lucinda, I'm pretty sure you don't think Kelli killed Hiram any more than I do. So who do you think did it?"

"I've spent many hours pondering that question."

"Someone who didn't want the mine reopened? Someone with an old grudge? Or a new grudge? A business matter? Or something personal?"

Lucinda drew check marks in the air with a finger. "Any of the above."

"Norman?"

"I don't like to think it, but the possibility has occurred to me. They were old friends, but that tequila is powerful stuff, and they both got pretty hot under the collar when they drank and argued."

"But it was apparently a planned murder, not an impulse thing."

"Why do you say that?" she asked with a sharpness that surprised me.

"For one thing, the fact that the murderer brought along a weapon rather than just using whatever was available to hit Hiram over the head with." I assumed the police had noted that point as readily as I had, but probably they hadn't stressed its importance when releasing information to the public.

"That's true, I suppose," she agreed. She sipped the coffee reflectively. "I'm inclined to think it must have been some outsider, someone who was bitter about some business deal with Hiram in the past and wanted to settle the score."

That sounded reasonable, and Lucinda was certainly in a position to know as much about Hiram's business affairs as anyone. "Someone such as that would most likely come prepared," I agreed.

"Hiram was . . . shrewd, you know. He was never stingy. Never. But he could drive a hard bargain when he was making a deal. So that's what I'm thinking, that it was someone who came, did the deed, and left as unnoticed as he came. And will probably never be caught."

"What about an old wife?"

"There's only one still around, number two, I think she

126

was, and I have a hard time suspecting her of anything." Lucinda chuckled, as if an inside joke were involved. "You can meet her tomorrow at the rehearsal. Doris Hammerstone. She's prompter for the skits."

Doris Hammerstone? Tiny, pink-scalped, bent-bodied Doris was one of Hiram's old wives? No, I couldn't see her whopping him over the head, at least not with anything more substantial than a celery stick. I couldn't, in fact, even see her making it up to the third floor of the house. "Actually, I've already met her."

Okay, cancel the old wives. Although I have to admit I did so reluctantly.

Lucinda left a few minutes later. I did some more vacuuming and dusting. Abilene got home just before dark, elated about her driving practice. "Dr. Sugarman says that I already drive well enough that after a little more practice next weekend I should be ready to take the test. The pickup is an automatic, which is a lot easier to drive than the stick shift on the old tractor."

I noted that he was still Dr. Sugarman, not Mike, to her.

We spent the evening with me going through the driver's license booklet and asking Abilene every question I could think might be on the test. Then I figured I'd better study that booklet myself, because she knew more than I did.

In the morning I used the cell phone to call the mail-forwarding outfit in Arkansas, give my password, and ask them to send my accumulated mail to general delivery in Hello. Mail wasn't delivered to homes here. Everyone had a P.O. box, but I was reluctant to do that. I suspected the Braxtons had tracked me down once by using the resources of a family member in the postal service. Maybe I was being paranoid, but I figure too much caution is better than too little.

Right after lunch I walked down to the old hotel building on Main Street. A gloomy blanket of clouds cut off the top half of the mountains on both sides of town, and dirty gray slush ridged the streets. The hotel had no doubt been impressive in its day, and it still maintained a stolid dignity. Four stories, all brick, still the tallest building in town. A couple of windows were boarded up on the second story, but above that everything appeared in good shape.

Activity buzzed around the front door, cars coming and going and dropping people off, and I followed several ladies inside. A wide stairway led off to the right of a shabbily carpeted lobby, but the stairs were blocked by a tasseled cord and a "Keep Out" sign. A plywood barrier and a similar sign, with the addition of a red-lettered "Danger," barred entrance to a single elevator on the left side. Ladies wrapped in a hum of busy chatter milled around the lobby.

The far side of the room opened onto what may once have been a large restaurant or even a ballroom. Now it held numerous rows of unpadded brown seats, the folding kind I remember from movie theaters when I was a girl. An impressively large stage covered the far end of the room, but the floor had been patched with plywood, and a crisscrossing of two-by-fours braced one end. The rod holding a gold curtain drifted downhill, and the floor felt uneven under my feet. To really refurbish the building, as Hiram had apparently promised to do, would surely take big bucks.

A slapstick skit was in progress on stage, three people shoving each other around. The actors were all women, but one of them yelled, "Soitenly!" in that old Three Stooges take on "certainly." As I recalled, the Three Stooges hadn't come along until later than the 1920s, but probably the Revue aimed for fun rather than fussy time details. Lucinda and another woman stood off to one side consulting a script. And there, right down front, was Doris Hammerstone, also a script in hand, her unexpectedly strong voice now bellowing out, "No, no, Emily, it's not Mel, it's Moe. Moe is one of the Stooges."

Off to one side, the chorus line was getting lined up, a tall woman in the center, height graduating unevenly down to the shortest ladies on either end. Tight leggings had been out of style for some time now, but they were in prominence in the chorus line, along with all the unflattering lumps and bumps tight leggings reveal.

"Mrs. Malone, I thought that was you!" I turned and saw a slim, blond woman rushing toward me. "Remember me? Char Sterling, Chris Sterling's mother. We met at the Historical Society the other day."

"Yes, of course." The ladies there had called her Charlotte, but apparently she preferred Char.

"How nice of you to come and watch our little production! So, what do you think?"

Charlotte was more casually dressed today, dark slacks and a ski sweater, but her oversized purse with the enigmatic letter was the same as before. Today her blond hair was in a sleek ponytail tied at the nape of her neck, casual but still elegant.

"Very interesting. You're not in the chorus line?" I asked, since she looked in better shape for it than most of the ladies in the lineup.

"I'm handling costumes again this year. And wigs." She held up a dark wig that looked as if it had been cut with a bowl as a pattern. "Moe's, I think. For the Three Stooges skit." She surprised me by draping the wig over her own elegant hairdo. It covered half her face. "What do you think?" she asked from beneath it. "Could I sell more real estate in this? Things are slow now."

We both laughed as she took the wig off, and I liked her better for being able to make a bit of fun of herself. Not nearly as stuffy and pretentious as I'd thought at our first meeting.

"Did someone at the Historical Society find information on the house you asked about? The Randolph house, I think you called it."

"Actually, I had to go back over there and do it myself." She wrinkled her nose with an air of exasperation, and I wondered if she also called this the "Ladies Hysterical Society." "Perhaps you'd like to see the house sometime? And some of the town's other historic old houses as well?"

"I would indeed. But I'm afraid I'm not in the market for real estate of any age at the moment."

She put a hand on my arm and laughed again. "Oh, I'm not trying to sell you anything. I just thought you might be interested. Although none of the other houses have the mystique of having a murder attached as Hiram's place does, of course. Do you really think you can uncover anything about his death?"

"The police apparently did a very thorough examination of the house and didn't find anything. There was fingerprint powder all over the third floor tower room, from where he was pushed."

Charlotte shuddered lightly. "I wouldn't want to live there."

"Really?" A thought occurred to me. "What about selling the place?"

She looked momentarily nonplussed. Then, assuming a polished real estate saleslady air, as if she were addressing prospective buyers, she said, "Oh, Mr. and Mrs. Johnson, I have just the place for you! It's this marvelous old Victorian home that belonged to one of our town's most illustrious citizens. Three stories, with enough bedrooms for all your

130

guests, fantastic views of the city and mountains, especially from your very own ballroom on the third floor! Plus a mysterious history that no other house in town can claim. A murder once happened there! I know you'll love it, and you won't believe the reasonable price they're asking for it."

She was laughing by the time she finished, and so was I. "Am I good, or what?" she asked.

"You're good."

Going more serious, she added, "Anyway, for a small town, we have a really competent police force. We had another murder three or four years ago, some drug-related thing, and they had the killer nailed within a week. So I'd guess they didn't leave anything undone on this one. Although I'm personally inclined to think Hiram was killed by some outsider who may be very difficult to track down."

An opinion that matched Lucinda's. "Not Kelli?"

She looked surprised that I'd even ask. "Definitely not Kelli. And I'd believe that even if she weren't my son's girlfriend. Kelli is no killer, and it just makes me furious how people have jumped to unfair conclusions about her." An apologetic smile erased the deep frown lines that had momentarily cut into her smooth complexion. "Sorry. I just get kind of worked up on this subject."

I changed the subject. "This is quite an impressive old building too."

She glanced overhead, as if suspecting something might come tumbling down. "As you may have heard, Hiram was planning to buy and renovate it, and then donate it to the Historical Society. But that won't happen now, of course, so this may be the last year for the Revue. The fire department has been warning for the last couple years that the building is unsafe and threatening to shut us down."

"That would be too bad. But I suppose officials have to be cautious about safety."

131

"Personally, I think it's a big to-do about nothing. This old building will still be standing when that young fire marshal is gray-haired and doddering."

"The stairs and elevator must be dangerous." I gestured toward the signs.

"I don't know that I'd call the elevator dangerous. It certainly isn't going anywhere. It's been stuck in the basement since last year. And the stairs might not support a crowd of people, but we use the third floor for storage for costumes and props, so someone is always running up or down the stairs, and we've never had any problems. We have to use the third floor because the second was vandalized years ago." She hesitated, one hand absentmindedly stroking the wig as if it were a pet. "I probably shouldn't say this, but I've sometimes wondered if there wasn't some collusion going on."

"Collusion? Between whom?"

"Well, for starters, maybe between Hiram and the fire department officials? Threats to condemn the building would certainly lower the value and might convince the elderly woman in Denver who owns it to sell cheap."

I was surprised at her suggestion of a shady business practice on Hiram's part, since her son had been his lawyer and presumably advising him. Although I realized I probably shouldn't be surprised. I'd already heard about Hiram's shrewdness, which might merely be a euphemism for any number of less complimentary adjectives.

She laughed and touched my arm again. "Oh, don't pay any attention to me. Probably just my imagination running amuck. Chris says I read way too many mystery novels, and he may be right."

"Mysteries are my favorite reading material too."

"Really? Maybe you won't think my suspicions completely weird, then." She stepped closer, her voice dipping confidentially low when she added, "Chris always thought so highly

132

of Hiram, but I had my doubts. Before my husband passed away, he also handled Hiram's legal affairs. He never actually told me anything specific, confidentiality between lawyer and client, you know. But I got the definite impression that it wasn't easy to keep Hiram on the up-and-up, that he often wanted to do things that weren't necessarily illegal but were definitely—" She broke off and made a little side-to-side wiggle with her hand.

"Definitely questionable?" I asked, wanting to make certain I wasn't misinterpreting the gesture. She nodded.

"And it could be all my imagination." She smiled. "Plus all those mystery and thriller novels, of course."

"Imagination can sometimes produce useful insights."

"You know, would you and your friend who works for Dr. Sugarman like to come over for dinner one night? Kelli and Chris can come too. We'll put our heads together and brainstorm a solution to Hiram's murder!"

"Sounds great. Chris doesn't live with you?"

Charlotte touched her cheek in a pretended gesture of horror. "A thirty-year-old man living with his mother? You must be joshing." She laughed again. "No, he has one of those new condos out beyond Safeway. Though they'll probably buy a new house before the wedding. The condo's a little small."

She made the wedding sound more imminent than Kelli had. I wondered if she knew Chris was pushing for an elopement, and Kelli was stalling.

Someone rushed up to Charlotte then, something about needing a screwdriver. I thought Charlotte would go off to help the woman find one, but instead she dug in her big purse and astonished me by hauling out an entire miniature tool kit.

The woman grabbed and waved it. "Charlotte is always prepared for any emergency. Stamps, Tums, Band-Aids, anything. Would you believe, once I needed a dab of blue nail polish, and she pulled it right out of her purse?" The woman was rushing off again even as she spoke.

Charlotte gave a little wave as she headed off in the direction the woman had taken. "I'd better go see what they're doing with my screwdriver. Not messing around with the electricity again, I hope." She rolled her eyes, as if in tribute to some previous disaster. "Nice talking to you! Don't forget, dinner some evening soon."

I didn't stay for all the rehearsal, although I did watch Paul Newman do his master of ceremonies bit between skits. I was astonished. The man who in the tow truck had acted as if it would take an IRS agent to pull a few reluctant words out of him was, on the stage, talkative and jovial. He told a joke about an old couple with hearing problems, complete with appropriate voices, did a funny little dance step, and joked about the hotel's deteriorating condition, a total about-face from his offstage personality.

I also watched the chorus line perform one number. After a moment I recognized the jazzy music as the old '20s tune, "Yes, Sir, That's My Baby." The chorus line lacked something in coordination as they kicked and turned, but their boisterous level of enthusiasm rivaled six-year-olds at a birthday party. Even when the statuesque central lady, who I now knew was Lulu Newman, the MC's wife, tumbled and the entire chorus line shrieked and tumbled with her, they simply untangled themselves, giggled, and regrouped.

Outside again, I wandered the full length of Hello's main street. There was indeed an oversupply of what Abilene had called "antique-y" shops, but I also passed the more practical necessities: a photo shop, Halburton's Hardware, the Café Russo, and a small flower shop.

I paused at the window. I didn't need flowers, of course. I couldn't afford flowers. But a bunch of yellow daffodils drew me inside. Daffodils always reminded me of Harley.

He used to grow beautiful daffodils. But they never seemed to bloom as lavishly back at the house on Madison Street after he was gone.

I asked the dark-haired young woman at the counter the price of a half dozen of the daffodils.

"There's a dozen there in the window," she said. "A dozen make a very nice arrangement."

"I know, but I just need a half dozen." I figured even that many was stretching my budget.

She tilted her head as she looked at me thoughtfully. "They're getting a little old. Three dollars?"

I was surprised. That sounded very reasonable for out-of-season daffodils. I nodded and got out my billfold as she went to the display window and removed six of the daffodils. Then something occurred to me, and I stopped short. "That isn't the real price, is it?"

"Are you implying I raise my price just because a customer needs daffodils, and I'm the only florist in town?" She touched her chest and managed to sound righteously indignant, but something in her hazel eyes gave her away as a phony.

"I'm implying you may go broke if you lower your price just because some little old lady looks wistful about a few daffodils."

She laughed. "Whatever." She handed over the flowers wrapped in green tissue paper. A calico cat wandered in from somewhere and jumped on the counter to rub its head under the girl's chin. "It's been a slow day. Enjoy."

"I'm Ivy Malone," I said impulsively. "We just moved into the old McLeod house, and I'm working on Hiram's books for the Historical Society library."

Her pretty face went a little stiff, but her "Oh" was non-committal. She became very busy micromanaging a display of small cards to accompany floral arrangements.

I felt at a peculiar loss for words, given the abrupt change in atmosphere, and I stumbled along with, "Did you know Hiram?"

"I'd met him."

"I suppose you know Kelli Keifer too, then? She's been very kind and helpful to us. And generous too."

The girl didn't say anything, just grabbed a cloth and started polishing the counter with a vigor that would have put a shine on a mud pie. The cat gave her a dirty look and jumped down. I felt as if I'd blundered into some social gaffe here, because she obviously didn't see Kelli as kind and helpful. Yet, as usual, I also felt defensive where Kelli was concerned.

"The town seems to have made some judgments about Kelli that I feel are unjustified."

She looked up at me, hazel eyes flashing in her heart-shaped face. She slammed the polishing cloth down on the counter. "I don't know about that, but I do know Kelli Keifer blew into town, sized up the eligible males, and grabbed mine."

I touched my throat in dismay. No wonder the atmosphere had plunged from friendly to frigid. Chris Sterling's former girlfriend!

13

While I was wondering how to get what felt like an oversized foot out of my mouth—praising current to former girlfriend is not a hallmark of tact—the young woman's expressive face changed again. "I'm sorry. That was totally uncalled for."

She grabbed my flowers, rushed over to the window display, and added the other six daffodils. "I really am so sorry," she repeated as she thrust the enlarged bouquet at me.

"I guess you must have been very much in love with Chris."

She smiled wryly. "I had my wedding gown picked out and our first two children named, if that tells you anything. Fortunately I found out what kind of man he is before I made the mistake of marrying him. So I probably should be grateful to Kelli for that."

"What kind of man is he?"

"Not a faithful one, that's for sure. He strung me along for weeks before he admitted he was seeing Kelli too, and dumped me. And not the greatest lawyer in the world, either.

A friend went to him and said he completely messed up a real estate contract. He'd never have gotten into that law firm if his father hadn't been a partner in it." She shook her head and smiled guiltily. "Sorry. Again. A woman scorned and all that, right?"

"A natural feeling, I'm sure."

"Does it feel . . . uncomfortable living there in a house where a man was murdered?"

"I don't really think about it. We don't hear creaks or groans or thuds in the night."

"I was there a couple of times with Chris, when he went to see Mr. McLeod about something. The place struck me as a little on the spooky side even then. The first thing I thought was, I wonder if there's a secret room around here somewhere?"

"A secret room? I'd never thought about that." But interesting, very interesting!

"Oh, I know, it's pretty far out, isn't it? But that old house just seems like the kind of place that would have a secret room."

I liked this lively touch of imagination. "With something hidden in it?"

"What good is a secret room if you don't hide something in it? I had a secret hidey-hole where a board had come loose in the back of my closet when I was a girl."

"What did you hide in it?"

"Oh, a two-dollar bill I got hold of somehow. A diary. A photo of an older guy I had a crush on. A piece of bubble gum he gave me. A letter my brother wrote to me when he was in college." Her chest rose and fell in a long breath. "Just before he was killed in a car accident."

I remembered Kelli saying Chris's mother hadn't liked this girl, hadn't wanted him to marry her. I liked her! The thought occurred to me that under different circumstances, she and

Kelli might well have been friends. I reached over and patted her hand. "Someone else will come along." I almost said "someone better," but that seemed disloyal to Kelli, who was in love with Chris now, so I skipped it.

"Actually, someone else kind of has." She sounded shy on this subject, but hopeful. "I'm seeing a guy who works for the State Forestry."

"Good. And thank you for the flowers." I wound the green tissue a little tighter around the stems, then paused at the door for a final question. "Do you think Kelli killed her uncle?"

The blunt question didn't seem to surprise her. She retrieved the cloth and started polishing again, although more slowly this time. "You can hardly expect an impartial opinion from the dumped ex-girlfriend. Even if she is now thankful she was dumped."

"You strike me as a person who'd try to be fair."

She lifted her gaze, her eyes steady on mine now. "I can't offer an opinion on the murder. But my personal experience says what Kelli Keifer wants, Kelli Keifer goes after. And if anything gets in her way—" She sliced a finger across her throat.

I wanted to disregard what the young woman—Suzy, I presumed her name was when I saw the "Flowers by Suzy" sign over the door of the tiny establishment when I went out—said about Kelli. As she'd pointed out herself, she was hardly the person to provide an impartial assessment.

Yet it was the first truly personal-experience assessment I'd heard about Kelli, and I kept thinking about it while I arranged the cheery daffodils in a vase at the house and set them on the card table. I was still thinking about it the following day when I decided Suzy's idea about a secret room wasn't all that far out and set out to do a little investigating.

I didn't get far. I thought it would be simple to measure floor areas and wall lengths and thickness to see if there were any discrepancies that would allow for an extra room, but either the house had settled over the years, or hadn't been built square to begin with, and every measurement was a little off. I couldn't find enough space for a room anywhere, but neither could I make the figures come out exactly right. I wound up not getting through more than a third of the first floor that day.

Koop followed me around for a while, but when I didn't go down in the basement, which was where he wanted to go, he got bored and retreated to his imitation bearskin rug. Eventually I gave up and took a bubble bath before Abilene got home. Today she was excited about Dr. Sugarman's project to provide a cat paralyzed in its hindquarters with mobility by fitting it with a little two-wheeled cart. What a fine veterinarian she'd have made if she'd ever had the chance, I realized regretfully.

Next day I gave in to Koop's pleading to open the basement door, but I quickly decided if there was a secret room down in that cobweb-infested area, I didn't want to find it.

By Thursday, when I settled down among the books at the Historical Society, I hadn't changed my mind about Kelli's innocence in Hiram's murder. A couple of alternate thoughts about ex-girlfriend Suzy had, in fact, occurred to me. She seemed like a sweet young woman, certainly not a murderess type, but would there have been any advantage in Hiram's death for her? I couldn't think of any, but I wasn't about to dismiss anyone as a suspect. I had the feeling there were undercurrents churning in Hello that I knew nothing about.

A second thought came when I remembered again that Kelli had said Chris's mother had been against his marrying the ex-girlfriend. Perhaps that had more to do with the breakup between Chris and Suzy than any "grabbing" by Kelli.

In spite of those thoughts, when Kelli stopped by the library later to see how my job was going, I realized uncomfortably that the certainty of her innocence had slipped a percentage point or two in my mind. I tried to cover the discomfort with vivacious chatter about the wonderful books and how the Ladies had agreed to order the software program I needed for the cataloging process. Kelli looked surprised at my un-characteristic effusiveness, but she didn't mention it, just said it looked as if I had everything under control.

And the discomfort I felt then was minuscule compared to the dismay I felt when I walked back to the house from the library on Saturday afternoon. Because there in the driveway, in all its mismatched, multicolored, mud-spattered glory, stood the Dorf. I'd doubted the thing would be ambulatory within this decade, and here it was. With Norman standing there grinning at me in all his bearded, ponytailed glory.

"Norman," I said. "I-I wasn't expecting you."

"I got the Dorf runnin'. 'Specially so I could come and see you."

Ivy Malone, the senior sexpot, inspiration to semi-eccentrics everywhere. Oh joy. Now I noted a bumper sticker I hadn't before. "Eat more possum."

Norman thrust a sack at me. "I brought you some eggs."

I accepted the sack and peered inside. Beautiful big brown eggs, with bits of straw from the nest still clinging to them. "Why, uh, thank you, Norman. That's very thoughtful of you."

"I figgered maybe you'n me could have dinner at the Café Russo."

Several thoughts splashed through my mind. One was that the Café Russo had looked quite elegant, undoubtedly the most expensive restaurant in town. Did they have a dress code? Norman was wearing a suit and tie, but his Nikes looked as if they had spent some time in a dumpster.

The second thought loomed even larger. What if we ran into some of the Historical Society ladies at the restaurant? I didn't know what had brought Norman up as a subject of conversation, but I'd overheard the two ladies on duty at the main desk yesterday laughing about how he'd brought his chickens in for the Fourth of July parade last summer. Not as participants, but so the chickens, safely wedged under Norman's arms, could watch the parade. Women of the Society would be aghast—and/or giggly—at my being out on what would surely look like a date with Nutty Norman the Chicken Man. And what if he did something outrageously strange at the restaurant?

Norman was waiting expectantly for my answer, and I was trying to think of a polite way to avoid this, but suddenly I was ashamed of myself. Yes, his old blue suit was shiny in places and long out of style, his shoes strange, and his beard as wild and bushy as ever, but there were no stray leftovers in it, and he'd obviously done all he could to spiff himself up for this occasion. His ponytail was neatly rubber-banded, his fingernails clean. The scent of cigarette smoke still clung to him, but the garlic was absent, and I even caught a whiff of aftershave lotion. I decided not to wonder where he'd put it, since he didn't shave.

I also decided I wasn't going to disappoint him or hurt his feelings by turning him down. He'd put a lot of effort into this. What did I care what anyone thought about my going to dinner with him? I thought about suggesting someplace cheaper than the Café Russo, but I suspected he'd find that insulting. I decided if he came up short on money, I could discreetly add a few dollars to make up the difference.

"The Café Russo sounds lovely," I said. "Would you like to come in while I freshen up?"

He grinned. "You already look mighty fresh to me, Ms. Ivy."

Norman may have his peculiarities, but he knew how to flatter a woman. I led him through to the kitchen, where I stashed the eggs in the refrigerator. Koop, who has no tolerance for cigarette smokers, even spiffed-up ones, took one sniff and headed out of the room.

To cover Koop's rude departure, I pointed to the jar on the windowsill. "Kelli brought your feathers here after the funeral. They're very nice."

I left Norman with a cup of coffee in the kitchen while I went to refresh my lipstick, fluff my hair, and change to a more up-to-date pair of dark slacks, my best imitation silk blouse, and seldom-worn, dressy high heels. If anyone saw us, I fully intended to look as if this was an important date, not something to be embarrassed about.

"You look beautiful, Ms. Ivy," Norman said when I returned.

"Thank you, Norman. You look very nice too."

There was an awkward moment when I remembered the doors of the Dorf didn't open. I was feeling kindly toward Norman, but not so kindly that I wanted him helpfully boosting me through a window.

"Why don't we walk?" I suggested. "We'll work up an appetite and enjoy our food more."

"Fine idea, Ms. Ivy."

The high heels weren't the best choice for walking, but Norman considerately took my elbow at curbs and over bumps of icy slush. At the Café Russo, the hostess led us to a small booth in the rear. I didn't know if that meant she preferred to hide us from public view, or if she thought we wanted something dim and intimate, but I was guiltily grateful. The hour was still early, only a few scattered diners present. I was grateful for that too.

We both declined drinks. I was apprehensive that Norman might demand possum, but he ordered red snapper en papillote by pointing to it on the menu. I chose the manicotti.

When our first-course minestrone arrived, Norman threaded his fingers together and looked at me expectantly. In surprise I realized he was waiting for me to offer a blessing, which I did.

Our conversation during the meal covered a wide range of topics from books he'd read, although I was relieved that he skipped the subject of UFOs this evening. One thing he asked about was the whistle I always carry on a chain around my neck. I'd forgotten to tuck it under my blouse, as I usually do.

I told him how, after a woman was mugged in a local parking lot back in Missouri, a friend had given me one to wear. Another friend replaced it when that first whistle was lost.

"Have you ever used it?" he asked.

"Not yet."

He considered the situation thoughtfully. "Keep wearing it," he advised.

"You think I might need it?"

"There's a killer around here somewhere."

"But there's no reason a killer would be interested in me," I protested.

"He might be real interested if you figger out who he is."

I swallowed. A thoughtful observation . . . or a personal warning?

I decided to detour that ominous line of thought and concentrate on dinner. "I'm certainly a long way from figuring out anything," I said brightly.

Norman's manners weren't exactly impeccable. He used a knife to scoot his vegetables onto his spoon. But he didn't do anything over-the-top nutty. One couple passing by glanced at Norman as if they recognized him, but I didn't spot anyone I knew.

I was, guiltily, relieved by this also. But disappointment unexpectedly overtook the guilt and relief, and I was defiantly prepared to acknowledge him as my good friend Norman. Actually, I rather missed the opportunity to do that.

Eventually, over tiramisu for dessert (which Norman recommended), I got around to asking him the question I asked almost everyone in one form or another. "Norman, who do you think killed Hiram?"

"Not Kelli," he said, his tone decisive. Apparently he knew the local gossip even if he didn't get to town often.

"Did Hiram ever mention anyone threatening him? Anyone unhappy with him over business or personal dealings?"

"No, though there must of been some bad feelings back there sometime. He did tell me once that I should never put money in a bank in the Bahamas, no matter how much interest they promised. He sounded real down-in-the-mouth about it, but I don't know why he was tellin' me. I don't need no bank. Any money I've got will fit in my shoe."

"Had Hiram been, um, enjoying his tequila at the time he gave you this advice?"

"Yes'm, I think he had."

"Perhaps that explains it, then."

"But I got enough to pay for this here meal," Norman assured me confidently. I had uneasy visions of him yanking off his shoe to do so, but when the bill came he made the normal gesture of pulling a billfold out of his pocket. He studied the bill carefully. "Fifteen percent, right?"

I nodded, and he carefully counted out a tip, right down to the quarter and three pennies laid on top of the bills to make an exact 15 percent. Then he sat there a moment, his expression thoughtful. I thought perhaps he was thinking about cutting back to 10 percent, but what he said was, "Maybe you oughta know some people think I killed Hiram. Or that Kelli and I were in it together."

Tears welled up in his eyes. He undoubtedly knew people called him Nutty Norman, which perhaps didn't bother him, but this did.

I started to assure him I didn't think that, but then I backed off. Because, in spite of the tears and his obvious regret that Hiram was gone, the thought occurred to me that homicide and regret aren't necessarily mutually exclusive. Norman could have killed Hiram in a fit of anger and still deeply regret it now. I didn't feel as if I'd been dining with a killer, but feelings can be deceptive. Still, I couldn't think I was in any danger from him. But a conspiracy between him and Kelli? Hmmm.

Norman paid for our dinner, and he did have sufficient money, though I felt guilty at how much the meal cost. I'd send the chocolate pie that was in the refrigerator home with him, I decided.

Then, just beyond the steps of the restaurant, he came to an abrupt halt. He carefully whirled three times, tapped his forehead once, then gave three energetic hops. I was startled.

"It keeps the brain waves going right, so they don't get all tangled up inside," he explained as he offered me his arm.

Nutty? Just a little, to my way of thinking. But what do I know about brain waves? Mine have occasionally felt tangled.

And lots of people have odd little rituals, I reminded myself. I always put my makeup on in a specific order. Eyebrows first, then eyeliner, blush, and lipstick. Maybe that was my subconscious keep-the-brain-waves-in-line system. I tucked my hand under his elbow and nodded genially to Victoria Halburton as she sailed by.

The Ladies Hysterical Society would have plenty to gossip about now, I knew, but I didn't care. And I was glad I'd worn my dress-up high heels.

14

On Sunday afternoon Abilene went out to the ranch with Dr. Sugarman for more driving practice, and on Tuesday afternoon she and I drove down to Hayward in his pickup so she could take the test for a driver's license.

Hayward was still in the mountains, but it was at a lower elevation and wasn't confined to a narrow valley as Hello was. It was also busier and more modern. Downtown Hayward actually had two one-way streets and a multiscreen movie theater. We found the DMV on the far edge of town, with a livestock auction building and stockyard just beyond it. A pungent scent of the occupants of those corrals added an earthy perfume on this surprisingly pleasant, almost spring-like day.

Written and driving tests together would take considerable time, and I didn't want to just sit and wait. I parked the pickup where it would be easily available for Abilene's test. It was one of those big "king" cab ones and took up a lot of space. I walked back to a shopping area. I bought a couple of mysteries at a used-book store, picked up a carton of plastic wrap at a dollar discount store, and marveled at the almost platter size of a silver belt buckle in the window of a tack shop.

Then I decided a cup of coffee would taste good, and my feet needed a rest too. I went into a café where the parking lot was filled with pickups and horse trailers, even a truck loaded with sweet-smelling hay. Inside, it was definitely a good-ol'-boys type place, with a big, round center table occupied by mostly older men in cowboy boots, with bellies overhanging their belt buckles. The men looked like a bunch that congregated regularly to exchange tall tales and enjoy the attention of a couple of pretty waitresses.

I slipped into a small booth and ordered coffee from an older waitress. It seemed the kind of place where customers were welcome to sit and sip, and I settled back to pass the time reading one of my new mysteries. Scraps of conversation reached me from the table, "that dingbat of a chestnut mare I had back in '87," and "the year my daddy like to kilt me 'cause I took off rodeoin' instead of helping with the haying."

I'd barely reached discovery of the body on page 7 of my book when a burst of laughter at the table made me look up. One of the younger waitresses was refilling cups and flirting lightly with the men. Teasing one of them about the sexy scent of a new shaving lotion brought on a fresh round of guffaws.

But what I suddenly noticed about the slim and attractive young woman were her earrings. Miniature carousel horses! They pranced and bounced as she swung her long blond braid and laughed and expertly twirled to evade a male arm trying to encircle her waist.

She was too far away for me to get a really good look at the earrings, but I was intrigued by them. Carousel horses are not a topic to which I've ever given much thought, but now carousel horses occupied my bedroom, and miniature carousel horses danced on the ears of this young woman. On impulse, when the waitress finished at the table, I motioned to her. "May I have a refill, please?"

"Sure."

She came to my booth, big blue eyes, long legs, short skirt, silver ankle bracelet, perky yellow bow tied at the end of the thick braid. Her walk was athletic but feminine, her smile friendly. Up close, I could see that the earrings were beautifully carved and painted, perfect miniatures of the real thing. Probably real wood too, definitely not junk.

"Those are beautiful earrings. I've never seen anything like them."

She smiled and fingered one of the tiny carved carousel horses. "Aren't they cute? I've always had this thing about merry-go-rounds. A friend had the earrings specially made for me, and I wear them all the time, but—"

"KaySue!" a male voice yelled from a door in the rear of the room. "Someone just backed into the side of your pickup!"

"Oh no!" The girl whirled and took off through the back way, blond braid flying. A couple of the men from the table, apparently concerned about their favorite waitress, went out to see what was going on.

I waited several minutes, but the girl didn't return. When I started back toward the DMV I peered into the parking lot. The back end of a Honda was still buried in the side of a red pickup, with curious onlookers, a tow truck, and a police car crowded around. KaySue and a young guy in baggy pants were squared off face-to-face, and then, to my astonishment, she hauled off and slammed a fist into his jaw. A real prize-fighter smackeroo, it looked like. He didn't go down, but he definitely wobbled. The police officer stepped between them.

Not a good time to be inquiring about earrings, I realized regretfully.

I expected I'd still have to wait a while at the DMV, and I was surprised to find Abilene pacing back and forth by Dr. Sugarman's pickup. Something in her expression told me she wasn't out here because she'd finished the tests already. The pickup didn't look as if it had been moved.

"Is something wrong?"

"I didn't even get to take the tests. If you don't have an old driver's license from some other state to turn in, you have to have a birth certificate. You can't get a license without it. And I don't have one."

"Oh, Abilene, I'm so sorry." I knew how much she'd counted on this. "We'll just have to get you one."

"How?"

Offhand, I didn't actually know. But . . . "We'll talk to Kelli. She'll know what to do."

Abilene's glum face brightened. "Hey, she will, won't she?"

I parked in front of Kelli's tiny office on a steep side street. A beauty shop occupied the other half of the stucco building. A discreet bell sounded when I opened the door. Kelli had said she'd let her receptionist go, but the computer at the reception desk was turned on, and papers were scattered as if the receptionist had just stepped out for a minute. Kelli came out of a room beyond this one.

"If you're busy, we can come back later—"

"No, not busy." She saw my glance at the receptionist's desk and gave me a sheepish smile. "Stage setting, so it will look as if my busy receptionist just left the desk for a moment

150

in case, wonder of wonders, a potential client wanders in. Is something wrong at the house?"

"Oh no, everything's fine. We're here to use your professional services. Abilene has a problem."

Kelli looked surprised, but she motioned us into the inner office. She scooted the papers on her desk to one side and motioned us to a pair of chairs. It was pleasant but not what I'd call a power office. A robust jade plant stood in one corner. Kelli apparently wasn't afflicted with the kiss-of-death thumb that I have. A couple of framed certificates hung on one wall, and several photos of old mining scenes, probably the Lucky Queen, decorated another wall. The carpet was generic tan. Abilene explained the problem with the birth certificate and a driver's license.

Kelli's eyebrows lifted. "You've never had a driver's license? Most kids get them the day they turn sixteen. And you're . . . ?"

"Twenty-three. I did drive, but it was only the tractor out on the farm, and I didn't need a license."

"Have you ever had a copy of your birth certificate?"

"My mom had it when they took me down to Texas to marry Boone. Afterward, I put it in a drawer with our marriage certificate. But there's no way I could get it from there now."

Right. Contacting Boone to ask for the certificate would be like lighting the fuse on a stick of dynamite.

"What about your parents? Would they have another copy?"

Abilene shook her head, eyes lowered. She no longer had contact with her mother and stepfather. We both knew that if they knew where she was, they'd probably rush to tell Boone. Unfortunately, that's the kind of people they were. They'd forced her into the marriage and then told her she should stay in it even when Boone was physically abusing her.

Kelli looked curious again, but she didn't ask questions about husband or parents. Instead she said, "Getting a copy of the birth certificate shouldn't be a problem. I'll just contact the vital records department of the state in which you were born." She went on to ask for the pertinent data about Abilene's birth and jotted it down. "I'll get right on it."

Abilene opened her purse, but Kelli shook her head. "Wait until we see what costs are involved. It shouldn't be much."

I stood up, presuming we were finished, but Abilene cleared her throat. "I'm, uh, also wondering . . ."

"Yes?" Kelli prompted when Abilene just sat there nervously toying with the zipper on her purse.

"About a divorce."

"You mean, obtaining a copy of a divorce decree also?"

"No, about getting a divorce."

It was my turn to be surprised now. Not that I didn't think the divorce was warranted. In general, I'm opposed to divorce. Biblical teaching is against it, and I think most couples should try harder to work things out. But in Abilene's situation, with the abuse and threats, plus the fact that she knew Boone had been unfaithful and had girlfriends while married to her, I had to think differently.

"How long have you lived in Colorado?" Kelli asked.

"About six weeks."

Right. We'd spent some time in the Colorado Springs area before getting stranded here in Hello. We'd celebrated Abilene's twenty-third birthday there.

Kelli shook her head regretfully. "Unfortunately, you have to be a resident of the state for at least ninety days to file for a divorce in Colorado. But we can certainly do it a little later on."

"Can it be done without my husband knowing where I am?"

152

"That would be difficult." Kelli tilted her head curiously. "Is that, um, important?"

"Extremely," I put in.

Kelli glanced at me, then back at Abilene. Hesitantly at first, then in a rush of words, Abilene told Kelli what she'd once told me. How her stepfather and mother had yanked her out of school at sixteen, taken her from Kansas down to Texas, and shoved her into instant marriage with Boone Morrison, a man with three children from a former marriage.

"Why in the world would they do that?" Kelli sounded appalled.

"I think my stepfather figured it was a good way to get rid of me. I would've walked out the first time Boone hit me, but I didn't know what he might do to the kids if I wasn't there to protect them. So I hung on."

"Even when he broke her arm," I put in. The faint ridge from where the break hadn't healed right, because Boone wouldn't let her get proper medical attention, still showed near her wrist.

"Hung on for how long?"

"Six years."

"Six years," Kelli echoed, a kind of horror in her voice.

"Until the children's mother went to court and got them back," I put in.

"Then I took off. Except I wrecked Boone's Porsche getting away, which made him kind of mad."

Kind of mad. The understatement of the year. I put it in more specific terms. "So he tracked her down in Oklahoma and threatened to kill her. And would have done it, too, if we hadn't run. Which is more or less how we wound up here in Hello."

"Boone doesn't quit until he . . . gets even with people," Abilene said, her words broken with a hard swallow.

The ominous statement hung in the air. Kelli tapped the

desk with a ballpoint pen. "Look, how about if I do some checking, very discreet checking, on the situation back in Texas, okay? After you have the proper residence established here, we'll think of some way to handle this without endangering you. My working through another lawyer in Texas might be a possibility. Give me names and dates and places, okay?"

Abilene did this, and Kelli jotted the facts down alongside the information for the birth certificate. She slipped the paper under the edge of the phone. "In the meantime, I'll get going on the birth certificate."

"Thank you," Abilene said.

I thought Kelli was going to shake hands with us, a formal conclusion to a business meeting, but instead she came around the desk and wrapped her arms around Abilene in a big hug. "I'll help you," she said almost fiercely.

At the door to the outer office, Kelli switched to a lighter mood. Her tone was teasing when she said, "I heard you and Norman had a romantic dinner at the Café Russo." At my surprised look that she knew about my dinner with Norman, but before I could deny that any romance was involved, she smiled and added, "Victoria Halburton told Chris's mother, and she mentioned it to me. There are no secrets in Hello."

"Except for who murdered Hiram," I murmured.

"True," Kelli admitted. "Did you and Norman talk about that?"

"He assured me you didn't do it, and neither did he." I paused, reconsidering that statement. Actually, Norman hadn't declared his innocence. I bypassed that now. "He also said that Hiram once told him never to put any money in a bank in the Bahamas. I'm wondering if that meant Hiram had some bad experience with a Bahamas bank."

"The Bahamas?" Kelli looked surprised. "No, I haven't

seen anything in his records about that, although I'm still not certain I have everything."

"It may have been a long time ago."

Kelli nodded. "Hiram made a lot of investments over the years. In spite of his general shrewdness, not all of them were exactly blue chip. He told me once about putting money in a company that claimed they could turn seaweed into fuel for cars."

"Did it work?"

"Apparently not. We're still buying barrels of oil from the Middle East, not boatloads of seaweed. But he might have gotten into some investment in the Bahamas. Some of those offshore banks do promise very high interest."

One other thought occurred to me. "Do you know anything about a secret room or passageway at the house?"

"No!" Kelli's blue eyes sparkled with interest. "Did you find one?"

"No. I've looked a little, but it's a big house."

"What makes you think there might be a secret room?"

I didn't want to tell her that ex-girlfriend Suzy had suggested it, so I detoured with, "Doesn't it just seem like the kind of creepy old place that would have a secret room?"

She laughed. "Well, now that you mention it, I guess it does."

"You don't mind if I keep poking around looking for a room then, do you?"

"Poke away. After all, Hiram did own what was once one of the richest gold mines in the state. Maybe it'll be full of gold bars or enormous nuggets or something."

Her light tone suggested she didn't think there was a high probability of this. I didn't either, but that mutant curiosity gene wanted to know if such a room existed, even if there was no treasure in it. It might hold any number of interesting things, from more old books to old photos or clothes. Maybe an old skeleton! My imagination, cousin to the curiosity gene, is always busy.

I went back to the original thought of treasure in a secret room. "Maybe the killer knew about a secret room full of something valuable, and that's why Hiram was killed. So the killer could take what he knew was hidden."

"But who could know about a secret room? Unless it was one of the old wives, and we've pretty well eliminated them as killers, haven't we?"

Yes, old wives would be the ones most likely to know about a secret room, if it existed. But were there other possibilities? Unless Hiram had simply told someone about the existence of a secret room, the person would have to be someone who had spent enough time in the house to discover such a room. Which led right back to people I didn't want to consider as potential murderers. Norman. Lucinda. And Kelli herself.

Another thought occurred to me. There wouldn't necessarily have had to be some valuable treasure hidden in the room. If someone simply knew about a secret room and *thought* something valuable was hidden there, and was willing to kill for it . . .

Since we had the pickup, we drove out to Nick's Garage to check on the motor home. Nick had dragged it around back of the shop, more out of the way. It looked the same as before, dejected. We went around by the post office before heading home. A few things had been sent on from the Arkansas mail-forwarding outfit. A letter from niece DeeAnn and another from grandniece Sandy, and one from old friend Magnolia Margollin too, with a Phoenix postmark. She and Geoff had been living full-time in their motor home since selling their home across from mine on Madison Street back in Missouri.

Oh, and a postcard sent direct to general delivery here in Hello. I didn't have to turn it over to know who it was from. Who else would send a postcard with the picture of a giant sponge—a giant sponge wearing giant sunglasses—on it? But I waited until we got home to read the message, savoring the anticipation.

15

Back at the house, I turned up the thermostat on the heat pump and read the postcard. Pleased as I was to hear from him, I still felt a twinge of annoyance. Mac MacPherson, the Postcard Man, has never written me a real letter.

This message was brief, as usual. It said he'd be leaving Florida soon. He had an assignment from a travel magazine for an article about an unusual theme park in Texas, and then he might head up to Colorado. Not a statement that he was definitely coming to Hello, of course. Mac tends to be very cagey about pinning himself down. But maybe he'd be here before long.

My first impulse was to call and tell him how to find us if he came to Hello. He did say he was very much looking forward to seeing me again, which, from Mac, qualifies as a fairly strong commitment. But on second thought I decided to leave finding me in Hello to Mac's ingenuity. If he wanted to find me, he certainly would. I wanted to see him again, but I wasn't going to look as if I were panting and drooling with expectation. (I wasn't, was I? Well, maybe just a tiny increase in respiration rate.) Then, after reading Magnolia's letter, I instantly grabbed our cell phone and punched in the numbers she'd provided.

"Ivy, it's so good to hear from you!" Magnolia exclaimed. I could see her in my mind's eye. Her formidable, Victorian-style figure enveloped in yards of gauzy swirls that always seemed to have a life of their own. Her changing hair color. Insulation Pink. Raspberry Red. Rainbow. And her accessories—earrings or hair decoration or necklace—all magnolias, of course. "Are you going to tell me where you are?"

I've been cautious about that. The Braxton mini-mafia surely knows about my relationship with Magnolia and Geoff, and I wouldn't put it past them to try to get to me through these friends. That wouldn't be easy, given that the Margollins are also often on the move, but they've had a couple of suspicious encounters. I've always figured it would be easier for them to keep the secret of my whereabouts if they didn't know where I was.

"Why don't you just tell me all about your new home? You're actually going to give up RVing and settle down in Phoenix?"

"Oh, Ivy, we love it here! Right now there's one of those roadrunner birds out in the yard. He comes almost every day to eat the hamburger balls I toss out for him." Magnolia gushed on about their southwestern-style home with tile roof, built-in barbecue, and a yard full of saguaro, cholla, and ocotillo. "And Geoff is going to try to get some magnolia trees started for me too."

Back home in Missouri, their lush stand of her namesake trees had been almost famous, and I figured if anyone could grow magnolias in the desert, it would be Geoff.

"So, what about your genealogical studies?" I asked. Mag-

159

nolia has long been involved in researching her family's history and happily claims connections to everyone from American Indians to French royalty. "Have you made any new family discoveries?"

"Oh my, yes. We have these wonderful Hispanic neighbors, and I do believe I've discovered a family connection from when one of my French ancestors married a Spanish adventurer. We may make a trip down to Mexico one of these days for further research. We aren't giving up the motor home just because we have a house now."

"You'll probably locate some distant cousins." Sometimes I wonder just how distant a connection can be and still be recognized as a cousin. Is there such a thing as a thirteenth cousin? Or a twenty-seventh?

"But that trip will have to wait. First we have to go back to Missouri to do something with all the things we left in storage there."

"When will you go?"

"Quite soon, probably. Although it depends on the weather."

I pulled up a rough mental map showing Phoenix, Hello, and Missouri. Connecting them didn't exactly make a straight line. "You know, if you didn't mind making a detour up into Colorado—"

"Ivy! You're in Colorado? Where? That's hardly out of our way at all!"

I hesitated, but a desire to see my old friends won out over worries about Braxtons. "It's this little town called Hello, up in the mountains."

I gave her instructions about how to find the McLeod house once they got here. "And it's possible Mac MacPherson may show up too."

"Mac," she marveled. "We haven't seen him in months. Is he still traveling the country in his motor home?"

"Still writing articles about odd events and places. Foot-loose and fancy-free."

Magnolia muttered something unintelligible but grumpy sounding, then added, "If that man had any sense, he'd grab you before someone else does."

Bless Magnolia. She's always had an exaggerated idea of my effect on elderly males and how eager they are to rush into wedded bliss with me.

We chatted a few more minutes, and then she ended with, "So we may see you before long."

"Come any time. I'm looking forward to it."

Kelli stopped by the library at the end of the week. I think she did that because she thought if she came to the house too often we'd feel she was snooping on us and how we were taking care of her house. I was at the computer installing the new software and figuring out how it worked. Someone had rounded up an old desk, and we'd moved the computer into the library section for my use. Victoria Halburton and Myra Fighorn were manning the reception desk today. Earlier, Victoria had made a sly remark about the Café Russo, to which I'd responded that Norman and I had greatly enjoyed our dinner there.

"You didn't find him just a little, oh, odd?"

"No odder than many people in Hello." I made a meaning-ful perusal of her overdyed black hair, which had a strong resemblance to dismembered crow wings.

Kelli ignored the main desk and strode through to my area. "Looking good," she said approvingly. "I just wanted to let you know that I called Kansas. I don't know if it will do any good, but I asked them to put a rush on the birth certificate."

"Thanks. We appreciate that."

"And I asked Chris if he knew anything about Hiram having money in a Bahamas bank, but he said he didn't. Actually, Hiram didn't necessarily involve either Chris or me in his financial affairs unless some legality was involved. And, as you said, it may have been a long time ago."

True. Although the whole Bahamas thing struck me as peculiar. "What about the divorce?"

"I have a lawyer friend in Texas checking for me. We may have to publish a legal ad in a newspaper down there when Abilene files for divorce, but we can do it using my friend's name and office address, and Boone will never find out anything about Abilene's whereabouts from her. I should know more in a day or two."

"Good."

Kelli smiled and gave a little wave as she left.

A big storm blew in on Saturday, and the ladies at the Historical Society decided to close at noon. Heavy white flakes were coming down like an overturned bucket of snow cones by then, but in spite of the weather I was surprised when Doris Hammerstone offered me a ride home. She'd never shown any sign of helpfulness before.

"Why, thank you. I'd appreciate that very much."

I helped Doris with her coat and steadied her going down the front steps, where three inches of snow had already accumulated. But once we were in her car, the situation changed. Doris might be tiny and bent over, and the streets might be slippery with snow, but she wheeled that big old Lincoln around as if we were in tryouts for the Indy 500. I gulped and clutched the seat belt as we squirreled around corners, barreled up the hill, and finally skidded into the driveway at the McLeod house.

Doris seemed unruffled by the fact that we'd barely missed the hedge around the yard. "I do like a car with power," she said, her tone complacent.

I hastily gathered my gloves and purse and wits, relieved to be home in one piece. I put my hand on the door handle, but she seemed in no hurry to rush off. She leaned forward and peered up at the third floor of the tower, where the raw blotch of plywood was faintly visible through the wind-driven blur of snow.

"That's where Hiram fell?"

"Yes. He landed on the brick walkway below. No one seems to know why he and whoever killed him were up there." I wanted to hear her thoughts on this, but I didn't want to let on that I knew she and Hiram had once been married, in case that was a touchy subject. So, in what I hoped was a discreet way, I added, "Have you ever been up there?" as if I thought she may have been a guest there sometime.

She skidded around my tactfulness the same way she'd skidded around street corners. "You mean up there to push Hiram out the window?" she snapped.

"Well, uh . . ."

"Or up there back when he and I were married? Because someone told you we were married, didn't they? Who was it? Lucinda?"

I dodged the question, not about to admit she was correct about Lucinda. "I'm sure no one thinks that you—"

"You don't have to murder someone personally, you know. You can hire a killer. I could have done that."

I had to make an effort to keep my mouth from dropping open at this surprise suggestion. But I managed to say, "Did you?"

"No, I didn't kill him, either personally or hired." She

sounded a little cross about it. "Though, if I'd thought of it, I might have back when Hiram and I were married. I certainly had reason enough." She leaned back, her momentary flash of spirit seeming to fizzle. The car was cooling rapidly, our breaths already clouding the windows.

I waited, hoping she'd elaborate, but what she said when she went on was, "But that was a long time ago, and it all turned out for the best. Dan and I had many happy years and four children together."

"I'm glad to hear that."

"So, to answer your question, yes, I've been in the ball-room, but no, not for many years. Hiram and I threw some rather lively parties up there. Hired a band and everything. Hiram was quite a fancy dancer back in those days."

"Something tells me you were probably a rather 'fancy dancer' yourself."

Doris's sly pixie smile confirmed that, although what she said was, "But I heard the ballroom had been closed off in recent years."

"Which makes it all the more puzzling why he was up there."

"Ask Kelli Keifer. She should know." The statement wasn't venomous, but it was certainly on the sour side. Doris lifted her elbow and swiped at the condensation on the window.

"You think Kelli killed him?"

"I don't see how it could be anyone else. She certainly had the means and motive, far more motive than anyone else, and isn't that what's important?"

"Motive meaning she wanted his assets? Or motive because she opposed him on the matter of reopening the mine?"

"Both. A win-win situation for Kelli."

"Isn't it possible Hiram made enemies in his business dealings over the years? Or he did seem to have . . . difficulties in his personal relationships."

Doris unexpectedly laughed at my delicate reference to Hiram's many wives and marital problems.

"Perhaps some other of his former wives was bitter enough to take drastic action even if you weren't," I suggested.

"That's possible, I suppose, but I don't think so."

"Why not?"

"On a practical basis, I'm the only former wife left around here. Except for Damaris, of course, but she's in the McLeod plot in Low Cemetery. And I don't believe in ghosts, so I don't think she came back to do him in."

I had to agree with Doris there.

"It's hard to explain," she went on, wrinkles multiplying on her brow. "Given Hiram's shortcomings as a husband, particularly his cavalier attitude toward faithfulness, you'd think we'd all have been delighted to do him in. Most of us probably felt that way at the time. But in the long run I don't think there were any big grudges against him. He was always generous in the divorces, even, in his own way, rather gallant. He never actually dumped any of us. He always let us divorce him and took all the blame." She smiled reminiscently, as if some private but pleasant memory had occurred to her.

"That's a very generous attitude on the part of the wives."

"As my husband used to say, life's too short to hold grudges. He and Hiram were friends. Although I'm not sure I could have as generous an attitude as Lucinda."

"In regard to marrying him, you mean, after he'd already been married so many times?"

"I mean in taking a second chance on him. I'd certainly never have married him again under any circumstances. I'd have thought Lucinda had learned her lesson too."

"But Lucinda was never actually married to him."

"No, but they were steadies all through their last year in high school and within a kiss of being married. And, even though he didn't dump any of the wives, he certainly did dump Lucinda."

"I didn't know that."

"Did he ever! Practically left her at the altar. The wedding was all set, but about a week before the date he ran off to somewhere, Reno, I guess it was, with a waitress he'd known only a month or so. So on the day that was supposed to be his and Lucinda's wedding day, here he was, cruising around town with his new bride in his new convertible, happy as a lark. Lucinda took off and went to visit some relatives back East for almost a year, then married Bill O'Mallory when she came back. Although that was a happy enough marriage, from everything I've heard, better and certainly more lasting than any of Hiram's."

"So the girl Hiram ran off with was wife number one?"

She nodded. "And I was wife number two. With the distinction of being the only wife who was older than Hiram." She smiled and shook her head of wispy white curls. "Do you ever look back on some time in your life and wonder, What was I *thinking*?"

Blessedly, for me there had been only Harley, and I'd never had a moment's regret about him.

"Anyway, I don't see how Lucinda could possibly have decided to marry him now, after what he did to her. It was so crushing, so humiliating, a scandal everyone talked about for weeks. She was totally devastated."

"As you also said, that was a long time ago. Things change. People change. Kelli seemed to think it was nice that they'd found each other again after all these years. Very romantic." Although I now had to wonder if Kelli knew the ugly details about that long-ago breakup between Hiram and Lucinda.

Doris snorted, an unlikely sound coming from such a fragile-looking little lady. "Romantic foolishness. Ridiculous at our age."

166

I didn't say anything, but I couldn't agree with that. I think romance and true love are possible at any age. Not that I'm prepared to take a high dive into that murky pool.

"Well, I'd better be going or I'll find myself snowed in right here in the driveway," Doris said briskly. "Sometimes I think about buying myself one of those Hummer things. I think they'll go anywhere. Oh, if you're interested, there'll be another rehearsal next week. I heard you came to the last one."

"It looked as if everything is coming along nicely."

"About as usual. Always some crisis lurking in the wings. Ben Simpson is supposed to do a Will Rogers monologue, and he's been down several times with back trouble. And Lulu Newman's hip is bothering her. She's the tallest one in the chorus line, and we really need her, but she took quite a tumble at that last rehearsal."

"They're fortunate to have you as a prompter."

"Why, thank you." Doris's wrinkled face bloomed in a smile of pleasure at the compliment. "Well, see you next week."

I opened the car door and headed toward the house, thinking about what Doris had said, something that hadn't occurred to me before. A hired killer. Was that possible, here in Hello? It seemed to me that a hands-on killing took a certain ruthlessness and steely guts. But a hands-off killing opened any number of possibilities.

Then I forgot that thought and cringed as tires squealed when Doris took the corner beyond the house. Doris Hammerstone in a Hummer? Run for your lives!

Dr. Sugarman brought Abilene home a few minutes later. He'd also decided to close early. Koop took time off from his job of holding down the imitation bearskin rug to look out the window for a while before going back to the rug.

Abilene and I decided to use the unexpected spare time to fulfill more of our housecleaning duties. We tackled the kitchen, washing woodwork, scrubbing out the refrigerator, and running the vacuum cleaner. Koop, unperturbed, snoozed peacefully even when I carried both him and the rug to a chair so we could strip the old layers of wax on the floor. He did deign to open his one good eye when we moved in a small dining table, one I'd spotted on the second floor, to replace the card table.

While Abilene tackled the oven, unfortunately not the self-cleaning variety, I went through the lower cabinets, scrubbing the shelves and separating items for discard or recycling. Plastic bags, which Hiram apparently never threw away, went in that room stuffed with his other discards. I carried a stack of old mining magazines upstairs and tossed old cleaning supplies, cartons of Ajax cleanser hardened rock solid, dried-up floor polish, and empty spray cans of room deodorant, into the outside garbage can. An old shoe box under the counter held a haphazard collection of monthly utility bills, which Hiram apparently hadn't considered important enough for filing in his office. I started to throw them out, then decided I should probably give them to Kelli. Maybe she'd have some use for them.

We didn't finish the kitchen cleaning until almost 8:30. By then we were both so tired we decided to splurge and order pizza delivered. While we ate our spicy pepperoni and Italian sausage combo, I idly browsed through the box of old utility bills. Hiram's electric bills were low. He must not have minded a chilly house. The trash collection bills were boringly similar, a set monthly rate. The phone bills were more interesting, with numerous long-distance calls both in and out of state. He'd often called Denver and Hayward here in Colorado, plus other numbers in Texas. Perhaps the company he'd been dealing with on reopening the mine? And then I came across some long-distance numbers that zapped my mutant curiosity gene into high gear.

16

These numbers definitely meant Kelli should see this box of bills. I tried to call her on the cell phone, but she wasn't at home. We skipped church the next morning. Snow had stopped falling, and snowplows were clearing the streets, but the wind was still whipping through town as if on a search-and-destroy mission. So I got out my Bible, and Abilene and I had an interesting session in Romans. I still couldn't get Kelli at home that afternoon on the cell phone. I hoped she hadn't decided to drive out to the mine and gotten stranded.

As for me, curiosity about the phone bills finally got the better of me. On Monday morning, after Dr. Sugarman came by to pick up Abilene, I gave in and dialed that faraway long-distance number.

A woman with a lovely lilt in her voice said, "Banco de Island Internacional." With a musical emphasis on the last syllable.

"You're in the Bahamas?" That was what the phone bill had said, but I wanted to be certain.

"Yes, ma'am."

Now what? Various ideas bloomed. I could announce that I was handling Hiram McLeod's estate and needed information about his account. Or claim I was his widow, maybe even his wife, and there was a mix-up in his finances. Or perhaps go authoritative: "This is a representative of the Banking Regulatory Committee and—"

I broke off the fanciful stories that often worked so well for the fictional sleuths in the stories I read. My tongue and my conscience are stuck with the truth.

"My name is Ivy Malone, and I'm connected with Hiram McLeod, a client of yours." (I was sleeping in his bed. That connected me, right?) "There are some, ummm, irregularities in the records on the account." I broke off to give that a check. True? Yes, something very irregular here.

Miss Lilting Voice, unimpressed, broke into my mental checkup. "Do you have an account number?"

"Well, no. But Mr. McLeod has been murdered, you see—"

"Murdered?" I heard a note of alarm. "Here in the Bahamas?"

"No, here in Colorado. But I'm almost certain he has an account with you, and it is imperative that I obtain information about it." I stomped down heavy on the imperative.

"One moment please."

A long hold, considerably more than a moment, while I felt the paid-for minutes on the cell phone dribbling away. Dribbling at some rate double or triple the usual speed, I figured, since this was an out-of-U.S. call.

A new woman came on. I repeated my spiel. She sounded wary, but she asked me to spell the name. After another wait she said, "Our records do not presently show an account in the name of Hiram McLeod."

The careful wording of that made me ask, "But he formerly had an account with you?"

Another delay, although I couldn't tell whether that meant the woman was looking up something or debating whether to tell me anything. "Any accounts we may have had in the name of Hiram McLeod are not now in existence. That is all I can tell you without authorization from Mr. McLeod."

"But I told you, he's *dead*. Murdered."

"Then it will be necessary for an authorized representative to contact us with proper documentation before we can release any information. Thank you for calling Banco de Island Internacional."

End of conversation.

Well, my sleuthing abilities weren't up there with Kinsey Millhone's or Jessica Fletcher's clever talents, but I was almost certain I'd found out one thing. Even though the woman wouldn't specifically verify it, Hiram had had an account with the bank at one time, something neither Chris or Kelli had known about. Which meant what? Weren't the Bahamas some kind of tax haven? Didn't people sometimes try to hide assets in offshore banks? Had Hiram been involved in something shady? I checked the dates on the calls made to the bank. They were all fairly recent, only about a month before his death, a whole flurry of them. Odd. But Kelli could no doubt get to the bottom of it.

Piles of snow from the industrious snowplows rose like miniature mountain ranges along the streets, but the storm was over. I took an invigorating walk all the way out to Safeway and picked up a few groceries. I'd have liked to have gotten a sack of bird seed too, to feed all the birds fluttering around, but it was too heavy to carry all that way. After dinner that evening, Kelli showed up.

"Good news!" she said while I was pouring her a cup of coffee in the kitchen. "At least I think you'll find it good. My friend Linda down in Texas called to tell me she's learned Boone has filed for divorce."

Abilene, doing dishes at the sink, whirled so quickly that dishwater suds flew. "Really?" She sounded hopeful but not quite believing, as if this was too good to be true.

"Can he do that, without Abilene being notified?" I asked. I was as hopeful as Abilene, but I didn't want some fine-print detail to sabotage everything at the last minute.

"It's a little more complicated, and takes longer than a regular divorce, but it can be done. Linda says that in Texas, after a 'diligent effort' is made to locate a missing spouse, notification can be made by newspaper ad. Then, if there's no response to the ad, the divorce can proceed without the missing spouse. She located a copy of the ad Boone's lawyer published."

"So all I have to do is wait?"

"That's all you have to do. I'm not sure how long it will take, but Linda will let us know when the divorce decree is issued."

Abilene looked so stunned that I had to ask, "This is what you wanted, isn't it?"

She blinked, as if coming out from under a trance. "Yes, oh yes! I-I just thought it would be a lot harder than this. Thank you!"

"No thanks to me," Kelli said. "Actually, I guess it's Boone you have to thank."

I doubted Boone Morrison deserved any thanks. He hadn't been trying to do Abilene any favors. I suspected his main motive in divorce was so he could drag some other poor woman into marriage to do his cleaning and cooking and take his abuse. But for whatever reason, hooray! The end of a marriage probably shouldn't be occasion for a happy dance, but I felt a little twinkly toed anyway.

"Hey, you've really been working in here." Kelli leaned over to peer at the kitchen floor. "I always thought this linoleum was yellow, and it's almost white!" Then she spotted the vase of daffodils on the table.

She touched a petal. "From Suzy's flower shop?"

"Why, yes, they are. I believe it's the only flower shop in town." Before we could get into messy details about what I was doing in there, and even more messy details about whether the Kelli-Chris-Suzy triangle had been discussed, I headed toward the shoe box of utility bills I'd set aside for her.

"I found something I think you should have." I thrust the box at her. "Hiram's old electric and phone and trash collection bills. He had them stuck away in one of the kitchen cabinets. I tried to call you over the weekend, but you were never home."

"I was home, but I had the phone shut off. I thought of this great twist for the story I'm working on, so I worked straight through on it."

She took the box and flipped through the old envelopes, although I had the feeling she was more interested in the fact that I'd been in Chris's ex-girlfriend's flower shop. "I don't think they're anything I need, but I suppose I'd better hang on to them for a while anyway."

"There are some phone calls that might interest you." I picked out one of the bills I'd marked with a paper clip and opened it for her.

She looked at it, then at me. "Phone calls to the Bahamas!" She looked at the bill again. "And made only a couple of months ago."

"I know it's probably none of my business, but I called,

and the number is to a bank down there. The woman didn't exactly say Hiram had an account there, but I think he did and it's closed now. But that's all they'd tell me."

"I'll contact them. I've been thinking all along that there's money missing, and this may explain it. Thank you!"

It wasn't until after Kelli was gone that another happy thought occurred to me. I mentioned it to Abilene.

"Hey, since Boone filed for divorce, maybe that means he's given up on revenge and chasing us down!"

"You think so?" She sounded doubtful.

"Even a guy like Boone has to go on with life."

"But Boone doesn't give up easy. I remember there was some guy who beat him in a drag race way back in high school, and he got even with him years later when he was a mechanic and worked on the guy's car."

That wasn't encouraging, but then Abilene added, "But even if he'd still like to get even, he has to keep his job to make payments on the farm. And it would probably cost him something too, to look for us."

I could see she was trying to talk herself into believing Boone was no longer after us, because then we might be able to stay here in Hello. And I thought it was a reasonable enough belief. Boone might have a vicious heart and a thirst for revenge, but he didn't have the resources the Braxtons did to run us down, particularly if his sheriff cousin tired of the chase. Yes, this looked good.

Now if I could only figure out a way to divorce the Braxtons, we'd be home free.

Charlotte Sterling came by the library Thursday afternoon. One thing about not having a phone: if someone wants to talk to you they have to make a real effort to do so. What she'd come for, she said, was to invite Abilene and me to dinner at her house Saturday night. Chris and Kelli would be there too. She said she knew we didn't have transportation, and Chris would be happy to pick us up. He'd come at seven o'clock.

On Saturday evening Abilene and I were in the living room, watching through the window for Chris's red Mustang, but it was Kelli who showed up. She was getting out of the Bronco when we went down the front steps. She looked at her watch.

"I need to talk to you for a minute, so I told Chris I'd pick you up. But I guess we can do it on the way."

I was relieved to see she was wearing slacks and sheepskin-lined boots. I hadn't known how dressy an evening Charlotte intended, and I'd gone for warmth with wool slacks and sweater. Abilene was in similar garb.

Once in the Bronco, Kelli sat there without starting the engine before finally saying, "This is awkward, but I want to ask you not to mention anything about Uncle Hiram's bank account in the Bahamas tonight."

I was mildly flabbergasted. "Why would I do that?"

"I don't suppose you would. I just want to make sure. You see . . ." She hesitated again, and I suspected she'd rather not tell us more but felt she had to. "The thing is, I talked to Chris again about an account down there, and this time he admitted he knew Hiram had put money in a bank there because it was offering such huge interest rates. But it turned out to be a fly-by-night outfit that completely scammed him. He lost almost everything he put in."

My first thought was, *So why didn't Chris say that to begin with?* but what I said aloud was, "But on the phone it sounded like a big international bank."

"Right. The bank you talked to is a big, legitimate bank. They took over the other outfit, the shysters, but not before Hiram's money was down the drain."

"So why did Chris earlier pretend he didn't know anything about this?" I asked bluntly.

"Because he was too ashamed and embarrassed." Kelli sounded distressed and embarrassed too. "Chris said Hiram had come to him for advice about putting money in this bank in the Bahamas. Chris checked them out, thought they were okay, and told Hiram that. So when it all went bust, Chris felt miserable, as if it were all his fault."

My thought was, *Maybe it was his fault*, but what I said was, "But how did Chris decide the first bank was okay if it wasn't?"

"They simply put a lot of careful time and effort into setting everything up so it would look legitimate. It was a very sophisticated scam. And Chris is really embarrassed that it fooled even him."

"I see."

"Hiram apparently tucked the records on all this away somewhere, maybe even threw them out, which is why I've never seen anything. He was probably embarrassed about it too, since he considered himself such a smart investor."

"That sounds reasonable."

"Anyway, this explains the money I was sure was missing but which I could never find any records on. Just don't bring it up, okay? Chris says his mother doesn't know anything about this, and she'd be horrified. He handles most of her investments and doesn't want to send her into a tailspin worrying he doesn't know what he's doing. His investments for her are, in fact, doing very nicely. Chris says he really learned his lesson on the Bahamas thing."

"That's good."

Kelli started the engine, and we headed for a newer area of town out beyond Safeway. I could see Kelli felt defensive and protective about Chris in this. She didn't want to believe he'd done anything wrong, and, I had to admit, he probably hadn't. Anyone, even an astute advisor, can make a financial mistake, and well-done scams have fooled even hotshot accountants in big corporations. But not being up-front with Kelli about what he'd done hadn't won Chris any points with me. Not a person from whom I'd ask financial advice. Not that I needed any, unless he had a hot tip on how to invest the coins in the special piggy bank I kept for found pennies.

"Did you contact the Bahamas bank?" Abilene asked, surprising all of us since she so seldom spoke up.

"No, I don't see any point in going through the hassle of documenting my status as executor of the estate just to confirm that the money's gone. If it's gone, it's gone."

I doubted documenting her status would be all that complicated, so I was momentarily puzzled. But then I realized what was going on here. Kelli was in love with Chris. She believed, as I do, that love includes trust. So she didn't want to be sneaking around behind his back checking up on his mistakes.

An admirable attitude. Yet I, who wasn't in love with Chris, didn't feel nearly as trusting. It all felt very . . . slippery. Yet what other version could there be? Chris had admitted he gave Hiram bad advice, and he felt properly guilty and responsible.

Dinner was lively and pleasant. Charlotte might give a good sales pitch on old Victorian houses, but her own home was modern, gleaming, and elegant. Lots of glass and pale peach carpet and white leather furniture. Charlotte exclaimed enthusiastically over our hostess gift. We couldn't finance wine or flowers, but I'd wrapped up a good mystery (bought new, read only once) by a new author. Conversation centered around the upcoming Roaring '20s Revue, my work at the library, and the real estate business.

I could see why Kelli was attracted to Chris. He was attentive to her, affectionate, well-mannered, nice to his mother, which is something I feel is always a point in a man's favor. He was nice to me and Abilene too, but not in a way that suggested he saw Abilene as anything other than a pleasant young lady. He made us laugh with funny stories about his lawyer experiences and even told one tear-jerker about a little girl injured in a car accident.

We did get into a brief discussion of Hiram's murder, although it could hardly be called "brainstorming." Again the conclusion was that some outsider must have come in with a deliberate plan of getting even because of something unscrupulous Hiram had done to him in the past. I supposed I should be relieved with this consensus of opinion, at least among those not already convinced Kelli was guilty, but instead I found it mildly annoying. Why was everyone so willing to pass the killer off as some unknown outsider and apparently not be all that anxious about whether he was identified and caught?

After dinner, we moved into the living room for coffee and a fresh fruit compote for dessert. It was good, apparently meant to satisfy Chris's only-fruit-for-dessert requirements, but I'd been hoping for something rich and chocolaty. Charlotte had flyers about various local houses for sale sitting on the coffee table. I browsed through them when I finished my compote.

"Char, have you ever run into any old house here in Hello with a secret room or passageway?" Kelli asked.

Charlotte looked interested, but she shook her head. "No, not really. Although when they tore down that old place on Cooper Street they found an actual mine shaft underneath. But no secret rooms that I know of. Why?"

"Someone mentioned to Ivy that there might be one in Uncle Hiram's place, and she's been looking for it."

Chris dropped his fork and leaned over to pick it up.

"A secret room. Really?" Charlotte said. "How exciting! Any luck in finding it?"

"Not so far. I haven't actually covered much of the floor space yet, but I'm working on it," I said.

"Need any help looking?" Charlotte sounded eager to come over and start shoving furniture around.

"Be careful, or Mom will be over there tearing down walls and ripping up floors. She reads all these murder mysteries, you know, and they're big on secret rooms, hidden passageways, conspiracies, long-lost heirs, dusty skeletons, etcetera." Chris sounded affectionately exasperated by his mother's reading preferences.

"Some of them do get a little far out," Charlotte admitted. "But they're certainly more entertaining than those boring legal things you are always reading."

"It's like beauty, Mother. All in the eye of the beholder," Chris said loftily, and we all laughed.

"I did go down to the basement—"

"You investigated the basement?" Kelli broke in, sounding horrified. "I wouldn't go down there with anything less than an assault rifle and a chemical bomb for protection. I saw a spider crawling up out of there that looked big enough to star in one of those monster-arachnid movies."

"It was kind of creepy," I had to admit. "But Koop enjoyed it. He caught three mice."

"Koop is Ivy's cat," Kelli said by way of explanation to Chris and his mother.

Charlotte wrinkled her nose. "Does he eat them?"

"Heavens, no. He brings them to me. I'm not sure if they're a gift or if he thinks maybe I'll make him a nice mouse casserole."

We all laughed, and Chris made some comment about Kelli's cat being too accustomed to caviar to be interested in mice, and she gave him a playful punch in the shoulder.

"One time, just once, I give Sandra Day a bare smidgen of caviar, and he's never going to let me forget it."

The evening ended with Charlotte saying we'd have to do this again soon. We trooped out to the Bronco, where Charlotte and I exchanged hugs, and Chris kissed Kelli lightly.

To me he said, "Are you going to keep looking for that mysterious secret room?"

"Probably. When I have some extra time."

"Be careful digging around in that old house. It could be dangerous. I wouldn't be surprised to see a floor or ceiling collapse in that old place."

"I'll be careful," I assured him.

Now, as earlier, nothing suggested he was anything other than a competent, caring son and lawyer and a fine prospect as a husband.

But I couldn't help thinking about former girlfriend Suzy's acid remarks about him, and, reflecting back on the evening, I thought Chris had acted a little odd when the "secret room" was mentioned. He'd dropped that fork as if he'd been jabbed with it. He'd covered what might have been agitation by taking an overlong time to retrieve the fork, and he'd made fun of looking for such a room. But I was almost certain he'd been nervous about the possibility that such a room existed.

Hmmm. Why would that be?

And on the drive home that old, definitely unflattering joke about lawyers unexpectedly dropped into my mind.

How can you tell when a lawyer is lying?

Answer: when his lips are moving.

Chris Sterling's lips had done a lot of moving. First denying he knew anything about money in a Bahamas bank, then admitting his poor judgment about advising Hiram that it was okay to put big money there.

Although, what I should probably be doing, I told myself, was giving Chris credit for 'fessing up instead of wondering if he was up to something. Admitting to the woman he loved that he'd made such a big mistake couldn't have been easy. And yet, wasn't there something a little fishy about a legitimate bank taking over a non-legitimate, shyster outfit? Although the big bank could have been trying to protect the area's reputation, not let word of a scam get out and scare off investors. But since Hiram hadn't gotten his money back, the bank's move really hadn't done much for the area's reputation.

17

The snow wasn't melting, but the streets had been snow-plowed down to bare pavement. Abilene managed to get some bird seed, and we set up a feeder outside the kitchen window, which was immediately popular. I went to another Roaring '20s Revue rehearsal and even had a chance to go with Lucinda up to the third floor, where the costumes and props were kept. It seemed in fairly good shape, although the hallway had a bit of downward slant.

It was an interesting place with clothing and props from various years spread out among several rooms. Movable metal racks were jammed with costumes for both this year's performance and performances past. For this year one rack was devoted to spangled chorus-line costumes, another to chemise-style dresses with matching feather boas. For previous years there was everything from men's knickers-style pants in a wild plaid to a somewhat moth-eaten fur coat and a rack of enormous layered petticoats.

"Every year I swear I'm going to come up here and get all

this stuff organized," Lucinda said, sounding frustrated as she searched for a hat for Stella in the street scene. "Someday I'm really going to do it."

There were shelves of hats for both men and women, a glass case of jewelry, and several racks of shoes. Props ranged from furniture and lamps to parasols and canes, a baseball bat and bowling ball, dishes, knickknacks, and an enormous dictionary. Though I had to wonder what they'd used the stuffed skunk and the lethal-looking Chinese sword for. And why the fire marshal or some other safety official wasn't raising a ruckus about blocking off the entrance to the non-working elevator with something more substantial than a piece of cardboard. With the doors frozen in an open position on the third floor, you could shove the cardboard aside and use the open drop to the basement for anything from bungee-jumping to disposal of incompetent actors or unruly patrons. The elevator opening was at the far end of the hall from the stairs, not something anyone would stumble into by accident, but it still looked as if it at least needed some solid barrier nailed over the opening.

At the library, I was making progress with cataloging and shelving the books. But at night I was having problems. I'd discovered a football-sized lump in the mattress, at least that's what it felt like. As large as the bed was, you'd think I could avoid the lump, but at some time in the night I'd invariably find myself draped over it. I uncovered the mattress, thinking perhaps I'd find a lumpy collection of hundred dollar bills or a missing clue to Hiram's murder. But it was just a lump, probably a broken spring, and not nearly as large as it had felt against my back. I tried to turn the mattress myself, which didn't work, so I called on Abilene for help.

Abilene is lean and strong, but even she puffed as we wrestled with the heavy, bulky old mattress. I've never tried to move a beached whale, but I figure I now have a pretty good idea what it would be like.

"Hey, what's this?" Abilene asked when we finally got the thing thumped in place. She knelt to look at something on the floor, and I circled the bed to see what it was.

At least a dozen letters lay scattered on the carpet, apparently dislodged from under the mattress during our struggle with it. There were no envelopes, just pages of yellow stationery with a row of chipmunks dancing across the top. I picked one up. It was dated June 10, but there was no year. The writing was large and loopy, feminine looking. The opening read "Dearest Hiram," and a tiny heart substituted for the dot over the *i*. I hesitated. These were obviously very private letters. They'd been carefully hidden from prying eyes. We probably shouldn't read them . . .

But Hiram was dead, murdered, and I decided that at this point the matter of his privacy was moot.

I read on, as Abilene was doing with another letter. We exchanged glances when we came to the signature at the end. It was just an initial, K, but it was surrounded by a heart and preceded by the words, "Love forever 'n ever."

"Hiram had a *girlfriend*," Abilene said. She sounded shocked.

"We don't know when the letters were written," I said, because I knew what she was thinking. "It may have been long before his engagement to Lucinda."

I picked up another letter. A small piece had been torn from one edge of it, accidentally, it appeared, since it slashed through the middle of a sentence. I'd tucked that scrap of paper I'd found in Hiram's office away somewhere, but I didn't have to see it again to know it would have fit here. The end of the torn sentence read, "Meet me at the Nu."

I mentally filled in the incomplete words from the scrap I'd found. Together they read, "Meet me at the Nugget at

3:30 Tu." A continuation of the sentence here made that Tuesday.

Abilene examined several more letters. "Too bad there aren't envelopes with postmarks."

I glanced at the carousel horses mysteriously placed in Hiram's bedroom. I thought about a young waitress down in Hayward with carousel-horse earrings given to her by a "friend." I thought of numerous long-distance calls to Hayward on Hiram's phone bills. I thought of the name of the café in Hayward where I'd had coffee. Had it been the Nugget? I looked at the signature on the letters again. K. KaySue?

Surely not. The girl had appeared to be in her midtwenties, a good forty years younger than Hiram. And even if they had known each other, it could have been simply a friendly relationship, a mutual interest in merry-go-rounds and carousel horses, perhaps, not some romantic involvement.

Yeah? the cynical part of me scoffed. *What about "Dearest Hiram," and "Love forever 'n' ever"? Not exactly platonic sounding.* Hiram, from what Kelli had said, had a strong preference for younger wives. The spitfire, hot-tempered kind. You couldn't get much more spitfire than slugging a guy in front of a police officer.

I sat on the edge of the mattress and read more letters. It had been a busy relationship. Movies, dinners, a rodeo, a county fair . . . where they'd ridden a merry-go-round, about which K. waxed ecstatic. Thanks for the carousel-horse earrings came a little later, and there were also thanks for yellow roses. "Yellow is my favorite color!"

I thought of a lone yellow silk rose in a vase on the windowsill in the kitchen. I thought of a yellow ribbon on KaySue's long blond braid, and a scrap of something yellow in Hiram's office sucked up into the vacuum cleaner.

"Are you going to show these to Kelli?" Abilene asked.

Should I? Probably. And yet, if the relationship was old, it

185

was irrelevant, and bringing it to light would serve no useful purpose. But if the relationship wasn't old . . .

"Not yet," I said. Because what I needed to do first was get down to Hayward and talk to a waitress named KaySue.

I figured getting to Hayward again would be a problem, but the arrival of Abilene's birth certificate a few days later solved that. Dr. Sugarman again loaned us his pickup so she could take the driving tests.

I was wondering if "Dr. Sugarman" would segue into "Mike" now that a divorce was in the works, but I saw no change. Dr. Sugarman was obviously interested in Abilene, and I felt in my bones that she was aware of him as something more than her employer. But the status quo between them wasn't going to change for conscientious Abilene until the decree was issued and the marriage legally over.

I parked the pickup at the DMV in Hayward, left Abilene, and headed directly for the restaurant down the street. I could now see the name that I hadn't noticed before. The Nugget, the name semicircled around a lumpy, gold-colored blob.

Inside, I looked for the waitress with a long blond braid, but all I saw were two other young waitresses. I approached one of them. "I'm looking for KaySue. Is she around?"

"She's off today," the young woman said. "But she'll be back for the early shift tomorrow."

"I'm only in town for the day, and it's important that I see her." I gave the waitress a hopeful smile and my most soul-fully pleading LOL look. "I'm not a bill collector or anything. It's just . . . really important that I see her."

The girl laughed and patted my arm. "You don't look like a bill collector. And I'm sure KaySue pays her bills anyway.

186

Why don't you call her? She's probably home. I don't think she planned to do anything special today."

I didn't want to admit I didn't know KaySue's last name. "Could you look up the number for me? It's so hard to read the small print in phone books these days." Another of my best LOL smiles. "Or better yet, just give me directions to where she lives, and I'll go over and surprise her."

"Sure." She turned her order pad over and drew a little map. It looked like a fair distance, but I figured I could hoof it.

I was there in twenty minutes. It was a two-story stucco apartment building built around a small courtyard with an assortment of nondescript bushes, a clean enough looking place but definitely not the high-end variety. I spotted a red pickup with a big dent in the passenger's side in the parking area. I rang the bell on 2C. A barefoot KaySue came to the door in low-cut jeans that showed her navel, and a yellow T-shirt. A towel was draped on her head.

"You probably don't remember me, but I was in the Nugget not long ago? I admired your earrings?"

Her look told me no, she didn't remember me. Not surprising, given all the people she undoubtedly waited on in the café. Plus the fact that age seems to create its own aura of invisibility. "Could I come in and talk to you for a minute?"

"What for?"

"It won't take long. I'm not selling anything."

"Sure, I guess so." She turned and I followed. A faint scent of floral shampoo trailed after her. She bent over and toweled her hair vigorously for a minute, then let it fall free. With the long blond hair around her shoulders, she looked even younger than she had at the café.

The apartment was one room divided into living, dining, and kitchen areas, with doors leading off to bedroom and bath. A very ordinary-looking place except for how she'd

decorated it. A miniature merry-go-round stood on a cabinet. Another merry-go-round formed the base of a lamp. A
carousel horse painted on black velvet hung over the sofa.
A collection of wooden and ceramic carousel horses filled
three shelves on a wall. Even the oversupply of throw pillows
that covered the sofa were decorated with carousel horses.
Yellow silk roses in a carousel-decorated vase stood on the
kitchen windowsill. The flowers matched the lone rose in
Hiram's kitchen.

"You said you had a thing for merry-go-rounds, and you
really do, don't you?" KaySue would love those carousel
horses in my bedroom. No doubt in my mind now but that
Hiram had acquired them with her in mind. I wondered if
she knew about them.

She laughed. "I don't know why, but I've always loved
them. It's like you could get on a carousel horse and just ride
off into some wonderful fairyland." Her tone went momentarily dreamy, but then she came back to earth with a roll
of expressive eyes. "My sister thinks they're dumb, but you
should see her stupid collection of doughy-faced old dolls."
KaySue wrinkled her nose.

"Hiram didn't think carousel horses were dumb, did
he?"

KaySue's big blue eyes got even bigger. "You knew
Hiram?"

"Well, um, in a way . . ."

Her expression changed, like a person who's suddenly
horrified to spot a cockroach crawling across her foot. "Are
you Lucinda?"

"You knew about Lucinda?"

"What's this about?" she demanded. "Who are you, and
why are you here?"

"May I sit down? It was a long walk over here. And no,
I'm not Lucinda."

KaySue's blond eyebrows scrunched together in a frown, but she tossed a couple of pillows aside to make room for me on the sofa.

"My name is Ivy Malone, and Hiram's niece is letting me and a friend live in Hiram's house. When we were turning the mattress in the bedroom, we found the letters you'd written to him hidden there. I suppose I should apologize, because we read them."

She swallowed, perhaps remembering some of the details of those letters, but her tone was challenging when she said, "So?"

"Hiram must have valued the letters very highly to save them so carefully."

Her expression softened. "We were going to get married this spring. On our honeymoon we were planning to visit all these fabulous merry-go-rounds all across the country."

"What about Lucinda? She thought Hiram was going to marry her this spring."

KaySue studied a fingernail, then bit off a smidgen of cuticle. More nervous than she was letting on, I guessed. "Hiram felt really bad about Lucinda. He said she was a nice woman, and he didn't want to hurt her. But he couldn't marry her once he'd met me. He was going to tell her very soon."

"But wasn't it . . ." I paused and searched for some suitable word. "Wasn't it frustrating that he hadn't yet told her? You must have been seeing him for some time."

She shrugged, her eyes not meeting mine, but the stiffened line of her body told me this had indeed been a point of contention between them.

"Did Lucinda know about you?"

"No, I told you, he hadn't told her yet. He wanted to let her down easy, he said."

Which didn't mean Lucinda didn't know about KaySue,

no matter what KaySue thought. Lucinda was neither stupid nor non-observant.

"You met Hiram when he came into the Nugget?"

"He came in quite a few times before we started seeing each other. He was always such a gentlemen, unlike most of the clods I meet. And he wasn't into drugs like so many guys my age."

"Did his smoking bother you?"

KaySue looked blank, and I realized that for her the smoking was a non-issue. I saw a green ashtray by the carousel lamp, although there was no sign that it had been used recently. I had to remember how, with Lucinda, Hiram's smoking had been relegated to her back porch.

"Did the police question you after Hiram was killed?"

"No. No one knew about us. Hiram wanted to wait until after he told Lucinda before he introduced me to people." She looked at her left hand. "And give me a ring."

"A carousel-horse ring?"

"No, a diamond. A big diamond."

"It seems someone in Hello would have known about you and Hiram. Didn't you ever run into any of his friends from up there? Hayward isn't all that far from Hello."

"Hiram liked it here in my apartment. He said it was cozy and soothing. So lots of times we wouldn't even go out. I'd cook dinner for him, and then we'd watch a video or something. When we did go out, Hiram liked to go to some other town. Once I went with him on a business trip to Denver."

Busy Hiram. Seeing both KaySue and Lucinda. Dodging people he knew. He must have spent a fortune on gas, dashing off to towns where he figured he wouldn't be identified. And with Lucinda and KaySue both feeding him, it was a wonder he could still make it up to the third floor of the house in Hello.

"Were you ever at the house in Hello?"

"Hiram didn't think that would be a good idea."

"But I found a yellow ribbon from your hair in his office, so you must have been there sometime."

That was a wild guess, because I couldn't be positive what the vacuum cleaner had sucked up, but my guess was on target. Her hand flew to her hair, as if checking for a missing ribbon. "Well, I, uh, did go there once. Though I don't remember losing anything."

"When was this?"

"A few days before he was killed."

"He invited you there after all?"

"No. I-I was kind of mad at him. He was supposed to come down, and I was going to cook dinner for him. Then we were going to watch *Sleepless in Seattle* together. I love it, and he'd never seen it."

"But?"

"He called and said he wasn't feeling good. That's when I got mad, because I figured the real reason he wasn't coming was because he was doing something with Lucinda. So I tore up there to—" She broke off, a flash in her eyes revealing her angry passions of the moment. She touched her lips with her fingertips, as if to close off whatever she'd started to say.

"To?"

"Not to murder him, if that's what you're thinking. This was before he was killed."

I didn't say anything. Sometimes it's more profitable to stay silent and see what fills the empty space.

"I just went up to tell him if he didn't tell Lucinda about us, I was going to. Or maybe I'd break up with him. Or both."

I thought of her altercation with the guy in the parking lot. Somehow I doubted she'd have confronted Hiram with a calm ultimatum. KaySue did fireworks. Even fisticuffs.

"And?"

"I wound up not saying anything about either one, because when I got there he really *was* sick. I was still a little mad because he and that old guy from the mine had been drinking together the night before, drinking *all night*, can you believe that? And he was sick because he still had an awful hangover." Another blue flash in her eyes. Apparently she disapproved of drinking and hangovers, which I found admirable. "But his telling me he was sick didn't have anything to do with Lucinda. So then I felt kind of awful, being so suspicious."

I murmured something noncommittal.

"I feel awful now too, with him . . . gone. I never saw him again after that night. It's still hard to believe somebody killed him."

"Do you know who could have done it?"

She shook her head.

"Did he ever mention anyone threatening him? Anyone he was afraid of? Anything?"

Another shake of head. "I don't know why anyone would want to kill Hiram. He was a wonderful man."

"Did he write you letters too?"

"No, Hiram wasn't a letter writer. But he had my carousel earrings especially made for me. And he gave me that lamp too." She pressed a button on the lamp with a merry-go-round base, and the carousel horses rose and fell to a tinny tinkle of music.

"You didn't go to the funeral?"

"I didn't even know he was dead until the funeral was over."

"How did you find out he was dead?"

"Those old guys in the Nugget were talking about this guy getting murdered up in Hello, and then one of them mentioned a name. And it was Hiram."

"That was a hard way to find out."

She nodded, and her throat moved in a swallow. "I know

you probably don't believe it, because of the difference in our ages and all, but I really, really did love him. And he loved me."

So young. So earnest. I sighed. "How much difference in age was there?"

"Well, he was fifty-seven and I'm twenty-six. So not all that much," she said defensively. "And age doesn't matter anyway."

Fifty-seven. I shook my head. Oh, Hiram. "You weren't concerned about his bad track record with all his marriages?"

"Two isn't all that many marriages. My mom's been married more than that."

So, dear ol' Hiram hadn't exactly been up front with her about his age or his marital history. Should I tell her? I also thought about the carousel horses in the bedroom back home. Were they to be a wedding surprise for her, after he dumped Lucinda? I didn't want to go there.

"Did anything come of your, um, altercation in the parking lot a while back?"

"Which one?"

With that answer, I decided there was no point in pursuing that line of inquiry. KaySue definitely met any requirements Hiram may have had for spitfire temperament.

KaySue started braiding her hair and unexpectedly became quite chatty about Hiram, telling me about all the things they had in common besides carousel horses. Perhaps, I thought, to convince me the relationship had been true love. They both liked Chinese food, long walks, rap music, and old John Wayne movies. I couldn't help but wonder who was fooling whom with that list, and in the end I didn't tell her about all the wives, Hiram's age, or the carousel horses. At this point, none of it seemed particularly relevant.

What was relevant was that my big question had been answered: this relationship had been going on parallel to

193

Hiram's relationship with Lucinda. Which raised the ominous question: had Lucinda found out about KaySue? And had she grimly decided that Hiram had dumped and humiliated her once, and he wasn't going to get away with it again?

She could have gotten him up to the third floor easily enough. Just told him she hadn't seen the view from up there since their high school days and wanted to see it again. She was strong and fit from her walking and health club workouts. She'd have no difficulty pushing him out the window.

Oh no. No, no. I didn't want to think such thoughts about Lucinda.

Another side of the coin occurred to me. What about the reverse of Lucinda finding out about KaySue and being angry enough to kill him? Maybe Hiram had decided he was going to marry Lucinda after all, and he'd broken it off with KaySue. How would she take the news? Calmly and graciously?

About as likely as Three Stooges Moe breaking into operatic aria.

18

Good news when I got back to the pickup. Abilene had passed both written and driving tests. She proudly showed me her new license, complete with terrible photo. I wouldn't have thought Abilene could look unattractive under any circumstances, but the curse of the DMV photo held true even for Abilene. Her mouth had an odd, off-center tilt, her eyes bulged in a way they never did in real life, and her hair looked like a blond wig one of Norman's chickens had been scratching in. She didn't mind, I knew. She'd have happily accepted a license that made her look like Frankenstein, just so she could now drive legally.

Which she did, all the way back to Hello, smiling all the way, wheeling that oversized pickup down the road as if she'd been driving all her life. Although she sobered when I gave her a brief rundown on my meeting with KaySue, whose last name I still didn't know, and my two-sided suspicions.

"So either one of them could have done it." Abilene sounded as dismayed as I felt. She liked Lucinda too.

But, I asked myself, wasn't KaySue the more likely perpetrator? She admitted to being in Hiram's house. She could have been fudging about when she was there. She could also have been lying about the drinking/hangover thing. If she'd gone up to Hello and found Hiram was with Lucinda that evening, she might have waited for him, her temper spiraling to the murderous level.

The scenario fell apart there. If KaySue was angry enough to kill Hiram, she'd have clobbered him right there in the driveway or kitchen. She wouldn't have wasted time luring him up to the third floor.

Abilene's next question, "Now what?" echoed my question to myself.

Yes, now what? Tell Kelli everything? Confront Lucinda? Go to the police? I felt squeamish about all these alternatives. I didn't want Lucinda to turn out to be a killer. But neither, I realized, did I want hotheaded but also naïve and optimistic KaySue to be the guilty person. Or, for that matter, Nutty Norman or Kelli or flower-shop Suzy or I-can-hire-a-killer Doris or anyone else I'd encountered so far.

So many suspects, so many conflicting motives and clues.

And then there was Chris, with his bad advice about the Bahamas bank. Could that have tangoed into murder? But in that situation, if someone was going to murder someone, it seemed more likely ol' Hiram would have been furious enough to do Chris in, not the other way around.

By now my head was pounding, as if those carousel horses were thundering around inside it, and I remembered a mystery I'd once read in which a character remarked about the victim, "What difference does it make who killed him? The old goat deserved killing. Why bother to figure out who did it?"

But I didn't feel that way. Old Hiram McLeod certainly

had his flaws and faults, but no one had the right to decide he should die for them. Not even one of the nice people on my list of suspects.

Abilene intended to drop me off at the house and go back to work, but a business card was wedged in beside the doorknob. It was from Nick's Garage, with a greasy message on the back about an available motor home engine, so we drove out to the garage.

A motor home—or, more accurately, what was left of a motor home—stood in the yard. Compared to this one, ours was almost roadworthy. The entire back half of it was simply gone, no bathroom, kitchen, or rear wheels, almost as if that half had been surgically removed. Part of a sofa dangled out of what had been the living room.

Nick came out to talk to us as we studied the mess.

"What happened to the occupants?" I asked, appalled.

"Funny thing. Brakes on an eighteen-wheeler went out, and the truck hit 'em dead-on sideways at a crossroads down south of here. You can see what it did. Sheared off the whole back half of the thing. Scattered it over half an acre down there. But those folks, couple about your age from New Jersey they are, had their seat belts buckled on tight, or the good Lord was with 'em or something, because they walked away with no more'n a few scratches. You can see how the driver's and passenger's seats weren't even touched."

"What about the truck driver?"

"He's okay too, but shook up as bad as they are. The thing is, these people never want to see this or any other motor home ever again. They just want to go home, and they're flying back to Jersey tomorrow. So if you want the engine, I figure we can get it for a bottom price, probably not over five hundred. They just want out from under."

"I don't want to take advantage of their misfortune!"

"You wouldn't be taking advantage. You'd be doing them

a favor. They have comprehensive and liability insurance, but no collision coverage, so there's nothing for them there. They'll probably get a good settlement from the truck company eventually, but who knows how long that will take? They want to wash their hands of what's left of the motor home *now*."

"The engine would work in our motor home?"

"It's a newer model, but it'll work. And it looks like it's in good condition, with a lot less miles on it than yours. A really weird accident, kind of like when a tornado demolishes one house and leaves the one next door untouched, the way the accident left the engine untouched."

"So how much would it cost altogether?"

"Well, with the installation charge, and probably some miscellaneous parts to buy, I'd say maybe twelve or thirteen hundred total. It's the best deal you're ever going to get on an engine, that's for sure, because we're not too busy now and I'm shaving the labor fee to the bone. If you can pay them for the engine now, you can take two or three months to pay me for the labor."

"Let us think about it for a few minutes, okay?"

"Sure." Nick walked back toward the open garage doors. Nothing was up on the rack today, and his helper was drinking coffee, which suggested business was indeed slow.

"So, what do you think?" I asked Abilene.

"I guess we ought to do it," she said, though she didn't look overjoyed. A few weeks ago we'd both have been thrilled by this unexpected opportunity, but circumstances were different now. Her job, my job. Dr. Sugarman? Mac coming to town? "I'll get paid in a couple days, and I can put that money in on it."

My Social Security check and CD interest were on direct deposit with the bank, and I hadn't touched that money yet this month. I could write a check against that and then pay

Nick off with part of next month's checks. "I can swing the rest of it."

Then Abilene asked the big question. "When we get it fixed, do we pick up and leave right away?"

Decision time. With the motor home in working shape, we'd no longer be stranded in Hello. We could head on down to Arizona, as we'd originally planned. Warm weather. Swimming pool. Sunshine. I figured Nick would trust us to send the balance of the money from there. We'd be putting distance between ourselves and anyone who was after us.

But we'd more or less decided the divorce meant Boone had given up on us, and the Braxtons hadn't shown their ugly faces since they'd chased me into Oklahoma some months ago. Maybe we didn't have to run.

There were good reasons to stay on. Abilene loved her job, and maybe something would develop between her and Dr. Sugarman after the divorce, which I thought would be a very good thing.

And it just wasn't in my genes to walk out on a murder unsolved.

"I think we could stay on here for a while," I said, and Abilene's grin surely qualified her for entry into some toothpaste ad hall of fame.

We went in and told Nick we wanted the engine and how we could pay for it, to which he was agreeable. He said he'd get right on it and be in touch later, and I told him where I was working now. On the way home, I made another decision.

"We won't tell anyone about the letters or KaySue yet, okay?" I added my reasoning. "The letters don't prove anything, and they might just cause innocent people embarrassment and trouble."

So, the problem now was, how to find out if Lucinda knew about KaySue. Because if she didn't know, she wouldn't have

199

had any reason to murder Hiram. Which would be a big, unpleasant weight off my mind, and I could go on to other possibilities from there.

I didn't want to ask any of the Historical Ladies if they'd heard rumors or gossip, because asking a question can all too easily *start* a rumor. Saying, "Have you ever heard anything about Hiram seeing a young blond down in Hayward before he was killed?" can, when it makes the jump in a gossip circle, take on a much more scandalous spin. "Hey," it becomes, "did you know Hiram was running around with a blonde a third his age down in Hayward?"

Lucinda came by the library a couple of afternoons later. She waved to Doris Hammerstone and Stella Sinclair at the main desk but bypassed them to come directly to my workspace. I was into setting up a separate section for Hiram's books on Egyptian archaeology, another of his varied interests.

"Big problem," Lucinda announced. I'm thinking murder and secret girlfriend and carousel horses, but what she said was, "Esther McIver has dropped out as our props person. She decided she's had it with snow and ice and took off yesterday to visit her son in California until spring. You'd think she could give us a little advance notice, but that's Esther for you." She gave the pages of a book an exasperated flip, then targeted me with an expectant look. "Anyway, I'm thinking you're the perfect person to take over."

"I don't know anything about props."

"If you can tell a doghouse from a policeman's nightstick, you're in."

"In that case, I'll give it a try." I was pleased with the idea of helping out on the Revue without flouncing around in the chorus line. I'd heard the money the Revue brought in was divided between a summer camp program for kids and helping out with the local meal delivery program for seniors.

"Nick has found a replacement for our motor home engine, but we've decided to hang around even after it's fixed."

"Good. I have a list of props we need. I was thinking, if you have time, we could go over to the hotel on Sunday and see what props Esther has lined up and what we still have to locate."

"Sunday afternoon would be fine. I'll go to church in the morning."

"I'll pick you up about 1:30, then, okay?"

This felt like an opening to me, and I had to ask, "Would you like to come to church with us?"

"No thanks." Her tone suggested she'd as soon spend the morning listening to reruns of political speeches from 1982 as listen to a Christian message from the pulpit with us.

I was pleased with her Sunday invitation anyway. Surely, with an entire afternoon to work with, I could think of some discreet way to find out if Lucinda knew about KaySue.

Dr. Sugarman sat with us at church on Sunday. Afterward he invited both of us to go to the Chuckwagon Buffet with him. I had my appointment with Lucinda, so I declined but added brightly, "But you two go ahead. I hear the food there is very good." But Abilene, without me along to make it a non-date, also declined. Though I did think she looked disappointed. Dr. Sugarman surely was.

After we got home, I asked if she'd like to come to the hotel with Lucinda and me. Her nod wasn't wildly enthusiastic, but it was a nod.

Lucinda had a key to the hotel, of course, and she talked about the hotel's history as we climbed to the third floor. How President Hoover was supposed to have stayed there at one time and movie star James Dean too, and that Gypsy

Rose Lee had been the star to christen the stage when it was first built and featured productions a bit more racy than the current Revue.

On the third floor Lucinda got out her list, and we started trying to locate the things on it. Thankfully, it appeared that Esther had lined up most of the necessary items, which was good because there was only a week and a half left before the big performance. She had a doghouse and a phony fountain with plastic "water" for the Three Stooges piece, a sign saying "Harry's Barber Shop" for the street scene, and a tall stool for Ben Simpson's Will Rogers monologue.

"Did Will Rogers use a stool on stage?"

"Beats me. But Ben is sure going to need one. I talked to him last night, and he could hardly get out of bed yesterday. We're always short on men for parts, of course. You know the statistics about older men and women." She sounded annoyed, as if the men died off early just to get out of appearing in the Revue.

We also found a needed bouquet of silk flowers, a fringed lamp, and a set of black masks for another chorus-line number. I kept trying to find out what Lucinda knew about Hiram's activities before his death, but it's not easy to work questions about someone's extracurricular love life into an ordinary conversation. And I had to be careful not to give anything away. If Lucinda didn't already know about KaySue, I didn't want to be the one to spill it to her.

"I found some of Hiram's old phone bills. He made a lot of long-distance calls," I observed. "Especially to Hayward." Would that elicit a response such as, "I think he may have been seeing another woman down there"?

No. Lucinda replied, "Yes, he was always talking with people from that mining company. They have offices in Texas and Denver and all over."

"Hayward?"

202

"Maybe there too. I don't know." No hint from her of anything else going on in Hayward.

I asked several more discreet questions, but discreet wasn't getting me anywhere. Getting more blunt, I asked, while we were plowing through a box of knickknacks, "Did you ever wonder, given Hiram's past, if he could really settle down with one woman?"

To which she answered cheerfully, "He knew if he didn't confine himself to one woman this time that he was going to find himself minus this woman." Lucinda sounded more concerned when she added, "You know one thing we're missing on the list is the fire hydrant for the street-scene skit."

"Would the city have an old one we could use?"

"Possibly. But it would probably be so heavy we'd need a crane to get it up here. And another one to get it down to the stage. Which is probably why Esther hadn't figured out what to do about it yet."

Abilene had been wandering around looking at costumes and peering down that elevator shaft to the basement, but now she said, "Maybe we could make one."

"Out of what?" I asked.

"There's those big chunks of Styrofoam in that trash room at the house. They're funny shaped because they must have been packed around something, but we could cut and glue them into a fire hydrant shape, then paint it red."

"Marvelous idea!" Lucinda applauded.

I've never been good at artsy-craftsy things, but if Abilene thought we could do it, maybe we could. We moved on to other items on the list, a live cactus plant and a Greta Garbo poster, me still trying to work in my sly questions.

Or maybe not so sly questions, considering that Lucinda finally planted her fists on her hips and looked at me over a lava lamp we'd just uncovered. "Ivy, are you trying to find out from me if Hiram was seeing some other woman while we were engaged?"

"Well, uh, no. Not really." True. I already knew what Hiram was doing. I was just trying to find out if Lucinda knew.

"Have you heard rumors?"

I shook my head. Definitely not. No rumors. Hiram had apparently been careful as the proverbial long-tailed cat in a roomful of rockers.

"I suppose you've heard what Hiram did to me years ago, how he left me at the altar and ran off to marry another woman?"

"Umm, uh, well . . ."

"For years after that, I wouldn't have trusted Hiram about anything. If he'd said it was Monday, I'd have looked at the calendar to be sure. If he'd said two plus two equals four, I'd have checked on my fingers. I had money I'd inherited invested in my husband's family's bank, and I warned Bill if they dealt with Hiram in any way I'd yank my money out. But Hiram changed in his later years." She smiled wryly. "Or maybe he just got too old for the chase. In any case, he was trustworthy now. We had a good thing going, and Hiram wouldn't have done anything to damage it."

"That's . . . comforting."

But not true. I still didn't know which woman Hiram intended to marry, Lucinda or KaySue, but I definitely knew he was up to his same old devious, womanizing tricks. And Lucinda's statement about money and the bank reinforced what I already knew, that she did have a temper when she was pushed hard enough, and she would retaliate.

By the end of the day, I had to admit Lucinda was either blithely unaware of KaySue's existence, or she'd simply outwitted me, because I didn't know any more than I did before.

Maybe I'd better give up sleuthing and take up fireplug construction.

19

When we got home, Abilene and I walked up to the corner to inspect the fire hydrant. It's odd how you see some ordinary thing such as a fire hydrant almost daily, and you can identify one instantly when you see it. But when you actually get down to making one, you realize you don't know the details at all.

So I took a tape measure and measured height and circumference, and Abilene sketched the hookups and various lumps and bumps, and I measured them too. Then we spent the next two evenings out in the trash room working on building a fire hydrant. We ruined several large pieces of Styrofoam until we got the knack of how to cut it without breaking it, but, fortunately, there were plenty more pieces to experiment with. We cut and glued and taped, tore apart and remeasured and cut again. It was not easy stuff to work with. Great sculptors, I suspect, are not soon going to switch to Styrofoam as a medium for their artistic work.

Koop batted bits of the stuff around for a while, then

found a place to sleep in some shredded newspaper that had probably also been packing material at one time. We did as much giggling as cutting, gluing, and painting, and we both wound up with splotches of red paint in odd places. We'd found a shelf with various partially full cans of paint in the laundry room.

"How did you get red paint behind your ear?" Abilene inquired.

"Probably the same way you got it on your right elbow."

Even Koop had a speck on his tail.

Up close, our fireplug certainly wouldn't fool anyone as authentic, but from a distance it was passable, bright red and light enough to toss around. I took it to the Wednesday afternoon rehearsal, getting a few odd looks as I carried it through town. I can usually walk anywhere without drawing any more attention than your average stray cat, but carrying a bright red fireplug does tend to increase one's visibility. Several people peered out from store windows. Suzy at the flower shop saw me, did a double take, and came to the door to laugh and call, "Going to a fire, Ivy?"

Fortunately I didn't run into any oversized dogs, or I might really have been in trouble.

This was a partial dress rehearsal, with a full dress rehearsal scheduled for Friday evening. Time was growing short, with the big performance only a week and a half away. There were two tiny dressing rooms behind the stage, although they were barely big enough to turn around in, and Charlotte was flying up and down the stairs, getting two sets of chorus-line costumes distributed and the ladies dressed, undressed, and dressed again. I lugged the imitation fountain down to the stage, and the ladies pranced an enthusiastic, if somewhat ragged, revolving wheel routine to the music of "Tiger Rag." Although they all had to stop and take a break when Lulu Newman's hip developed a glitch. She was the centerpiece in all the circular movements, her statuesque figure holding everything together.

Stella Sinclair, who was in the street scene, had brought her potbellied pig, DaisyBelle. DaisyBelle took an unfortunate dislike to our fireplug, and I had to rush onstage and rescue it from being trampled into Styrofoam bits when she charged, tossed it a good ten feet, and charged again. No one seemed particularly fond of DaisyBelle, who liked to run up behind people and stick her snout where it didn't belong, but the fact that Stella had personally paid for the new set of spangled chorus-line costumes apparently insured the pig's welcome.

On the night of the performance all the props would already have to be downstairs, crowded in behind the stage. Otherwise I'd be carrying them right through the audience since there was only that one stairway up to the third floor. The first row of seats would be reserved for actors and chorus-line ladies to sit in when they weren't performing, because there was so little space backstage. I had to wonder if things hadn't been somewhat more upscale when Gypsy Rose Lee was here.

After the rehearsal, everyone gathered in the lobby for coffee, cookies, and a rehash of the evening's successes and problems. The fireplug drew praise, as did the Three Stooges' rendition of "Three Little Fishies." Ben Simpson had given a well-memorized if, to my mind anyway, not particularly rousing impersonation of Will Rogers, but now he kept arching and rubbing his back. Charlotte Sterling, looking frazzled from all her trips up and down the stairs, came up and leaned against the wall beside me. Across from us, Stella was feeding DaisyBelle dainty bites of cookie and cooing about what a good pig she was.

"Good pig, my eye," Charlotte muttered. "If that ugly creature gets a little too cozy with her snout just one more time—" She hacked the air with one hand. "Instant pork chops."

After DaisyBelle's attack on our fireplug, I also wasn't feeling too kindly toward her. A couple of small hams in addition to pork chops would be nice, I decided.

"Don't tell anyone," Charlotte added in a confidential tone, "but dressing sixteen not-so-young ladies is more work than dressing sixteen two-year-olds. At least the two-year-olds don't keep worrying about how big their butts look."

I was scarfing down chocolate chip cookies, but Charlotte just had coffee, black. She looked as if she needed the caffeine to keep her going.

"It's great how everyone works in unison to pull this all together," I offered as a generic soother.

"Although we may wind up pulling each other's hair before this is all over. If Emily complains about that Moe wig one more time . . ." She rolled her eyes. Then, as if she'd like to think about something other than costumes, pigs, and wigs, she asked, "So, how's the search for the secret room coming?"

"So far it isn't. I've been too busy. But I'll probably get back to it within the next few days."

"If you find a secret room, are you going to have a grand unveiling like that guy did on TV when they whacked into some old gangster's vault?"

"I hadn't thought about that, but it could be fun, couldn't it?" I smiled. "Maybe we could make it a money-raising event for the Ladies Historical Society."

Charlotte laughed. "Great idea." She gave DaisyBelle another venomous glance. "We could sell barbecued ham sandwiches on the side."

"Actually, by now I'm pretty sure there isn't any secret room," I admitted, "but I'm going to keep looking. I did find a cartoon from the 1930s under a baseboard. Maybe, if nothing else, I'll find a gold nugget Hiram had hidden away somewhere."

"Oh, much to my surprise, I had a bite on the Randolph place. Some Texas people on their way to ski at Aspen."

Someone came up then, looking for a can opener, which Charlotte promptly pulled out of her apparently bottomless purse.

I was feeling frazzled too, by the time I got home. I'd jaunted up and down those stairs to the third floor quite a few times myself. I was happy just to plop in front of the TV for the evening. Abilene reported that Dr. Sugarman had sent her on several errands with the pickup that afternoon, so she was happy too.

We went to bed about 9:30, rather earlier than usual. We left the bedroom doors open, as we usually did, because Koop likes to prowl around in the night, sometimes sleeping on Abilene's bed, sometimes on mine, sometimes getting a midnight snack. I was in the midst of a pleasant dream about pork chops smothered in mushroom gravy when something landed in the middle of my chest.

I oofed and floundered awake. "Koop, what's the matter with you?"

I sat up and tried to push him off my chest, but he seemed to have developed Velcro paws. His fur felt electrified.

Now he added a hiss and growl to his stiff-legged stance, then suddenly leaped off me and skittered toward the doorway, yowling.

At that moment I became aware of a peculiar smell. Smoke! And a strange flickering light in the hallway. I dashed to the doorway in my nightgown, then started screaming.

"Abilene! Abilene, we're on fire!"

The flickering light—oh, and now a tongue of flame!—came from the trash room where we'd been working. Abilene's bedroom was closer to it than mine. I dashed down the hallway, screaming at the top of my lungs. More tongues of flame. A faceful of smoke that made me cough.

Abilene met me at her doorway in her flannel pajamas. Koop whipped around her feet, then tore down the hallway away from the fire. The fire crackled hungrily now as it licked around the door frame. Dark smoke billowed out of the room. Bicycle tires, I remembered.

"I'll call 911!" The cell phone, where was it? I couldn't seem to think straight. *Lord, help me! Where is it? Oh yes, my purse.* Where was my purse? In the bedroom. I backed toward the door, afraid to take my eyes off the leaping flames for fear they'd explode into a firestorm behind my back.

"I'll get water! There's a bucket in the kitchen—"

"No!" Water buckets weren't going to do it. Maybe a hose would, but we didn't have one. And I wasn't going to let Abilene risk her life for this old house! I grabbed her hand, yanked her down the hallway, then gave her a shove. "You find Koop, then go out the front way. I'll get the cell phone and meet you there."

Abilene, unshovable when she doesn't want to be shoved, dug in her heels. She looked back at the fire. The kind of person who'd stand and fight till the walls crumbled to ashes around her, I thought, partly exasperated, partly admiring. But I shoved again, and she reluctantly moved on down the hallway, calling for Koop.

I flicked the switch in my bedroom, and the light came on. The electricity was still working. *Thank you, Lord!* The red numbers on the digital clock read 12:02. I spotted my purse on a chair, grabbed it, then hesitated momentarily. We might lose everything. What else should I save?

Clothes? Mementos? No, not stuff. My few important papers and records were still in the motor home, and all that really mattered were Abilene and Koop. I left everything behind and raced for the front door, frantically fumbling for the cell phone as I ran. The hall was filling with smoke now. I had the feeling the flames were right behind me, a fiery demon on my tail, but when I glanced back I saw they were still back at the doorway to the trash room. But becoming bolder as they edged along the carpet like dancing elves. Evil elves.

I glanced up the stairs as I flew by, then stopped short. What if Koop had gone up there? And Abilene went after him.

"Abilene!" I yelled. I peered up the stairs, ascending into blackness. Much as I loved dear Koop, I couldn't have Abilene risking her life getting trapped up there while looking for him.

"Out here!" She was at the door, her shoulder holding it open, an iron arm clasped around a squirming Koop, the other hand reaching for me.

Outside . . . yes, we were safely outside! *Thank you, Lord* . . . I took several deep breaths of unsmoky air and punched in the numbers on the cell phone. Then I wondered, did Hello even have a 911 system? I'd never checked. Would a call go through to a local 911 system, or was I calling some other city, some other state?

A voice answered, and I yelled, "Where are you? Are you in Hello?"

"Yes."

Another grateful *Thank you, Lord*, and then I yelled "Fire!" and gave the address.

From the front of the house, except for a bit of flickering light behind the etched glass in the doors, everything looked oddly normal.

"Maybe it isn't as bad as we thought," Abilene said. "Isn't there a fire extinguisher in the laundry room? I could go back and—"

I grabbed her arm again. "No!" Yes, there might be a fire extinguisher in the laundry room, but the door was only a few feet up the hallway from the trash room. Too dangerous. "Just hold on to Koop."

I suddenly realized I should call Kelli too. This was her house. But I didn't have the number . . . Yes, I did. I'd dialed it any number of times that weekend when I'd tried to call her about the utility bills and finally added it to my list on the cell phone. With shaky hands, I pulled it up from the list and dialed it. Ring, ring, ring, ring. *C'mon, Kelli, answer!* Finally she did, after a good dozen rings, a sleepy, "Hello?"

"Kelli, this is Ivy. The house is on fire—"

"On fire? Oh no! Where are you? Are you okay?"

"We're outside, all three of us. We're okay. I've called 911—"

"I'll be right over."

Then we retreated to the far side of the hedge and watched and waited. I could feel Abilene still wanting to rush inside and do something, and I held on tight to her arm to keep her from it. Koop kept squirming, but Abilene held on tight to him too. The glow behind the etched windows in the double front doors grew brighter, and now it flickered through the living room windows too.

Finally, finally, somewhere in the distance I heard the wail of a siren. At the same time I realized we were both barefoot, me still in my nightgown, Abilene in her pajamas. But firemen had undoubtedly seen underdressed people before. I was just grateful I wasn't wearing those skimpy things from Victoria's Secret that Sandy had once given me.

The fire engine arrived. Some of the men ran through the front door dragging a hose. Others raced around the back way. Crashing noises. Glass breaking. Yells. With the front door open, we could see full-fledged flames down the hallway, like looking into a roaring furnace.

Kelli arrived a few seconds later, running. "I parked down the street so I wouldn't be in the way!" By now, other people were congregating on the street. I didn't realize I was shivering until Kelli whipped off her coat and wrapped it around me.

"What happened?" she asked.

"I don't know. We were asleep. Koop woke me up—" I broke off, for the first time realizing Koop may well have saved our lives. Thankfully for us, his aversion to cigarette smoke apparently extended to other kinds of smoke as well.

"Where did it start?"

"In the trash room. We've been working in there on a Styrofoam fire hydrant for the '20s Revue—" I broke off again. Had we somehow started the fire? But we hadn't been in there since last evening. Unless we'd somehow started something smoldering then, and tonight it had burst into flame . . .

"I was in there earlier this evening to get some plastic bags to take to the clinic. I didn't see anything then, no smoke, nothing," Abilene said.

"It doesn't matter. Just so you're both safe. And Koop too." Kelli put an arm around my shoulders and squeezed reassuringly. "If the house burns, let 'er burn."

As well it might. Flames shot up from the back side of the house, and the crackle exploded to a roar. Smoke rose, a black blot against the starry sky. Sparks created stars within the blot. Ashes fell around and on us. I smacked one that burned my arm.

Koop wasn't acting like a hero at the moment. He squirmed and twisted in Abilene's arms, even hissed at a passing fireman.

"Why don't you put him in the Bronco?" Kelli said. "He'll be safe there and can't run away."

Abilene left to do that, her tread steady in spite of the bare feet. A second fire engine arrived. More firemen dragged another hose around to the back of the house.

I don't know how long we stood out there. Not as long

as it felt, I'm sure. But long enough for my toes to feel like something out of the freezer case at the supermarket. Gradually the flames at the rear of the house died back. The roar dropped to a pop and crackle. It was some minutes after all sign of flames had disappeared when a stocky man in fireman's gear came up to us. He loosened the strap on his sloping yellow hat. An ugly scent of burned, wet wood hung in the air.

Kelli stepped forward. "I'm Kelli Keifer, the owner of the house."

"The McLeod place, isn't it? Where old Hiram McLeod was killed a while back?"

He didn't say it, but I wondered if he was connecting the two, the death and the fire.

"Yes. Hiram was my uncle. Great-uncle, actually. Ivy Malone and Abilene Tyler have been living here." Kelli motioned to us. "Is everything okay?"

They didn't seem to know each other, because he also introduced himself. "Fire Chief Wally Burman. The fire's out, but we'll leave a man on watch for the night just to be sure."

"Ivy says it started in the room my uncle used for storing all kinds of discarded materials and trash. Paper and plastic, pieces of wood, rags. Everything. I should have hauled it all to the dump a long time ago."

He asked more questions. Kelli answered some, I answered others.

"Can you tell yet what started the fire?" she asked. "I'm thinking it may have been something electrical. The wiring in the house is really old."

"That's possible. We'll do a more complete investigation in the morning. The back door on the house was locked, and we had to break our way in." He looked at me. "You said you'd been working with paint in that room?"

"Yes, but—"

"And paint thinner?"

"Yes, but we didn't spill any, and we didn't have matches anywhere near the room."

"Do either of you smoke?"

"No. Never."

"What about a heater? Wasn't it cold working out there?"

"Yes, we did have an electric heater with us. But we didn't leave it there. And Abilene said she was out there earlier in the evening, and there was no sign of fire then."

"The paint and paint thinner weren't even in the trash room," Abilene added. "I'd moved them back to the shelf in the laundry room."

"Well, as I said, we'll investigate further in the morning."

"Don't oily old rags sometimes spontaneously combust?" Kelli asked. "Uncle Hiram could have used some of those old rags for most anything." I could see she didn't want the fire chief blaming us. Neither did she want us to feel as if we were to blame.

"We'll consider that when we investigate. It's possible." He started to turn away, then turned back as if he'd just thought of something. He gave Kelli a calculating appraisal. "Do you still have a key?"

"Yes, of course."

"Were you in the house this evening?"

Kelli looked startled, as I was. Was he shifting from thinking accident as cause of the fire to a possibility of arson? And was he thinking about Hiram's death here, and the town's pre-judgment of Kelli as murderer? Murderer now turned arsonist?

"No, I haven't been here in several days."

"That's right," I put in.

"Is the house insured?"

"Yes. Of course. Putnam's Insurance Agency, over on Calvin Street. Are you thinking it could be arson?"

"Our investigation will cover all possibilities."

"If you're thinking arson . . ." I began.

The fire chief and Kelli had been regarding each other warily, but now they both turned to look at me.

"Yes?" the fire chief prompted.

"The thing is, Abilene and I have reason to believe that someone could have, ummm, traced us here to Hello. Someone—someones, actually—who might start a fire. Actually, that's why we're here, because we were running away from . . . them."

I stumbled through the awkward statement because I could see doubt written on the fire chief's face.

"They could have traced you?"

"Yes. Possibly."

"How? Why?"

"Well, I'm, uh, not sure. They had someone working in the post office once, I think, or they might use the license plate on our motor home . . . or something." The statement sounded more flimsy and less believable the further I went.

"And you think these, ah, someones, got into the house and tried to burn it with you in it?"

"Yes. Exactly. They tried to do it to my house back in Missouri, and there have been threats on both our lives." I made a little gesture toward Abilene.

"What she's saying is true," Abilene put in, which swiveled the fire chief in her direction. "My former husband . . . I mean, we're in the process of getting a divorce, so he's almost my former husband . . . has threatened to kill me. Kill both of us."

"Maybe you should be telling this to the police chief."

"Well, uh . . ." Now it was Abilene's turn to stammer. "If

216

Boone doesn't already know where I'm at, he might find out, because his cousin is the sheriff, and then—"

"But the house wasn't broken into. How could they have gotten inside?"

"We haven't figured that out yet," I put in.

"Look, it's been a stressful night for all of you. Why don't you just get a good night's sleep, and things will look different in the morning."

I got an instant glimpse of us through his eyes. One LOL, which here meant "loony old lady," and one younger woman, paranoid about an ex-husband, both imagining bogeymen in the dark. And what we really were, to his mind, were two scatterbrained women careless with paint thinner and flammable trash trying to wiggle out of responsibility for the fire with a wild story about being tracked down by killers and arsonists.

The only time our stories were going to be taken seriously, I could see, was after we were dead, when someone might say, "Well, how about that? Someone *was* out to get them."

"Is the house livable?" I asked, partly as distraction, partly because his suggestion about getting a good night's sleep reminded me we had no place to do that.

"The house isn't a total loss, as you can see." The fire chief motioned toward the untouched towers and gingerbread across the front porch. "But most of it is smoke and water damaged, and the addition on the back side is pretty well destroyed." To Kelli he said, "I'd suggest you get your insurance people out here as soon as possible. We can't allow anyone to stay here tonight, of course."

Abilene and I looked at each other, with the question that passed between us every once in a while in our uncertain lives looming again. *Now what?*

Kelli had a quick answer. "You can stay at my place. I have an extra room with twin beds."

I didn't protest that we didn't want to put her to any bother. I was just grateful for her continuing generosity. "Can we go inside long enough to get a few things?" I asked.

The fire chief looked over our bare feet and night clothes. He called another fireman over and told him to escort us inside.

The wet, burned smell expanded to a nose-clutching stench as we made our way down the hall. The electricity had gone out by now, and the fireman used a flashlight to guide our way. The actual fire didn't appear to have extended more than a half dozen feet forward in the hallway, but starlight made murky by lingering smoke showed through the roof farther back. The back door at the end of the hallway, with only a skeleton of a wall around it, dangled on its hinges. If the fire had moved forward rather than to the rear, and if Koop hadn't awakened us . . .

The Lord had been looking out for us, and one of my favorite verses from Hebrews came to me, as it often did: "Never will I leave you; never will I forsake you." *Thank you for that promise, Lord. Thank you for fulfilling it.*

Water squished in the carpet under our bare feet. Fire hadn't harmed the bedrooms, although water from the hoses had drenched everything. The carousel horses glowed like eerie apparitions in the beam of the flashlight. The fireman actually jumped when he saw them.

We didn't bother to dress, except to put on shoes. We grabbed only basic necessities: clothes, other shoes, toiletries, Koop's cat carrier. We had nothing to carry anything in, but Kelli efficiently yanked sheets off the beds, and we bundled everything in those. All three of us were weighed down with the makeshift bags slung over our shoulders, Abilene with the addition of the cat carrier in one hand, by the time we staggered out of the house and down the street to the Bronco.

Abilene and I stayed in the vehicle while Kelli went back to the house to check with the fire chief again and make sure it was okay to leave. Koop had calmed down, and we put him in the cat carrier.

Abilene forcefully repeated what she'd said earlier. "There was nothing, nothing burning in the trash room when I went out there. However the fire got started, it was after that."

Neither of us had been out there flinging matches around. So how had the fire started? I remembered that shredded newspaper where Koop had napped. Oily rags. Old egg cartons. Plastic.

An arsonist's delight. And, even if Fire Chief Wally Burman thought my story of being traced to Hello was just a loony old lady's imagination, I had a pretty good idea who'd gleefully tossed a burning match into the trash room.

20

Kelli quickly got us settled in her guest room. It was a cozy
room, chinked logs on the outside wall, painted wood pan-
eling on the interior walls. Patchwork quilts covered the
beds. Braided rag rugs beside each bed made colorful ovals
on the wooden floors. Koop got a bed of his own, a plastic
laundry basket filled with a pillow, although I doubted that
was where he'd sleep.

Sandra Day had met us at the front door when we first
arrived. She looked as if God had used creative imagination
when putting her together: mottled Siamese coloring but
long hair, six toes on each front foot, and a pug face, the odd
combination all nicely held together with a queenly grace.
She and Koop had sniffed warily through the screen of the
cat carrier. No fireworks, but we were keeping him in the
room with us for the time being.

We dug in our makeshift bags until I found a nightgown,
Abilene another pair of pajamas. They were dampish but
clean. The ones we had on were speckled with ashes and

pocked with burn holes. We scattered our other damp clothes around the room to dry. The smell of smoke clung to both of us, and we took turns in the shower down the hall. We got in bed, but both of us felt too wired to turn out the ruffled lamps on the nightstands.

"I think we should thank the Lord for bringing us through safely," I said. "And for again providing us with a safe place for the night, as he has done so many times before."

Abilene made a peculiar noise, which it took me a moment to decipher as a clearing of her throat. Then she said, "I-I could do that."

You could? I was surprised. But I didn't want to make a big deal out of it, so all I said was, "That would be nice."

"Dr. Sugarman always says a blessing before we have lunch."

She'd been taking a sack lunch, but I hadn't realized she and the veterinarian ate together. "Dr. Sugarman brings a sack lunch too?"

"Lately he has been. He says it's quicker than going out to eat like he used to."

I didn't comment, but I suspected time wasn't the real reason for Dr. Sugarman's switch to sack lunches.

"I've been thinking maybe I should say the blessing sometimes before we eat, so he wouldn't be doing it all the time. I'm thankful for the food too."

"That sounds like a great idea." I also suspected Dr. Sugarman would be as pleased with her offering a blessing before lunch as I now was with her offer of a prayer of thanks for tonight.

Her prayer wasn't smooth or elegantly worded, not what you might hear in church or on a Christian radio program. She stumbled and ummm-ed and paused to swallow. It was also brief. But it was heartfelt, and I followed with an amen.

And a silent thanks of my own for this big step Abilene had taken.

It was getting close to 5:30 a.m., but we still didn't turn out the lights. Too much still hung unfinished.

"So," I said tentatively, "about the fire."

Abilene raised up on one elbow. "I don't care what that fire chief thinks, I don't think the fire was an accident. Somebody started it."

"He said the back door was locked, and the firemen had to break their way in," I reminded.

"So someone got in by picking the lock. Then he . . . or she . . . started the fire and locked the door again when he went out."

I certainly didn't doubt but what the Braxtons had someone, male or female, with lock-picking talent, and they'd be happy to trap us in a killer blaze. I shivered in spite of the comfortably warm room. If it were the Braxtons, which meant they had our location pinpointed and would probably try again, what did that do to our plan to remain here in Hello?

Abilene must have been thinking the same thought, and wanting to dodge it, because she asked, "Could someone from right around here have done it?"

"Like who?"

She answered that with another question. "Who knew about that trash room?"

"Kelli, of course," I answered reluctantly. But she surely couldn't have set the fire and gotten home in time to answer the phone. Or could she? The phone had rang and rang, and she'd sounded just wakened when she answered it. But maybe she was slow answering not because she was asleep, but because she was just dashing in the door and pretending the phone had wakened her. Yet what reason would she have to do it? Insurance? I couldn't believe the insurance money would amount to that much, and I definitely couldn't believe she'd endanger our lives for any amount of money. Not Kelli.

Yet a tiny suspicion slithered in, unwanted as a snake at a garden party. Could there be something in the house concerning Hiram's death that she wanted destroyed? Something she was desperate enough to get rid of that she was willing to risk our lives?

No. I'd already decided Kelli was no killer. Or arsonist.

"Lucinda?" Abilene suggested, her tone uneasy.

Yes, Lucinda knew about that inflammable trash. Could she have realized that we suspected she may have killed Hiram because of KaySue and decided it was time to get rid of us? Or at least scare us into moving on? She knew about the engine Nick was installing in the motor home. Had she decided we needed a strong nudge to get us on our way? She quite likely had a key to the house. But she couldn't have known the house wouldn't be totally engulfed by a fire, us with it. Was she willing to risk our lives to get us to move on? I didn't want to think so, and yet it was possible.

"Norman?" I added to the list.

"He had to know about the trash room," Abilene agreed.

But surely not Norman! He had a crush on me. He was miles from town. He couldn't even harm his chickens. But crushes were notoriously fickle, the Dorf was in running condition, and maybe Norman was more ruthless about people than chickens. He may also have a key Hiram had given him at some time. If he thought I was about to figure out he was the killer . . .

"I don't want to think about this any more tonight," I muttered finally. I reached up and turned off the lamp.

"Me neither." The other lamp also clicked off.

But in the morning, the problem was still with us. Kelli was already gone by the time we got up, which was a much later hour than usual because it had been so close to the end of the night before we'd gotten to sleep. She'd left a note saying she wanted to talk to the insurance people as early as possible. "Help yourself to anything edible," the note ended. "Coffee's hot in the coffeemaker."

We fixed scrambled eggs and toast. Koop and Sandra Day looked each other over and, dignified creatures that they were, decided the two-cat situation was tolerable. Abilene called Dr. Sugarman, explained what had happened, and told him she'd be in a little later. I could tell from her end of the conversation that he was worried and wanted to come pick her up, but she told him she'd walk.

We settled at the kitchen table with second cups of coffee. Neither of us really believed someone local had sneaked in and set the house on fire. Abilene offered the first gloomy possibility.

"Maybe Boone hasn't given up after all," she said.

"Could be." Although I thought Boone would be more apt to try something direct, something face-to-face where he could be certain Abilene knew it was him getting even. Running her down with a vehicle. Sticking a gun in her face. Whacking her over the head with a tire iron. Not something as anonymous as a fire in the night.

But the Braxtons just wanted me dead, any way they could do it. Maybe by this time it had become a matter of family pride. It was, at least, definitely a family project. "Maybe the Braxtons haven't given up either."

Abilene nodded. Both of us had just stated the obvious.

The only problem was, neither Boone nor the Braxtons could have known about that trash room and how easy starting a fire would be there. Wasn't it more likely that if either of them wanted to burn the house they'd simply have splashed gasoline on an outside wall and tossed a match? Why bother to get inside?

"The thing is," Abilene went on slowly, "if it was Boone, he's going to be really mad his scheme didn't work. If he's here, he'll try again. And next time I-I'm afraid he might do something at the vet clinic."

"But he wouldn't get me there."

"The big thing that matters to Boone, as he put it back there in Oklahoma, is making mincemeat out of me. It's just that he doesn't care if you get hurt or killed in the process. He also wouldn't care if Dr. Sugarman got killed if he got in the way. Dr. Sugarman would try to protect me, I know he would. And Boone might kill him."

That was what worried her more than her own safety, I realized. Dr. Sugarman, even if she hadn't yet admitted it to herself, was more to her than just an employer.

"What do you think we should do?" I asked.

Her answer was immediate. "Go talk to Nick. See how soon he can get that engine installed so we can get out of here."

Keeping Dr. Sugarman safe meant more to Abilene than the job she loved, which told me a lot.

The only way we had to get out to Nick's Garage was walk. I hoped we'd find him putting finishing touches on transferring the engine from the wrecked motor home to ours. But the half motor home, looking like something chewed on by some monster in a horror movie, still stood in the yard, and our lifeless motor home was still out back.

"Problem," Nick said when we approached him in the shop, where he was doing something to a green pickup.

He wiped his hands on a greasy rag and slammed the hood down. "Someone from the truck company's insurance wants to examine the wrecked motor home before anything is done to it. I guess I should have expected that. They're probably anticipating a big claim from the New Jersey folks, mental anguish and all that, and they want to see exactly what the accident did to the motor home."

"How long will this take?"

"Hard to say."

"Things have changed, and we're in kind of a hurry now."

He nodded, but I suspected wanting something done yesterday was par for the vehicle repair business, not something he was going to get worked up about. "Say, I heard there was a fire at the McLeod place last night. What happened?"

"Just a blaze that got started in a roomful of trash. The back section of the house is heavily damaged, but we're fine. Kelli is talking to the insurance company this morning."

"That's good. Kind of a bad luck place, though, isn't it? Old Hiram getting killed there, now this." He looked us over appraisingly, his tone speculative.

I did not intend to encourage speculation. "It's a beautiful old house," I said. "Very spacious."

Nick apparently took that non sequitur to mean "mind your own business," which it did. He jumped back to the subject of the motor homes. "Well, hey, I'm real sorry about the delay on the engine, but there's nothing I can do about it. I'll get on it soon as I can. I just hope some of the lawyers involved don't decide the motor home has to be preserved as is for a trial or something."

"You mean the whole deal might fall through?" Abilene doesn't tend to gasp, but this was definitely a gasp.

"Possible."

Nick went back to the pickup, and Abilene and I moved slowly toward the gate out to the road.

Abilene jammed her hands in her pockets and looked at the ground in front of her feet. "I guess we don't have to make a decision about whether to leave now," she said.

Right. No decision necessary. We were still stranded in Hello.

Abilene went on to work. I waved her off and figured with her long strides she'd be at the vet clinic before I made it to the Historical Society, even though the distance was much farther.

I didn't get much done with the books that day. Doris Hammerstone and Victoria Halburton were on duty at the main desk, and various other Historical Society ladies wandered in and out, not something they usually did. It didn't take a prompter in the wings to tell me I was the major attraction. Each lady came by my desk with expressions of shock and horror but also eager for a firsthand report on the fire.

What caused the fire, of course, was everyone's openly asked question, although penny-pinching Victoria also pointed out that I hadn't put in a full day's work today and would be docked for the hours I'd missed. Everyone skirted around the bigger, underlying questions, as if it would be indelicate to ask: did the fire have something to do with Hiram's murder? Was Kelli involved? Was something scandalous going on?

Which raised a dilemma for me. My personal opinion was still that the fire had to be arson, but I didn't want to spread details about the Braxtons and Boone Morrison. Yet if I mentioned the possibility of arson and didn't mention them, Kelli would undoubtedly be Suspect #1. So I finally just downplayed the situation as much as possible and said the fire chief was taking care of things, which I hoped was less incendiary wording than the more ominous "investigating."

If I'd hoped to quell gossip with my verbal tap dance, I was mistaken. Several times ladies gathered around the main desk, gossip humming like a live wire connecting them, surreptitious glances shooting my way like sparks out of a malfunctioning toaster. The Ladies Hysterical Society in high gear.

Doris Hammerstone offered me a ride at the end of the afternoon. I thanked her but declined for two reasons. One was that I figured the offer was mostly because she wanted to pump me for more information, maybe pick up something no one else had. The other was that, after last night's excitement, I didn't feel up to another death-defying whirl in Doris's Lincoln.

Back at Kelli's house that evening, she reported that the fire department, in spite of the chief's doubts, hadn't ignored the possibility of arson. They'd rushed in a sniffer dog from out of town but had found no trace of gasoline or other accelerants popular with arsonists. That, along with the fact that there was no sign of forced entry into the house, had made them decide against arson. The room, with so much highly inflammable trash, had been so thoroughly burned that they couldn't even determine exactly where in it the fire had originated.

"So what they finally decided was that there was probably some malfunction in the old wiring, with sparks igniting the trash."

Even so, I wasn't convinced. I wasn't sure Kelli was either when she gave me a surreptitious sideways glance. We were eating at the small table in the kitchen as we talked. I'd found hamburger in the refrigerator and made a meatloaf and creamed potatoes. The cats had gotten quite cozy and were sharing the sofa in the other room.

"There really are these . . . people after you, like you told the fire chief?" Kelli asked.

"Yes. I suppose we should have warned you about that when you first offered to let us live in the house."

"But they seem quite convinced it wasn't arson."

My first thought was, even experts make mistakes. But on second thought, I had to admit I could be the one who was mistaken. I was paranoid about the Braxtons and Boone, no doubt about it, and could be seeing arson where none existed. Maybe it was faulty old wiring. There were mazes of uncovered wires all over the house, and we avoided using a couple of electrical outlets in the kitchen because they always shot sparks.

"I guess I'm just relieved that they didn't think I'd deliberately set the fire, considering how ready most people have been to think I'm a murderer," Kelli said. "If necessary, I was counting on you to back up my alibi that I was at home when you called to tell me about the fire. But that didn't turn out to be necessary."

I didn't want to think it, but the slithery thought was there: could she have rushed home deliberately to be there when someone called?

"It's helpful that they concluded the investigation so quickly. It probably makes dealing with the insurance and repairs easier."

"Right."

I supposed Abilene and I should also be grateful that the fire department wasn't putting blame on us for carelessly, or even purposely, setting the fire.

"If the fire department's investigation is finished, can we go back to the house tomorrow?" I asked.

"I'm afraid it will be a lot longer than tomorrow before the house can be lived in again. The first floor, maybe the entire house, will have to be cleaned and repainted because of the smoke and water damage. I'll have the back side boarded up as soon as possible, but Burman said that won't be enough to make it 'acceptable for occupation.' It has to meet building department requirements before it can be lived in."

"So how long will repair work take?"

"I talked on the phone with a contractor today. I'm meeting him at the house tomorrow. We're looking at anywhere from a month to several months, depending on whether I have that whole back section rebuilt. And on how fast the insurance company moves too, of course." She paused, brow wrinkling. "Although there is a possibility inspection will determine that the old place is structurally unsound and should simply be torn down."

I must have looked dismayed, because she reached across the table and patted my hand. "Don't worry. You can stay right here."

"But we can't impose on you for a month, let alone several months or more! And don't tell me two strangers and a cat aren't an imposition."

"You aren't, but . . . okay, I'll make you a deal. If there's one thing I'm tired of, it's my own cooking. How about you take over the job for a month? Then, at the end of that time, we'll see how things stand and reevaluate."

"Done!" Maybe the motor home would be ready by then. Which would mean another decision about staying or leaving, but we'd face that when we came to it.

"What about me?" Abilene asked. "What can I do?"

"You can give Sandra Day her worm medicine pill and bath. She usually won't speak to me for a couple days after I do it."

Another done. We beamed at each other as if we'd just solved the major problems of the world, up to and including bad hair days.

Except that conscience made me give Kelli a reluctant

230

warning. "If it was the Braxtons or Boone, they might try again. Right here at your cabin. Having us here could be dangerous."

"There's something I never told you, either," Kelli said. "With Uncle Hiram dead, I'm the last in the McLeod line."

"Is that important?"

"I don't know. People think I killed Uncle Hiram, but I know I didn't. Which means the real killer is still out there. And, since I don't know why Uncle Hiram was killed, I keep wondering if maybe I'm next on the killer's hit list. Staying here with me may put you in danger too."

Maybe the killers would have to take a number and get in line.

21

Gloomy clouds spit icy snowflakes the following morning. Kelli drove Abilene and me to the house to pick up the remainder of our belongings and clean out the refrigerator and freezer.

The old house still had that ugly, dead-campfire scent of wet, burned wood, and the interior was as cold as the frigid air outdoors. I stomped the floor and hammered a wall with my fist, and everything still felt solid to me, certainly no reason for the entire house to be condemned, but I was no expert, of course. I sent thought-vibes of encouragement: *Hang in there, house. Don't let 'em scare you into giving up.*

Fortunately, with the below-freezing temperatures, the lack of electricity to refrigerator and freezer hadn't damaged the contents. The carousel horses had been drenched by the firemen's hoses, but they didn't appear damaged. I knew it was probably foolish, but I rather wished KaySue could have them. They'd surely mean more to her than anyone else.

Kelli took Abilene on to the vet clinic and me to the Historical Society. She planned to take the Bronco back to the log cabin and unload, then keep the appointment with the contractor at the house.

Myra Fighorn and Charlotte Sterling were on desk duty today. I knew most of the Historical Society ladies took turns at the desk, but I hadn't seen Charlotte on duty before. When she came over to offer her sympathies about the fire, I also found out why she was here.

"Victoria Halburton called up and jumped all over me for not doing my share, so I said I'd do it every day this week." She rolled her eyes and sounded put upon, then shrugged and changed the subject. "It must have been terrifying, waking up to find the house burning all around you. I've always figured drowning would be the worst way to go, but getting trapped in a burning house is certainly right up there at the top of the list too."

"We never were actually trapped, but it was kind of terrifying."

"I feel so bad about this for Kelli too. She's been under so much stress, and now this. Will you be able to go back to the house soon?"

"Not for quite some time, apparently. There's a lot of cleanup and repair work to be done, plus safety regulations about occupying a house that's been badly damaged by fire. But, as you probably know, we're staying with Kelli at her cabin."

"Yes, that's what Chris said. She's so good-hearted, isn't she? But I'm thinking, Kelli's place is so tiny. Why don't you and Abilene come stay with me? There's all kinds of room. You could each have a bedroom of your own. I remember you said you liked mystery novels, and I have shelves and shelves of them. Oh, and satellite TV too."

I was surprised, both by the offer and by how attractive she was trying to make staying with her sound. "Why, thank you, Charlotte. Char," I corrected, knowing that was the name she preferred even though no one else used it. Char Sterling was what she had on her real estate business card. "That's so very kind and generous of you. But I'm not sure—"

"Actually, I'd love to have the company. Chris is so wrapped up in his work, you know. A workaholic just like his father." She gave a half-affectionate, half-exasperated shake of head. "I do wish he and Kelli would hurry up and get married and bring me some grandchildren. So, how about it? Want to come stay for a while? I could take you around to see some of the town's old houses. We talked about that once."

"Actually, we're hoping to get a new engine in our motor home soon, and then we can live in that again. And we do have a cat, you know." Remembering how shiny and spotless the house had been, I suspected that could be important.

"Oh? I'd forgotten the cat." She frowned lightly. Apparently I'd been right. A cat was a problem. "Doesn't that vet Abilene works for board animals? Perhaps you could keep the cat there. I think Stella left that smelly DaisyBelle there when she went to Maui last year."

DaisyBelle had her faults, but I thought "smelly" a bit unfair. Actually, the only scents I'd smelled during our scuffle over the fire hydrant was baby powder and maybe a hint of Eternity.

"Well, uh, let us think about it."

My back was to the front door as we talked, but Charlotte was facing in that direction. Her eyebrows lifted. "Well, looks as if we have visitors. I'd better get back to the desk and give them a big Hello welcome. She looks a little mature for a ski bunny, but we get all kinds, don't we?"

I turned to look and saw a formidable Victorian figure in a pink ski outfit decorated with dramatic slashes of black and gold. Plus a peaked Tyrolean hat with a frisky blue feather atop fire-truck red hair, and a ski pole as a walking stick.

234

Followed by a wiry man in totally neutral gray slacks and windbreaker.

I left Charlotte standing there and rushed toward the couple. "Magnolia!"

"Ivy!"

We met in a flurry of hugs, me dodging the ski pole swinging wildly around us. Then I had to hug Geoff too.

"It's so good to see you! It's been so long. How long can you stay?" I grabbed Magnolia's hands again and stepped back to take a better look at her. She does tend to go for the dramatic, but this outfit was a bit over the top even for her. So far as I know, the closest she's ever been to a ski slope is watching Winter Olympics on TV.

"Oh, we'll be here a few days. Long enough to have a good visit. We'll stay at the RV park we passed out on the south side of town. We're headed for our storage unit in Missouri, of course, but we aren't on a set schedule."

"I'm so glad. I've missed you."

"I'm looking forward to meeting that young woman traveling with you."

"Abilene Tyler. You'll like her." I hesitated, still wondering about the pink outfit and ski pole. "Have you taken up skiing?"

"Well, I may." She gave the ski pole an airy twirl. "You never know. At our age, we need to keep active, and I thought, since we were coming here into snow and ski country, that I should consider it. Although at the moment I'm just trying things out."

She wiggled her shoulders inside the jacket. I was pleased to see that the sharp end of the ski pole had been flattened, so she wasn't walking around poking holes in things, including me.

I knew what "trying things out" meant with Magnolia. Back in Missouri she'd briefly taken up horseback riding but quit when she realized jodhpurs made her back side look broader than the horse's. I'd never consider Magnolia shallow. She's too good-hearted for that. But she isn't about to devote herself to activities that feature unflattering fashions.

In all honesty, this ski fashion was not particularly flattering. It made her look a bit like a top-heavy, pink Popsicle. But I figured Magnolia would discern that for herself soon enough, so all I said was, "This isn't really a ski area, I'm afraid. There's lots of snow, but no one's ever built ski runs."

"Really?" As if that meant she could relax, she unzipped the jacket. "But Ivy, what's going on with you? We followed your directions and drove straight to the house. Only to find that the place had been in some sort of ghastly conflagration. We were so afraid something terrible had happened to you! But then this nice young woman came out and told us we could find you here."

"That was Kelli Keifer. She's been letting us live in the house. She's the niece of the man who—" I broke off, not wanting to get into details about Hiram and murder just yet. Magnolia tends to fuss when I get involved in these things. "The fire was just an accident that got started in a room where a lot of inflammable trash was stored."

Magnolia frowned. "An accident? Are you sure?"

Magnolia knew all about the Braxtons, although I had yet to tell her about Boone.

"The fire department has already investigated. Probably something to do with a malfunction in the old wiring." I still didn't go along with that 100 percent, but I didn't intend to fuss at the fire department about it. I changed the subject. "I'm so glad you got here today! I don't suppose you'll be able to stay for the Roaring '20s Revue next weekend, but we're having a dress rehearsal tonight. Would you like to come?"

Magnolia looked at Geoff. Some people think flamboy-

236

ant Magnolia runs everything, but quiet Geoff is really boss behind the scenes.

"Sounds interesting. We'll go get registered at the RV park," he said.

I didn't realize until then that Charlotte had been standing there with us all the time, looking curious, and I finally collected my manners and made introductions. Charlotte echoed my invitation to the rehearsal. We were going to pretend she'd never made that snide ski bunny remark, I realized.

"And you're both in the Revue?" Magnolia asked. She sounded doubtful, because she knows I'm not the performing type.

"Oh no. I'm costumes and Ivy is props." Charlotte laughed. "But the whole production would surely fall apart without us."

Actually, that evening the whole production appeared on the edge of falling apart even with us.

By then, Magnolia and Geoff had gotten parked and hooked up at the RV park. Chris, Kelli, and Charlotte were going to the Chuckwagon Buffet for dinner, and Magnolia, Geoff, Abilene, and I met them there before the rehearsal. The Margollins were pulling a small Honda behind their motor home now, so they had transportation to get around. We made quite an exuberant group all gathered around one big table at the Chuckwagon. Chris entertained us with tales from a law school friend who now worked in L.A. and dealt with the high jinks legal affairs of various celebrities. ("Would you believe this one actress has written into all her contracts that she gets approval on bosom measurements of all the other actresses?") Magnolia had a small genealogical gaffe to admit concerning a cat named Molly that had somehow gotten written into the family line as an ancestor. Charlotte had a real-estate story about people who took their poodle along to look at a house and then rejected the house because the poodle didn't like it. ("And I'm not going to tell you how that miserable creature expressed his disapproval.") I was pleased that we made such a compatible group. Kelli didn't have much to say, but she and Chris were holding hands under the table.

After the meal Kelli and Chris went back to his office to look up a fine-print technicality on the insurance on Hiram's house, and Charlotte said, with what I thought was more pride than exasperation, "See? What did I tell you? Always wrapped up in work."

The rest of us went on to the rehearsal. I got Magnolia and Geoff settled in one of the rows of folding seats, and then Abilene helped me carry more props down from the third floor. We had backstage lined with everything from a policeman's nightstick to a phony ham.

The first thing that went wrong was when DaisyBelle wiggled her leash out of Stella's grasp, snatched a feather boa from one of the chorus-line dancers, and raced up the aisle with it. Charlotte took off in hot pursuit, her yells blasting even over the sound of music and dancing feet.

I thought I'd do my part and barricaded the end of the aisle with my arms spread wide. A great move, except that DaisyBelle didn't aim for my spread arms. She dove between my knees, and down I went. Charlotte crashed on top of me, and the three of us wallowed in the aisle like three hogs in a mud hole. DaisyBelle then made sharp little pig prints across both of us and sprinted on up the aisle, feather boa flying victoriously.

All was not lost, however. Abilene, coming down the aisle behind me, grabbed DaisyBelle. The pig squealed objections, but Abilene, who I sometimes think could calm a charging

238

hippopotamus, soothed her and carried her back to a grateful Stella, who was also running up the aisle now. They met where Charlotte and I were disentangling ourselves, and a Pig War appeared on the verge of erupting. All this time the chorus line had kept right on dancing, shimmying up a storm in their chemises and feather boas, apparently oblivious to the pig drama going on offstage. I was thinking Charlotte had been right. Pork chops it was. Maybe decorated with tiny feather boas.

But Abilene won Stella's gratitude forever, I think, by yelling over the music, "She's a really nice pig, isn't she? How old is she?"

Even I, now that DaisyBelle was safely snuggled in Abilene's arms, had to admit she looked kind of cute all wrapped up in a feather boa.

Charlotte was not so easily soothed, and she definitely did not think DaisyBelle was cute. She snatched back the boa and marched up to Lucinda, waving it like a war flag. The two of them stood face-to-face just below the stage, Charlotte's words coming through like the boom of a loudspeaker when the music and dancing suddenly ended. "Either the pig goes or I go."

"We'll work it out," Lucinda soothed. "Stella, perhaps DaisyBelle could go out to the car for the rest of rehearsal tonight?"

Stella momentarily looked as if she might grab the boa and wrap it around Charlotte's neck, but Abilene again came to the rescue.

"I'll help you take her out," she offered to Stella. "We can run the heater for a few minutes so she'll be warm." And off they went, two new buddies discussing how wonderfully sweet and intelligent potbellied pigs were.

I hoped this meant DaisyBelle was banned from the main performance, but I could see Lucinda had a problem here.

Retain the pig, lose Charlotte. Ban the pig, lose Stella. Charlotte was essential with the costumes, but Stella, singing a solo of "Five Foot Two, Eyes of Blue" couldn't be replaced in the street scene.

Magnolia was applauding the performance now as she helped me to a seat and scooted in beside me. "Ivy, that was marvelous! Is that part of the show? The audience will love it. But how did they ever train the pig to do that?"

I decided I hadn't the energy just then to tell her that the pig caper wasn't part of the regular performance. Getting run over by the duet of an escaping pig and an angry Historical Society lady is somewhat debilitating for an LOL.

The next thing that went wrong was Ben Simpson's performance as Will Rogers. He got through the monologue itself okay, sitting on his tall stool, but as he was getting off the stool something in his back locked up and he couldn't straighten up. And there the poor guy stood, looking rather like a bent toothpick.

"Is that part of the performance?" Magnolia whispered doubtfully.

"I'm afraid not." From all appearances, I'd say Ben Simpson and Will Rogers were now kaput as far as the Revue went.

The third and worst disaster happened during the final chorus-line number, the one where the dancers circled around like a revolving wagon wheel, Lulu Newman the statuesque hub of the wheel. Lulu kicked, crumpled, and didn't get up, her spangled costume puddled around her. People crowded around, but her husband shoved them aside to get to her. Poor Paul looked terrified as he knelt by his wife. A few minutes later an ambulance arrived, and the EMTs carried her out on a stretcher, Paul running along beside them.

Lucinda waved a hand as if in defeat. "Okay, everybody can go home now." She plopped into a seat beside me. "Her doctor's been telling her for months something like this could happen."

"What now?" I said.

"It'll shorten the program, but we can just cancel Ben Simpson's spot. But without Lulu the chorus line falls apart. She's like the heart of it. The centerpiece. The flagpole."

"Can't you just rearrange the line and put the tallest person in her spot?"

Lucinda shook her head. "There's too much rivalry among the others. I pick one of them, and someone else will have a hissy fit. What I need is someone new . . ." Suddenly she looked beyond me to Magnolia. "Stand up, would you please?"

Magnolia looked a little surprised, but she stood up, and I suddenly saw her through Lucinda's eyes. Tonight she was wearing a white pantsuit of some silky material that flowed around her body, and she had her trademark silk magnolia tucked in her red hair. Tall. Imposing. Regal. Yes, even statuesque.

"How about you? You want to be in the chorus line?"

Magnolia is not easy to flabbergast, but this definitely flabbergasted her. "Me?" she squeaked in a voice totally unlike her own. "Dance in the chorus line? Oh, I don't think so—"

"Yes, you. You'd be perfect. Can you dance?"

In a split second, Magnolia did an about-face. The impossible suddenly shifted to possible. "I've never performed on stage, but I did have a few dancing lessons. Back when I was . . . younger."

"Good," Lucinda said. She didn't inquire how many years ago those lessons were, but I knew. Tap dance lessons back in grade school. "You and Lulu are about the same size. Her costumes should fit you."

"But it's only a week before the performance!" I objected.

"There are all the dance routines she'd have to learn, all those steps, and Lulu was such a . . . a centerpiece of the line. She'd been doing it for years, and there's only a week—"

Magnolia drew herself up to her full height. "I think I can manage," she said loftily, with a downward glance at me, and I felt properly chastised. Confidence has never been a problem for Magnolia, and I could see that she did not appreciate my throwing roadblocks in the path of this new venture. "I'm quite musical you know, and Geoff has always said I'm light on my feet, haven't you, dear?"

Geoff blinked as if trying to remember ever making such a statement, and I tried to remember if Magnolia had ever exhibited any musical talent. All I could think was that she did play a radio reasonably well, which didn't seem terribly relevant.

"And the costumes are quite lovely, aren't they?" Magnolia added.

Yes, quite lovely. Okay, I granted reluctantly, if the clothes were right, maybe Magnolia could do it. Maybe.

Then the big problem apparently occurred to her. She looked at Geoff. "But we weren't planning to stay here in Hello that long, were we?"

Geoff came through, as he always does, even the time Magnolia decided she wanted to make a quick side trip by dogsled when they were doing genealogical research in Alaska.

"I'm sure staying a few days longer than we planned won't be a problem," he said.

"Okay, it's all set then." Lucinda stood up. "The next regular rehearsal isn't until Monday afternoon, but I'll get the girls from the chorus line together tomorrow afternoon. I'll go up to the hospital and see how Lulu is and get her costume. Can you make it tomorrow, say two o'clock?"

"Oh yes," Magnolia said. "Perhaps you have diagrams of the chorus line's movements? Something I could study?"

I was astonished by this bit of insight into the workings of a chorus line, but Lucinda didn't seem surprised. "Why, yes, I do. That's a good idea. I'll go get them."

"Actually," Magnolia confided to me as we were headed back to the cabin a few minutes later, "I've always wanted to be in a chorus line."

News to me. She'd never mentioned it. But then, I've always had a smidgen of secret desire to be one of those glamorous barrel racers in a rodeo, tearing around the arena in a rhinestone-studded cowboy hat, and I've never mentioned that to anyone either.

"I'm sure I'll be quite good at it," Magnolia added serenely. "A much better choice than skiing, actually."

I remembered a phrase of Norman's that seemed appropriate now. "Glory be."

22

I had to work on Saturday, but I rushed over to the hotel as soon as I got through at the library at four o'clock. The old building felt hollow and empty today without the usual bustle of activity in the lobby and people wandering in and out, but music and thump of feet echoed from the stage.

And yes, there was Magnolia right in the midst of it, half a head taller than anyone else, flagpoling the wagon-wheel routine as if she'd been doing it for weeks instead of only a couple of hours. The audience area was dim, but the stage brightly lit. Lucinda called directions, her hand motioning for emphasis. The taped music wasn't quite as loud today as it usually was.

"To the right now. One, two, three, kick. Back up now, keep your heads up. Kick. *Higher!* Dance like you're trying out for the Rockettes!"

Magnolia wasn't perfect, but neither was anyone else. She made some missteps, bumping hips and stepping on the foot of the dancer next to her when she went left instead of right. She was a little low and wobbly on the kicks and uncertain on the part where the dancers turned their backs to the audience and gave a little flounce of skirts. Or what would be skirts when they were in costume. But when they came to the part where the line broke into individual dancers doing a Charleston shimmy, she shimmied right in there with the best of them.

When the music ended on that routine, I gave a one-woman standing ovation.

"Okay, break time," Lucinda called. She came up to where I was sitting and dropped down beside me. She wiped a hand across her forehead as if she'd been working as hard as the dancers themselves, which she probably had. "She's going to be okay.

I was glad to hear that, for both Lucinda's and Magnolia's sakes. "How's Lulu?"

"They took her on down to Hayward instead of keeping her at the local hospital last night. She had surgery early this morning. Good specialist down there. Paul said she broke her hip in two places when she fell. Or maybe the hip broke, and that caused the fall. I understand that's how it happens sometimes."

"Osteoporosis?"

"Right. Take your calcium. She was still a little dopey from the anesthetic when I saw her a few hours ago, but the only thing she was worried about was the chorus line. I told her she could never be replaced, but we'd found someone to fill in for her. And I picked up the costume."

Diplomatic Lucinda, always thinking of how to keep someone's feelings from being hurt.

"Charlotte and Magnolia will have to get together to see if the costume needs alterations. You don't happen to have any more talented friends tucked away somewhere, do you?

I talked to Ben today too, and he's definitely out. No Will Rogers monologue."

"Did you get Charlotte and Stella's ruffled feelings about DaisyBelle taken care of?"

"I think I've convinced Stella that DaisyBelle might accidentally get hurt if something went wrong at one of the performances, and she'd be safer at home."

Diplomatic Lucinda at work again. Appealing to Stella's affection for her pig rather than laying down hostile rules. And it was true. DaisyBelle might get hurt. Charlotte definitely had mayhem in mind where the pig was concerned.

"Oh, I didn't have breakfast before I went down to Hayward, so I stopped at a little café," Lucinda said. "They have the biggest cinnamon rolls you've ever seen. Enormous! You should try the place sometime, if you get down that way. It's called the Nugget, out near the stock auction yards."

She went back to the stand she had set up just below the stage, and I sat there with my jaw going a little slack. Was her going to that café and telling me about it just some odd coincidence? Or was she subtly letting me know that she knew I knew about KaySue? Which meant what? And did this have anything to do with the fire . . . or Hiram's murder?

No way, I scoffed. My imagination working overtime again. If I could just get paid for all that overtime, I could retire with a menu of lobster and prime rib, a Dior wardrobe, and shoes from Manolo Blahnik. And, more importantly, hire a body-guard built like a Sherman army tank and thumb my nose at the Braxtons. But an overactive imagination, unfortunately, is not exactly a marketable skill. I squelched mine.

Lucinda surely wouldn't be telling me about the Nugget if she was guilty of anything. The only thing on her mind here was an oversized cinnamon roll. *Don't make more out of it than that*, I told myself.

A few minutes later, Lucinda had the chorus line back

at work. I could see Magnolia making progress even as I watched. Her kicks got higher, in line with the other dancers, and she spent less time peeking sideways at the other ladies to make certain she was doing the right steps.

"How come you aren't up there?"

The whisper spoke directly in my ear. It sounded like . . . but it couldn't be . . .

I whirled in the seat, then jumped to my feet. Even in the dim room there was no mistaking the thick, silver-white hair, break-your-heart blue eyes, and big smile. Behind him Geoff was smiling too.

"Mac!" The back of the seat was between us, but he gave me a hug over it. A rather awkward hug, although I didn't know whether the awkwardness was because of the seat or because of us.

"I don't understand." The music ended, and I lowered my voice to normal. "How . . . ? Where . . . ?"

"I told you I was coming," Mac said. He sounded mildly reproachful, as if he'd made a promise, so how come I was doubting him? "So here I am."

Yes, here he was. No knobby knees today, not in this weather. Today he wore jeans and a bulky tan vest, long-sleeved blue shirt hiding the blue tattoo of a motorcycle I knew was on his forearm. He'd shaved off the beard he'd had the last time I'd seen him. He'd looked good with it. He looked good without it. The contrast between his Florida tan and his white hair definitely put him over into Senior Hunk status.

"I was walking around the RV park, looking things over, and there he was," Geoff said. "Just pulling into the park." He spoke with a kind of pride, like a fisherman who's just landed the biggest fish of the day.

"I thought I'd find a space and get settled in before trying to locate you," Mac said. "Which turned out to be not as dif-

247

ficult as I thought it might be, since I ran into Geoff. It's good to see you, Ivy." He reached over and squeezed my hand.

"Good to see you too."

It was good to see him, yet at the same time I felt the familiar ambivalence I always feel with Mac. Ambivalence in him, ambivalence in me. The pull of attraction, the push of wariness of getting too involved.

Forget it, I told myself firmly. *He's here. Enjoy the moment.*

"What is this, anyway?" Mac motioned toward the stage as the chorus line regrouped.

I explained about the skits and chorus line, and what the proceeds from the Revue went for. "The main performances are scheduled for next Friday and Saturday evenings. Can you stay to see one of them?"

"Oh, I think I probably can. I'm in no big rush to get anywhere. You and Abilene plan to stay around here for a while?"

"She's working on another murder," Geoff said.

"What?" Mac and I yelped the word simultaneously. I was startled because I didn't know how Geoff could know about the murder, since I certainly hadn't mentioned it. Mac wasn't so much startled, I suspected, as exasperated with the news. Was that part of his ambivalence? He didn't want to get too closely involved with a woman who seemed to stumble into murders as easily as other women stumble into some new boutique selling cashmere bargains?

"Mag was talking to the people who run the RV park," Geoff said. "She mentioned that we didn't know anyone here in town except you, and they were telling her about the murder and how you were looking for the killer."

I mentally groaned. Me and my rash statement about being a criminal investigator, which had apparently taken wings around Hello. Fortunately, the music started again, loud enough to discourage conversation. The chorus line moved sideways, forward and backward, their whirls and kicks not exactly in precision time, but reasonably close to it.

After a few minutes, Mac raised his voice over the music. "They're pretty good. Like I said, why aren't you up there?"

"I'm doing props."

"I didn't know Mag could do that," Geoff said as his wife went into the shimmy that was the highlight of the final routine. I couldn't tell if he was startled, admiring, or just bemused. Probably some of all.

My reaction, even though I'd earlier had my doubts Magnolia could carry this off, was *humph*. Women can do all sorts of things men don't know they can.

That routine ended the afternoon's practice session. Magnolia accepted congratulations from the other dancers, then made her way to the steps at one side of the stage and up the aisle to us.

"You were fantastic," I said sincerely. "Awesome, as my grandniece would say."

She was a little out of breath and her color high. Magnolia isn't a couch potato, but she isn't a lightweight, and I guessed this was more activity than she'd had in some time. She put a hand on the small of her back and groaned. "I'm going to be sore all over by morning."

"Probably not as sore as when you took up horseback riding," I pointed out. "And the costumes are much nicer."

She brightened. "True."

Suddenly a thought dropped out of nowhere into my head. I turned to Mac. "How do you feel about Will Rogers?"

I expected a noncommittal answer. Who doesn't like Will Rogers's folksy humor? Then I'd try to use my persuasive powers to get him to try the monologue.

But Mac went into a cowboy slouch and put an aw-shucks grin on his face. "There's two theories about how to argue with a woman," he drawled. He pushed back a pretend hat. "Unfortunately, neither one works."

It was one of the very lines from Ben Simpson's monologue of Rogers's sayings. I stared at him in surprise.

"I was Will Rogers in some playacting thing Margarite got us into years ago. I wanted to be George Burns because Margarite was playing Gracie Allen, but they already had a George Burns, so I wound up as ol' Will."

"You must have been very good."

"Afterwards people were always after me to do the Will Rogers thing. It's been a long time though. I'm not sure I even remember any of the other lines. Oh yeah, there's this one." He went into the slouch and grin again. "I never met a man I didn't like."

I couldn't believe it. Ben Simpson had said the lines competently enough, but Mac had a warmth and style that went beyond reciting words. He made you believe he really had never met a man he didn't like. I grabbed his hand and dragged him down the aisle toward Lucinda.

"You asked if I had any other talented friends lurking in the wings? Well, I do. Meet Will Rogers."

"Hey, wait a minute," Mac protested. "I'm not getting involved in—"

"Just do it," I said.

He did the slouch and grin and hat pushed back. "After eatin' an entire bull, a mountain lion felt so proud of himself he started roarin'. He kept at it until a hunter came along and shot him. The moral is, folks, when you're full of bull, keep your mouth shut."

Lucinda gaped at him.

"Though I'm not sure those are exactly the right words," he said.

"Close enough," Lucinda breathed, as if the skies had just

opened and showered her with stardust. To me, as if I were his keeper, she said, "Will he do it?"

Mac, who is definitely his own man, wasn't about to let me decide anything for him. "Do what?"

"A local man was supposed to do a Will Rogers monologue for the Revue," I explained. "But his back gave out, and we need a replacement."

Lucinda was already rummaging in the stand where she kept everything. "I have the script in here somewhere . . ."

"Hey, wait a minute—"

"Rehearsal Monday afternoon." Lucinda handed Mac the script and then turned and gave me a hug as if I'd just solved all her problems.

I held my breath. Mac and I keep running into each other here and there across the country. There's this *something* between us. But in all honesty, I didn't really know him well enough to predict how he'd react in this situation.

Then Lucinda said, "You will do it, won't you? We really need you."

Mac smiled, and I relaxed. "Well, yeah, I guess I will. It's for a good cause and all, isn't it? Though if I'm going to do this I really think Ivy should have to be in the chorus line too."

Lucinda saved me. "That would be nice, but we can't do without her as our props person."

I started to say, "Maybe next year." Magnolia seemed to be having great fun in the chorus line. But honesty made me remain silent. Some of us are chorus girls, and some of us are props people.

Lucinda had already dashed on to a new problem. "Which reminds me. It isn't on the list, but, Props Person, we need a rope."

"A rope?"

"A rope. A cowboy-type rope. Charlotte located a photo of Will Rogers on the Internet. He always carried a rope and kind of played with it during a performance." She gave me a glance as if expecting I might pull one out of my pocket, like I'd produced Magnolia and Mac.

"We'll locate one," Mac said.

Magnolia and Geoff were sitting in the back row, and we made our way up to them. I announced Mac's part in the production. They didn't seem nearly as surprised as I was by this. They were headed back to their motor home, Geoff said.

"Ben-Gay," Magnolia groaned as she stood up. "I need Ben-Gay."

"I'll take Ivy home and see you later," Mac said.

"It isn't exactly home," I admitted. "We're staying with Kelli temporarily. There was this fire where we were living—"

"Ah yes. A fire. A fire and a murder, I believe. Ivy, we need to talk."

"Maybe you could stay for dinner?"

"Peach cobbler?"

He never forgot that peach cobbler was what I'd brought the first time we met at one of Magnolia's barbecues back in Missouri. There's something heartwarming about that kind of memory.

"Peach cobbler," I agreed.

I didn't think until we got outside just how he planned to take me home. He'd never pulled a vehicle behind his motor home as many people, now including Magnolia and Geoff, did, just had a bicycle mounted on a frame on the back of the motor home.

Now I saw what our transportation was to be. It stood angled into the curb right outside the hotel, chrome gleaming. I swallowed, hard.

Although I should have guessed, I realized. Sooner or later a man with a blue tattoo of a motorcycle on his forearm is going to show up with the real thing.

23

I'll say one thing for my first motorcycle ride. It had its heart-in-the-throat moments, but it wasn't as wild as riding with Doris Hammerstone in her Lincoln. Mac had produced a helmet for me out of a luggage box mounted on the back of the motorcycle. (Which made me wonder: how many other LOLs, with arms clasped around him as mine were, was he giving rides to?) I was both chilled and windblown when we arrived at the log cabin, but it was a short trip, and all was well otherwise.

I slid off the padded seat, feeling a little shaky anyway. "You carry the motorcycle with you on the motor home now?"

"I had a special rack built on back for it, with a little ramp so I can zip right up on it. No lifting." Mac opened the luggage box, and I dropped the helmet inside. He smiled as if he knew what I'd been thinking. "In case you're wondering, I bought the helmet especially for you just before I left Florida."

"How did you even know I'd ride on this thing?" I don't know much about motorcycles. This one was relatively small, certainly not as big and mean as some I've seen, but it had a lot of racy-looking chrome.

Mac grinned. "Ivy Malone, you're the woman who jumps into murder and mayhem the way some women jump into a shopping spree. I didn't think you'd turn down this new adventure."

Hmmm. I decided to let that one go.

Kelli had given Abilene and me each a key, and I led the way inside the cabin, where Koop and Sandra Day met us. Do cats remember people? I'd swear Koop remembered Mac from when he'd visited us in Oklahoma. As soon as Mac sat down, Koop jumped on his shoulder, rubbed his whiskers on Mac's ear, and revved up his purr.

I started making the peach cobbler immediately, though I had to do it with canned peaches, of course. We caught up on what Mac's daughters and their husbands and the grandchildren were doing, and the travel article assignments he'd done about sponges in Florida and the theme park in Texas. I told him about my job setting up books for the new Historical Society library and a little more about the Revue and the people in it.

Finally, as I was checking the cobbler in the oven to see how it was coming along, he said, "I do believe you're avoiding telling me about this murder. And the fire."

"Not avoiding," I protested. "It's just that it's no big deal. And you seem so . . . disapproving. It's not that I go around looking for murders, you know," I added defensively. "I just kind of . . . stumble into them."

"Ivy, I admire your sleuthing abilities. I'm amazed by them, in fact. So it isn't really disapproval—" He broke off as if checking that statement for validity. "Well, maybe it is disapproval in a way. But it's only because I worry about you."

"Worry? About me?" I was astonished.

"Yes, worry. Because murderers are dangerous. And you always seem to wind up in some weird situation."

Truth in that, I had to admit. But the worry element was a new and not displeasing thought. You don't worry about someone unless you care, do you? While I was contemplating that, the phone rang.

I had assumed both Kelli and Abilene would be home soon, but this call was from Kelli saying she and Chris were going to have dinner with Charlotte, and she wouldn't be home until later. Then, no more than a minute after that, Abilene called and said she was going with Dr. Sugarman out to a ranch to look at a sick horse.

So there we were. Just Mac and me. Although that was not to hold true for long.

I got out pork chops to cook for dinner, feeling a little guilty about my earlier hostile thoughts toward DaisyBelle. I really wouldn't want to see her cute little chops in my frying pan. I was peeling potatoes, Mac sitting at the kitchen table keeping me company, when the back door rattled under the pounding of a fist.

Someone coming to the back door wasn't unusual. It was the entrance everyone used. But the pounding . . . "Now who could that be?"

I wiped my hands on a kitchen towel and went to the door. I'd no sooner cautiously opened it than I was engulfed in an enormous, smoke-and-garlic-scented bear hug.

Norman drew back and looked down at me. "Ms. Ivy! Glory be! You're all right! I went over to Hiram's house lookin' for you, and I saw all that mess from a fire, so I come over here to see Kelli and find out what happened to you—" He broke off when he looked over my shoulder and saw Mac.

I glanced back too. Mac had risen from the chair, his expression somewhere between alarmed and puzzled. My first inclination was to ease Norman politely out to the Dorf,

255

which was sitting in the driveway, and send him on his way. Which wasn't possible, I realized with an inner groan, because the Dorf stood there as lopsided as a woman with a missing high heel.

"There's a flat tire on your pickup."

"Yep. Found that tire layin' along the road a few months back, so I figure I got my money's worth out of it." He grinned cheerfully.

I wouldn't simply have sent Norman on his way anyway, I realized. He was a good guy, in his own eccentric way, and I couldn't do that to him.

"Come on in, Norman," I said. "I'll introduce you and Mac."

Norman clumped in, his beat-up old Nikes leaving a trail of ashes from the house, and I introduced them. Mac MacPherson, Norman—Norman what? I realized I'd never heard anything past Norman. Nutty Norman.

Norman held out his hand. "Norman Pierson. You kin of Ms. Ivy's?" He sounded hopeful.

"No. No kin." Not a common word in Mac's vocabulary, I suspected, but he used it as if it were. "Just . . . good friends."

The two men regarded each other warily. Norman hadn't worn his suit today, so apparently he hadn't intended to take me to the Café Russo again. Tonight he was wearing black denim pants, ragged around the bottom, and a heavy jacket a couple sizes too large for him. Cold or wind had fluffed his beard to electrified-cat proportions, which made his ponytail look skinny as a twisted string hanging down his back.

"Did you come to town for some special reason?" I asked. "I hope you're not ill?"

"No, I'm fine. I had to come in to the hardware store. Ginger died, but my shovel handle broke, and I couldn't dig any more till I got a new one. I brought you some eggs. They're out in the Dorf."

Mac looked even more puzzled, and there were, I realized, various elements in those statements that were as mysterious as some Dead Sea language unless you knew Norman. A Dorf. A dead Ginger. Well, I'd explain some other time.

"I'm sorry to hear about Ginger," I said.

"What about that fire?"

I explained about the blaze in the trash room that had expanded to engulf the whole back side of the house, with the fire department's conclusion about what had started it. "So then Kelli invited Abilene and me to stay with her here at the cabin for a while."

All the while we were talking I could practically hear Mac's puzzled thoughts: *Who is this guy? How come he shows up and hugs you like some long-lost sweetheart?*

Okay, I didn't want Mac thinking Norman was some sort of love interest, though that bear hug might take some explaining. But neither did I want Norman's feelings hurt thinking I was embarrassed about him and anxious to get rid of him. So I did the only thing I could think to do.

"Would you like to stay for dinner, Norman? I'm fixing pork chops and gravy, and there's peach cobbler for dessert." I'd already put on a couple of extra chops in case Abilene came home hungry, so there was plenty of food for one more.

Norman's eyes lit up. "Glory be, I sure would like that, Ms. Ivy."

Norman immediately took off his jacket and sat down at the table across from Mac, ashes fluttering around his feet. Green suspenders held up the black pants, and his sweatshirt had a NASA logo. And a few unidentifiable stains. I put on an extra place setting and poured coffee for both men. Koop, objecting to Norman's cigarette scent, pulled one of his stiff-tailed departures. Mac eyed Norman speculatively.

Maybe this would work out just fine, I decided. Arousing a bit of jealousy is a rather immature ploy, but it wasn't as if I'd set it up on purpose, and maybe it wouldn't hurt for Mac to see another man was interested. Even if that man wasn't exactly Senior Hunk of the Year.

Was that what happened? Guess.

"You ain't from around here, are you?" Norman inquired of Mac.

Norman had this peculiar blend of reasonably correct and considerably flawed English in his speech, and it was odd, but I was never quite certain which was the real Norman. Was he basically uneducated but had picked up some correct wording from all the reading he did? Or was he a lot educated and deliberately plugged himself into hermit-from-the-hills speech much of the time?

"No. I'm traveling," Mac said. "I just got in from Florida."

"Florida, eh? I was there, long time ago, down in those Keys. Quite a place. All those bridges hoppin' from island to island."

That surprised me. I'd never pictured Norman as having a life before his hermit existence out at the mine, and certainly not one that had taken him to the Florida Keys. This obviously interested Mac too.

"I didn't get down to the Keys, but I wish I had. I'll have to go back someday. I spent most of my time around Tarpon Springs."

"Hey, I worked on a sponge boat outta there for a while."

And they were off, talking sponges, boats, Florida Keys, and motorcycles. Then they got started on the Lucky Queen and its history, which brought in Hiram McLeod, of course, and soon they were into his mysterious murder.

I sat there thinking, *Well, this is good, isn't it?* No unpleasant jealousy scene, just friendly talk, like two old buddies who haven't seen each other in months. I wouldn't have wanted them pulling guns and having an old-fashioned shootout or fistfight over me, would I? Of course not. Although would it have hurt if one of them exhibited just a *smidgen* of jealousy or hint of competitiveness for my affections? But neither did. Their appetites were just fine too. They both chowed down on pork chops and gravy as if they hadn't had a solid meal in days, passing platters back and forth and talking all the time.

Then I sighed. I should have known this was what would happen. I already knew Mac was the kind of guy who could talk to anybody and found everybody interesting. No reason to think he'd be any different with Norman. And Norman, for all his peculiar ways, had a core of what I could only call gentlemanliness.

"Good peach cobbler, Ivy," Mac said over dessert.

"The best," Norman echoed.

So there it was, a unanimous vote of approval from my non-suitors.

Afterward, they went out together to fix Norman's flat tire. Norman came in to wash up, and then I walked out to the Dorf with him to pick up the eggs he'd brought. I noted he didn't do his little whirl and hop as he had when leaving the Café Russo. Perhaps that ritual was necessary only after being in some public place.

"Right nice fellow you've got there, Ms. Ivy," Norman said.

"He's not my . . . We're just friends."

"He's thinkin' more than that."

"What makes you say that?"

Norman tapped his temple. "A man can tell."

I'd have had more faith in that knowledgeable-sounding statement if that tap on the temple hadn't been the same

259

gesture he'd used to indicate how he contacted the aliens flying around in their UFO.

"You're kind of soft on him too, ain't you?" Norman asked.

"Just friends," I repeated.

"Well, I'll be going now. But if he don't treat you right, you let me know, okay?" He momentarily got an almost ferocious scowl around his eyes.

"Okay. I'm glad you came, Norman." And I was, I really was.

He twisted and jumped and flung himself through the window of the Dorf but sat there without turning on the engine, something obviously on his mind. I didn't know whether to encourage him or not.

Finally he said, "I figure I oughtta mention something, Ms. Ivy. I didn't want to say anything inside, 'cause it's kinda personal. You might even say it speaks ill of the dead. And Hiram was my friend and always done right by me."

I had no idea where this was going, so I just shifted the sack of eggs from one arm to the other.

"The thing is, when I was over at the house lookin' for you, I went inside, trying to figure out what happened. The front door's locked, but anyone could go in the back way, like I did. You might mention that to Kelli. There's a lot of valuable antique stuff in there yet."

"I'll do that. But I think she plans to have it boarded up temporarily within the next few days."

"Anyway, I saw them fancy carousel horses, like on merry-go-rounds, there in the bedroom. And they reminded me of something." Pause. "Someone."

I made a neutral murmur.

"This is the part that's kind of hard, Ms. Ivy, because it don't speak well of Hiram. But he had a girlfriend on the side, someone besides Lucinda. Which I never thought was right, not right at all." It was hard to tell what his face was doing under the beard, but his brow wrinkled with disapproval.

"He told you about her?"

Norman nodded. "One night when we were drinkin' tequila. The reason this come to mind now is that he said she was just crazy about merry-go-round horses. And I seen them carousel horses, and I figure he must of bought 'em for her. So now I'm wondering . . . well, I'm not quite sure what I'm wonderin'."

"He'd never mentioned the carousel horses to you?"

"No, and I never saw 'em at the house before. Which makes me think he hadn't had 'em very long."

"Did Lucinda know about this other woman?"

"Well, now, I've wondered about that."

"Did Hiram intend to abandon her and marry the other woman?"

"I've wondered about that too."

"Or maybe he was having a final fling before he married Lucinda?"

"Could be."

Now that he'd told me this bad thing about Hiram, Norman seemed reluctant to commit himself on what it might mean.

"Did he ever tell you this woman's name?"

"No. Never did. All he said was she had a real spitfire temper. It tickled him, I think. He was laughin' about it 'cause she'd got mad and thrown a bowl of soup at him."

"For some particular reason? Or just because she liked to throw soup?"

"He said she had a jealous streak." Unlike two men of my acquaintance, I thought irrelevantly. "Lucinda could get a little hot too, of course. Though I don't know as she ever threw things."

No, but she wasn't above acting on her feelings when she

261

got irked, as Kelli said she'd done when she'd once fed Hiram's dinner to a couple of miner bums. And maybe she'd do a lot more than that if she really got angry. More than ever, those carousel horses in the bedroom, especially if only recently purchased, suggested that Hiram had planned to dump Lucinda and marry KaySue, with the horses a wedding surprise for her. Not a pleasant surprise for Lucinda.

I jumped to the bottom line. "Do you think this could have something to do with Hiram's death? Or the fire?"

"You said the fire was from bad wiring. An accident."

"Hiram's death wasn't."

He nodded, his expression troubled. He started the engine. Pop. Bang. Burst of smoke. "Well, I'm just thinking, you should take care, Ms. Ivy. Funny things goin' on. People ain't always what you think they are."

So very true. "I'll be careful."

He'd been so somber with what he had to say, but all of a sudden he brightened. "But I figure you'll be okay, with Mac here lookin' out for you now." He gave me a little wave, not a heartbroken wave, I noted, and the Dorf roared backward out of the driveway. At the street he braked to yell, "Thanks for dinner, Ms. Ivy. You tell Mac he wants to come out to the mine any time and look around, he's welcome."

"Thanks, Norman."

The Dorf drove off, with a rattle like a junkyard symphony, one taillight winking with a peculiar irregularity, as if it might be receiving messages from outer space. I went back inside. Mac was in the bathroom washing off grease and dirt from fixing the flat tire. He came out of the bathroom with his sleeves rolled up.

"Who's Ginger?" he asked.

"One of Norman's chickens. They're all named for movie stars, past and present. He never kills them to eat, so when they die he buries them. He has a little cemetery." I wondered if he had a funeral for them. I hadn't thought of that before.

Mac didn't guffaw or say anything to make fun of Norman. I was, in fact, prepared to give a fiery defense of Norman's ways, if he did. But all he did was say reflectively, "Ms. Ivy. You like that?"

"It's a Norman exclusive, if you don't mind." I paused, thinking. "Some people think he could be the one who murdered Hiram."

"Really? I thought he sounded rather fond of the guy. What do you think?"

"I consider everyone a suspect."

Mac threw up his hands. "But I just got here!"

"Okay, everyone but you is a suspect."

Mac laughed. "He's an interesting guy. More to him than you might think at first glance."

That sounded more curious and thoughtful than jealous. Which might have been disappointing except that I'd lost interest in the jealousy angle. What interested me now was that Norman had seen the same possibilities in the Lucinda-Hiram-KaySue triangle that I had. Both women had tempers. Both women were capable of acting on those tempers. One of them could have done him in.

And might not be shy about doing the same to me if I looked like a problem.

24

We all went to church together the next morning, all except Kelli. She and Chris, who were spending more time than ever together, were going to brunch at the Chuckwagon. She'd developed an I-have-a-secret glow about her, which made me suspect she and Chris would soon have an important announcement to make. I was glad for her, even though I hadn't yet been able to warm up to Chris myself.

Magnolia and Geoff, Mac, Abilene, and I all went, using the Margollins' car for transportation. Dr. Sugarman joined us at the church, and we filled up a good share of a pew. I felt gratified by how raptly our whole lineup listened to the message about the dangers of false teachers, taken from Jude, a short book of the New Testament that is too often overlooked.

Afterward, with sudden inspiration, I asked Dr. Sugarman if he had a cowboy rope Mac could use for the Will Rogers monologue.

"Sure. I've got several old ropes out in the barn. I used

to do some calf roping in college rodeos back when I was in vet school. Come on over after church, and I'll find one for you."

I looked at Mac.

"Sounds good to me," he said. "Although I have to admit I don't know one end of a rope from the other."

My own thought was, *How much can there be to know?* Although that was to prove overly optimistic.

We arranged that Dr. Sugarman would take Abilene and me back to the house to change clothes, and Abilene would go on with him to his place. They were going out to treat the sick horse again that afternoon. Mac would go back to the RV park with the Margollins, get his motorcycle, and come by for me. At the cabin, I fixed a quick sandwich lunch for Dr. Sugarman, Abilene, and me. Dr. Sugarman, ever the vet, gave both cats a quick going-over while he waited for us.

Today, when Mac picked me up, I was better prepared for a motorcycle ride. I'd put on thick socks, long underwear under my jeans, a heavy sweatshirt over my sweater, plus a wool scarf wrapped around my neck, and gloves lined with fake fur for my hands. And I recklessly dabbed on a few drops of that perfume grandniece Sandy had sent me a while back, the Catch Your Man stuff. I was pretty sure I smelled good, although I was afraid I looked like a short, overstuffed teddy bear. For whatever reason, Mac nodded approvingly.

Dr. Sugarman had given me directions on how to get to his house, which was about a mile out of town, and I yelled them to Mac as we rode. You don't talk in normal tones on a moving motorcycle, I discovered. I also discovered I didn't really have to wrap my arms around Mac. Bracing myself against the sturdy backrest and just grabbing his jacket lightly made me feel quite stable and secure.

Hmmm. I decided I'd pretend I'd never discovered that. Wrapping my arms around him felt too good to discard. I actually managed to enjoy riding the motorcycle this day. It puts you right out there with the fresh scent of snow and trees, the shrieks and laughter of children sledding on a hill, plus the discovery that there were odd pockets of warmer air even on this cold day that you never noticed in a car.

Dr. Sugarman's house was bigger than I expected, two stories with a covered deck and cozy-looking dormers on the second floor. There were no flowers at this time of year, and the lawn showed brown and flattened between patches of snow, but rototilled spaces that were surely flowerbeds in spring edged the walkway to the front door. Did flowerbeds signify a woman's presence recently? I wondered if Abilene had asked Dr. Sugarman if he'd ever been married. Knowing Abilene, I guessed not.

Dr. Sugarman and Abilene were headed out to the barn when we zoomed into the yard on the motorcycle. A couple of big chestnut horses trotted along a corral fence, tails flagged high. Abilene had mentioned Dr. Sugarman had taken in two other horses to care for in their old age, and they were out in a larger pasture area. One had a decided limp, but it snorted and kicked like a colt when the motorcycle pulled into the yard. Cats perched on the corral fence, peeked out of the barn, and played tag on the deck. An Australian shepherd with white eyes and a three-legged poodle came over to check us out.

"Glad you found the place okay," Dr. Sugarman called.

Inside the roomy barn, he led us to a tack room, neat but not fanatically clean. He examined several ropes, chose one, and tossed a loop at an upright bale of hay in the alleyway. The coils of rope in his left hand unfurled smoothly, and he jerked the loop taut around the bale. He coiled the rope again before handing it to Mac. "Need a roping lesson?"

"I don't have to rope anything. I just need to know how to

266

keep from accidentally hanging myself with the thing. I practically choked myself hanging up a clothesline one time."

Dr. Sugarman laughed. "It's not like a gun. It isn't going to go off accidentally. Say, why don't you two ride out to the Everlys' ranch with us? Even if a sick horse doesn't interest you, it's a nice drive out to their valley."

I made up my mind I was going even if Mac decided to go back to town, but without a moment's hesitation he said, "Sure. Interesting country around here."

We headed for Dr. Sugarman's big pickup then, and, with the prerogative of LOLs, I came right out and asked, "Have you ever been married—" I started to call him Dr. Sugarman, because Abilene always did, but I remembered he'd once said to call him Mike. Which seemed like a good idea, since I was getting into nitty-gritty nosiness here. Unable to think of more tactful phrasing, I repeated the question. "Have you ever been married, Mike?"

He looked a little surprised, since there had been nothing leading up to the subject, but he said, "No, never have. I came close once when I was in vet school, but we both backed off when I realized she was thinking city vet clinic for lapdogs, and she realized I was thinking country clinic for anything four-legged. And since then . . ." He didn't finish the sentence, but he gave Abilene a sideways glance that I thought was meaningful. She, of course, was busy petting one of the cats.

Dr. Sugarman and Abilene sat up front, Mac and I in the backseat of the king cab. Up front, they talked about the sick horse's problem, something called impaction colic. Abilene was fascinated, of course, asking questions about various medications she'd been reading about. I knew that's what she did in her spare time at the office: read Dr. Sugarman's old vet books. But I had to admit, when it finally registered to me what impaction colic was, that I had only limited interest in what boiled down to a severe case of horse constipation. Though I was glad for the horse's sake that Dr. Sugarman seemed so knowledgeable and competent, since I don't like to see any creature suffer and this could be life-threatening.

The gravel road out to the ranch passed several other ranches, some with prosperous-looking red barns and expansive houses, some with rickety sheds and a single-wide trailer. A trio of high-spirited horses raced around one snowy pasture, and a black bull regarded us with kingly superiority from atop a small rise in another field. Dr. Sugarman pointed out some long-abandoned mining shacks clinging to a steep hillside, and a pair of snowmobiles whizzed across an open field.

In spite of the interesting sights, I was glad when we reached the Everlys' ranch. I'd dressed for motorcycle riding, not the warm interior of a pickup, and I was beginning to feel like a hot dog steaming in a bun. I was also afraid an overheated-LOL scent might be canceling out the Catch Your Man.

Dr. Sugarman and Abilene went off to run a tube into the horse's stomach where they would let off gas and administer mineral oil, not a process I particularly wanted to watch. Mac had brought his newly acquired rope, and we strolled over to the fence where a half dozen cud-chewing steers didn't bother to stand up when we approached.

Mac made a loop with the rope as Dr. Sugarman had done and tossed it at a fence post, but he neglected to let loose of the coil, and the loop flopped around his feet. Where he immediately got a foot entangled in it, then a leg, and finally nearly managed to hog-tie himself before he got out. I could see how the clothesline had given him problems.

"What did ol' Will do with the rope onstage anyway?" Mac grumbled as his second toss went no better than the first.

"I'm not sure. Didn't he kind of spin the loop back and forth or something?"

Mac tried that, only to find the rope wound around shoulders and knees like a web trying to strangle him. The rope had appeared cooperatively limber and manageable in Dr. Sugarman's hands, but now it seemed to have gone stiff and contrary, with a stubborn will of its own.

"Perhaps this rope didn't come with the spinning feature," I suggested, trying to be tactful. Mac's look suggested I knew even less about ropes than he did. True. I tried again. "You know the old saying, practice makes perfect."

"At least I do have most of the monologue learned."

"Already?"

He launched into a handful of Will Rogers's folksy sayings, and again I marveled at how smoothly he slipped into the persona. Although somehow I doubted the real Will whopped himself on the head with the rope hard enough to make him blink, as Mac did.

"Good thing I never wanted to be a cowboy," he muttered.

Altogether, in spite of the unruly rope, it was a most enjoyable day. With a most satisfactory good-night kiss at the end of it.

Monday afternoon was another rehearsal, and it was a hectic time because Lucinda wanted it done with a full setup of props. So I lugged props onstage for each skit, offstage after the skit was over, plus dashed up to the third floor numerous times because some little thing always seemed to be missing. Then someone bumped into the lamp in the parlor scene skit and smashed the shade. A loose board popped up and ripped one of the spangled costumes. Doris prompted one of the Stooges with the wrong lines. Tempers flared several times.

Mac's performance went off great as far as his lines went, not so great with his rope performance. It tangled around his feet. It snagged on his belt buckle. It wrapped around his body and knocked his hat off. Everyone was tittering rather than laughing outright, because this wasn't the part that was supposed to be funny, and Mac looked thoroughly frustrated.

The chorus line had a few glitches too, with the revolving wagon wheel looking more like the flat tire on Norman's Dorf. One woman seemed to have forgotten the difference between left and right, and soon the whole lineup was more like a traffic jam than a chorus line. Stella had a cold, and her song in the street scene sounded as if she was gargling the words underwater.

Lucinda dropped her head on her director's stand at the end of the rehearsal. "I keep telling myself that it's always like this, and there's nothing to worry about. Always, just a few days before performance, it seems like everything is falling apart. But then it all works out okay."

I wanted to say that I was sure it would all work out okay this year too, but my tongue tangled in doubt because the chorus line was beginning to look more like a choreographed riot and the skits as if a traitor had sabotaged the scripts. But I put the best spin I could on it and said hopefully, "Everyone's working very hard. Mac says he can fix the lamp shade."

Which he did, with duct tape that he ran out to the hardware store and bought. Though I have to admit I half-expected Charlotte to produce a roll of it from her purse.

A full dress rehearsal was scheduled for Wednesday, but Tuesday everyone got a day off to recuperate from Monday's near fiasco. Mac and I spent the morning wandering through Hello's antique and gift shops. Posters about the coming Revue were up everywhere, prints made from a photo of a previous year's chorus line in an organized moment. In the afternoon Magnolia decided she wanted to drive down to Hayward because someone in the RV park had told her about a yarn shop there and she needed some special yarn for a project at the house in Phoenix. She and Geoff invited Mac and me to ride along.

When we reached Hayward, Mac and Geoff headed for a car parts store. Something about needing windshield wipers and spark plugs, although I suspected they were just avoiding yarn. Posters about the Revue were in windows everywhere here too. I went with Magnolia to the yarn shop, but I'm about as good with yarn as Mac is with rope, and I slipped away for a quick side trip to the Nugget. I'd been wondering if KaySue had come up with any ideas about who'd murdered Hiram, and I also wanted to see if she was doing okay. And, though she wasn't high on my list of suspects, she hadn't slipped off it.

In midafternoon, business was light in the Nugget, and I found KaySue drinking a soda and leafing through a *People* magazine at the far end of the counter. She was still wearing the carousel earrings. I walked up behind her and tugged her long blond braid lightly.

"Hi, KaySue. Remember me?"

She swiveled on the counter stool. "Hey, I sure do." I was surprised at how pleased she seemed to see me.

"I just happened to be down this way with some friends, so I thought I'd drop in and see you."

"Want a cup of coffee?"

"No, thanks anyway. Is everything going okay?"

"I guess." She shrugged in a so-so way. "I've been out with a guy who works at the Ford dealership a couple times." She

271

wrinkled her nose. "But he's no Hiram. They haven't caught Hiram's killer yet?"

"Not yet. There was also a fire at the house the other night. It destroyed the back side of the house. Abilene and I had to move out."

"Why would someone want to burn the house down?"

The first question most people asked was about how the fire got started. But KaySue's first thought was that the fire had been set on purpose. Hmmm. Interesting.

"The fire department says it was probably caused by the old wiring. But I keep thinking maybe there's something in the house that the killer doesn't want found, and the fire wasn't an accident."

"Like what?"

My turn to shrug.

"I think Lucinda knew about me," she said slowly. She twisted her feet childlike around the stool's center pedestal and fingered the thick braid hanging over her shoulder.

"What makes you think that?"

"I hadn't thought about it before you were here last time, but then I got to thinking about something Hiram said once, not long before he was killed. That he'd bought something special for me, something I was really going to like, and he thought maybe she'd found out about it."

Carousel horses. Lucinda had said she hadn't known anything about them until after Hiram's death, but was that true?

"And so you think . . . ?"

She jumped to her feet, blue eyes blazing in one of those spitfire swings of temper I'd heard about. "Sometimes I think I'll just go up there and face her down. Do whatever it takes to get the truth out of her about how she killed him!"

She loomed over me, tall and blond and strong, a Viking in a mini skirt, and I felt a spurt of alarm at what she might do. Something stronger than throwing soup in Lucinda's face, I was afraid.

"Oh no, KaySue, I don't think that would be a good idea." I pushed her back toward the stool because she looked as if she might dash out to her pickup and roar up to Hello right now. "If she's guilty the police will figure it out. Don't do anything you might regret." As an afterthought I added, "Lucinda's taken karate lessons, you know."

"I'm not afraid of her," KaySue scoffed. "And if she did kill Hiram, she shouldn't get away with it."

I agreed with that, but I still wasn't ready to erase KaySue's name completely from my list. She might be naïve, but she wasn't dumb, and she looked at me as if she guessed what I was thinking.

"You don't think I went up there and started the fire, do you?"

"The thought has occurred to me," I admitted.

"Why would I do that?"

"Maybe Hiram dumped you, and you wrote him a threatening letter before you went up there and killed him. And you were afraid we might find that letter too, and it would be quite incriminating. So you decided you'd better make sure it was destroyed."

It was a possibility that had just occurred to me. She blinked once as if flabbergasted by my accusation, then blinked harder to hold back the tears glistening in her eyes. I felt a stab of remorse. She was really upset that I'd think such a thing.

Or maybe she was a really great actress . . .

"That's crazy," she said finally with a vehement shake of head that swung the braid like a blond whip. "He didn't dump me. We loved each other. He had something . . . something nice for me."

I knew that to be true. And in all honesty it did make my accusation look a little far out. Unless Hiram had planned the carousel horses as a parting gift because he was going to marry Lucinda . . .

"You're on Lucinda's side, aren't you?" she accused suddenly. She planted her fists on her hips. "Because you're her age, and I'm not. And you don't figure anyone as young as I am could really be in love with someone Hiram's age!"

I also blinked, uneasily wondering if there could be truth in that. Ageism in reverse? "I'm not on anyone's side. I just want to find out who killed Hiram."

"It wasn't me!" She squared her shoulders, her eyes blue ice now. "And don't come back again."

She turned and stalked off toward the kitchen, exit punctuated by the swinging of the door behind her. I was sorry our brief relationship had ended this way.

I was also sorry that deep down inside, I was now almost certain Lucinda was the killer. I'd tried my best to wiggle around it, but there it was.

The full dress rehearsal started at one o'clock Wednesday afternoon. There were several crises. The tape with the music for Stella's "Five Foot Two, Eyes of Blue" number in the street scene exploded.

"A tape can't explode," Lucinda protested.

The woman handling the sound equipment lifted a handful of stuff that certainly looked like exploded tape. "No?"

The chorus line did fairly well, except when a tumble by a woman on one end rippled through the line like falling dominos. Except the ripple stopped at Magnolia, who stood firm as a redheaded statue.

I tried not to think about murder every time I looked at Lucinda. A killer? No, she couldn't be. Yet the thoughts wouldn't go away. Instead of seeing her waving her hand to direct the chorus line, I saw her waving something behind Hiram's head, bringing it down hard . . .

Someone produced a second tape for Stella. Her cold was gone now, and she no longer sounded as if she was gargling underwater. Good. That much was encouraging.

But Mac's battle with the rope was no more successful than before. Finally he tossed it aside in disgust. Lucinda waved him on. But a few moments later a voice broke into the monologue.

"Bring back the rope!" The hoarse yell boomed from Doris Hammerstone, in that voice that sounded more longshoreman than LOL. She pounded her fist on her clipboard. "Bring back the rope!"

Someone else took up the cry. "It's better with the rope!"

Hey, I realized, they were right! Maybe getting tangled in the rope wasn't authentic Will Rogers, but with Mac it added a charm all his own. The cowboy bumbler spouting words of wisdom. I added my own cry. "Bring back the rope!"

Lucinda, with a kind of resignation, waved toward the rope, and Mac retrieved it. "Just do whatever comes natural," she said.

What came natural to Mac with a rope was getting his feet, arms, and neck tangled in it, and he started adding a few comments of his own to those of the original Will. "This thing's as tricky as a politician writing a new law, ain't it?" he suggested.

About that time, I made a decision. I was not going to think about murder and Lucinda now. After the Revue, yes, I'd have to do something about my suspicions then. I wasn't certain what. Talk to Kelli, probably. But Lucinda wasn't going to take off and disappear in the next few days, so there'd be time enough after the Revue.

Then, two things happened.

The first was that evening when Kelli came home and handed Abilene several folded sheets of paper. "My friend Linda in Texas faxed that to me today."

Abilene unfolded the pages. She got a strange look on her face, a light of happiness and yet uncertainty too, as if the pages were a wonderful gift, but she wasn't certain it belonged to her. "This is it? It's all legal?"

"It's all legal," Kelli assured her. "She'll send a certified copy in the mail, but this says it all."

Abilene read the papers and then handed them to me. Yes, there it was. The divorce was final. It took everything of any material value away from her and gave her nothing, but I knew that didn't matter to her because it gave her what really mattered: an end to any tie to Boone. I went over and wrapped my arms around her in a big hug. She wiped a knuckle below her eye.

"I kept thinking somehow . . . somehow it would all fall through. That maybe some unknown law would turn up that said I had to go back to him."

The tears weren't unhappiness, I knew. Nor were they joy. They were simply relief. The long nightmare of being married to Boone Morrison was over.

"You're single, girl," Kelli said. "Announce it to the world! Celebrate!"

No celebration, I knew. No announcement. Just that sweeping sense of relief for Abilene. But I did hope she'd tell Mike Sugarman. One question, however.

"And this all happened without Boone ever knowing where Abilene is?" I asked Kelli.

"Linda said she had no contact with either Boone or his lawyer. She watched the local newspaper, and when she saw the divorce listed in the court proceedings she got a copy of the decree directly from the court records. I don't see any way anyone could use any of that to trace Abilene."

I hoped that was true, and I so much wanted to believe the divorce meant Boone had abandoned the hunt for Abilene. I could see a new day dawning for her now, and from the look on her face she could too.

"I have an announcement of my own to make," Kelli added. She tried to sound offhand, but a whoop of glee burst through. "Chris and I have set the date! June 17."

She lifted her left hand, and I was surprised to see not an enormous diamond but a small one in an old-fashioned white-gold setting. "It was his grandmother's. Char said she'd been saving it for him to give to the right girl."

Okay, Chris Sterling went up a notch in my estimation. I'd thought him the kind of guy who'd have to advertise his superiority and success with a flashy car, big house, and certainly a show-off diamond for his fiancée, but this was really sweet. And not only nice of Charlotte but a big vote of confidence from her too, in passing the family ring along to Kelli.

I gave Kelli a hug. "Congratulations!"

"We haven't even started to think guest list yet, but you're both invited, of course."

I didn't want to throw any wet blanket on her joy, but I had to ask, "You're sure, Kelli? Really sure?"

Her smile would have lit up the dark tunnel of a mine. "Really sure."

The next thing happened the following day at the library. Charlotte and a woman I hadn't met before, Anne Perkins, were on desk duty this day. About three o'clock, Charlotte brought over an older man who wanted to check out a book from Hiram's library. We weren't set up for loaning books out yet, but I let him have it, *An Old-Timer's Memories of Early*

Colorado Days. I put a due date on a slip to stick in the book and made a note of his name, address, and driver's license number for myself.

He seemed tickled by my precautions, as if I thought he might be planning to grab the book and hightail it across the border. He came up with a tale about some guy he'd known who'd done that after embezzling a fortune, then went on with reminiscences about Hiram and good times they'd had prospecting together.

"Even though he was already rich, Hiram never gave up hoping he might strike another one like the Lucky Queen."

"He wanted more riches?"

"Oh, I suppose. Who doesn't? But mostly, I think, he just wanted the thrill of finding a big new vein of gold. He told me once he'd invested money with some guy searching for a sunken galleon in the Caribbean, and he sounded as if he'd like to go off to sea and help search himself."

I asked the question I always asked. "Have you any idea who might have killed him?"

"Not a clue. Though it was something about money, I figure. Isn't it most always about money?"

The old guy may have been right about Hiram mostly wanting the thrill of finding some new treasure, but from what I'd seen, he was plenty fond of money and making more. I'd set aside a whole stack of books he'd collected on assets and investing, and I decided now that I'd set up a separate section on one of the shelves for these books.

I brought a load of the books to my desk and started the process of cataloging them on the computer. Some of the titles were stuffy and serious: *Understanding Investing in Futures* and *Sound Investment Strategies*. But there was also *Investing for Dummies*, and *Scammers and You: Don't Be the Scammee!*

I was intrigued by that one. I opened the book. Actually it fell open by itself because several envelopes had been stuffed

278

inside. When I saw the return address and foreign stamps, I felt a strange flutter of misgiving.

By the time I'd read the first letter, I was startled. By the second letter I was stunned. And by the third letter I knew this changed everything.

25

I glanced up when I heard footsteps approaching my desk. I hastily jammed the letters and envelopes back in the book.

"Charlotte," I said a little breathlessly. Charlotte was the last person I wanted to see.

"I was just wondering if I need to come up with a costume for Mac's monologue."

"No. He said he has some old clothes that will do fine. And he picked up a scruffy-looking hat and cowboy boots at a secondhand store."

"He's such a natural as Will Rogers. I'm especially glad, for Lucinda's sake, that he showed up when he did. So many things have gone wrong with the Revue this year. But that rope bit is a stroke of genius. He just lights up the stage with it! I laughed until my side hurt." She laughed now, as if just thinking about Mac and his wayward rope tickled her.

I nodded, still clutching the book, my own smile anemic. I hoped nothing was sticking out of the book. Especially nothing showing the name or address of the sender.

Charlotte leaned over to look at me more closely. "Are you okay? You look a little feverish."

Did what I knew show like a rash on my face? Was it sprouting in a big wart on my nose? I did feel warm. Perspiration ran down my ribs as if the book in my hands had turned into a nuclear-powered heating pad.

"Oh, sure, I'm fine!" I managed a cough. Hack-hack. Phony as a kid trying to stay home from school for the day. "It's just that some of these old books are so dusty." That was true enough, and sometimes I really did cough.

"If you're going to come down with anything, hold off until after Saturday night. Lucinda's about to go into meltdown as it is. I think she used to take things in stride better than she does now. Maybe age does that."

Only a few minutes ago I'd have been certain any problems Lucinda had were because she was stressed out with guilt and worry about murder and arson. With the information I now held in my hands, I knew murder, at least her involvement in murder, had nothing to do with her level of stress. But all I said was, "Is there some new problem?"

"She had to get carpenters in to fix those loose boards and brace up the stage this morning. I think our chorus line may be getting a little tubby. She's already said that even if the fire department doesn't shut us down that this is going to be her last year directing the Revue."

"Well, I'm no problem for her. I'm fine," I repeated. I straightened in my chair and widened my smile to prove it. "Did you get the ripped costume repaired?"

"No, it was worse than I thought. But a seamstress down in Hayward is doing a rush job on a new costume and making some minor alterations on Magnolia's costume too. I have to run down there in the morning and pick them up. Cross your fingers that I don't have car trouble or something."

Under other circumstances I might have pointed out that

281

I trusted in God, not crossed fingers, but the book felt as if it were growing in my hands, doing some Jack-and-the-Beanstalk thing right there in my hands to a size Charlotte couldn't help but notice. I waited until she was back at the main desk talking to Victoria Halburton, who had just come in, before opening the book again. There were six envelopes in all, the last letter and enclosures dated only a month or so before Hiram's death. I held everything down below desk level so I could read without anyone at the desk being able to see what I was doing.

The revelation in the letters was clear. And that revelation would surely devastate Charlotte. She thought the sun rose and set on Chris. Chris, her handsome, smart, personable, workaholic son, hopefully soon to be father of her grandchildren. But what I had here definitely dimmed that glowing vision of Chris.

Then the second phase hit me. Kelli would be devastated too. She'd been slow in coming to a decision about Chris, taken her time until she was certain, but she'd given her heart to him now.

This would shatter both Kelli and Charlotte.

Because Chris Sterling hadn't just given Hiram faulty advice about putting money in a Bahamas bank. He'd personally set up the account and then embezzled the money. Drained the account, shaken it as clean as a kid emptying his brother's piggy bank.

Copies of Hiram's side of the correspondence weren't here. Perhaps he'd called the bank instead of writing. But the responses from the bank told it all. How Hiram had become suspicious of what Chris had told him about his money being lost in a bank disaster. How he'd contacted the bank directly about the account, and how they'd told him there had been no problem at the bank. The money had simply been withdrawn by his "authorized representative," Christopher

Sterling II. Included was a copy of the legal form Hiram had signed making Chris the authorized representative. Photocopies of other documents, with Chris's signature, proved how he'd abused that status. He'd done it over a period of time, early small withdrawals escalating into large ones. Hiram had never known the money was missing because all the bank statements went to Chris's office.

I couldn't tell from this what had eventually made Hiram aware the money was gone or what had prompted him to become suspicious of Chris's explanation for its disappearance. From the bank's point of view, it was all quite legal, as they firmly pointed out. They'd done nothing wrong. But Chris certainly had. Although he may have been Hiram's "authorized representative" with legal access to the account, Hiram obviously had not authorized him to remove the money. Money that Chris had just as obviously diverted to himself rather than passing on to Hiram. The final letter showed that Hiram himself had closed the account and withdrawn the minuscule amount remaining in it.

I'd like to be able to think I'd cleverly had some intuition or hunch about Chris's treachery, but I'd had nothing at all. I hadn't been able to like Chris, but I'd accepted at face value what I'd heard from Kelli about Hiram losing money in an unwise investment in an offshore bank. Irrelevantly, I thought old Hiram's haphazard filing system made a certain sense after all. All his papers about being scammed on an investment were right here in a book on that very subject. The thought also occurred to me that ex girlfriend Suzy probably wasn't going to be surprised when all this came out.

Now what? Should I first show all this to Kelli or go directly to the authorities with it?

Because these letters suggested much more than the proof of embezzlement. Hiram obviously hadn't yet gone to the authorities with this information before his death, which made it a powerful motive for murder. Murder done by Chris Sterling to hide his other crime of embezzlement before Hiram went public with it.

Had Chris known these letters and documents existed somewhere? Was that the motive for arson as well as murder? He could have had a key copied from one Kelli had. Or Hiram may even have given him one, since he apparently was at the house fairly often. Which meant he surely also knew about the trash room and its easy flammability.

He'd needed to make certain these letters and documents never came to light. Perhaps he'd been afraid that in my search for a "secret room" I might run across this incriminating evidence. Burning the house and all its contents was the way to get rid of it. Never mind that Abilene and I might lose our lives too. We were expendable. He'd apparently never guessed the incriminating papers had already been removed from the house.

I started to shove the book in a plastic bag to take with me, but then I hesitated. Kelli didn't rummage in our things in the cabin, of course, but I didn't want her to somehow accidentally stumble across this. The front of my mind told me this was because I wanted to protect her, perhaps break the news to her gently. The darker side of my mind suggested something different. What if she found the incriminating papers and decided to destroy them? She was, after all, in love with Chris. Maybe a desire to protect him would prove stronger than bringing Hiram's killer to justice.

Another point. Charlotte was going to fall apart when her beloved son was accused of embezzlement or murder, or both. If it happened immediately, tomorrow, or in the midst of the Revue, her collapse might take the Revue down too, because she'd never be able to manage her responsibilities with the costumes when this hit her. What then? Could Lucinda manage without her?

284

Even after the practice of full-dress rehearsals, with Charlotte trying her best to get everyone organized, she was still the one who kept things running smoothly in the dressing rooms and made certain the costumes were ready for the right person at the right moment and accessories were all in place. Lucinda couldn't be backstage doing that.

Okay, maybe making a success of the Revue wasn't a matter of world-crisis proportions. But, as Charlotte had said, Lucinda was already near "meltdown" because of problems on it. And I was already awash in guilt for how I'd unfairly, if only in my mind, labeled Lucinda a killer. I didn't want further guilt by ruining her last Revue with this revelation.

Quickly, instead of bagging the book to take with me, I tucked it and its incriminating contents in the bottom drawer of my desk and packed an assortment of software instructions, pamphlets, and computer printouts over it. Because so many of the Historical Society ladies were involved in the Revue, they'd decided the building would not be open on Friday and Saturday, as it usually was. So the book and its contents would be locked up and safe here until after the Revue was over.

Which would be soon enough to bring Chris to justice and rip Charlotte and Kelli's worlds apart.

Mac came by to pick me up at closing time so I wouldn't have to walk all the way to Kelli's cabin. I watched Victoria, Charlotte, and Anne Perkins leave the building right behind me, Victoria locking the door and giving the handle an extra shake to be sure it was locked. Usually her fussiness irritated me, but now I was grateful for it.

I couldn't tell Mac what I'd just discovered while we were whizzing through town on the motorcycle, and by the time we got to Kelli's I'd had second thoughts about telling him at all. Mac was a great guy, but the people involved weren't as special to him as they were to me, and he'd probably want me to rush to the authorities immediately.

"You seem quiet today," Mac observed after we left the motorcycle at the back gate and I was unlocking the cabin door.

I was thinking how to answer that, but I didn't have to because he added, "But handling all the props for the Revue is pretty stressful, isn't it? I'd never have guessed how much detail is involved. Look, why don't we go over to my motor home, and I'll do the cooking tonight so you can just relax?"

Sounded good to me. I'd invited him this morning to have dinner here at the cabin with Abilene, Kelli, and me, but his offer relieved me. Getting away from the cabin would be good. I wasn't sure I could face Kelli's happy chatter about Chris, knowing what I did about him.

Which perhaps meant I was wrong not telling her immediately what I knew. The truth wasn't going to be any easier for her to take next week than right now. Maybe I was being unfair or foolish not letting her know.

While I was contemplating that, the phone rang. It was Kelli asking if it would be okay if she brought Chris home for dinner. My heart did an imitation of Mac's rope and tangled somewhere around my kneecaps. The very last person I wanted to see was Chris Sterling.

Yet this was Kelli's home, and I was the designated cook while we were enjoying her hospitality. I couldn't just blurt out what I knew over the phone. "Sure," I said brightly. "That'll be great. There's a chicken in the fridge. I'll roast it. Mashed potatoes and gravy?"

"Sounds great. Don't bother with anything fancy for dessert. Chris doesn't eat dessert, you know."

Right. Chris Sterling could commit murder and arson, but

eating a piece of cheesecake or pecan pie was a moral no-no. But what I said was just, "Okay. See you later."

"Change of plans?" Mac asked when I hung up the phone. I explained why. With Koop in his lap, he said, "I get the impression you're not overly fond of this Chris guy."

I was so startled I stumbled over my own feet going to the fridge. Was I that transparent? If I was, would Chris realize the minute he walked in that I knew what he'd done? I opened my mouth, on the verge of telling Mac everything. But I closed it. If Mac knew, that would just make one more of us with the secret to keep.

Because I was not going to run the risk of ruining the Revue for Lucinda and a lot of other people who'd put so much hard work into it.

Yet at the same time I found myself muddling around in another dilemma. Didn't my not telling Mac say something not good about our relationship? In a loving relationship, wouldn't people share something as important as this?

Okay, Mac would be the very first person I'd confide in, I promised myself. Just as soon as the Revue was over.

But first I had to get through this evening.

Not going to be easy, I realized as soon as Kelli and Chris arrived while I was putting mushroom dressing in the oven to go with the already nicely browned chicken. Abilene had come home a half hour earlier and was making salad. She'd reported the sick horse was doing fine now.

Chris gave me a solid hug, as if we were old friends. "Ivy! Good to see you again. This is really great, your fixing dinner for us on such short notice. Kelli tells me you're a wonderful cook."

My nerves tightened, and my stomach felt as if I might be coming down with an oversized case of horse-sized colic myself. It took all my self-control not to jerk away from him. No doubt God can love even an arsonist/murderer, but it was taking all my willpower just to be civil to him. I was so nervous I forgot to introduce Mac, and Kelli had to do it.

"Mac is doing the Will Rogers monologue for the Revue," she added to Chris. "Ben Simpson had to back out because of his back problems."

"I guess we'd better go, then, hadn't we?" Chris said. He sounded put-upon.

I was surprised. "You weren't planning to go to the Revue?"

Kelli rolled her eyes. "Of course we're going. Everybody goes. My fiancé, the big kidder." She slugged him lightly on the shoulder. "We don't go, and your mother will boycott our wedding. She's worked her fingers to the bone with those costumes."

Chris grinned. "Yeah, you're right. I just like to tease both of you. It's like lighting a match to a puddle of gasoline."

My own grim thought was, *I wouldn't count on there being any wedding*. Then I quickly turned back to the stove, afraid my thoughts might be spraying out like some messy sneeze.

The thought that had been hiding in the back of my mind ever since I found those incriminating letters now shot to the surface. If Chris knew I had them, my life wouldn't be worth any more than the mushrooms I'd tossed in the dressing. If he was capable of killing Hiram and trying to burn the house down, getting rid of one LOL wouldn't be any big deal for him.

That thought made me so jittery I found myself mashing potatoes as if they were some mortal enemy.

I calmed myself with another thought. Chris couldn't possibly do me in right here at dinner in front of three people. He surely couldn't choke, shoot, or clobber me with some heavy object with everyone looking on. There was no high place from which he might push me off, nothing flammable nearby to set fire to.

But maybe he could come up with something creative. A little poison in my coffee cup? A foot artfully positioned so I'd stumble over it and crash into the open oven?

No, of course not. He couldn't, I reminded myself, even have any idea I'd found those incriminating papers. So this entire panic trip was unnecessary.

Eat, drink, and be merry, I told myself firmly. Which didn't mean I didn't keep a wary eye on him all through dinner.

Actually, Chris was at his best tonight. Quite scintillating, in fact, with stories about judges and odd clients. Everyone was laughing and having fun, but my laugh was hollow. It made my heart ache to see how much in love with him Kelli was. She'd held back until she was sure, and now . . . *Oh, Kelli, what's it going to do to you when you find out what he is and what he did to Hiram?*

I was relieved when the evening finally ended. Relieved that I could finally unwind the smile on my face. Relieved that Chris hadn't figured out some sly way to do me in. Relieved that he surely didn't even suspect what I knew.

26

Showtime.

I peeked out from behind the gold curtain. Tomorrow night was supposed to be the big night for the Revue, but the seats were already filling for this Friday night performance. I spotted Kelli and Chris in a center row. I looked away. I didn't want to think about Chris tonight. And there was no need for my sudden shivers. He couldn't, I reminded myself, do anything to me with Kelli right beside him. And there were Abilene and Dr. Sugarman on their very first real date together! Was she calling him Mike yet? I hoped so. A strip of yellow plastic cordoned off the front row of seats, reserving them for the chorus ladies and other cast members to sit when they weren't onstage. A yellow strip that looked exactly like crime scene tape, almost like a warning that something bad was going to happen . . .

No, no! This wasn't yellow tape. I blinked and refocused. It was yellow, but it was *ribbon*. Ribbon tied into a nice big bow. Get thee behind me, paranoia.

I went backstage to check props again. I had everything divided into sections. Each skit had its own space, all organized.

The lightweight fire hydrant had fallen over, and I stood it upright. Paul Newman was standing under a light, studying his master-of-ceremonies script, busily penning in last-minute changes. The ladies were getting ready in the dressing rooms amid giggles and heady drifts of perfume and flying feather boas. DaisyBelle was safely at home, probably sitting in her favorite chair and watching Animal Planet.

I was checking the duct-taped lamp shade to be sure it was holding together when Mac came up beside me and leaned his rope against the wall.

"Nervous?" he asked.

Well, yeah. I was still thinking crime-scene tape and wondering if Chris was making murderous plans for me for later. I pushed that aside. "Not as much as I would be if I had to go onstage. Though I keep thinking maybe I'll hand someone the wrong prop, and maybe the policeman will be out there in the street skit with this lamp shade instead of a nightstick. How about you?"

"A little nervous," he admitted.

He didn't look it. He looked cowboy rumpled in his old clothes and scruffy cowboy hat, as if he'd just ridden in off a hard day on the range. Although a rather foxy rumpled old cowboy, I decided. I stretched up and gave him a quick kiss on the cheek. "You'll do great."

"You got a minute?" he asked.

I looked at my watch. "Sure."

He led me to an empty corner beyond the dressing rooms.

"I was planning to wait until after the last performance tomorrow night to give you this. But maybe now would be a good time. Close your eyes."

I did. He took my hand. I could feel him fumble in his shirt pocket for something. Then he pressed whatever it was into my hand and closed my fingers around it.

"There. You can open your eyes now."

I kept my eyes squeezed shut, feeling oddly wary. I fingered the object. Small, metallic, round. With a hole in the center.

A ring.

My heart jumped with an adolescent twang of surprise and joy. A ring! Mac had finally gotten around to making that commitment he'd always avoided.

Just as quickly I felt a surge of dismay and a shiver of panic, as if I were about to be swept over Niagara Falls. A ring. Wanting commitment from me.

Hold on now, Ivy, I chastised myself. *You can't feel both ways.*

But I could. One part of me wanted to yell, *Yes, Mac, yes I'll marry you!* But another part was muttering, *No, I can't do this. You're a wonderful man, Mac. I enjoy you when we're together. I miss you when we're apart. Sometimes I think I love you. But lifetime commitment? No, no, no, not now, not yet!*

But wait. My brow wrinkled over my closed eyes, and I explored the object further with my fingertips. Yes, the object was round and metallic and had a hole in the center. But there was a chain attached . . .

My eyes flew open, and I lifted my hand.

"I saw you admiring it when we were in one of those antique and gift shops. So I went back and bought it for you."

I angled the circle toward the dim backstage light. Yes, I had admired the necklace in a glass case in one of the shops. It was a circular pendant of southwest Native American design, beautiful, delicate yet bold and striking. A circle of sterling silver inset with alternating bands of turquoise, polished coral, mother-of-pearl, and black onyx.

Beautiful. Very beautiful. But not a ring. Actually, now that I saw it, I didn't know how I could have mistaken it for a ring. The center hole was too large, the silver circle too flat. And there was the attached chain, of course.

Maybe I'd made the mistake because I'd wanted it to be a ring?

Oh, Ivy, get your act together. What do you want?

"Want to put it on?"

That much I knew I did want. "Oh yes!"

I turned around and leaned my head forward. He draped the chain around my neck and fastened the latch. I adjusted the circular pendant at my throat. I was wearing a black sweater and pants, good, inconspicuous backstage wear, but perfect for showing off the striking colors of the necklace.

"Thank you, Mac. It's a wonderful gift."

I was also thankful I hadn't made an idiot of myself by throwing myself in his arms and yelling that ridiculous, "Yes, Mac, yes, I'll marry you!"

Okay, down to the nitty-gritty here: was I disappointed? Another of those seesaw emotions. Yes, one part of me was a little disappointed. Sometimes Mac's ambivalence, his three steps forward and two steps backward in our relationship, was frustrating, and a ring would mean all those steps were forward now. But another part of me felt almost giddy with relief that he hadn't offered a commitment I couldn't accept.

They balanced out, I realized. Disappointment. Relief. Which left us both free to explore where, if anywhere, we wanted to go from here.

I stood on tiptoe and gave him another kiss. "Thank you, Mac." With thanks for more than he probably realized.

The music signaling the show was about to begin started, and we edged over to the side of the stage where we could see onstage. The curtain was still closed, but the chorus line stood poised and ready to go, draped arms uniting them. Magnolia looked glorious, hair piled high, a white magnolia perched on top making her look like a centerpiece in a flower arrangement. Paul Newman stood right behind where the curtain would split when it opened. His face looked as grim as if he were about to face an IRS audit, but his black suit looked sharp and sophisticated.

I could hear Lucinda's voice from in front of the curtain. I couldn't see her, but I knew she had a special gown for the occasion, a slinky satin '20s thing decorated with seed pearls. She welcomed everyone to the Revue, thanked all those who had worked hard to make it a success, and remembered Lulu and Ben as casualties along the way.

"So, without further ado, to get our show under way, here is our master of ceremonies, our very own Paul Newman!"

Paul swaggered through the curtain, and we could no longer see him, but I could tell from his voice that his onstage personality transformation had kicked in again. He gave a brief, lively history of the Revue, tossing in jokes here and there, finally saying, "But that's enough from me, because I know what you all really want to see are the lovely ladies in our Hello chorus line. And here they are!"

The big moment. Except that nothing happened. The curtain didn't sweep open. It just hung there like a dishrag.

More loudly, as if he thought the person operating the curtain perhaps hadn't heard, Paul repeated his dramatic words. "And here they are!"

The music for the first chorus-line number began, but no curtain flew open. On the far side of the stage I could see the woman who was supposed to operate the curtain struggling with a tangle of ropes. Mac leaped away from me and raced across the stage. The chorus line shifted like a breaking wave as everyone tried to see what was going on.

Mac might have trouble with a cowboy rope, but he worked a miracle with the ropes on the stage curtain. It flew open, catching the surprised-looking chorus ladies standing there as disorganized as a flock of Norman's chickens. Magnolia took charge. "C'mon, ladies," she boomed. "Let's go!"

The chorus ladies whipped into a ruler-straight line, and they were off, kicking and sidestepping and whirling.

And from that point on, everything went like clockwork.

With Mac's help, I got the props on and offstage in record time for each skit. His monologue and bumbling with the rope brought whoops of approval and applause.

I did have to make two quick runs up to the third floor to get a dog collar that had somehow disappeared, and a replacement for a dish that had been stepped on. They were awkward trips because I had to sneak along an outside aisle beside the audience to get to the stairs in the lobby, but no one seemed to pay much attention. Charlotte was up there once, frantically looking for a boa to replace one that had unexpectedly started to shed feathers.

"I know we had a couple extras. I ordered them because I knew some dumb thing would happen. It always does," Charlotte moaned as she tossed costumes like confetti. "But where are they?"

I finally found one of them for her. Someone had draped it around the stuffed skunk. "Bless you, Ivy," she said and raced for the stairs.

Paul was there the second time, fretting about a lost cuff link and looking for a replacement in the glass jewelry case.

When the final curtain closed on the chorus line, and Paul, complete with two cuff links, stepped out to wrap things up, we all knew the evening had been a big success. The applause proved it.

Everyone was hugging everyone else backstage as the audience milled around and out into the lobby. I hadn't thought since opening curtain about murder and Chris, but when he and Kelli came backstage to give Charlotte a congratulatory hug, the truth hit me hard.

On Monday, when I went to the authorities with the evidence about Chris, another curtain would be closing. And that time there'd be no applause and congratulations.

27

With Friday night's successful performance behind us, the high-energy atmosphere backstage just before the Saturday night show was more party time than performance. A celebration party for the cast was, in fact, scheduled for later.

The curtain had been tried and pronounced in perfect working order for tonight. Laughter but no squabbles were issuing from the dressing rooms. Magnolia had had her hair coloring refreshed this afternoon, and it looked like a royal flame piled atop her head. Even Paul Newman was smiling and cracking jokes.

I was wearing my new necklace again, and I'd made a wonderful discovery. Mac had had the back side of the silver circle engraved! *To Ivy from Mac.*

Earlier, when I'd showed it to Kelli, she'd said, with a knowing nod, "When a man gives a woman a piece of jewelry, it means something. And engraved, that really means something."

I wasn't examining what the necklace or the engraving might mean, but both brought me great chunks of joy.

I checked my props carefully to make certain nothing had gone astray overnight. I spotted Lucinda standing at the edge of the curtain. It was surprisingly chilly backstage tonight, and she was wearing a jacket over the satin gown. She still looked slim and slinky, but there was a peculiar stiffness to her stance as she peered around the curtain at the audience. I walked up behind her.

"Everything okay?" I asked.

She jumped, her expression oddly guilty, as if she'd been doing something illicit, but her smile flashed spotlight bright. "Oh yes. Fine! We're sold out tonight."

Unconvinced that she was as fine as she said, I stood on tiptoe to look over her shoulder. I saw Geoff, of course, right up front. The fire chief was there. Oh, and there was Nick from Nick's Garage, along with a chunky, red-haired wife. I was surprised to see Kelli and Chris in the audience again tonight. Then I realized Lucinda's gaze wasn't targeted on any of these people. She was staring at a young woman alone in the back row. There wasn't enough light to see the woman clearly, but I could see enough to flutter my toes. I knew I shouldn't ask, but that curiosity gene got to me again.

"Is that, uh, someone you know?" I asked cautiously.

"The woman with dark hair in the third row? She looks familiar, doesn't she? I think she's someone's granddaughter."

An adroit detour and a safe enough comment. Isn't every woman someone's granddaughter?

"No, the one in the back row. With the long blond braid."

Lucinda gave me a sharp glance, spotlight smile turned off now. "Do you know her?"

"She looks familiar."

"Yes, she does, doesn't she?" Lucinda said in a tone that held enough acid to dissolve every hair in that blond braid.

Before I could think what to say next, a frantic voice interrupted.

"Lucinda, help! Stella is saying she can't possibly wear that black dress again tonight! This afternoon someone told her it made her look like a hooker in mourning, and she's all in a tizzy. I don't know what to do!"

"For goodness sake, who'd say such a terrible thing? And why? She looks great in that dress."

"I have no idea." Charlotte threw up her hands in helpless exasperation. "Would you talk some sense into her? We have nothing else for her to wear. Nothing. She's too short and chubby for any other dress in our wardrobe."

Thank you, Charlotte, I murmured silently, because Lucinda, distracted, rushed off to soothe Stella.

I peered out again. No doubt about it. The young woman was definitely KaySue. What was she doing here? The Revue posters, of course. They'd been plastered all over Hayward, with Lucinda's name as director in small print down near the bottom.

Had KaySue come here with the idea of carrying out her threat, confronting Lucinda, and making her confess to killing Hiram? Did she intend to sit through the performance and then seek out her former rival? Or, remembering KaySue's soup-tossing, fist-throwing temper, did she plan some spitfire drama backstage . . . or even onstage?

Frantically I scrambled around the curtain, down the side steps, and up the aisle. The seats were now filling rapidly. By the time I reached KaySue, she'd moved down three rows. Oh yes, she had something in mind. I scooted in beside her.

"KaySue!" I whispered.

"Oh. You." She gave me a look as if I were a sack of garbage that had just been dumped beside her. "What are you doing here?"

"I'm the props person for the show. What are you doing here?"

"It's a free country. I bought a ticket." She held up a torn stub.

"KaySue, I don't know why you're here tonight, but if it's to cause Lucinda trouble, she didn't kill Hiram—"

"You're just saying that because you're afraid I might do something to mess up your big show!"

I thought she might do something, all right. Anything from an onstage Perry Mason–type confrontation to a catfight in the aisle. "No, KaySue, it's true. I found some papers and letters that I'm sure prove someone else did it. Someone who also set the fire at the house."

"Yeah?" she challenged. "Who?"

"I can't tell you yet. I haven't told anyone yet. But I'm taking everything to the authorities soon. Very soon."

"Why haven't you done it already?"

"Because I didn't want to ruin the Revue."

She gave me a look that would wither an oak tree. Not ruining the Revue was right up there with a Save the Cockroaches campaign on KaySue's list of concerns. But then her head tilted with reluctant interest. "It's someone else in the Revue?"

"I can't explain now, but please, KaySue, please don't do anything awful tonight. Just enjoy the show. We've all worked very hard on it. A friend of mine does a great Will Rogers impersonation. And come Monday—"

"Who's Will Rogers?"

Generation gap. I squelched a sigh. "An entertainer from a long time ago, someone I'm sure Hiram liked very much."

The music was starting. The seats were almost full, and people were settling down. Anticipation danced in the air.

"Please, KaySue? Promise, no fireworks tonight, okay?"

"Does this mean you don't think I killed Hiram?"

"Exactly! Not Lucinda, and not you either!"

Paul Newman stepped out from behind the curtain. "Ladies and gentlemen, welcome! So good to see you all here tonight!"

I was out of time. I jumped up, gave KaySue a hopeful thumbs-up gesture, and hastily scurried to my position backstage.

The show moved along nicely. The Three Stooges skit drew enthusiastic applause. The chorus line still wasn't precision-perfect, but the big smiles and enthusiasm made up for any glitches in timing. I kept dashing over to the side of the stage to peer around the edge of the curtain at KaySue, still afraid she might do something drastic. Lucinda was busy keeping everyone organized, but once I spotted her peering around the curtain on the far side. Did she think KaySue had killed Hiram?

Mac helped me get props on and offstage, but there was no time for personal conversation, and I was too busy checking on KaySue every few minutes. I did manage to give him a quick good-wishes kiss before he sauntered onstage. I claimed a good spot off to the side of the stage to watch. I didn't want to miss a minute of this.

"Howdy, folks." He pushed back the hat. "You're all lookin' good!"

Oh, that grin! Pure devastation. But I missed whatever he said next because Lucinda grabbed my arm. "Ivy, can you run upstairs and find another purse for Stella?" she whispered frantically. "Something's happened to the one she's supposed to carry, and she's gone all prima donna and says she can't go onstage without one. Charlotte has to fix a split seam before the next chorus-line number, and she's about to go into orbit."

"But I don't want to miss Mac!"

"Oh, maybe I can get someone else." Lucinda lifted her head and scanned the backstage crowd, frown lines cut into her forehead.

Plenty of people were milling around, but the chorus-line ladies were all in costume and couldn't go sneaking up the aisle through the audience, and everyone else looked occupied. Duty called.

"Okay, I'll go." If I hurried, maybe I could get back before Mac's performance was over. "Where can I find a purse?"

"Maybe in that big old chest of drawers by the bed. There must be several that we've used in other years. And hurry!"

My usual invisibility helped, and no one seemed to notice as I scurried up the side aisle. I peered back over my shoulder a couple of times. Mac was chatting in Will Rogers's folksy style, doing his thing with the rope, acting mystified by its antics, and the audience loved it. I looked for KaySue but couldn't see her, which made me wonder nervously if she'd sneaked off to do something drastic. I almost turned back, thinking I'd better warn Lucinda . . . but no time for that now. I'd tell her as soon as I got back. I hurried on out to the lobby and up the stairs.

Upstairs, puffing from the fast climb, I raced for the chest of drawers. It stood at the foot of a bed they'd used in a scene in some other year. I started at the top drawer, frantically clawing through gloves and scarves. No purses.

Second drawer was gourds. Gourds? Yes, a zillion gourds, rattling like some mariachi band gone berserk as I scrabbled through them. Wigs filled the third drawer. A wig with eyes? No, a mouse! I slammed the drawer shut.

I knelt to get the bottom drawer open. Yes, purses! What color? Lucinda hadn't said. I grabbed a red one. It would show up nicely against Stella's black—

The thought ended there. Vanished in a crashing thunder of whirling stars and something weighing me down and darkness . . .

Darkness of length unknown, maybe a minute, maybe an hour. Then I was looking groggily at something that didn't make sense. Two pointed black somethings. My dazed mind finally identified them as shoes, toes pointed upward. *Now, that isn't right*, my mind argued dizzily. *Toes don't point up toward the ceiling . . .*

It got through to me. Those were my toes. I was lying on my back on the floor looking at them.

No, not just lying . . . the floor was moving!

Wrong. It was me moving. Someone, I realized, had hold of the back of my sweatshirt and was dragging me down the hallway.

"Hey!" I protested. Gurgled, actually, because the front of the sweatshirt was pulled so tightly against my throat that I was almost choking. I clawed at it weakly.

The dragging stopped. Fingers felt at my throat. Looking for a pulse, I realized. What had happened? Was I being rescued after some catastrophe? I had a vague memory of something crashing down on me. Building collapse? Earthquake?

I heard a muttered grunt, not a particularly pleased-sounding grunt, and then the dragging started again. It felt faster than before, as if the person felt some new need for speed. But the person had a different grasp now, so the sweatshirt wasn't quite so tight around my neck, and there was a certain dreamy pleasantness to the movement, no effort required. I had a new perspective on the faded wallpaper and scuffed baseboards. One piece of advice, however. If you're going to be dragged around, wear something more substantial than thong panties.

I was conscious enough to know I was being dragged, but not conscious enough to feel more than a puzzled bewilderment by what was going on. We must be headed toward the stairs. I felt a first twinge of alarm. Did this person intend to drag me bumping and bouncing right down the stairs?

Indignantly I tried to protest. *If you'll just give me a minute to get my bearings, maybe I can walk.* But my groggy brain and my tongue couldn't seem to connect, and nothing but a garble came out.

Then I realized something even more puzzling. We weren't headed toward the stairs. We were headed the opposite direction, down the long hallway toward that old elevator shaft. *Hey, no, turn around, this direction is a dead end! And it's dangerous—*

The fog in my brain finally lifted, cleared by alarm over something more important than uncomfortable thong panties. What was going on here?

Something had knocked me out. A blow to the head? No, I vaguely recalled something crashing down on me. The chest of drawers. Yes, that was it. The chest of drawers had accidentally fallen on me.

Or not so accidentally?

Twisting my head, I got a glimpse of the legs of the person dragging me. Dark pant legs.

With sudden panic I tried to dig in my heels and elbows and stop this relentless drive toward the far end of the hall. Another grunt, and then a ruthless kick knocked my elbow out from under me. The dragging started again.

And now I knew one thing for certain: this was no rescue.

303

28

Full consciousness blasted through. With it came realization of what was going on here. Chris Sterling must have spotted me coming up here alone. Somehow he knew or suspected I'd found those incriminating letters and decided he had to get rid of me. While I was searching for the purse, he'd sneaked in behind me, climbed on the bed behind the chest of drawers, and shoved it over on me. And he was planning a deadly fall for me, the same way he'd gotten rid of Hiram.

I dug in my heels again, but all that happened was a shoe flew off and slammed into the wall. The dragging didn't slow, though it was more jerky now, and his breathing was labored. Maybe he wasn't in as good shape as he looked. Or maybe I'd put on a few pounds. But obviously not enough pounds to stop what he intended doing.

Frantically I dug for the whistle caught under my sweatshirt. Norman had warned I might need it. If I could just alert someone to what was going on . . .

There, I had it! I put it to my lips. I couldn't blow strongly, given my awkward position, but in the empty hallway my blast made as much noise as a blaring siren. My dragger paused and grabbed at the whistle. He got both chains, the one for the whistle and the one for my necklace too. One chain alone might have broken when he yanked, but two held firm!

"It . . . doesn't . . . matter," the dragger gasped, breathing hard from the effort of pulling me. "Blow all . . . you want! No one can hear you."

Unfortunately, that was correct. There was a kind of vibration coming up from below, applause perhaps, or maybe the chorus line doing their thing. I must have been out long enough for Mac's performance to be over. In any case, any noise I made wasn't going to reach anyone three stories below. Then a different kind of realization hit me.

The voice wasn't identifiable because of the gasped breaths, but it was definitely not Chris Sterling's voice. It was female. I also caught a flowery scent that was not male. Perfume.

Lucinda? KaySue? Kelli?

I struggled to a sitting position. I swung around, and we stared at each other. She was leaning over to catch her breath, left hand on the thigh of her dark pants, right hand on the prop from some long-gone Revue.

"You're supposed to be fixing a split seam on a costume!"

"A minor deception." She gave me a wry smile. "Surprised?"

I eyed the baseball bat as the pieces of this puzzle finally snapped into place. Great sleuth I was. Headed down the wrong trail entirely. "You made a mistake last time, didn't you? You intended it to look like an accident, but the police could tell it was murder."

"Not this time."

No, this time she'd used a falling chest of drawers for the

preliminary blow, something that probably wouldn't look all that different than injuries from a fatal fall.

"I really didn't want to do anything to you, Ivy," Charlotte said, her tone reproachful, as if I'd brought this on myself. "I rather like you. Although you're much too nosy for your own good, of course."

"You invited us to stay at your place because you like me?"

"Well, mostly I thought if you were at my place I could keep an eye on what you were up to."

"And have a private, convenient setting in which to get rid of me if you figured I was getting too close to the truth."

Charlotte sighed. "You're putting such an ugly spin on this, Ivy. It's just that I don't have any choice now that you've found those letters from the bank about Chris. I can't let you expose him any more than I could let Hiram do it, and I'm sure that's what you intend to do."

"What makes you think I found anything?" I tried to sound innocent.

She laughed. The woman is up to her elbows in murder and attempted murder, out of breath from dragging her latest victim, me, down a hallway, but she can laugh. "Oh, Ivy, you should have seen yourself. You looked so guilty sitting there at your desk clutching that book. I knew something was up. So I went back later and looked. I have a key to the building, you know."

"And you took the letters, I suppose."

"Of course. And now all I have to do is get rid of you."

Charlotte's preference for Kelli over Suzy the florist as a daughter-in-law made dreadful sense now. There was the big danger, once Kelli took over Hiram's legal affairs, that she'd discover the embezzlement. But Charlotte had figured that if Kelli was in love with, or better yet, married to Chris, she wouldn't expose him.

306

"And once you're rid of me, no one will ever know your son is an embezzler."

"It isn't fair to look at it that way!" Charlotte protested vigorously. "Chris is no embezzler. He just borrowed the money to take advantage of an incredible opportunity on some oil stocks. He intended to put it back. Everything would have been fine if old Hiram hadn't decided he needed the money to buy this stupid building." She banged the baseball bat against the floor, as if both the old hotel and Hiram were to blame for everything.

"Did Chris make a fortune on the oil stocks?"

"Unfortunately, he'd received some bad information, and the stock tanked. But he'd have put the money back eventually anyway."

So, when Hiram wanted his money and couldn't get it, Chris had hastily made up that phony story about a bank scam, which hadn't satisfied Hiram for long. "And Hiram intended to expose what Chris had done, so you had to kill him."

"It would have destroyed Chris's life! I couldn't let that happen. Could you, if it were your son?"

I'd have figured out an alternative to murder, that's for sure. "You set the fire at the house too?"

She frowned. "No, that was Chris's idea. I really didn't approve. But he didn't plan to kill you and Abilene, you know. He's . . . squeamish that way. He figured you'd get out. He just wanted to destroy the house. He really thought there might be a secret room where Hiram had hidden the letters."

"But Chris wasn't squeamish about letting you commit murder for him," I pointed out.

"He didn't know about it until after Hiram was dead." Ever the protective mother.

"How did you get Hiram up there to the third floor?"

"I knew he was thinking about selling the house after he

307

and Lucinda were married." She was still breathing hard from the exertion of dragging me, and she paused, hand on her chest, to take in a deep breath. Probably she wouldn't be carrying on this conversation if she hadn't needed a rest from the hard labor of dragging me. All work and no play, if you're a murderess. "I told him I'd like to list it and asked if I could see the view from the third floor so I could use that in promoting the sale."

"Did you try to talk him out of revealing what Chris had done?"

"He'd already made plain to Chris that his mind was made up. He didn't even know I knew about the missing money."

"And you hit him with . . . ?"

"A salami." She smiled, seeming quite pleased to share this bit of creativity with me. "My idiot 'secret sister' in the Historical Society gave it to me last year. The ugly thing must have been a foot and a half long. As if I'd ever eat garbage like that! So I froze it, and it came in quite handy."

Yes, several pounds of frozen salami might indeed make a formidable weapon. And it had been easily concealed in Charlotte's oversized purse, of course.

"Afterward I just let it thaw out and put it through the garbage disposal." She still sounded pleased with herself, but she suddenly jabbed me with the baseball bat. "Get up. We're wasting time. I didn't think you'd regain consciousness so soon. But since you did, you can walk the rest of the way."

Walk to the elevator shaft, where she intended to shove me to my death in a fall to the basement level. She was on a roll with this hit-and-shove murder system. No need to change tactics now. Her breathing was almost back to normal.

Lord, I need some help here!

As with so many times in my life, I was totally dependent on him. Would he send a contingent of angels to whisk me off to safety? Probably not. But he wouldn't abandon me, of that I was certain.

So what now, Lord? A nice verse from Psalms surfaced: "When I am afraid, I will trust in you." *Okay, Lord, I'm afraid, but I'm trusting in you.*

Delay. Stall. Procrastinate.

I blinked. *Really?* Not the words you expect to hear from an all-powerful Lord, but, as the old saying goes, the Lord works in mysterious ways. I put on my best chatty demeanor. "You and I were alone up here during last night's performance. Why didn't you do this then?"

"A dead body here in the hotel would have ruined tonight's show." She sounded shocked that I'd even consider such a thing. "I didn't want that to happen."

Right. The show must go on. I'd thought that too, and now here I was, facing a murderer with a baseball bat.

"Tonight it won't matter," she added. "The show will be over before the body is found. Everything will work out fine. In fact, with luck, the body may not be found for days."

The body. Hey, we're talking about me here. And I might add that her definition of "fine" differed considerably from mine.

"Maybe the fall won't kill me. I'll be lying down there groaning and moaning, and everyone will hear me."

"I doubt that. The fall should do it. But if not, the crowd going out is always so noisy they'll never hear a thing." But she frowned, apparently not as certain of that as she'd like to be. She picked the bat up and examined it as if checking to see if it would fit an LOL. "I don't want to use this, but I will if I have to."

Great. I'd just convinced her she'd better bash me with the baseball bat after all.

"Women don't kill people with baseball bats," I protested. "Haven't you read enough mysteries to know that? Women use more . . . ladylike methods." Although I had to admit that probably didn't apply to a woman who'd already used a salami.

No response to that. I tried another approach. "Don't you think the authorities are going to wonder what I was doing way down at the far end of the hall?" I added. "And how I happened to fall into the shaft?"

"Everyone knows how nosy you are. And everyone knows, too, how older people get addled and lose their sense of direction and balance. Especially after you knocked that chest of drawers over on yourself."

Epitaph: Here lies Ivy Malone. She had a bad sense of direction.

New tactic. "Maybe I've already told someone about the letters."

"No, you wouldn't do that without the letters in hand to prove it. And you don't have them, I do." She sounded smugly victorious, quite sure of herself. She gave me another jab with the bat to hurry me along. "C'mon, get up."

"I can't walk," I muttered. I wasn't certain of that, but I was certainly feeling shaky enough, with all this talk about my imminent demise. I also didn't feel obliged to make some big effort just to simplify things for her. I kept my thong-clad bottom obstinately planted on the carpet.

The thought occurred to me that surely carpet fibers would show up on my slacks when my body was found. "You can't get away with this, you know," I warned.

"We'll see."

"Hey, Ivy, you up here?"

Charlotte and I both jumped at the sound of Mac's voice from the head of the stairs. Charlotte dropped the bat. It rolled down the uneven hallway. For a moment I thought that meant she realized she was caught and was ready to surrender. I was mistaken. The well-equipped murderer always has a backup weapon, a weapon far more deadly than a bat, and she was no exception. A gun, suddenly pulled from a pocket of her hooded sweatshirt. No doubt brought to the performance in that carry-everything purse.

Mac's head appeared at the far end of the hall. Charlotte lifted the gun, desperation on her face. I could read her thoughts: *Okay, two bodies down the elevator shaft! So what if it was obviously murder . . . Worry about that later!*

Any ideas, Lord?

Advice from the Lord, perhaps filtered through a TV ad: just do it.

I braced my hands on the hall carpet, lifted my legs, and swung, spinning on my bottom. I caught her in the shins, the blow ricocheting through my own legs up to my already battered head. She oofed and went down, face first. The gun flew out of reach down the hallway. *Thank you, Lord!*

"Mac!" I screamed.

I could go after the bat . . .

No, she'd surely beat me to it. And she surely wouldn't hesitate to use it on Mac as well as me. I scrambled on my hands and knees and went after Charlotte instead. I plopped in the middle of her back. She oofed again. I really am putting on weight. But I wasn't heavy enough to keep her down, and her back rose under me like a bucking bronc. I hung on with one fist and pounded the top of her head with the other.

Footsteps thundered to a halt a few feet in front of the two of us. "Ivy, what's going on?" Mac asked, his tone aghast. "What are you *doing*?"

"She killed Hiram. She was trying to kill me! Grab the baseball bat."

Mac, bless him, didn't ask for confirming details. He grabbed the bat. I slid off Charlotte's back.

Charlotte swung around to a sitting position. I retrieved my lost shoe, then stood up a little unsteadily and used a tissue to pick up the gun. Mac held out his hand, and I gave it to him. In a minimum of words I told him about embezzlement, murder, and attempted murder.

Charlotte started to get up, but Mac's gesture with the bat changed her mind. "This is all a terrible misunderstanding," she said.

"We'll see what the police think. Ivy, perhaps you could go call them?"

I headed for the stairs. Behind me I heard Charlotte say, "You wouldn't really use that bat on me. You're surely too much of a gentleman for that."

"Try me," Mac returned cheerfully. "And I now have a gun too."

Downstairs, Stella was onstage in the beaded black dress, purse in hand, belting out "Five Foot Two, Eyes of Blue." I doubted now that Stella had ever been missing a purse. That was just another of Charlotte's "minor deceptions" to get me up to the third floor.

I'd have to find someone with a cell phone because there wasn't a regular phone in the old hotel. I knew there were probably deputies right here in the audience, but I didn't know any of them. Then, remembering who I'd spotted earlier, I scooted down the aisle and tapped Fire Chief Burman on the shoulder.

"Emergency," I whispered. He followed me up to the lobby, where I gave him a quick rundown on the situation. He went back into the audience and collected two out-of-uniform deputies. We all trooped upstairs as the chorus line swung into their final number. A few members of the audience were obviously curious, but there was no big uproar.

And, as I spelled out the details, the police didn't seem to think this was all just a terrible misunderstanding.

29

"Are you going to be okay with this?" I asked.

Kelli draped a tablecloth over the card table pushed up against the dining table. With seven for dinner, we needed more space. This farewell get-together for Magnolia and Geoff had been Kelli's idea, but I wasn't so sure we should have gone ahead with it.

"I'm fine."

Kelli didn't look fine. The revelations about both Chris and Charlotte had hit her like a world collapsing around her. Shadows smudged her eyes, and her jeans hung loose at the waist. She wasn't acknowledging yet that she believed them guilty, perhaps because memory of the town's hasty jump to conclusions about her was still fresh in her mind. Or perhaps because of the straightforward loyalty of her character and her strong belief in "innocent until proven guilty."

But neither, I knew, could she disbelieve my account of what Charlotte had said and what she'd tried to do to me, an account underlined by a body rife with scrapes and bruises from the overturned chest of drawers, plus carpet burns on my slacks. (To say nothing of carpet burns underneath my slacks, thanks to that now-discarded thong.) Nor could she disregard the fact that a police search of Charlotte's house had turned up the incriminating letters from the bank. I was surprised that she hadn't already burned them, but criminals make mistakes.

"Did you go down to Hayward today?" I asked. That was where Chris and Charlotte were being held. So far neither had been released on bail. I opened the oven and basted the ham again. Kelli started putting plates on the table. Abilene had gotten home late from work and was still in the shower.

"I saw Chris. Charlotte refused to see me. Chris said their lawyers are going for plea bargains, which would mean an agreed-upon sentence without going to trial." She swallowed. "He admitted to me today he was the one who broke into the house shortly after Hiram was killed. He was looking for those letters. He had a key, but he broke in so it would look like an outsider did it." Another rough swallow. "He used the key when he went in to set the fire."

"What do you think about the plea bargains?"

"They'll both get prison sentences, a much longer one for Charlotte. But, I think, under the circumstances, it's probably the best course of action. They can probably do better with plea bargains than with a jury." She spoke in a neutral, lawyerly tone as she gave a neutral, lawyerly opinion. But she blinked, cutting off tears, and briskly changed the subject. "I went by the house today. The workmen have the back side all boarded up now."

"Have you decided to rebuild the addition?" I checked the scalloped potatoes. I'd sprinkle grated cheese on top a few minutes before they came out of the oven.

"No, I'm going to let it go. I'm going to donate the antiques and the carousel horses to the Historical Society and let them

314

do whatever they want with them. Then I'll put the house up for sale in the spring." She gave me the ghost of one of her mischievous smiles. "Want to buy it? I'm willing to let it go at a bargain price, with excellent terms."

She wasn't asking the question seriously, and the idea of my buying the place was surely out of the question. And yet . . .

A knock sounded at the door, and I went to open it. I was expecting Mac and the Margollins, or Dr. Sugarman, so I stared in surprise at Lucinda.

"Am I interrupting something?" she asked. Over my shoulder she could undoubtedly see the table set for dinner.

"No! We're having a little farewell doings for my friends from Arizona, but no one's here yet. Come on in." I didn't like the way that came out, as if, if anyone had been here, she wouldn't be welcome. I pulled her inside and closed the door behind her. "We'd love to have you stay for dinner. There's plenty of food. And raspberry cheesecake for dessert."

"That sounds lovely, but thanks, no. I'm on my way to the health club to get going on my karate lessons again. I missed them when we were working so hard on the Revue. What I came for . . ." She pulled out what she'd been holding behind her. "I was down at the hotel gathering things up backstage and came across Mac's rope. I wanted to give it back to him. I thought he might be leaving before long."

"The rope! I guess in all the, um, excitement we forgot all about it." I certainly had, and apparently Mac had too. "Actually, it's Dr. Sugarman's rope. He'll be here later, and we'll give it to him."

"Okay. Good. And tell Mac again how much I appreciate his wonderful performance. Maybe he'll come back again next year?"

"Will there be a Revue next year?"

"Yes," she said with surprising conviction. "I figure I'm

315

good for another show or two after all. We may have to move it to some location other than the hotel, but I'll start working on that right away. And we'll need a good props person too."

"I'm glad to hear the show will go on." I wondered if she knew about KaySue. I guess I'll never know for certain. I'm certainly not going to tell her.

"Ivy, I also want to say how much I admire how you handled such a dangerous situation. If I'd had any idea that Charlotte . . ." She shook her head as if she still couldn't quite believe what Charlotte had done to Hiram or to me.

"I asked the Lord for help, and he gave it."

She nodded. "I figured that. Well, I'll be going."

I touched her arm. "Stay. Please do. We'd love to have you."

Again she shook her head. "No, but I'll see you on Sunday."

Sunday. I tried to remember. Had we some leftover details to finish up at the hotel?

She smiled. "You'll be in church, won't you?"

"Yes, but—"

"So I'll see you then. I've been thinking about you . . . and everything . . . and decided I was a bit premature in giving up on God and prayer. He never gave up on me, and I finally realized it's harder to believe prayer doesn't change things than to believe that it does."

Right. I gave her a hug. "See you Sunday."

Mac and the Margollins arrived just as Lucinda was pulling out of the driveway. Dr. Sugarman came a few minutes later, and then our farewell celebration got into high gear. Kelli was reserved, of course, and once I caught a farewell sadness in her eyes that I suspected had nothing to do with Magnolia and Geoff, but she was careful not to put a damper on anyone else's fun.

With sparkling apple juice, she even managed a toast to them. "To Magnolia and Geoff, new friends of some of us, old friends to others. Come back to us soon."

"How about you, Mac?" Magnolia said after Kelli sat down. "What are your plans now?"

"I'm thinking."

Magnolia isn't easily detoured. "About what?"

"Oh, I might head for warmer country and do a couple of Arizona articles my editors want. I might head for Montana and play with my grandkids in the snow. Or I'm also thinking Hello might not be a bad place to settle down. I could go out and do some gold panning with ol' Norman." He gave me a sideways glance. "Like I said, I'm thinking."

Magnolia turned to me. "And the two of you?"

"Our motor home should have the new engine installed within the next couple of days. I talked to Nick today, and he said he'd gotten the okay to take it out of the wrecked motor home."

"Actually, Abilene won't be leaving Hello," Dr. Sugarman said.

I looked at her. She didn't say anything, but she was blushing and glowing all at the same time.

"I guess this is as good a time as any to announce our plans. We're getting married at Mountain Community Church next month." He smiled. "And I think it's going to work. She's finally calling me Mike instead of Dr. Sugarman."

Then we were all congratulating both of them, and Magnolia was saying maybe they'd be coming back from Missouri about the time of the wedding, but finally the question got back to me. Magnolia asked it. "So, with the motor home engine fixed, what are you going to do now?"

"I need a couple more weeks to finish with the books at the library."

"And then?"

"I'm trying to talk her into buying the house. Nothing down," Kelli wheedled. "I might even throw in those carousel horses if she really wants them."

"Can't beat a deal like that," Geoff said.

I nodded. But I knew something none of them did.

The *Hello Telegraph* had published a front-page article about the arrests and my part in them, and, incredibly, some tabloid had picked up the one-line mention of the salami and run with it. I hadn't seen the headline myself, but I'd heard that it said, "Widow Kills with Salami!" Shortly afterward an inquiry had come to the *Telegraph* from some other publication about my availability for an interview. I had no proof this was the Braxtons, of course, and the inquiry had come from California, not Braxton territory. It could be a legitimate inquiry. But somehow it smelled Braxton to me, and down deep I knew they were still after me.

But maybe it was time to stop running. Maybe it was time to dig in my heels and turn and face the enemy.

But there was a whole clan of Braxtons, people capable of arson, dynamite, and who knew what else.

Yet if Mac decided to stay here in Hello . . . My thought when Charlotte yanked the chains around my neck, and they didn't break, came back to me. Two chains are stronger than one.

"Well?" Mac prodded.

"I'm thinking."

Contact the author:

Lorena McCourtney
P.O. Box 773
Merlin, OR 97532
Email: lorena2@earthlink.net

She's not your average crime fighter!

D espite her age, Ivy Malone's unconventional sleuthing and unmatched determination make her one spunky sleuth that just won't quit. Don't miss Ivy's other hilarious escapades!